PENGUIN CANADA

D1132463

World of Wonders

ROBERTSON DAVIES (1913–1995) was born and raised in Ontario, and was educated at a variety of schools, including Upper Canada College, Queen's University, and Balliol College, Oxford. He had three successive careers: as an actor with the Old Vic Company in England; as publisher of the Peterborough *Examiner*; and as university professor and first Master of Massey College at the University of Toronto, from which he retired in 1981 with the title of Master Emeritus.

He was one of Canada's most distinguished men of letters, with several volumes of plays and collections of essays, speeches, and *belles lettres* to his credit. As a novelist he gained worldwide fame for his three trilogies: *The Salterton Trilogy*, *The Deptford Trilogy*, and *The Cornish Trilogy*, and for later novels *Murther & Walking Spirits* and *The Cunning Man*.

His career was marked by many honours: He was the first Canadian to be made an Honorary Member of the American Academy of Arts and Letters, he was a Companion of the Order of Canada, and he received honorary degrees from twenty-six American, Canadian, and British universities.

Also by Robertson Davies

NOVELS

Tempest-Tost

Leaven of Malice

A Mixture of Frailties

Fifth Business

The Manticore

The Rebel Angels

What's Bred in the Bone

The Lyre of Orpheus

Murther & Walking Spirits

The Cunning Man

SHORT FICTION

High Spirits

CRITICISM

A Voice from the Attic

ESSAYS

One Half of Robertson Davies

The Enthusiasms of Robertson Davies

The Merry Heart

Happy Alchemy

ROBERTSON DAVIES

World of Wonders

With an Introduction by M.G. Vassanji

**PENGUIN
CANADA**

PENGUIN CANADA

Published by the Penguin Group

Penguin Group (Canada), 90 Eglinton Avenue East, Suite 700, Toronto, Ontario,
Canada M4P 2Y3 (a division of Pearson Penguin Canada Inc.)

Penguin Group (USA) Inc., 375 Hudson Street, New York, New York 10014, U.S.A.
Penguin Books Ltd, 80 Strand, London WC2R 0RL, England
Penguin Ireland, 25 St Stephen's Green, Dublin 2, Ireland (a division of Penguin Books Ltd)
Penguin Group (Australia), 250 Camberwell Road, Camberwell, Victoria 3124, Australia
(a division of Pearson Australia Group Pty Ltd)
Penguin Books India Pvt Ltd, 11 Community Centre, Panchsheel Park,
New Delhi — 110 017, India
Penguin Group (NZ), cnr Airborne and Rosedale Roads, Albany, Auckland 1310,
New Zealand (a division of Pearson New Zealand Ltd)
Penguin Books (South Africa) (Pty) Ltd, 24 Sturdee Avenue, Rosebank, Johannesburg 2196,
South Africa

Penguin Books Ltd, Registered Offices: 80 Strand, London WC2R 0RL, England

First published in Canada by The Macmillan Company of Canada Limited, 1975
First published in the United States of America by The Viking Press, 1976
Published in Penguin Canada paperback by Penguin Group (Canada),
a division of Pearson Penguin Canada Inc., 1977, 1996
Published in this edition, 2005

(WEB) 10 9 8 7 6 5 4 3 2 1

Copyright © Robertson Davies, 1975
Introduction copyright © M.G. Vassanji, 2005

*Publisher's note: This book is a work of fiction. Names, characters, places and incidents
either are the product of the author's imagination or are used fictitiously, and any
resemblance to actual persons living or dead, events, or locales is entirely coincidental.*

Manufactured in Canada.

ISBN 0-14-305140-7

Library and Archives Canada Cataloguing in Publication data available upon request.

Visit the Penguin Group (Canada) website at **www.penguin.ca**

Contents

Introduction by M.G. Vassanji   *vii*

1   *A Bottle in the Smoke*   *3*
2   *Merlin's Laugh*   *138*
3   *Le Lit de Justice*   *290*

Introduction

by M.G. Vassanji

He was beloved in his lifetime and became an icon of Canadian high culture, yet Robertson Davies's proclivities as a writer were far from the trendy or fashionable. He even called himself a moralist, balking only slightly at this uncool term of description for anybody, especially in the sixties. Of course he astutely defined the term "moralist" to suit his purpose. When the prevailing literary view of man or woman was that of a creature caught in a despair not of his or her making; when that creature was held up as merely an involuntary blink of consciousness, or as someone pitted in a struggle against an over-bearing world, or as a victim of historical circumstance, Davies wrote a novel about moral responsibility. That novel was *Fifth Business*. Overnight it became a bestseller and a classic of modern literature.

On a winter's day in Deptford, a village of five hundred in southern Ontario, Percy Boyd Staunton, a boy of about eleven, throws a barrage of snowballs out of spite at his friend and rival Dunstan Ramsay, who is on his way home for dinner following an afternoon of sledding. The last snowball contains hidden in it a stone. Dunstan ducks the ball and it hits the young bride Mrs. Dempster, out on a walk with her husband, the Baptist minister. The pregnant Mrs. Dempster gives birth prematurely by three months; the baby, Paul, barely survives; and the woman becomes "simple." Dunstan Ramsay is wracked with guilt.

The throw of a stone, literally and metaphorically, sets the novel in motion; a trilogy is born. But in the universe that unfolds for us, this simple act is seen as nothing comparable to the proverbial butterfly's innocent flutter that will cause an atmospheric disturbance halfway round the world. It is wilful, childishly cruel, and thoughtless. It determines the life trajectories of two of the Deptford boys, Dunstan Ramsay and Paul Dempster, and it will return to demand a reckoning from the third, the privileged "Boy" Staunton.

Fifth Business has the most powerfully haunting prelude one is ever to find in a modern novel. "I began it," Davies said, "because for many years I had been troubled by a question: to what extent is a man responsible for the outcome of his actions, and how early in life does the responsibility begin?"

We are all responsible for our actions, even as children, the book suggests; no, it proclaims. Our deeds bear consequences, trivial or profound, and we are accountable. However, what is proposed is not retribution or punishment, justice in a simple sense. We are given a simple observation. But while we may not be judged by a higher court—parental, religious, or state—we may judge ourselves. And this is what Ramsay does: he did not throw the stone, but he moved aside and it hit someone else who suffered instead. The Christian symbolism therein is unmistakable.

It should come as no surprise to find in a writer's work various forms of the more enduring myths and symbols of our shared humanity, especially a writer brought up on popular theatre and fairy tale and the Bible. Davies himself made much of myth and fairy tale, calling them "the distilled truth about what we call 'real life,'" meaning that they illustrate the significant events of our lives in pure imaginative form; which, in a sense, is what a work of fiction often also does. In exploring his personal experiences and traumas, Davies took a keen interest in Freud, and a greater one in Jung, who explained the development of human personality in terms of universal archetypes. He found Jung particularly useful in understanding the transformations of middle age. But it would be misleading to conclude that he simply pegged his plots to a series of archetypes and myths, or that his writerly importance lies merely in his making use of them, however wonderfully. He was far too serious and conscious a writer to be reducible to a one-trick magician.

Davies's somewhat Magian appearance in old age, his sense of humour, and his forthrightness may have created the impression of a likeable, idiosyncratic, and out-of-fashion old uncle; a woman sighting him in a public place, for example, is said to have grabbed his abundantly flowing white beard, assuming thereby a certain familiarity. But behind that jolly facade—for he was first a man of the theatre, an actor, playwright, and director—lurked a complex personality, fighting many demons. He trawled his life's experiences for the substance of his novels and delved deep into what he called his "writer's conscience" for the psychological depth and the moral dilemmas he depicted. This conscience, he said in a revealing essay, "is the writer's inner struggle toward self-knowledge and self-recognition, which he makes manifest through his art." It is, said Davies, quoting Ibsen's chilling description of the writer's calling, "a man's self-judgment / As Doom shall judge the Dead."

Robertson Davies did not come from a privileged background or even a very happy family. He would recall his father's "appalling black moods which were terrifying—utterly terrifying." "All Welshmen are manic depressives," he said, and admitted to his own depressions—as which writer hasn't? He remained haunted by certain childhood traumas, for example when he had to physically abase himself before his mother for impudence, a scene that finds a strong and touching parallel in *Fifth Business*. He could never forgive his parents for having him late, and his mother for having been so old (she was forty-three, and nine years older than his father). He was never sure he had been wanted. In a 1966 diary entry he wrote, "My deep buried anxiety manifests itself in dreams of loss, of rejection, of love denied."

Life in school had its successes and its failures. He loved drama, and his knowledge of it was prodigious. At Upper Canada College, which he attended during his later years of schooling, he was a fascinating character unforgettable to his contemporaries; but this was the carefully cultivated persona of a gifted young actor who worked at his speech and demeanour. He performed brilliantly at the school's drama productions, became editor of the school paper and a prefect. But he was awful at sports, made much of at this boys' college even to this day, and prone to illnesses, and he could not pass mathematics, even after great effort. According to his biographer, this failure continued to haunt him into his later years. Without the requisite credits, he could not attend a degree program at any Ontario university, and Queen's accepted him only as a special, non-degree student. Salvation came when he was admitted to Oxford on the recommendation of his professors. He was now at the centre of the universe, as it were, and it came as a liberating, exhilarating experience, as it has done for many a colonial from the outer reaches of the Empire. He comported himself with elegance and style, and was an exuberant success in dramatics, but this persona, an extension of the one at UCC, hid a deeper problem. At the end of his first year he was diagnosed with a "severe nervous breakdown" and a heart condition. The depression was partly brought on by rejection in love; but the psychiatrist who treated him, and apparently alleviated his suffering, discovered another source for his condition, concluding, "You have been disastrously badly brought up."

His childhood was perhaps no more disastrous than many others; it was also, in many ways, privileged. Good and bad, it was experienced by a remarkable child, and it is from that childhood that Robertson Davies drew the core material for his Deptford novels.

Deptford is based on the town of Thamesville, Ontario, where Davies spent the first five years of his life. His father, Rupert, born a Welshman, published the local weekly newspaper, which he initially rented using all the money he had saved, having worked previously as a tailor, an errand boy, and a typesetter. Davies's two elder brothers helped part-time in the press, and his mother with keeping the accounts, setting type, and proofreading. When Davies was five, the family moved north to Renfrew, a larger town, where Rupert again published the local weekly. The family's fortunes were now on the rise. Still later they moved to Kingston, where Rupert took over the *Daily British Whig*, which combined with another paper to become the *Kingston Whig-Standard*.

The Deptford that Davies portrays was perhaps not untypical of a fairly prosperous Canadian village of those times (the trilogy begins in 1908); nowhere has he suggested that it was an exaggeration, and critics have hailed his faithful depictions of Canadian life. It was, on the one hand, a small, intimate place in which a sensitive child, a future author, could observe all the vagaries of human existence at close range and store them away for future use. It was, on the other hand, a village of narrow-minded and bigoted Christian sects where the public show of emotion or joy, a strand of hair out of place, even the bloom on the pregnant young Mrs. Dempster's face, were regarded as unbecoming. In Deptford you were Anglican, Baptist, Methodist, Presbyterian, Roman Catholic; each group a distinct identity and in its own eyes superior to the rest. "The Scots, I believed until I was aged at least twenty-five," writes Ramsay, "were the salt of the earth." A Presbyterian child, in particular, "knew a good deal about damnation." A Dante's *Inferno*, with lurid illustrations of hell's tortures, was a popular household object, "and probably none of us was really aware that Dante was an R.C." Deviancy in Deptford was meted out with harsh, unmitigated cruelty. Two of the victims of such cruelty were Paul Dempster and his mother.

"That horrid little village" is how one of the characters, Liesl, describes Deptford in the third book, *World of Wonders*. It is a place that has maimed the three men united by that fateful snowball, and to which none of them has formed an attachment: Ramsay and Staunton return only for brief periods initially, and Paul Dempster stops over once, just long enough to jump out onto the railway platform and spit twice in "loathing" in the direction of the village. All three change their names, thus giving themselves a second birth. Staunton and Ramsay abandon the Presbyterian Church, the former to join the Anglicans and the latter by discovering his own form of religious worship. Dempster seems to be an atheist, though he can quote passages from the Bible in profusion, thanks to the fanatical injunctions received in childhood from his father, the Reverend Amasa Dempster.

But of course, the central point of *Fifth Business* is that, as he admits, Ramsay never leaves Deptford in spirit. The incident of the stone weighs him with guilt; and guilt is imbibed with mother's milk in a town like Deptford. Ramsay's sense of sin and guilt has been compounded by Mrs. Dempster's dreadful fate subsequent to his departure. As a boy and later as an adult he attributes intercessional powers to her and comes to believe that she is a saint. Once, at a critical moment during his service in the Great War, he even sees her face on a statue of the Madonna. Later, when he is working as a teacher, he goes off on various sojourns in Europe in search of that statue, and finally becomes a full-fledged hagiologist, a specialist in European saints.

The second novel of the trilogy, *The Manticore,* is a charming, Jungian journey of a well-known middle-aged Toronto lawyer into his own psyche; it begins with the impact of a stone—the same fateful object that launched its predecessor. After a traumatic incident in which this stone prominently figures, Boy Staunton's son, David, sets off to Zürich's Jung Institute to undergo treatment. As the attractive Swiss doctor Johanna von Haller walks him through his life's experiences, we are given another perspective on Boy Staunton's career, and the effect his dominating personality has had upon his family, especially David. We also catch another look at Deptford, and meet the world of upper-class Toronto, for the Stauntons have done exceedingly well. In the process of this examination, David is made to acknowledge all the archetypes that have shaped his personality. However, just as for Ramsay, it is the European "ogress" Liesl who provides David with his epiphany, in this case when he acknowledges his ancestors: the ancient people who inhabited the caves of Europe, and also, significantly, Maria Dymock, an English servant girl who emigrated with her bastard son to Canada, having named him Staunton after her native village.

Finally, in *World of Wonders* it is Paul Dempster's turn to tell his story. He is now Magnus Eisengrim, the world's most accomplished magician—a career in which Ramsay as "fifth business" has also played a part. Dempster is a charismatic, self-made, and arrogant man, having transformed himself from the prematurely born weakling son of a tragic village woman. But he is not free of his wounds. In his creation, Robertson Davies has used his knowledge and experience of popular theatre to provide a vivid description of the travelling entertainment scene before the intrusion of television. It is with him that we first meet Liesl, and it is she who enables him to realize his full potential with the new name that she selects for him.

In this artfully layered trilogy, the impact of a single event reverberates throughout. The past is continually revisited and reinformed; the pursuit of a hobby—the study of saints—becomes in a sense a pursuit of Deptford. Ramsay finds Deptford in himself, and also in Dempster and Staunton; and in a far-off mountain retreat in Switzerland we leave this gentle man who was not a mover but a facilitator, now older and wiser.

DAVIES'S WORLD IS DEPTFORD and the other Canadian towns of his novels, based on the places he has known; it includes certain aspects of Toronto, where he spent a large portion of his life. This is the world of "English" (meaning British and all that entails) Canada. There is to it, in my reading of this world, a distinct sensibility of the other, the colonial, manifest in a cultural nostalgia, a longing for what is authentically European and British. "I think it was loneliness," says Magnus Eisengrim, of the Canadians he sees during his tour of the country, "not just for England ... but for some faraway and long-lost Europe."

Davies's Thamesville was a village close in recent memory to the British roots of its people. Besides its own weekly paper, it had music and drama societies and the Ferguson Opera House. Theatrical pictures adorned his father's study, including those of the famous theatre personality Sir Thomas Irving. Rupert Davies, who had first arrived in Canada at fifteen, felt deeply nostalgic about his native Wales, and Robertson spent many hours hearing stories about that land. In his old age, Rupert finally accomplished his dream of buying himself a house in Wales. His famous son never considered himself as anything but Canadian; he had wise words to say about that. Yet as a student at Upper Canada College he had worked assiduously to rid himself of his Ontario accent. How familiar that sounds in the annals of empire.

In *Fifth Business* Davies describes the mindset of many a Canadian lad who went off to the Great War. It was not to save the world, as wishful—though understandable—modern hindsight would have it. It was to fight for England against Germany that they went. "None had any clear idea what the war was about, though many felt that England had been menaced and had to be defended...."

Simultaneously, the demonization of the Germans and the Kaiser was complete: "These Germans, I gathered, were absolute devils; not winning campaigns, but maiming children, ravishing women...."

This connectedness to Britain perhaps might embarrass a new Canadian sensibility, groomed on a more modern sense of the nation. But it can be freely admitted in a world that is, as we now realize, so interconnected and filled with memories of departure and arrival.

Robertson Davies was of the generation previous to the one that in the seventies rallied against British and (especially) American cultural domination to promote an independent Canadian culture. Davies himself, having written at that time one of the defining books of Canadian literature, felt comfortable with American and British admirers. American readers seem to have loved him. Speaking to an American audience, he compared Canada to the daughter who stayed behind with Mother while Columbia went away, became independent, and prospered. Mother and the renegade later formed a close bond. What of the stay-at-home? She grew up and went her own way, discovered herself. The Deptford Trilogy is one of those moments during her maturing, when an author held up a mirror of some complexity for her to look at.

My point in pursuing Davies's Anglo-rootedness, and the Anglo and Euro cultural nostalgia of his books, is to hold them up as an example of the cultural multiplicities that our world has become aware of. In his imaginative exploring of where he came from, he becomes remarkably contemporary, joining the company of many a writer who arrives at new shores (often from a colony) to dissect the life and place he or she has left behind. As such, Davies is not from the mainstream of a once-dominant, now receding, irrelevant, and quaint past, but from a larger, diverse mainstream of the present-day.

For details about Robertson Davies's private life I am indebted to the excellent biography *Robertson Davies: Man of Myth* by Judith Skelton Grant. Many of Davies's own comments on his life and work have been collected in *One Half of Robertson Davies* and *The Enthusiasms of Robertson Davies* (edited by J.S. Grant). The quotations employed here have been taken from these books as well as the Trilogy.

World of Wonders

1

A Bottle in the Smoke

(1)

"Of course he was a charming man. A delightful person. Who has ever questioned it? But not a great magician."

"By what standard do you judge?"

"Myself. Who else?"

"You consider yourself a greater magician than Robert-Houdin?"

"Certainly. He was a fine illusionist. But what is that? A man who depends on a lot of contraptions—mechanical devices, clockwork, mirrors, and such things. Haven't we been working with that sort of rubbish for almost a week? Who made it? Who reproduced that *Pâtissier du Palais-Royal* we've been fiddling about with all day? I did. I'm the only man in the world who could do it. The more I see of it the more I despise it."

"But it is delightful! When the little baker brings out his bonbons, his patisseries, his croissants, his glasses of port and Marsala, all at the word of command, I almost weep with pleasure! It is the most moving reminiscence of the spirit of the age of Louis Philippe! And you admit that you have reproduced it precisely as it was first made by Robert-Houdin. If he was not a great magician, what do you call a great magician?"

"A man who can stand stark naked in the midst of a crowd and keep it gaping for an hour while he manipulates a few coins, or cards, or billiard balls. I can do that, and I can do it better than anybody today or anybody who has ever lived. That's why I'm tired of Robert-Houdin and his Wonderful Bakery and his Inexhaustible Punch Bowl and his Miraculous Orange Tree and all the rest of his

3

wheels and cogs and levers and fancy junk."

"But you're going to complete the film?"

"Of course. I've signed a contract. I've never broken a contract in my life. I'm a professional. But I'm bored with it. What you're asking me to do is like asking Rubinstein to perform on a player-piano. Given the apparatus anybody could do it."

"You know of course that we asked you to make this film simply because you are the greatest magician in the world—the greatest magician of all time, if you like—and that gives tremendous added attraction to our film—"

"It's been many years since I was called an added attraction."

"Let me finish, please. We are presenting a great magician of today doing honour to a great magician of the past. People will love it."

"It shows me at a disadvantage."

"Oh, surely not. Consider the audience. After we have shown this on the B.B.C. it will appear on a great American network—the arrangements are almost complete—and then it will go all over the world. Think how it will be received in France alone, where there is still a great cult of Robert-Houdin. The eventual audience will be counted in millions. Can you be indifferent to that?"

"That just shows what you think about magic, and how much you know about it. I've already been seen all over the world. And I mean *I've been seen,* and the unique personal quality of my performance has been felt by audiences with whom I've created a unique relationship. You can't do that on television."

"That is precisely what I expect to do. I don't want to speak boastfully. Perhaps we have had enough boasting here tonight. But I am not unknown as a film-maker. I can say without immodesty that I'm just as famous in my line as you are in yours. I am a magician too, and not a trivial one—"

"If my work is trivial, why do you want my help? Film—yes, of course it's a commonplace nowadays that it is an art, just as people used to say that Robert-Houdin's complicated automatic toys were art. People are always charmed by clever mechanisms that give an effect of life. But don't you remember what the little actor in Noel Coward's play called film? 'A cheesy photograph.'"

"Please—"

"Very well, let's not insist on 'cheesy'. But we can't escape 'photo-graph'. Something is missing, and you know what it is: the inexplica-ble but beautifully controlled sympathy between the artist and his audience. Film isn't even as good as the player-piano; at least you could add something personal to that, make it go fast or slow, loud or soft as you pleased."

"Film is like painting, which is also unchanging. But each viewer brings his personal sensibility, his unique response to the completed canvas as he does to the film."

"Who are your television viewers? Ragtag and bobtail; drunk and sober; attentive or in a nose-picking stupor. With the flabby concen-tration of people who are getting something for nothing. I am used to audiences who come because they want to see *me,* and have paid to do it. In the first five minutes I have made them attentive as they have never been before in their lives. I can't guarantee to do that on TV. I can't see my audience, and what I can't see I can't dominate. And what I can't dominate I can't enchant, and humour, and make part-ners in their own deception."

"You must understand that that is where my art comes in. I am your audience, and I contain in myself all these millions of whom we speak. You satisfy me and you satisfy them, as well. Because I credit them with my intelligence and sensitivity and raise them to my level. Have I not shown it in more than a dozen acknowledged film master-pieces? This is my gift and my art. Trust me. That is what I am asking you to do. Trust me."

(2)

This was the first serious quarrel since we had begun filming. Should I say "we"? As I was living in the house, and extremely curious about everything connected with the film, they let me hang around while they worked, and even gave me a job; as an historian I kept an eye on detail and did not allow the film-makers to stray too far from the period of Louis Philippe and his Paris, or at least no farther than artistic licence and necessity allowed. I had foreseen a quarrel. I was not seventy-two years old for nothing, and I knew Magnus Eisengrim very well. I thought I was beginning to know a little about the great director Jurgen Lind, too.

The project was to make an hour-long film for television about the great French illusionist, Jean-Eugène Robert-Houdin, who died in 1871. It was not simply to mark this centenary; as Lind had said, it would doubtless make the rounds of world television for years. The title was *Un Hommage à Robert-Houdin*—easily translatable— and its form was simple; the first twelve minutes were taken up with the story of his early life, as he told it in his *Confidences d'un prestidigitateur,* and for this actors had been employed; the remainder of the hour was to be an historical reproduction of one of Robert-Houdin's *Soirées Fantastiques* as he gave it in his own theatre in the Palais-Royal. And to play the part of the great conjuror the film-makers and the British Broadcasting Corporation had engaged, at a substantial fee, the greatest of living conjurors, my old friend Magnus Eisengrim.

If they had filmed it in a studio, I do not suppose I should have been involved at all, but the reproduction of Robert-Houdin's performance demanded so much magical apparatus, including several splendid automata which Eisengrim had made particularly for it, that it was decided to shoot this part of the picture in Switzerland, at Sorgenfrei, where Eisengrim's stage equipment was stored in a large disused riding-school on the estate. It was not a difficult matter for the scene designers and artificers to fit Robert-Houdin's tiny theatre, which had never seated more than two hundred spectators, into the space that was available.

This may have been a bad idea, for it mixed professional and domestic matters in a way that could certainly cause trouble. Eisengrim lived at Sorgenfrei, as permanent guest and—in a special sense—the lover of its owner and mistress, Dr Liselotte Naegeli. I also had retired to Sorgenfrei after I had my heart attack, and dwelt there very happily as the permanent guest and—in a special sense—the lover of the same Dr Liselotte, known to us both as Liesl. When I use the word "lover" to describe our relationship, I do not mean that we were a farcical *ménage à trois,* leaping in and out of bed at all hours and shrieking comic recriminations at one another. We did occasionally share a bed (usually at breakfast, when it was convenient and friendly for us all three to tuck up together and sample things from one another's trays), but the athleticism of love was a thing of the past for me, and I suspect it was becoming an infrequent adventure for Eisengrim. We loved Liesl none the less—indeed rather more, and differently—than in our hot days, and what with loving and arguing and laughing and talking, we fleeted the time carelessly, as they did in the Golden World.

Even the Golden World may have welcomed a change, now and then, and we had been pleased when Magnus received his offer from the B.B.C. Liesl and I, who knew more about the world, or at least the artistic part of it, than Eisengrim, were excited that the film was to be directed by the great Jurgen Lind, the Swedish film-maker whose work we both admired. We wanted to meet him, for though we were neither of us naive people we had not wholly lost our belief that it is delightful to meet artists who have given us pleasure. That was why Liesl proposed that, although the film crew were living at an inn not far down the mountain from Sorgenfrei, Lind and one or two of his immediate entourage should dine with us as often as they pleased, ostensibly so that we could continue discussion of the film as it progressed, but really so that we could become acquainted with Lind.

We should have known better. Had we learned nothing from our experience with Magnus Eisengrim, who had a full share, a share pressed down and overflowing, of the egotism of the theatre artist? Who could not bear the least slight; who expected, as of right, to be served first at table, and to go through all doors first; who made the most unholy rows and fusses if he were not treated virtually as royalty? Lind had not been on the spot a day before we knew that he was just such another as our dear old friend Magnus, and that they were not going to hit it off together.

Not that Lind was like him in external things. He was modest, reticent, dressed like a workman, and soft of speech. He always hung back at doors, cared nothing for the little ceremonials of daily life in a rich woman's house, and conferred with his chief colleagues about every detail. But it was clear that he expected and got his own way, once he had determined what it was.

Moreover, he seemed to me to be formidably intelligent. His long, sad, unsmiling face, with its hanging underlip that showed long, yellow teeth, the tragedy line of his eyelids, which began high on the bridge of his nose and swept miserably downward toward his cheeks, and the soft, bereaved tone of his voice, suggested a man who had seen too much to be amused by life; his great height—he was a little over six feet eight inches—gave him the air of a giant mingling with lesser creatures about whom he knew some unhappy secret which was concealed from themselves; he spoke slowly in an elegant English only slightly marked by that upper-class Swedish accent which suggests a man delicately sucking a lemon. He had been extensively educated—his junior assistants all were careful to speak to him as Dr Lind—and he had as well that theatre artist's quality of seeming to know a great deal, without visible study or effort, about whatever was necessary for his immediate work. He did not know as much about the politics and economics of the reign of Louis Philippe as I did, for after all I had given my life to the study of history; but he seemed to know a great deal about its music, the way its clothes ought to be worn, the demeanour of its people, and its quality of life and spirit, which belonged to a sensibility far beyond mine. When historians meet with this kind of informed, imaginative sympathy with a past era in a non-historian, they are awed. How on earth does he know that, they are forced to ask themselves, and why did I never tumble to that? It takes a while to discover that the knowledge, though impressive and useful, has its limitations, and when the glow of imaginative creation no longer suffuses it, it is not really deeply grounded. But Lind was at work on the era of Louis Philippe, and specifically on the tiny part of it that applied to Robert-Houdin the illusionist, and for the present I was strongly under his spell.

That was the trouble. To put it gaudily but truly, that was where the canker gnawed. Liesl and I were both under Lind's spell, and Eisengrim's nose was out of joint.

That was why he was picking a quarrel with Lind, and Lind, who had been taught to argue logically, though unfairly, was at a disadvantage with a man who simply argued—pouted, rather—to get his own way and be cock of the walk again.

I thought I should do something about it, but I was forestalled by Roland Ingestree.

He was the man from the B. B.C., the executive producer of the film, or whatever the proper term is. He managed all the business, but was not simply a man of business, because he brooded, in a well-bred, don't-think-I'm-interfering-but manner, over the whole venture, including its artistic side. He was a sixtyish, fattish, bald Englishman who always wore gold-rimmed half-glasses, which gave him something of the air of Mr Pickwick. But he was a shrewd fellow, and he had taken in the situation.

"We mustn't delude ourselves, Jurgen," he said. "Without Eisengrim this film would be nothing—nothing at all. He is the only man in the world who can reproduce the superlatively complex Robert-Houdin automata. It is quite understandable that he looks down on achievements that baffle lesser beings like ourselves. After all, as he points out, he is a magnificent classical conjuror, and he hasn't much use for mechanical toys. That's understood, of course. But what I think we've missed is that he's an actor of the rarest sort; he can really give us the outward form of Robert-Houdin, with all that refinement of manner and perfection of grace that made Robert-Houdin great. How he can do it, God alone knows, but he can. When I watch him in rehearsal I am utterly convinced that a man of the first half of the nineteenth century stands before me. Where could we have found anyone else who can act as he is acting? John? Too tall, too subjective. Larry? Too flamboyant, too corporeal. Guinness? Too dry. There's nobody else, you see. I hope I'm not being offensive, but I think it's as an actor we must think of Eisengrim. The conjuring might have been faked. But the acting— tell me, frankly, who else is there that could touch him?"

He was not being offensive, and well he knew it. Eisengrim glowed, and all might have been well if Kinghovn had not pushed the thing a little farther. Kinghovn was Lind's cameraman, and I gathered he was a great artist in his own right. But he was a man whose whole

9

world was dominated by what he could see, and make other people see, and words were not his medium.

"Roly is right, Jurgen. This man is just right for looks. He compels belief. He can't go wrong. It is God's good luck, and we mustn't quarrel with it."

Now Lind's nose was out of joint. He had been trying to placate a prima donna, and his associates seemed to be accusing him of underestimating the situation. He was sure that he never underestimated anything about one of his films. He was accused of flying in the face of good luck, when he was certain that the best possible luck that could happen to any film was that he should be asked to direct it. The heavy lip fell a little lower, the eyes became a little sadder, and the emotional temperature of the room dropped perceptibly.

Ingestree put his considerable talents to the work of restoring Lind's self-esteem, without losing Eisengrim's goodwill.

"I think I sense what troubles Eisengrim about this whole Robert-Houdin business. It's the book. It's that wretched *Confidences d'un prestidigitateur*. We've been using it as a source for the biographical part of the film, and it's certainly a classic of its kind. But did anybody ever read such a book? Vanity is perfectly acceptable in an artist. Personally, I wouldn't give you sixpence for an artist who lacked vanity. But it's honest vanity I respect. The false modesty, the exaggerated humility, the greasy bourgeois assertions of respectability, of good-husband-and-father, of debt-paying worthiness are what make the *Confidences* so hard to swallow. Robert-Houdin was an oddity; he was an artist who wanted to pass as a bourgeois. I'm sure that's what irritates both you men, and sets you against each other. You feel that you are putting your very great, fully realized artistic personalities to the work of exalting a man whose attitude toward life you despise. I don't blame you for being irritable—because you have been, you know; you've been terribly irritable tonight—but that's what art is, as you very well know, much of the time: the transformation and glorification of the commonplace."

"The revelation of the glory in the commonplace," said Lind, who had no objection to being told that his vanity was an admirable and honest trait, and was coming around.

"Precisely. The revelation of the glory in the commonplace. And you two very great artists—the great film director and (may I say it) the great actor—are revealing the glory in Robert-Houdin, who perversely sought to conceal his own artistry behind that terrible good-citizen mask. It hampered him, of course, because it was against the grain of his talent. But you two are able to do an extraordinary, a metaphysical thing. You are able to show the world, a century after his death, what Robert-Houdin would have been if he had truly understood himself."

Eisengrim and Lind were liking this. Magnus positively beamed, and Lind's sad eyes rolled toward him with a glance from which the frost was slowly disappearing. Ingestree was well in the saddle now, and was riding on to victory.

"You are both men of immeasurably larger spirit than he. What was he, after all? The good citizen, the perfection of the bourgeoisie under Louis Philippe that he pretended? Who can believe it? There is in every artist something black, something savouring of the crook, which he may not even understand himself, and which he certainly keeps well out of the eye of his public. What was it in Robert-Houdin?

"He gives us a sniff of it in the very first chapter of his other book, which I have read, and which is certainly familiar to you, Mr Ramsay"—this with a nod to me—"called *Les Secrets de la prestidigitation et de la magie*—"

"My God, I read it as a boy!" I said.

"Very well. Then you recall the story of his beginnings as a magician? How he was befriended by the Count de l'Escalopier? How this nobleman gave a private show in his house, where Robert-Houdin amused the guests? How his best trick was burning a piece of paper on which the Archbishop of Paris had written a splendid compliment to Robert-Houdin, and the discovery of the piece of paper afterward in the smallest of twelve envelopes which were all sealed, one inside the other? It was a trick he learned from his master, de Grisy. But how did he try to make it up to l'Escalopier for putting him on his feet?"

"The trap for the robber," I said.

"Exactly. A thief was robbing l'Escalopier blind, and nothing he tried would catch him. So Robert-Houdin offered to help, and what did he do? He worked out a mechanism to be concealed in the

Count's desk, so that when the robber opened it a pistol would be discharged, and a claw made of sharp needles would seize the thief's hand and crunch the word 'Voleur' on the back of it. The needles were impregnated with silver nitrate, so that it was in effect tattoo-ing—branding the man for life. A nice fellow, eh? And do you remember what he says? That this nasty thing was a refinement of a little gubbins he had made as a boy, to catch and mark another boy who was pinching things from his school locker. That was the way Robert-Houdin's mind worked; he fancied himself as a thief-catcher. Now, in a man who makes such a parade of his integrity, what does that suggest? Over-compensation, shall we say? A deep, unresting doubt of his own honesty?

"If we had time, and the gift, we could learn a lot about the inner life of Robert-Houdin by analysing his tricks. Why are so many of the best of them concerned with giving things away? He gave away pastries, sweets, ribbons, fans, all sorts of stuff at every performance; yet we know how careful he was with money. What was all that generosity meant to conceal? Because he was concealing something, take my word for it. The whole of the *Confidences* is a gigantic white-wash job, a concealment. Analyse the tricks and you will get a subtext for the autobiography, which seems so delightfully bland and cosy.

"And that's what we need for our film. A subtext. A reality running like a subterranean river under the surface; an enriching, but not necessarily edifying, background to what is seen.

"Where are we to get it? Not from Robert-Houdin. Too much trouble and perhaps not worth the trouble when we got it. No. It must come from the working together of you two great artists: Lind the genius-director and Eisengrim the genius-actor. And you must fish it up out of your own guts."

"But that is what I always do," said Lind.

"Of course. But Eisengrim must do it, as well. Now tell me, sir: you can't always have been the greatest conjuror in the world. You learned your art somewhere. If we asked you—invited you—begged you—to make your own experience the subtext for this film about a man, certainly lesser than yourself, but of great and lasting fame in his special line, what would it be?"

I was surprised to see Eisengrim look as if he were considering this question very seriously. He never revealed anything about his past life, or his innermost thoughts, and it was only because I had known him—with very long intervals of losing him—since we had been boys together, that I knew anything about him at all. I had fished— fished cunningly with the subtlest lures I could devise—for more information about him than I had, but he was too clever for me. But here he was, swimming in the flattery of this clever Englishman Ingestree, and he looked as if he might be about to spill the beans. Well, anyhow I would be present when, and if, he did so. After some consideration, he spoke.

"The first thing I would tell you would be that my earliest instructor was the man you see in that chair yonder: Dunstan Ramsay. God knows he was the worst conjuror the world has ever seen, but he introduced me to conjuring, and by a coincidence his textbook was *The Secrets of Stage Conjuring*, by the man we are all talking about and, if you are right in what you say, Mr Ingestree, serving! Robert-Houdin."

This caused some sensation, as Eisengrim knew it would. Ingestree, having forced the oyster to yield a little, pressed the knife in.

"Wonderful! We would never have taken Ramsay for a conjuror. But there must have been somebody else. If Ramsay was your first master, who was your second?"

"I'm not sure I'm going to tell you," said Eisengrim. "I'll have to think about it very carefully. Your idea of a subtext—the term and the idea are both new to me—is interesting. I'll tell you this much. I began to learn conjuring seriously on 30 August 1918. That was the day I descended into hell, and did not rise again for seven years. I'll consider whether I'm going to go farther than that. Now I'm going to bed."

(3)

Liesl had said little during the quarrel—or rivalry of egotisms, or whatever you choose to call it—but she caught me the following morning before the film crew arrived, and seemed to be in high spirits.

"So Magnus has come to the confessional moment in his life," she said. "It's been impending for several months. Didn't you notice? You didn't! Oh, Ramsay, you are such a dunce about some things. If Magnus were the kind of man who could write an autobiography, this is when he would do it."

"Magnus has an autobiography already. I should know. I wrote it.

"A lovely book. *Phantasmata: the Life and Adventures of Magnus Eisengrim*. But that was for sale at his performance; a kind of super-publicity. A splendid Gothic invention from your splendid Gothic imagination."

"That's not the way he regards it. When people ask he tells them that it is a poetic autobiography, far more true to the man he has become than any merely factual account of his experience could be."

"I know. I told him to say that. You don't suppose he thought it out himself, do you? You know him. He's marvellously intelligent in his own way—sensitive, aware, and intuitive—but it's not a literary or learned intelligence. Magnus is a truly original creature. They are of the greatest rarity. And as I say, he's reached the confessional time of life. I expect we shall hear some strange things."

"Not as strange as I could tell about him."

"I know, I know. You are obsessed with the idea that his mother was a saint. Ramsay, in all your rummaging among the lives of the saints, did you ever encounter one who had a child? What was that child like? Perhaps we shall hear."

"I'm a little miffed that he considers telling these strangers things he's never told to you and me."

"Ass! It's always strangers who turn the tap that lets out the truth. Didn't you yourself babble out all the secrets of your life to me within a couple of weeks of our first meeting? Magnus is going to tell."

"But why, now?"

"Because he wants to impress Lind. He's terribly taken with Lind, and he has his little fancies, like the rest of us. Once he wanted to impress me, but it wasn't the right time in his life to spill the whole bottle."

"But Ingestree suggested that Lind might do some telling, too. Are we to have a great mutual soul-scrape?"

"Ingestree is very foxy, behind all that fat and twinkling bonhomie. He knows Lind won't tell anything. For one thing, it's not his time; he's only forty-three. And he is inhibited by his education; it makes people cagey. What he tells us he tells through his films, just as Ingestree suggested that Robert-Houdin revealed himself through his tricks. But Magnus is retired—or almost. Also he is not inhibited by education, which is the great modern destroyer of truth and originality. Magnus knows no history. Have you ever seen him read a book? He really thinks that whatever has happened to him is unique. It is an enviable characteristic."

"Well, every life is unique."

"To a point. But there are only a limited number of things a human creature can do."

"So you think he is going to tell all?"

"Not all. Nobody tells that. Indeed, nobody knows everything about themselves. But I'll bet you anything you like he tells a great deal."

I argued no further. Liesl is very shrewd about such things. The morning was spent in arrangements about lighting. A mobile generator from Zürich had to be put in place, and all the lamps connected and hung; the riding-school was a jungle of pipe-scaffolding and cable. Kinghovn fussed over differences which seemed to me imperceptible, and as a script-girl stood in for Eisengrim while the lighting was being completed, he had time to wander about the riding-school, and as lunchtime approached he steered me off into a corner.

"Tell me about subtext," he said.

"It's a term modern theatre people are very fond of. It's what a character thinks and knows, as opposed to what the playwright makes him say. Very psychological."

"Give me an example."

"Do you know Ibsen's *Hedda Gabler*?"

He didn't, and it was a foolish question. He didn't know anything about any literature whatever. I waded in.

"It's about a beautiful and attractive woman who has married, as a last resort, a man she thinks very dull. They have returned from a honeymoon during which she has become greatly disillusioned with him, but she knows she is already pregnant. In the first act she is talking to her husband's adoring aunt, trying to be civil as the old woman prattles on about the joys of domesticity and the achievements of her nephew. But all the time she has, in her mind, the knowledge that he is dull, timid, a tiresome lover, that she is going to have a child by him, and that she fears childbirth. That's the subtext. The awareness of it thickens up the actress's performance, and emphasizes the irony of the situation."

"I understand. It seems obvious."

"First-rate actors have always been aware of it, but dramatists like Shakespeare usually brought the subtext up to the surface and gave it to the audience directly. Like Hamlet's soliloquies."

"I've never seen *Hamlet*."

"Well—that's subtext."

"Do you think the circumstances of my own life really form a subtext for this film?"

"God only knows. One thing is certain: unless you choose to tell Lind and his friends about your life, it can't do so."

"You're quite wrong. I would know, and I suppose whatever I do is rooted in what I am, and have been."

It was never wise to underestimate Magnus, but I was always doing so. The pomposity of the learned. Because he didn't know *Hamlet* and *Hedda* I tended to think him simpler than he was.

"I'm thinking of telling them a few things, Dunny. I might surprise them. They're all so highly educated, you know. Education is a great shield against experience. It offers so much, ready-made and all from the best shops, that there's a temptation to miss your own life in pursuing the lives of your betters. It makes you wise in some ways, but it can make you a blindfolded fool in others. I think I'll surprise them. They talk so much about art, but really, education is just as much a barrier between a man and real art as it is in other parts of life. They don't know what a mean old bitch art can be. I think I'll surprise them."

So Liesl had been right! He was ready to spill.

Well, I was ready to hear. Indeed, I was eager to hear. My reason was deep and professional. As an historian I had all my life been aware of the extraordinary importance of documents. I had handled hundreds of them: letters, reports, memoranda, sometimes diaries; I had always treated them with respect, and had come in time to have an affection for them. They summed up something that was becoming increasingly important to me, and that was an earthly form of immortality. Historians come and go, but the document remains, and it has the importance of a thing that cannot be changed or gainsaid. Whoever wrote it continues to speak through it. It might be honest and it might be complete: on the other hand it could be thoroughly crooked or omit something of importance. But there it was, and it was all succeeding ages possessed.

I deeply wanted to create, or record, and leave behind me a document, so that whenever its subject was dealt with in future, the notation "Ramsay says ..." would have to appear. Thus, so far as this world is concerned, I should not wholly die. Well, here was my chance.

Would anyone care? Indeed they would. I had written an imaginative account of the life of Magnus Eisengrim, the great conjuror and illusionist, at his own request and that of Liesl, who had been the manager and in a very high degree the brains of his great show, the *Soirée of Illusions*. The book was sold in the foyers of any theatre in which he appeared, but it had also had a flattering success on its own account; it sold astonishingly in the places where the really big sales of books are achieved—cigar stores, airports, and bus stops. It had extravagantly outsold all my other books, even my *Hundred Saints for Travellers* and my very popular *Celtic Saints of Britain and Europe*. Why? Because it was a wonderfully good book of its kind. Readable by the educated, but not rebuffing to somebody who simply wanted a lively, spicy tale.

Its authorship was still a secret, for although I received a half-share of the royalties it was ostensibly the work of Magnus Eisengrim. It had done great things for him. People who believed what they read came to see the man who had lived the richly adventurous and macabre life described in it; sophisticates came to see the man who had written such gorgeous, gaudy lies about himself. As Liesl said, it was Gothic, full of enormities bathed in the delusive lights of nineteenth-century romance. But it was modern enough, as well; it touched the sexy, rowdy string so many readers want to hear.

Some day it would be known that I had written it. We had already received at Sorgenfrei a serious film offer and a number of inquiries from earnest Ph.D. students who explained apologetically that they were making investigations, of one kind or another, of what they called "popular literature". And when it became known that I had written it, which would probably not be until Eisengrim and I were both dead, then—Aha! then my document would come into its own. For then the carefully tailored life of Magnus Eisengrim, which had given pleasure to so many millions in English, French, German, Danish, Italian, Spanish, and Portuguese, and had been accorded the distinction of a pirated version in Japanese, would be compared with the version I would prepare from Eisengrim's own confessions, and "Ramsay says ..." would certainly be heard loud and clear.

Was this a base ambition for an historian and a hagiologist? What had Ingestree said? In every artist there is something black, something savouring of the crook. Was I, in a modest way, an artist? I was beginning to wonder. No, no; unless I falsified the record what could be dishonest, or artistic, about making a few notes?

(4)

"I have spent a good deal of time since last night wondering whether I should tell you anything about my life," said Eisengrim, after dinner that evening, "and I think I shall, on the condition that you regard it as a secret among ourselves. After all, the audience doesn't have to know the subtext, does it? Your film isn't Shakespeare, where everything is revealed; it is Ibsen, where much is implied."

How quickly he learns, I thought. And how well he knows the power of pretending something is secret which he has every intention of revealing. I turned up my mental, wholly psychological historian's hearing-aid, determined to miss nothing, and to get at least the skeleton of it on paper before I went to sleep.

"Begin with going to hell," said Ingestree. "You've given us a date: August 30, 1918. You told us you knew Ramsay when you were a boy, so I suppose you must be a Canadian. If I were going to hell, I don't think I'd start from Canada. What happened?"

"I went to the village fair. Our village, which was called Deptford, had a proud local reputation for its fair. Schoolchildren were admitted free. That helped to swell the attendance, and the Fair Board liked to run up the biggest possible annual figure. You wouldn't imagine there was anything wrong in what I did, but judged by the lights of my home it was sin. We were an unusually religious household, and my father mistrusted the fair. He had promised me that he might, if I could repeat the whole of Psalm 79 without an error, at suppertime, take me to the fair in the evening, to see the animals. This task of memorizing was part of a great undertaking that he had set his heart on: I was to get the whole of the Book of Psalms by heart. He assured me that it would be a bulwark and a stay to me through the whole of my life. He wasn't rushing the job; I was supposed to learn ten verses each day, but as I was working for a treat, he thought I might run to the thirteen verses of Psalm 79 to get to the fair. But the treat was conditional; if I stumbled, the promise about the fair was off."

"It sounds very much like rural Sweden, when I was a boy," said Kinghovn. "How do the children of such people grow up?"

"Ah, but you mustn't misunderstand. My father wasn't a tyrant; he truly wanted to protect me against evil."

"A fatal desire in a parent," said Lind, who was known throughout the world—to film-goers at least—as an expert on evil.

"There was a special reason. My mother was an unusual person. If you want to know the best about her, you must apply to Ramsay. I don't suppose I can tell you my own story without giving you something of the other side of her nature. She was supposed to have some very bad instincts, and our family suffered for it. She had to be kept under confinement. My father, with what I suppose must be described as compassion, wanted to make sure I wouldn't follow in her ways. So, from the age of eight, I was set to work to acquire the bulwark and the stay of the Psalms, and in a year and a half—something like that—I had gnawed my way through them up to Psalm 79."

"How old were you?" said Ingestree.

"Getting on for ten. I wanted fiercely to go to the fair, so I set to work on the Psalm. Do you know the Psalms? I have never been able to make head or tail of a lot of them, but others strike with a terrible truth on your heart, if you meet them at the right time. I plugged on till I came to *We are become a reproach to our neighbours, a scorn and derision to them that are round about us.* Yes! Yes, there we were! The Dempsters, a reproach to our neighbours, a scorn and derision to the whole village of Deptford. And particularly to the children of Deptford, with whom I had to go to school. School was to begin on the day after Labour Day, less than a week from the day when I sat puzzling over Psalm 79. Tell me, Lind, you know so much about evil, and have explored it in your films, Liesl tells me, like a man with an ordnance map in his hand; have you ever explored the evil of children?"

"Even I have never dared to do that," said Lind, with the tragic grin which was the nearest he ever came to a laugh.

"If you ever decide to do so, call me in as a special adviser. It's a primal evil, a pure malignance. They really enjoy giving pain. This is described by sentimentalists as innocence. I was tormented by the children of our village from the earliest days I can remember. My mother had done something—I never found out what it was—that made most of the village hate her, and the children knew that, so it was all right to hate me and torture me. They said my mother was a hoor—that was the local pronunciation of whore—and they tormented me with a virtuosity they never showed in anything else they did. When I cried, somebody might say, 'Aw, let the kid alone; he can't help it his mother's a hoor.' I suppose the philosopher-kings who struggled up to that level have since become the rulers of the place. But I soon determined not to cry.

"Not that I became hard. I simply accepted the wretchedness of my station. Not that I hated them—not then; I learned to hate them later in life. At that time I simply assumed that children must be as they were. I was a misfit in the world, and didn't know why.

"Onward I went with Psalm 79. *O remember not against us former iniquities: let thy tender mercies speedily prevent us: for we are brought very low.* But as soon as I put my nose into the schoolyard they would remember former iniquities against me. God's tender mercies had never reached the Deptford schoolyard. And I was unquestionably brought very low, for all that desolation would begin again next Tuesday.

"Having got that far with me, Satan had me well on the path to hell. I knew where some money was kept; it was small change for the baker and the milkman when they called; under my mother's very nose—she was sitting in a chair, staring into space, tied by a rope to a ringbolt my father had set in the wall—I pinched fifteen cents; I held it up so that she could see it, so that she would think I was going to pay one of the delivery-men. Then I ran off to the fair, and my heart was full of terrible joy. I was wicked, but O what a delicious release it was!

"I pieced out the enjoyment of the fair like a gourmet savouring a feast. Begin at the bottom, with what was least amusing. That would be the Women's Institute display of bottled pickles, embalmed fruit, doilies, home-cooking, and 'fancy-work'. Then the animals, the huge draught-horses, the cows with enormous udders, the prize bull (though I did not go very near to him, for some of my schoolmates were lingering there, to snigger and work themselves up into a horny stew, gaping at his enormous testicles), the pigs so unwontedly clean, and the foolish poultry, White Wyandottes, Buff Orpingtons, and Mrs Forrester's gorgeous Cochin Chinas, and in a corner a man from the Department of Agriculture giving an educational display of egg-candling.

"Pleasure now began to be really intense. I looked with awe and some fear at the display from the nearby Indian Reservation. Men with wrinkled, tobacco-coloured faces sat behind a stand, not really offering slim walking-canes, with ornate whittled handles into which patterns of colour had been worked; their women, as silent and unmoving as they, displayed all sorts of fancy boxes made of sweet-grass, ornamented with beads and dyed porcupine quill. But these goods, which had some merit as craftwork, were not so gorgeous in my eyes as the trash offered by a booth which was not of local origin, in which a man sold whirligigs of gaudy celluloid, kewpie dolls with tinsel skirts riding high over their gross stomachs, alarm-clocks with *two* bells for determined sleepers, and beautiful red or blue pony-whips. I yearned toward those whips, but they cost a whole quarter apiece, and were thus out of my reach.

"But I was not cut off from all the carnal pleasures of the fair. After a great deal of deliberation I spent five of my ill-gotten cents on a large paper cornet of pink candy floss, a delicacy I had never seen before. It had little substance, and made my mouth sticky and dry, but it was a luxury, and my life had known nothing of luxuries.

"Then, after a full ten minutes of deliberation, I laid out another five cents on a ride on the merry-go-round. I chose my mount with care, a splendid dapple-grey with flaring nostrils, ramping wonderfully up and down on his brass pole; he seemed to me like the horse in Job that saith among the trumpets, Ha, ha; for a hundred and eighty seconds I rode him in ecstasy, and dismounted only when I was chased away by the man who took care of such things and was on the look-out for enchanted riders like myself.

"But even this was only leading up to what I knew to be the crown of the fair. That was Wanless's World of Wonders, the one pleasure which my father would certainly never have permitted me. Shows of all kinds were utterly evil in his sight, and this was a show that turned my bowels to water, even from the outside.

"The tent seemed vast to me, and on a scaffold on its outside were big painted pictures of the wonders within. A Fat Woman, immense and pink, beside whom even the biggest pigs in the agricultural tents were starvelings. A man who ate fire. A Strong Man, who would wrestle with anybody who dared to try it. A Human Marvel, half man and half woman. A Missing Link, in itself worth more than the price of admission, because it was powerfully educational, illustrating what Man had been before he decided to settle in such places as Deptford. On a raised platform outside the tent a man in fine clothes was shouting to the crowd about everything that was to be seen; it was before the days of rnicrophones, and he roared hoarsely through a megaphone. Beside him stood the Fire Eater, holding a flaming torch in front of his mouth. 'See Molza, the man who can always be sure of a hot meal,' bellowed the man in the fine clothes, and a few Deptfordians laughed shyly. 'See Professor Spencer, born without arms, but he can write a finer hand with his feet than any of your schoolteachers. And within the tent the greatest physiological marvel of the age, Andro, the Italian nobleman so evenly divided between the sexes that you may see him shave the whiskers off of the one side of his face, while the other displays the peachy smoothness of a lovely woman. A human miracle, attested to by doctors and men of science at Yale, Harvard, and Columbia. Any local doctor wishing to examine this greatest of marvels may make an appointment to do so, in the presence of myself, after the show tonight.'

"But I was not very attentive to the man in the fine clothes, because my eyes were all for another figure on the platform, who was doing wonders with decks of cards; he whirled them out from his hands in what appeared to be ribbons, and then drew them—magically it seemed to me—back into his hands again. He spread them in fans. He made them loop-the-loop from one hand to another. The man in the fine clothes introduced him as Willard the Wizard, positively the greatest artist in sleight-of-hand in the world today, briefly on loan from the Palace Theatre in New York.

"Willard was a tall man, and looked even taller because he wore what was then called a garter-snake suit, which had wriggling lines of light and dark fabric running perpendicularly through it. He was crowned by a pearl-grey hard hat—what we called a Derby, and known in Deptford only as part of the Sunday dress of doctors and other grandees. He was the most elegant thing I had ever seen in my life, and his thin, unsmiling face spoke to me of breathtaking secrets. I could not take my eyes off him, nor did I try to still my ravening desire to know those secrets. I too was a conjuror, you see; I had continued, on the sly, to practise the few elementary sleights and passes I had learned from Ramsay, before my father put a stop to it. I longed with my whole soul to know what Willard knew. As the hart pants after the water brooks, even so my blasphemous soul panted after the Wizard. And the unbelievable thing was that, of the fifteen or twenty people gathered in front of the platform, he seemed to look most often at me, and once I could swear I saw him wink!

"I paid my five cents—a special price for schoolchildren until six o'clock—and entered in the full splendour of Wanless's World of Wonders. It is impossible for me to describe the impression it made on me then, because I came to know it so well later on. It was just a fair-sized tent, capable of holding ten or twelve exhibits and the spectators. It was of that discouraged whitey-grey colour that such tents used to be before somebody had the good idea of colouring canvas brown. A few strings of lights hung between the three main poles, but they were not on, because it was assumed that we could see well enough by the light that leaked in from outdoors. The exhibits were on stands the height of a table; indeed, they were like collapsible tables, and each exhibit had his own necessities. Professor Spencer had the blackboard on which he wrote so elegantly with his feet; Molza had his jet of flaming gas, and a rack to hold the swords he swallowed; it was really, I suppose, very tacky and ordinary. But I was under the spell of Willard, and I didn't, at that time, take much heed of anything else, not even of the clamorous Fat Woman, who seemed never to be wholly quiet, even when the other exhibits were having their turn.

"The loud-voiced man had followed us inside, and bellowed about each wonder as we toured round the circle. Even to such an innocent as I, it was plain that the wonders were shown in an ascending order of importance, beginning with the Knife Thrower and Molza, and working upward through Zovene the Midget Juggler and Sonny the Strong Man to Professor Spencer and Zitta the Serpent Woman. She seemed to mark a divide, and after her came Rango the Missing Link, then the Fat Woman, called Happy Hannah, then Willard, and finally Andro the Half-Man Half-Woman.

"Even though my eyes constantly wandered toward Willard, who seemed now and then to meet them with a dark and enchantingly wizard-like gaze, I was too prudent to ignore the lesser attractions. After all, I had invested five ill-gotten cents in this adventure, and I was in no position to throw money away. But we came to Willard at last, and the loud-voiced man did not need to introduce him, because even before Happy Hannah had finished her noisy harangue and had begun to sell pictures of herself, he threw away his cigarette, sprang to his feet, and began to pluck coins out of the air. He snatched them from every-where—from the backs of his knees, from his elbows, from above his head—and threw them into a metal basin on his little tripod table. You could hear them clink as they fell, and as the number increased the sound from the basin changed. Then, without speaking a word, he seized the basin and hurled its contents into the crowd. People ducked and shielded their faces. But the basin was empty! Willard laughed a mocking laugh. Oh, very Mephistophelian! It sounded like a trumpet call to me, because I had never heard anybody laugh like that before. He was laughing at us, for having been deceived. What power! What glorious command over lesser humanity! Silly people often say that they are enraptured by something which has merely pleased them, but I was truly enraptured. I was utterly unaware of myself, whirled into a new sort of comprehension of life by what I saw.

"You must understand that I had never seen a conjuror before. I knew what conjuring was, and I could do some tricks. But I had never seen anybody else do sleight-of-hand except Ramsay here, who made very heavy weather of getting one poor coin from one of his great red hands to the other, and if he had not explained that the pass was supposed to be invisible you would never have known it was a trick at all. Please don't be hurt, Ramsay. You are a dear fellow and rather a famous writer in your own line, but as a conjuror you were abject. But Willard! For me the Book of Revelation came alive: here was an angel come down from heaven, having great power, and the earth was lightened with his glory; if only I could be like him, surely there would be no more sorrow, nor crying, nor any more pain, and all former things—my dark home, my mad, disgraceful mother, the torment of school—would pass away."

"So you ran away with the show," said Kinghovn, who had no tact.

"Ramsay tells me they say in Deptford that I ran away with the show," said Eisengrim, smiling what I would myself have called a Mephistophelian smile, beneath which he looked like any other man whose story has been interrupted by somebody who doesn't understand the form and art of stories. "I don't think Deptford would ever comprehend that it was not a matter of choice. But if you have understood what I have said about the way Deptford regarded me, you will realize that I had no choice. I did not run away with the show; the show ran away with me."

"Because you were so utterly entranced by Willard?" said Ingestree.

"No, I think our friend means something more than that," said Lind. "These possessions of the soul are very powerful, but there must have been something else. I smell it. The Bible obsession must somehow have supported the obsession with the conjuror. Not even a great revelation wipes out a childhood's indoctrination; the two must have come together in some way."

"You are right," said Eisengrim. "And I begin to see why people call you a great artist. Your education and sophistication haven't gobbled up your understanding of the realities of life. Let me go on.

"Willard's show had to be short, because there were ten exhibits in the tent, and a full show was not supposed to run over forty-five minutes. As one of the best attractions he was allowed something like five minutes, and after the trick with the coins he did some splendid things with ribbons, pulling them out of his mouth and throwing them into the bowl, from which he produced them neatly braided. Then he did some very flashy things with cards, causing any card chosen by a member of the audience to pop out of a pack that was stuck in a wineglass as far away from himself as his platform allowed. He finished by eating a spool of thread and a packet of needles, and then producing the thread from his mouth, with all the needles threaded on it at intervals of six inches. During the Oohs and Aahs, he nonchalantly produced the wooden spool from his ear, and threw it into the audience—threw it so that I caught it. I remember being amazed that it wasn't even wet, which shows how very green I was.

"I didn't want to see Andro, whose neatly compartmentalized sexuality meant nothing to me. As the crowd moved on to hear the loud-mouthed man bellow about the medical miracle called hermaphroditism—*only one in four hundred million births, ladies and gentlemen, only six thoroughly proven hermaphrodites in the whole long history of mankind, and one of them stands before you in Deptford today!*—I hung around Willard's table. He leapt down from it and lighted another cigarette. Even the way he did that was magical, for he flicked the pack toward his mouth, and the cigarette leaped between his lips, waiting for the match he was striking with the thumbnail of his other hand. There I was, near enough to the Wizard to touch him. But it was he who touched me. He reached toward my left ear and produced a quarter from it, and flicked it toward me. I snatched it out of the air, and handed it back to him. 'No, it's for you, kid,' he said. His voice was low and hoarse, and not in keeping with the rest of his elegant presentation, but I didn't care. A quarter! For me! I had never known such riches in my life. My infrequent stealings had never, before this day, aspired beyond a nickel. The man was not only a Wizard; he was princely.

"I was inspired. Inspired by you, Ramsay, you may be surprised to hear. You remember your trick in which you pretended to eat money, though one could always see it in your hand as you took it away from your mouth? I did that. I popped the quarter into my mouth, chewed it up, showed Willard that it was gone, and that I had nothing in my hands. I could do a little magic, too, and I was eager to claim some kinship with this god.

"He did not smile. He put his hand on my shoulder and said, 'Come with me, kid. I got sumpn to show ya,' and steered me toward a back entry of the tent which I had not noticed.

"We walked perhaps halfway around the fairground, which was not really very far, and we kept behind tents and buildings. I would have been proud to be seen by the crowd with such a hero, but we met very few people, and they were busy with their own affairs in the agricultural tents, so I do not suppose anybody noticed us. We came to the back of the barn where the horses were stabled when they were not being shown; it was one of the two or three permanent buildings of the fair. Behind it was a lean-to with a wall which did not quite reach to the roof, nor fully to the ground. It was the men's urinal, old, dilapidated, and smelly. Willard peeped in, found it empty, and pushed me in ahead of him. I had never been in such a place before, because it was part of my training that one never 'went' anywhere except at home, and all arrangements had to be made to accommodate this rule. It was a queer place, as I remember it; just a tin trough nailed to the wall, sloping slightly downward so that it drained into a hole in the ground. A pile of earth was ready to fill in the hole, once the fair was over.

"At the end of this shanty was a door which hung partly open, and it was through this that Willard guided me. We were in an earth closet, as old as Deptford fair, I should judge, for a heavy, sweetish, old smell hung over it. Hornets buzzed under the sloping roof. The two holes in the seat were covered by rounds of wood, with crude handles. I think I would know them if I saw them now.

"Willard took a clean white handkerchief out of his pocket, twisted it quickly into a roll, and forced it between my teeth. No: I should not say 'forced'. I thought this was the beginning of some splendid illusion, and opened my mouth willingly. Then he whirled me round, lifted me up on the seat in a kneeling position, pulled down my pants and sodomized me.

"Quickly said: an eternity in the doing. I struggled and resisted: he struck me such a blow over the ear that I slackened my grip with the pain, and he had gained an entry. It was rough: it was painful, and I suppose it was soon over. But as I say, it seemed an eternity, for it was a kind of feeling I had never guessed at.

"I am anxious you should not misunderstand me. I was no Greek lad, discovering the supposed pleasures of pederastic love in a society that knew it and condoned it. I was a boy not yet quite ten years old, who did not know what sex was in any form. I thought I was being killed, and in a shameful way.

"The innocence of children is very widely misunderstood. Few of them—I suppose only children brought up in wealthy families that desire and can contrive a conspiracy of ignorance—are unknowing about sex. No child brought up so near the country as I was, and among schoolchildren whose ages might reach as high as fifteen or sixteen, can be utterly ignorant of sex. It had touched me, but not intimately. For one thing, I had heard the whole of the Bible read through several times by my father; he had a plan of readings which, pursued morning and evening, worked through the whole of the book in a year. I had heard the sound as an infant, and as a little child, long before I could understand anything of the sense. So I knew about men going in unto women, and people raising up seed of their loins, and I knew that my father's voice took on a special tone of shame and detestation when he read about Lot and his daughters, though I had never followed what it was they did in that cave, and thought their sin was to make their father drunk. I knew these things because I had heard them, but they had no reality for me.

"As for my mother, who was called hoor by my schoolmates, I knew only that hoors—my father used the local pronunciation, and I don't think he knew any other—were always turning up in the Bible, and always in a bad sense which meant nothing to me as a reality. Ezekiel, sixteen, was a riot of whoredoms and abominations, and I shivered to think how terrible they must be: but I did not know what they were, even in the plainest sense of the words. I only knew that there was something filthy and disgraceful that pertained to my mother, and that we all, my father and I, were spattered by her shame, or abomination, or whatever it might be.

"I was aware that there was some difference between boys and girls, but I didn't know, or want to know, what it was, because I connected it somehow with the shame of my mother. You couldn't be a hoor unless you were a woman, and they had something special that made it possible. What I had, as a male, I had most strictly been warned against as an evil and shameful part of my body. 'Don't you ever monkey with yourself, down there,' was the full extent of the sexual instruction I had from my father. I knew that the boys who were gloating over the bull's testicles were doing something dirty, and my training was such that I was both disgusted and terrified by their sly nastiness. But I didn't know why, and it never would have occurred to me to relate the bull's showy apparatus with those things I possessed, in so slight a degree, and which I wasn't to monkey with. So you can see that without being utterly ignorant, I was innocent, in my way. If I had not been innocent, how could I have lived my life, and even have felt some meagre joy, from time to time?

"Sometimes I felt that joy when I was with you, Ramsay, because you were kind to me, and kindness was a great rarity in my life. You were the only person in my childhood who had treated me as if I were a human creature. I don't say, who loved me, you notice. My father loved me, but his love was a greater burden, almost, than hate might have been. But you treated me as a fellow-being, because I don't suppose it ever occurred to you to do anything else. You never ran with the crowd.

"The rape itself was horrible, because it was painful physically, but worse because it was an outrage on another part of my body

29

which I had been told to fear and be ashamed of. Liesl tells me that Freud has had a great deal to say about the importance of the functions of excretion in deciding and moulding character. I don't know anything about that; don't want to know it, because all that sort of thinking lies outside what I really understand. I have my own notions about psychology, and they have served me well. But this rape—it was something filthy going in where I knew only that filthy things should come out, as secretly as could be managed. In our house there was no word for excretion, only two or three prim locutions, and the word used in the schoolyard seemed to me a horrifying indecency. It's very popular nowadays in literature, I'm told by Liesl. She reads a great deal. I don't know how writers can put it down, though there was a time when I used it often enough in my daily speech. But as I have grown older I have returned to that early primness. We don't get over some things. But what Willard did to me was, in a sense I could understand, a reversal of the order of nature, and I was terrified that it would kill me.

"It didn't, of course. But that, and Willard's heavy breathing, and the flood of filthy language that he whispered as a kind of ecstatic accompaniment to what he was doing, were more horrible to me than anything I have met with since.

"When it was over he pulled my head around so that he could he see my face and said, 'You O.K., kid?' I can remember the tone now. He had no idea at all of what I was, or what I might feel. He was obviously happy, and the Mephistophelian smile had given place to an expression that was almost boyish. 'Go on now,' he said. 'Pull up your pants and beat it. And if you blat to anybody, by the living Jesus I'll cut your nuts off with a rusty knife.'

"Then I fainted, but for how long, or what I looked like when I did it, I of course can't tell you. Perhaps I was out for a few minutes, because when I became aware again Willard was looking anxious, and patting my cheeks lightly. He had taken the gag out of my mouth. I was crying, but making no noise. I had learned very early in life not to make a noise when I cried. I was still crumpled up on the horrible seat, and now its stench was too much for me and I vomited. Willard sprang back, anxious for his fine trousers and the high polish on his shoes. But he dared not leave me. Of course I had no idea how frightened he was. He felt he could trust in my shame and his threats up to a point, but I might be one of those terrible children who go beyond the point set for them by adults. He tried to placate me.

"'Hey,' he whispered, 'you're a pretty smart kid. Where'd you learn that trick with the quarter, eh? Come on now, show it to me again. I never seen a better trick than that, even at the Palace, New York. You're the kid that eats money; that's who you are. A real show-business kid. Now look, I'll give you this, if you'll eat it.' He offered me a silver dollar. But I turned my face away, and sobbed, without sound.

"'Aw now, look, it wasn't as bad as that,' he said. 'Just some fun between us two. Just playing paw and maw, eh? You want to grow up to be smart, don't you? Want to have fun? Take it from me, kid, you can't start too young. The day'll come, you'll thank me. Yes sir, you'll thank me. Now look here. I show you I've got nothing in my hands, see? Now watch.' He spread his fingers one by one, and magically quarters appeared between them until he held four quarters in each hand. 'Magic money, see? All for you; two whole dollars if you'll shut up and get the hell outa here, and never say anything to anybody.'

"I fainted again, and this time when I came round Willard was looking deeply worried. 'What you need is rest,' he said. 'Rest, and time to think about that money. I've gotta get back for the next show, but you stay here, and don't let anybody in. Nobody, see? I'll come back as soon as I can and I'll bring you something. Something nice. But don't let anybody in, don't holler, and keep quiet like a mouse.'

"He went, and I heard him pause for a moment outside the door. Then I was alone, and I sobbed myself to sleep.

"I did not wake until he came back, I suppose an hour later. He brought me a hot dog, and urged me to eat it. I took one bite—it was my first hot dog—and vomited again. Willard was now very worried indeed. He swore fiercely, but not at me. All he said to me was, 'My God you're a crazy kid. Stay here. Now *stay* here, I tell ya. I'll come back as soon as I can.'

"That was not very soon. Perhaps two hours. But when he came he had an air of desperation about him, which I picked up at once. Terrible things had happened, and terrible remedies must be found.

He had brought a large blanket, and he wrapped me in it, so that not even my head was showing, and lugged me bodily—I was not very heavy—out of the privy; I felt myself dumped into what I suppose was the back of a buggy or a carry-all, or something, and other wraps were thrown over me. Off I went, bumping along in the back of the cart, and it was some time later that I felt myself lifted out again, carried over rough ground, and humped painfully up onto what seemed to be a platform. Then another painful business of being lugged over a floor, some sounds of objects being moved, and at last the blanket was taken off. I was in a dark place, and only vaguely conscious that some distance away a door, like the door of a shed, was open, and I could see the light of dusk through it.

"Willard lost no time. 'Get in here,' he commanded, and pushed me into a place that was entirely dark, and confined. I had to climb upward, boosted by him, until I came to what seemed to be a shelf, or seat, and on this he pushed me. 'Now you'll be all right,' he said, in a voice that carried no confidence at all that I would be all right. It was a desperate voice. 'Here's something for you to eat.' A box was pushed in beside me. Then a door below me was closed, and snapped from the outside, and I was in utter darkness.

"After a while I felt around me. Irregular walls, seeming to be curved everywhere; there was even a small dome over my head. A smell, not clean, but not as disgusting as the privy at the fair. A little fresh air from a point above my head. I fell asleep again.

"When I woke, it was because I heard the whistle of a train, and a train-like thundering nearby. But I was not moving. I was wretchedly hungry, and in the darkness I explored Willard's box. Something lumpy and sticky inside it, which I tried to eat, and then greedily ate it all. Sleep again. Terrible fatigue all through my body, and the worst pain of all in my bottom. But I could not move very much in any direction, and I had to sit on my misery. At last, a space of time that seemed like a geological age later, I felt movement. Banging and thumping which went on for some time. A sound of voices. The sound of another whistle, and then trundling, lumbering movement, which increased to a good speed. For the first time in my life I was on a train, but of course I didn't know that.

"And that, my friends, is the first instalment of my subtext to the memoirs of Robert-Houdin, whose childhood, you recall, was such an idyll of family love and care, and whose introduction to magic was so charmingly brought about. Enough, I think, for one evening. Good-night."

(5)

When I made my way to bed, some time later, I tapped at Eisengrim's door. As I had expected, he was awake, and lay, looking very fine, against his pillows, wearing a handsome dressing-robe.

"Kind of you to come in and say good-night, Dunny."

"I expected you'd be waiting up to see what your notices were."

"A disgusting way of putting it. Well, what were they?"

"About what you'd expect. Kinghovn had a fine sense of the appearance of everything. I'll bet that as you talked he had that fair all cut up into long shots, close-ups, and atmosphere shots. And of course he's a devil for detail. For one thing, he wondered why nobody wanted to use the privy while you were left in it for so long."

"Simple enough. Willard wrote a note which said 'INFECTION: Closed by Doctor's Order', and pinned it to the door."

"Also he was anxious to know what it was you ate when you found yourself in the curious prison with the rounded walls."

"It was a box of Cracker-Jack. I didn't know what it was at the time, and had never eaten it before. Why should I have included those details in my story? I didn't know them then. It would have been a violation of narrative art to tell things I didn't know. Kinghovn ought to have more sense of artistic congruity."

"He's a cameraman. He wants to get a shot of everything, and edit later."

"I edit as I go along. What did the others say?"

"Ingestree talked for quite a while about the nature of puritanism. He doesn't know anything about it. It's just a theological whimwham to him. He's talked about puritanism at Oxford to Ronny Knox and

Monsignor D'Arcy, but that stuff means nothing in terms of the daily, bred-in-the-bone puritanism we lived in Deptford. North American puritanism and the puritanism the English know are worlds apart. I could have told him a thing or two about that, but my time for instructing people is over. Let 'em wallow in whatever nonsense pleases 'em, say I."

"Did Lind have anything to say?"

"Not much. But he did say that nothing you told us was incomprehensible to him, or even very strange. 'We know of such things in Sweden,' he said."

"I suppose people know of such things everywhere. But every rape is unique for the aggressor and the victim. He talks as if he knew everything."

"I don't think he means it quite that way. When he talks about Sweden, I think it is a mystical rather than a geographical concept. When he talks of Sweden he means himself, whether he knows it or not. He really does understand a great deal. You remember what Goethe said? No, of course you don't. He said he'd never heard of a crime of which he could not believe himself capable. Same with Lind, I suppose. That's his strength as an artist."

"He's a great man to work with. I think between us we'll do something extraordinary with this film."

"I hope so. And by the way, Magnus, I must thank you for the very kind things you said about me tonight. But I assure you I didn't especially mean to be kind to you, when we were boys. I mean, it wasn't anything conscious."

"I'm sure it wasn't. But that's the point, don't you see? If you'd done it out of duty, or for religious reasons, it would have been different. But it was just decency. You're a very decent man, Dunny."

"Really? Well—it's nice of you to think so. I've heard dissenting opinions."

"It's true. That's why I think you ought to know something I didn't see fit to tell them tonight."

"You suggested you had been editing. What did you leave out?"

"One gets carried away, telling a story. I may have leaned a little too heavily on my character as the wronged child. But would they have understood the whole truth? I don't after fifty years when I have thought of it over and over. You believe in the Devil, don't you."

"In an extremely sophisticated way, which would take several hours to explain, I do."

"Yes. Well, when the Devil is walking beside you, as he was walking beside me at that fair, it doesn't take a lot of argument to make him seem real."

"I won't insult you by saying you're a simple man, but you're certainly a man of strong feeling, and your feelings take concrete shapes. What did the Devil do to you that you withheld when you were talking downstairs?"

"The whole nub of the story. When Willard gave me that quarter in the tent, we were standing behind the crowd, which was gaping at Andro who was showing his big right bicep while twitching his sumptuous left breast. Nobody was looking. Willard had slipped his hand down the back of my pants and gently stroked my left buttock. Gave it a meaning squeeze. I remember very well how warm his hand felt."

"Yes?"

"I smiled up into his face."

"Yes?"

"Is that all you have to say? Don't you see what I'm getting at? I had never had any knowledge of sex, had never known a sexual caress before, even of the kind parents quite innocently give their children. But at this first sexual approach I yielded. I cosied up to Willard. How could I, without any true understanding of what I was doing, respond in such a way to such a strange act?"

"You were mad to learn his magic. It doesn't seem very strange to me."

"But it made me an accomplice in what followed."

"You think that? And you still blame yourself?"

"What did I know of such things? I can only think it was the Devil prompting me, and pushing me on to what looked then, and for years after, like my own destruction."

"The Devil isn't a popular figure nowadays. The people who take him seriously are few."

"I know. How he must laugh. I don't suppose God laughs at the people who think He doesn't exist. He's above jokes. But the Devil isn't. That's one of his most endearing qualities. But I still remember that smile. I had never smiled like that before. It was a smile of complicity. Now where would such a child as I was learn such a smile as that?"

"From that other old joker, Nature, do you suppose?"

"I don't take much stock in Nature ... Thanks for coming in. Good-night, decent man."

"Magnus, are you becoming sentimental in your old age?"

"I'm fully ten years younger than you, you sour Scot. Good-night, kind man."

I went to my room, and to my bed, but it was a long time before I slept. I lay awake, thinking about the Devil. Many people would have considered my bedroom at Sorgenfrei a first-class place for such reflection, because so many people associate the Devil with a high standard of old-fashioned luxury. Mine was a handsome room in a corner tower, with an area of floor as big as that of a modest modern North American house. Sorgenfrei was an early-nineteenth-century construction, built by a forebear of Liesl's who seemed to have something in common, at least in his architectural taste, with the mad King of Bavaria; it was a powerfully romantic Gothic Revival house, built and furnished with Teutonic thoroughness. Everything was heavy, everything was the best of its kind, everything was carved, and polished, and gilded, and painted to the highest possible degree, and everything would drive a modern interior decorator out of his tasteful mind. But it suited me splendidly.

Not, however, when I wanted to think about the Devil. It was too romantic, too Germanic altogether. As I lay in my big bed, looking out of the windows at the mountains on which moonlight was falling, what could be easier than to accept an operatic Devil, up to every sort of high-class deception, and always defeated at the end of the story by the power of sheer simple-minded goodness? All my life I have been a keen operagoer and playgoer, and in the theatre I am willing to accept the notion that although the Devil is a very clever fellow, he is no match for some ninny who is merely good. And what is this goodness? A squalid, know-nothing acceptance of things as they are, an operatic version of the dream which, in North America, means Mom and apple pie. My whole life had been a protest against this world, or the smudged, grey version of it into which I had been born in my rural Canada.

No, no; that Devil would never do. But what else is there? Theologians have not been so successful in their definitions of the Devil as they have been in their definitions of God. The words of the Westminster Confession, painstakingly learned by heart as a necessity of Presbyterian boyhood, still seemed, after many wanderings, to have the ring of indisputable authority. God was *infinite in being and perfection, a most pure spirit, invisible, without body, parts or passions, immutable, immense, eternal, incomprehensible, almighty, most wise, most holy, most free, most absolute, working all things according to the counsel of his own immutable and most righteous will, for his own glory.* Excellent, even if one is somewhat seduced by the high quality of the prose of 1648. What else? *Most loving, most gracious, merciful, long-suffering, abundant in goodness and truth, forgiving iniquity, transgression and sin; the rewarder of those that diligently seek him.* Aha, but where does one seek God? In Deptford, where Eisengrim and I were born, and might still be living if, in my case, I had not gone off to the First World War, and in his case, if he had not been abducted by a mountebank in a travelling show? I had sought God in my lifelong, unlikely (for a Canadian schoolmaster) preoccupation with that fantastic collection of wise men, virtuous women, thinkers, doers, organizers, contemplatives, crack-brained simpletons, and mad mullahs that are all called Saints. But all I had found in that lifelong study was a complexity that brought God no nearer. Had Eisengrim sought God at all? How could I know? How can anybody know what another man does in this most secret part of his life? What else had I been taught in that profound and knotty definition? That God was *most just and terrible in his judgements, hating all sin, one who will by no means clear the guilty.* Noble words, and (only slightly cloaked by their nobility) a terrifying concept. And why should it not be terrifying? A little terror, in my view, is good for the soul, when it is terror in the face of a noble object.

The Devil, however, seems never to have been so splendidly mapped and defined. Nor can you spy him simply by turning a fine definition of God inside out; he is something decidedly more subtle than just God's opposite.

Is the Devil, then, sin? No, though sin is very useful to him; anything we may reasonably call sin involves some personal choice. It is flattering to be asked to make important choices. The Devil loves the time of indecision.

What about evil, then? Is the Devil the origin and ruler of that great realm of manifestly dreadful and appalling things which are not, so far as we can determine, anybody's fault or the consequence of any sin? Of the cancer wards, and the wards for children born misshapen and mindless? I have had reason to visit such places— asylums for the insane in particular—and I do not think I am fanciful or absurdly sensitive in saying that I have felt evil to be palpable there, in spite of whatever could be done to lessen it.

These are evil things within my knowledge: I am certain there are worse things I have never encountered. And how constant this evil is! Let mankind laboriously suppress leprosy, and tuberculosis rages: when tuberculosis is chained, cancer rushes to take its place. One might almost conclude that such evils were necessities of our collective life. If the Devil is the inspirer and ruler of evil, he is a serious adversary indeed, and I cannot understand why so many people become jokey and facetious at the mention of his name.

Where is the Devil? Was Eisengrim, whose intuitions and directness of observation in all things concerning himself I had come to respect, right in saying the Devil stood beside him when Willard the Wizard solicited him to an action which, under the circumstances, I should certainly have to call evil? Both God and the Devil wish to intervene in the world, and the Devil chooses his moments shrewdly.

What had Eisengrim told us? That on 30 August 1918, he had descended into hell, and did not rise again for seven years? Allowing for his wish to startle us, and his taste for what a severe critic might call flashy rhetoric, could what he said be discounted?

It was always a mistake, in my experience, to discount Magnus Eisengrim. The only thing to do was to wait for the remainder of his narrative, and hope that it would make it possible for me to reach a conclusion. And that would be my much-desired document.

(6)

I knew nothing about filming, but Lind's subordinates told me that his methods were not ordinary. He was extremely deliberate, and because he liked careful rehearsal and would not work at night he seemed to take a lot of time. But as he wasted none of this time, his films were not as devastatingly expensive as impatient people feared they might be. He was a master of his craft. I did not presume to question him about it, but I sensed that he attached more importance to Eisengrim's story than ordinary curiosity would explain, and that the dinners and discussions at Sorgenfrei fed the fire of his creation. Certainly he and Kinghovn and Ingestree were anxious for more as we settled down in the library on the third night. Liesl had seen to it that there was plenty of brandy, for although Eisengrim drank very little, and I was too keen on my document to drink much, Lind loved to tipple as he listened and had a real Scandinavian head; brandy never changed him in the least. Kinghovn was a heavy drinker, and Ingestree, a fatty, could not resist anything that could be put into his mouth, be it food, drink, or cigar.

Magnus knew they were waiting, and after he had toyed with them for a few minutes, and appeared to be leading them into general conversation, he yielded to Lind's strong urging that he go on with his story or—as Ingestree now quite seriously called it—"the subtext".

"I told you I was on a train, but didn't know it. I think that is true, but I must have had some notion of what was happening to me, because I had heard the whistle, and felt the motion, and of course I had seen trains. But I was so wretched that I couldn't reason, or be sure of anything, except that I was in close quarters in pitchy darkness. My mind was on a different unhappiness. I knew that when I was in trouble I should pray, and God would surely help me. But I couldn't pray, for two reasons. First, I couldn't kneel, and to me prayer without kneeling was unknown. Second, if I had been able to kneel I could not have dared to do it, because I was horribly aware that what Willard had done to me in that disgusting privy had been done while I was in a kneeling posture. I assure you, however strange it may seem, that I didn't know what he had done, but I felt strongly that it was a blasphemy against kneeling, and if I knew nothing of sex I certainly knew a lot about blasphemy. I guessed I might be on a train, but I knew for a certainty that I had angered God. I had been involved in what was very likely the Sin against the Holy Ghost. Can you imagine what that meant to me? I had never known such desolation. I had wept in the privy and now I could weep no more. Weeping meant sound, and I had a confused idea that although God certainly knew about me, and undoubtedly had terrible plans for me, He might be waiting for me to betray myself by sound before He went to work on me. So I kept painfully still.

"I suppose I was in a state of what would now be called shock. How long it went on I could not then tell. But I know now that it was from Friday night until the following Sunday morning that I sat in my close prison, without food or water or light. The train had not been travelling all that time. All day Saturday Wanless's World of Wonders had a day's work at a village not many miles from Deptford, and I was conscious of the noises of unloading the train in the morning, and of loading it again very late at night, though I could not interpret them. But Sunday morning brought a kind of release.

"There were more men's voices, and more sounds of heavy things being methodically moved near where I was. Then after a period of silence I heard Willard's voice. 'He's in there,' it said. Then sounds somewhat below me, and a hand reached up and touched my leg. I made no sound—could not make a sound, I suppose—and was rather roughly hauled out into a dim light, and laid on the floor. Then a strange voice. 'Jesus, Willard,' it said, 'you've killed him. Now we're all up the well-known creek.' But then I moved a little. 'Christ, he's alive,' said the strange voice; 'thank God for that.' Then Willard's voice: 'I'd rather he was dead,' it said; 'what are we going to do with him now?'

"'We got to get Gus,' said the strange voice. 'Gus is the one who'll know what to do. Don't talk about him being dead. Haven't you got any sense? We got to get Gus right now.' Then Willard spoke. 'Yeah, Gus, Gus, Gus; it's always Gus with you. Gus hates me. I'll be outa the show.' 'Leave Gus to me about you and the show,' said the other voice; 'but only Gus can deal with this right now. You wait here.'

"The other man went away, and as he went I heard the heavy door of the freight-car—for I was in a freight-car in which the World of Wonders took its trappings from town to town—and I was for a second time alone with Willard. Through my eyelashes I could see him sitting on a box beside me. His Mephistophelian air of command was gone; he looked diminished, shabby, and afraid.

"After a time the other man returned with Gus, who proved to be a woman—a real horse's godmother of a woman, a little, hard-faced, tough woman who looked like a jockey. But she inspired confidence, and while it would be false to say that my spirits lightened, I felt a little less desolate I have always had a quick response to people, and though it is sometimes wrong it is more often right. If I like them on sight they are lucky people for me, and that's really all I care about. Gus was in a furious temper.

"'Willard, you son-of-a-bitch, what the hell have you got us into now? Lemme look at this kid.' Gus knelt and hauled me round so that she could see me. Then she sent the other man to open the doors further, to give her a better light.

"Gus had a rough touch, and she hurt me so that I whimpered. 'What's your name, kid?' she said. 'Paul Dempster.' 'Who's your Dad?' 'Reverend Amasa Dempster.' This pushed Gus's rage up a few notches. 'A reverend's kid,' she shouted; 'you had to go and kidnap a reverend's kid. Well, I wash my hands of you, Willard. I hope they hang you, and if they do, by God I'll come and swing on your feet!'

"I can't pretend to remember all their talk, because Gus sent the unknown man, whom she called Charlie, to get water and milk and food for me, and while they wrangled she fed me, first, sugared water from a spoon, and then, when I had plucked up a little, some milk, and finally a few biscuits. I can still remember the pain as my body began to return to its normal state, and the pins-and-needles in my arms and legs. She put me on my feet and walked me up and down but I was wobbly, and couldn't stand much of that.

"Nor can I pretend that I understood much of what was said at that time, though later, from knowledge I picked up over a period of years, I know what it must have been. I was not Gus's chief problem; I was a complication of a problem that was already filling the foreground of her mind. Wanless's World of Wonders belonged to Gus, and her brothers Charlie and Jerry; they were Americans, although their show toured chiefly in Canada, and Charlie ought to have been in the American Army, for the 1917 draft had included him and he had had his call-up. But Charlie had no mind for fighting, and Gus was doing her best to keep him out of harm's way, in hopes that the War would end before his situation became desperate. Charlie was very much her darling, and I judge he must have been at least ten years younger than she; Jerry was the oldest. Therefore, involvements with the law were not to Gus's taste, even though they might bring about the downfall of Willard. She detested him because he was Charlie's best friend, and a bad influence. Willard, in his panic, had abducted me, and it was up to Gus to get me out of the way without calling attention to the Wanless family.

"It is easy now to think of several things they might have done, but none of those three were thinkers. Their obsession was that I must be kept from running to the police and telling my tale of seduction, abduction, and hard usage; it never occurred to them to ask me, or they would have found out that I had no clear idea of who or what the police were, and had no belief in any rights of mine that might have gone contrary to the will of any adult. They assumed that I was aching to return to my loving family, whereas I was frightened of what my father would do when he found out what had happened in the privy, and what the retribution would be for having stolen fifteen cents, a crime of the uttermost seriousness in my father's eyes.

"My father was no brute, and I think he hated beating me, but he knew his duty. 'He that spareth his rod hateth his son; but he that loveth him chasteneth him betimes'; this was part of the prayer that always preceded a beating and he laid the rod on hard, while my mother wept or—this was very much worse, and indeed quite horrible—laughed sadly as if at something my father and I did not and could not know. But Gus Wanless was a sentimentalist,

American-style, and it never entered her head that a boy in my situation would be prepared to do anything rather than go home.

"There was another thing which seems extraordinary to me now, but which was perfectly in keeping with that period in history and the kind of people into whose hands I had fallen. There was never, at any time, any reference to what had happened in the privy. Gus and Charlie certainly knew that Willard had not stolen a boy, or thought it necessary to conceal a boy, simply as a matter of caprice. As I grew to know these carnival people I discovered that their deepest morality was precisely that of the kind of people they amused; whatever freedom their travelling way of life might give them, it did not cut far into the rock of North American accepted custom and morality. If Willard had despoiled a girl, I think Gus would have known better what to do, but she was unwilling to strike out into the deep and dirty waters that Willard's crime had revealed in the always troubled landscape of Wanless's World of Wonders.

"I think she was right: if Willard had fallen into the hands of the law as we knew it in Deptford, and in the county of which it was a part, the scandal would have wrecked the World of Wonders and Charlie would have been shipped back to the States to face the music. A showman, a magician at that, a stranger, an American, who had ravaged a local child in a fashion of which I am certain half the village had never heard except as something forbidden in the Bible—we didn't go in for lynchings in our part of the world, but I think Willard might have been killed by the other prisoners when he went to jail; jails have their own morality, and Willard would have found himself outside it. So nothing was said about that, then or afterward. This was all the worse for me, as I found out in the years to come. I was part of something shameful and dangerous everybody knew about, but which nobody would have dreamed of bringing into the light.

"What were they to do with me? I am sure Willard had spoken truly when he wished me dead, but he hadn't the courage to kill me when he had his chance. Now that Gus, who was the whole of the law and the prophets in the World of Wonders, knew about me, that moment had passed. As I have said, none of them had any capacity for thought or reasoning, and as they talked on and on Gus's mood turned from rage to fear. Willard was more at home in the air of fear than in that of anger.

"'Honest to God, Gus, nothing would ever have happened, if the kid hadn't shown some talent.'

"This was a lucky string to touch. Gus was sure she knew everything there was to know about Talent—a word she always pronounced with the air of one giving it a capital letter. And so it came out that when Willard had given me a quarter, out of pure open-heartedness, I had immediately done a trick with it. As neat a palm-and-pass as Willard had ever seen. Good enough for the Palace Theatre in New York.

"'You mean the kid can do tricks?' It was Charlie who spoke. 'Then why can't we fix him up a little with some hair-dye and maybe colour his skin, and use him as a Boy-Conjuror—Bonzo the Boy Wonder, or like that?'

"But this did not sit well with Willard. He wanted no rival conjurors in the show.

"'Jeeze, Willard, I only meant as a kind of assistant to you. Hand you things and like that. Maybe do a funny trick or two when you're not looking. You could plan something.'

"Now it was Gus who objected. 'Charlie, you ought to know by now that you can't never disguise anybody from somebody that knows him well. The law's going to follow the show; just keep that in mind. The kid's Dad, this reverend, comes into the show, sees a kid this size, and no hair-dye and blackface is going to hide him. Anyway, the kid sees his Dad, this reverend, and he gives him the high-sign. Use whatever head you got, Charlie.'

"Now it was Willard's turn to have a bright idea. 'Abdullah!' he said.

"Even though I was busy with the biscuits I stopped eating to look at them. They were like people from whose minds a cloud had lifted.

"'But can he handle Abdullah?' said Gus.

"'I betcha he can. I tell you, this kid's Talent. A natural. He's made for Abdullah. Don't you see, Gus? This is the silver lining. I made a little slip, I grant ya. But if Abdullah's back in the show, what does it matter? Abdullah's the big draw. Now look; we put Abdullah back, and I go to the top of the show, and let's not hear any more about Happy Hannah or that gaffed morphodite Andro.'

"'Just hold your horses, Willard. I'll believe a kid can handle Abdullah when I've seen it. You got to show me.'

"'And I'll show you. Gimme time, just a very little time, and I'll show you. Kid, can you handle a pack of cards?' Nothing could make me admit that I could handle a pack of cards. Ramsay had taught me a few card tricks, but when my father found it out he gave me such a beating as only a thoroughgoing Baptist can give a son who has been handling the Devil's Picture Book. It had been thoroughly slashed into my backside that cards were not for me. I denied all knowledge of cards before I had thought for an instant. Yet, immediately I had spoken, the four suits and the ways in which they could be made to dance began to rise in my memory.

"Willard was not troubled by my lack of knowledge. He had the real showman's enthusiasm for a new scheme. But Gus was dubious.

"'Just give me today, Gus,' said Willard. 'Only just this one Sunday, to show you what can be done. I'll work him in. You'll see. We can do it right here.'

"That was how I became the soul of Abdullah, and entered into a long servitude to the craft and art of magic.

"We began at once. Gus bustled away on some of the endless business she always had in hand, but Charlie remained, and he and Willard began to uncover something at the very back of the car—the only object in it which the handlers had not unloaded for Monday's fair—which was under several tarpaulins. Whatever it was, this was the prison in which I had spent my wretched, starving hours.

"When it was pulled forward and the wraps thrown aside, it was revealed as, I think still, the most hideous and offensive object I have ever seen in my life. You gentlemen know how particular I have always been about the accoutrements of my show. I have spent a great deal of money, which foolish people have thought unnecessary, on the beauty and workmanship of everything I have exhibited. In this I have been like Robert-Houdin, who also thought that the best was none too good for himself and his audiences. Perhaps some of my fastidiousness began with my hatred of the beastly figure that was called Abdullah.

"It was a crude effigy of a Chinese, sitting on top of a chest, with his legs crossed. To begin with, the name was crassly wrong. Why call a Chinese figure Abdullah? But everything about it was equally inartistic and inept. Its robes were of frowsy sateen; its head was vulgarly moulded in papier mâché with an ugly face, sharply slanted eyes, dangling moustaches, and yellow fangs which hung down over the lower lip. The thing was, in itself, reason for a sharp protest from the Chinese Ambassador, if there had been one. It summed up in itself all that spirit combined of jocosity and hatred with which ignorant people approach whatever is foreign and strange.

"The chest on which this monster sat was in the same mode of workmanship. It was lacquered with somebody's stupid notion of a dragon, half hideous and half cute, in gaudy red on a black background. A lot of cheap gold paint had been splashed about.

"Neither Willard nor Charlie explained to me what this thing was, or what relationship I was expected to bear to it. However, I was used to being ignored and rather liked it; being noticed had, in my experience, usually meant trouble. All they told me was that I was to sit in this thing and make it work, and my lesson began as soon as Abdullah was unveiled.

"Once again, but this time in daylight and with some knowledge of what I was doing, I crawled into the chest at the back of the figure, and thence upward, rather like an old-fashioned chimney-sweep climbing a chimney, into the body, where there was a tiny ledge on which I could sit and allow my feet to hang down. But that was not the whole of my duty. When I was in place, Willard opened various doors in the front of the chest, then turned the whole figure around on the wheels which supported the chest, and opened a door in the back. These doors revealed to the spectators an impressive array of wheels, cogs, springs, and other mechanical devices, and when Willard touched a lever they moved convincingly. But the secret of these mechanisms was that they were shams, displayed in front of polished steel mirrors, so that they seemed to fill the whole of the chest under the figure of Abdullah, but really left room for a small person to conceal himself when necessary. And that time came after Willard had closed the doors in the chest, and pulled aside Abdullah's robes to show some mechanism, and nothing else, in the figure itself. When that was happening, I had to let myself down into the secret open space in the chest and keep out of the way. Once Abdullah's mechanical innards had been displayed I crept back up into the figure, thrust aside the fake mechanism, which folded out of the way, and prepared to make Abdullah do his work.

"Willard and Charlie both treated me as if I were very stupid, which God knows I was not. However, I thought it best not to be too clever in the beginning. This was intuition; I did not figure it out consciously. They showed me a pack of cards, and painstakingly taught me the suits and the values. What Abdullah had to do was to play cards, on a very simple principle, with anybody who would volunteer from an audience to try their luck with him. This spectator—the Rube, as Willard called him—shuffled and cut a deck which lay on a little tray across Abdullah's knees. Then the Rube drew a card and laid it face down on the tray. At this point Willard pulled a lever on the side of Abdullah's chest, which set up a mechanical sound in the depths of the figure, which in fact I, the concealed boy, set going by pumping a pedal with my left foot. While this was going on it was my job to discover what card the Rube had drawn—which was easy, because he had put it face downward on a ground-glass screen, and I could fairly easily make it out—and to select a higher card from a rack concealed inside Abdullah ready to my hand. Having chosen my card, I set Abdullah's left arm in motion, slipping my own arm into the light framework in its sleeve; at the far end of this framework was a device into which I inserted the card that was to confound the Rube. I then made Abdullah's right arm move slowly to the deck of cards on the tray, and cut them; this was possible because the fingers had a pincers device in them which could be worked from inside the arm by squeezing a handle. When Abdullah had cut the cards his left hand moved to the deck and took a card from the top. But in fact he did nothing of the sort, because his sleeve fell forward for a moment and concealed what was really happening; it was at this instant I pushed the little slide which shot the card I had chosen from the rack into Abdullah's fingers, and it seemed to the spectators that this was the card he picked up from the deck. The Rube was then invited to turn up his card—a five, let us say; then a spectator was asked to turn up Abdullah's card. A seven in the same suit! Consternation of the Rube! Applause of the audience! Great acclaim for Willard, who had never touched a card at any time and had merely pulled the lever which set in motion Abdullah, the Card-Playing Automaton, and Scientific Marvel of the Age!

"We slaved away all of that Sunday. I lost my fright because Willard and Charlie were so pleased with what I could do, and although they still talked about me as though I had no ears to hear them, and no understanding, the atmosphere became cheerful and excited and I was the reason for it. I must not pretend that I mastered the mechanisms of Abdullah in an instant, and even when I had done so I had to be taught not to be too quick; I thought the essence of the work was to do it as fast as possible. Willard and Charlie knew, though they never bothered to tell me, that a very deliberate, and even slow, pace created a far better effect on the spectators. And I had much to learn. When I sat inside Abdullah my head was at the level of his neck, and here his robes parted a little to allow me to see through a piece of wire mesh that was painted the colour of his gown. It was by observing the actions of the Rube that I timed my own work. I had to learn to pump the little treadle that made the mechanical noise which simulated the finely scientific machinery of the automaton, and it was easy to forget, or to pump too fast and make Abdullah too noisy. The hardest part was ducking my head just enough to see what card the Rube had chosen and laid on the tray; as I said, this was ground glass, and there was a mirror underneath it so that I could see the suit and value of his card, but it was not as easy or as convenient as you might suppose, because the light was dim. And I had to be quick and accurate in choosing a card of greater value. A deck identical with the one used by the Rube was set up in a rack concealed by Abdullah's folded legs; it had eight pigeon-holes, in which each suit was divided into the cards from two to ten, and the Jack, Queen, King, and Ace by themselves. It was dark in Abdullah, and there was not much time for choosing, so I had to develop a good deal of dexterity.

"It was thrilling, and I worked feverishly to make myself perfect. How many times we went through the routine, when once I had mastered the general principle of it, I cannot guess, but I remember well that it was the management of the arms that gave me the most trouble, and any mistiming there made a mess of the whole deception. But we toiled as only people toil who are busy at the delicious work of putting something over on the public. There was a short noonday pause for a picnic, of which my share was milk and a lot of sticky buns; Gus had left instructions that I was not to be starved or overworked, because I was still weak, and I certainly was not starved.

"It was a hot day, and hotter still inside Abdullah. Also, Abdullah had a heavy smell, because of all the papier mâché and glue and size with which he was made. During my thirty-six hours or so of imprisonment I had been compelled to urinate, in spite of my awful thirst, and this had done nothing to freshen the atmosphere of that close confinement. Moreover, although I did not know it then, I learned later that the former operator of Abdullah had been a dwarf who cannot have been fastidious about his person, and there was a strong whiff of hot dwarf as I grew hotter myself. I suppose I became rather feverish, but although I would not describe my emotion as happiness I was possessed by an intensity of interest and ambition that was better than anything I had ever known in my life. When you were teaching me magic, Ramsay, I felt something like it, but not to the same degree, because—please don't be hurt—you were so tooth-achingly rotten at all your simple tricks. But this was the real thing. I didn't know quite what this reality was, but it was wonderful, and I was an important part of it.

"Charlie, who was as good-hearted as he was soft-headed, did all he could to make a game of it. He played the part of the Rube, and he did his best to include every kind of Rube he could think of. He was a terrible ham, but he was funny. He approached Abdullah as Uncle Zeke, the euchre champion of Pumpkin Centre, and as Swifty Dealer, the village tinhorn sport, and as Aunt Samantha, who didn't believe she could be bested by any Chinaman that ever lived, and as a whole gallery of such caricatures. I had to beg him not to be so funny, because I couldn't concentrate on my work when I was laughing so much. But Willard never laughed. He was the taskmaster, demanding the greatest skill I could achieve in the management of the mechanism. Charlie was a hearty praiser; he would gladly tell me that I was a wonderful kid and a gift to the carnival business and the possessor of a golden future. But Willard never praised a good piece of management; he was sharp about mistakes, and demanded more and more refinement of success. I didn't care. I felt that inside Abdullah I had entered into my kingdom.

"Come five o'clock Willard and Charlie thought we were ready to show our work to Gus. I had never been associated with any kind of show folk, and I thought it quite wonderful the way Gus climbed into the freight-car and behaved as if she had never seen any of us before; Willard and Charlie too behaved as if it were a real show and Gus a stranger. Willard gave a speech that I had not heard before, about the wonders of Abdullah, and the countless hours and boundless ingenuity that had gone into his construction; during all of it I kept as still as a mouse, and fully convinced myself that Gus did not know I was anywhere near; perhaps she thought I had run away. Then Gus, at the right time, came forward reluctantly and suspiciously, like a real Rube and not one of Charlie's comic turns, and cut the deck and chose a card: either Gus knew some sleight-of-hand herself or Willard had prepared a sharp test for me, because it was the Ace of Spades; there was no card to top it. And then I had one of those flashes which, I think I may say without boasting, have lifted my work above that of even a very good illusionist. At the bottom of the tray that held the court-cards in spades, there was a Joker, and that was what I caused Abdullah to put down on the tray to top Gus's Ace. Of course it would not do so, but it showed that I was able to meet an unexpected situation, and Charlie gave a whoop that would have drawn a crowd if there had been anybody hanging around the railway siding on a late Sunday afternoon.

"Gus was impressed, but the expression of her jockey's face did not change. 'O.K. I guess it'll do,' was what she said, and immediately the three began haggling again about some of the questions that had come up in the morning. I did not understand them then, but they concerned Abdullah's place in the show, which Willard insisted should be next to last, the place of honour reserved for the top attraction. It was now held by Andro, against whom Willard harboured a complicated grudge. Gus did not want to be rushed, and insisted that Abdullah should not be shown for a while, until we were far from Deptford.

"Charlie begged very hard that Abdullah should go into the show at once. Business wasn't good; they needed a strong attraction, especially now Hannah was getting out of hand and would have to be sat on; nobody would know the kid was in Abdullah because they would all be convinced Abdullah was a mechanical marvel. Yes, countered Gus, but how was she going to explain to the Talent a kid who turned up without warning and whom they would certainly know was the secret of Abdullah's card-playing genius? Would they just tell her that? A kid out of nowheres! Especially if there was any inquiry by Nosey Parkers and policemen. Could Hannah be trusted not to spill the beans? She was a religious old bitch and would love to do a mean thing for a holy reason. Ah, said Charlie, Gus surely knew how to handle Hannah; if Hannah had to go for as much as eight hours without the assistance of Elephant Gus, where would she be? And here Willard struck in to say that he knew a thing or two about Hannah that would keep her in order. And so on, at length, because they all argued in a circle, enjoying the contention rather than wishing to reach a conclusion. I had had a hard day, and the inside of Abdullah was like a Turkish bath; they had quite forgotten the living reality of the thing they were discussing. So I fell into an exhausted sleep. I did not understand it at the time, but I came to understand it very well later: when I was in Abdullah, I was Nobody. I was an extension and a magnification of Willard; I was an opponent and a baffling mystery to the Rube; I was something to be gawped at, but quickly forgotten, by the spectators. But as Paul Dempster I did not exist. I had found my place in life, and it was as Nobody."

The film-makers sipped their brandy for a time before Lind spoke. "It would be interesting to do a film about Nobody," he said. "I know I mustn't hurry you, so I won't ask you if you were Nobody for long. But you are going to continue, aren't you?"

"You must," said Ingestree. "Now we are getting a true story. Not like Robert-Houdin's faked-up reminiscences. He was never Nobody. He was always triumphantly and self-assuredly Somebody. He was charming, lively little Eugene Robert, the delight of his family and his friends; or he was that deserving young watch- and clock-maker; or he was the interesting young traveller who extracted the most amazing confidences from everybody; or he was the successful Parisian entertainer, drawing the cream of society to his little theatre, but always respectful, always conscious of his place, always the perfect bourgeois, always Somebody. Do you suppose many people are Nobody?"

Eisengrim looked at him with a not very agreeable smile. "Have you any recollection of being Nobody?" he said.

"Not really. No, I can't say I have."

"Have you ever met anyone who was Nobody?"

"I don't believe so. No, I'm sure I haven't. But then, if one met Nobody, I don't suppose Nobody would make much of an impression on one."

"Obviously not," said Eisengrim.

It was I who saw the film-makers to their car and watched them begin the descent from Sorgenfrei to the village where their inn was. Then I went back to the house as fast as my artificial leg would carry me and caught Eisengrim as he was getting into bed.

"About the Devil," I said, "I've been thinking more about what we said."

"Have you pinned him down, then?"

"Nothing like it. I am simply trying to get a better hold on his attributes. The attributes of God have been very carefully explored. But the Devil's attributes have been left vague. I think I've found one of them. It is he who puts the prices on things."

"Doesn't God put a price on things?"

"No. One of his attributes is magnanimity. But the Devil is a setter of prices, and a usurer, as well. You buy from him at an agreed price, but the payments are all on time, and the interest is charged on the whole of the principal, right up to the last payment, however much of the principal you think you have paid off in the meantime. Do you suppose the Devil invented numbers? I shouldn't be surprised if the Devil didn't invent Time, with all the subtle terrors that Time comprises. I think you said you spent seven years in hell?"

"I may have underestimated my sentence."

"That's what I mean."

"You're developing into a theologian, Dunny."

"A diabologian, rather. It's a fairly clear field, these days."

"Do you think you can study evil without living it? How are you going to discover the attributes of the Devil without getting close to him? Are you the man for that? Don't bother your old grey head, Dunny."

That was Magnus all over. He simply had to be the damnedest man around. What an egotist!

(7)

We were eating sandwiches and drinking beer at a lunch-break the following day. Magnus was not with us, because he had gone off to make some repairs and alterations in his make-up, about which he was extremely particular. Robert-Houdin had been a handsome man, in a French style, with strong features, a large, mobile mouth, and particularly fine eyes: Magnus would make no concession to a likeness, and insisted on playing the role of the great illusionist as his handsome self, and he darted away to touch up his face whenever he could. As soon as he was out of the way, Kinghovn turned the conversation to what we had heard the night before.

"Our friend puzzles me," he said. "You remember that he said the image of Abdullah was the ugliest thing he had ever seen? Then he described it, and it sounded like the sort of trash one would expect in such a poor little travelling show, and just what would seem marvellous to a small boy. How much is he colouring his story with opinions he formed later?"

"But inevitably it's all coloured by later opinions," said Ingestree. "What can you expect? It's the classic problem of autobiography; it's inevitably life seen and understood backwards. However honest we try to be in our recollections we cannot help falsifying them in terms of later knowledge, and especially in terms of what we have become. Eisengrim is unquestionably the greatest magician of our day, and to hear him tell it, of any day. How is he to make himself into a photo-graphic record of something that happened fifty years ago?"

"Then how can we reconstruct the past?" said Kinghovn. "Look at it from my point of view—really my point of view, which is through the camera. Suppose I had to make a film of what Eisengrim has told us, how could I be sure of what Abdullah looked like?"

"You couldn't," said Lind. "And you know it. But you and I and a good designer would work together, and we would produce an Abdullah that would give the right effect, though it might be far, far away from the real Abdullah of 1918. What would the real Abdullah be? Perhaps not as ugly as Eisengrim says, but certainly a piece of cheap junk. You and I, Harry, would show the world not simply what little Paul Dempster saw, but what he felt. We would even get that whiff of hot dwarf across to the public somehow. That's what we do. That's why we are necessary people."

"Then the truth of the past can never be recovered?"

"Harry, you should never talk. Your talk is the least useful part of you. You should just stick to your cameras, with which you are a man of genius. The truth of the past is to be seen in museums, and what is it? Dead things, sometimes noble and beautiful, but dead. And cases and cases of coins, and snuffboxes, and combs, and mirrors that won't reflect any more, and clothes that look as if the wearers had all been midgets, and masses of frowsy tat that tells us nothing at all. Once a man showed me a great treasure of his family; it was a hand-kerchief which somebody, on 30 January 1649, had dipped in the blood of the executed English King Charles I. It was a disgusting, rusty rag. But if you and I and Roly here had the money and the right people, we could fake up an execution of King Charles that would make people weep. Which is nearer to the truth? The rag, or our picture?"

I thought it was time for me to intervene. "I wouldn't call either the rag or your picture truth," I said; "I am an historian by training and temperament, and I would go to the documents, and there are plenty of them, about the execution of Charles, and when I had read and tested and reflected on them, I would back my truth against yours and win."

"Ah, but you see, my dear Ramsay, we would not dream of making our picture until we had consulted you or somebody like you, and given the fullest importance to your opinion."

"Well, would you be content to film the execution on a grey day? Wouldn't you want a shot of the sun rising behind Whitehall as the sun of English monarchy was setting on the scaffold?"

Lind looked at me sadly. "How you scholars underestimate us artists," he said, with wintry Scandinavian melancholy. "You think we are children, always beguiled by toys and vulgarities. When have you ever known me to stoop to a sunrise?"

"Besides, you don't understand what we could do with all those wonderful pearly greys," said Kinghovn.

"You will never persuade me to believe that truth is no more than what some artist, however gifted he may be, thinks is truth," I said. "Give me a document, every time."

"I suppose somebody has to write the document?" said Lind. "Has he no feeling? Of course he has. But because he is not used to giving full weight to his feelings, he is all the more likely to be deluded into thinking that what he puts into his document is objective truth."

Ingestree broke in. "Eisengrim is coming back from tarting himself up for the next few shots," he said. "And so far as his story is concerned, we might as well make up our minds that all we are going to get is his feeling. As a literary man, I am just pleased that he has some feelings. So few autobiographers have any feeling except a resolute self-protectiveness."

"Feeling! Truth! Balls! Let's get a few hundred good feet in the can before our star decides he is tired," said Kinghovn. And that is what we did.

A good day's filming put Magnus in an expansive mood. Ingestree's flattery about the quality of his acting had also had its effect on him, and that night he gave us a gallery of impersonations.

"Charlie had his way, and I was soon on the show. Charlie was right; Abdullah pulled them in because people cannot resist automata. There is something in humanity that is repelled and entranced by a machine that seems to have more than human powers. People love to frighten themselves. Look at the fuss nowadays about computers; however deft they may be they can't do anything that a man isn't doing, through them; but you hear people giving themselves delicious shivers about a computer-dominated world. I've often thought of working up an illusion, using a computer, but it would be prohibitively expensive, and I can do anything the public would find amusing better and cheaper with clockwork and bits of string. But if I invented a computer-illusion I would take care to dress the computer up to look like a living creature of some sort—a Moon Man or Venusian—because the public cannot resist clever dollies. Abdullah was a clever dolly of a simple kind, and the Rubes couldn't get enough of him.

"That was where Gus had to use her showman's discretion. Charlie and Willard would have put Abdullah in a separate tent to milk him for twenty shows a day, but Gus knew that would exhaust his appeal. Used sparingly, Abdullah was good for years, and Gus took the long view. It appeared, too, that I was an improvement on the dwarf, who had become unreliable through some personal defect—booze, I would guess—and was apt to make a mess of the illusion, or give way to a fit of temperament and deal a low card when he should have dealt a high one. Willard had had no luck with Abdullah; he had bought the thing, and hired the dwarf, but the dwarf was so unreliable it was risky to put the automaton on the show, and then the dwarf had disappeared. It had been months since Abdullah was in commission, and so far as the show was concerned it was a new attraction.

"I was anxious to succeed as Abdullah, though I had no particular expectation of gaining anything thereby. I had no notion of the world, and for quite a long time I did not understand how powerful I was, or that I might profit by it. Nor did anyone in the World of Wonders seek to enlighten me. So far as I can recall my feelings during those first few months, they were restricted to a desire to do the best I could, lest I should be sent back to my father and inevitable punishment. To begin with, I liked being the hidden agent who helped in the great game of hoodwinking Rubes, and I was happiest when I was out of sight, in the smelly bowels of Abdullah.

"When I was in the open air I was Cass Fletcher. I always hated the name, but Willard liked it because he had invented it in one of his very few flights of fancy. Willard had no imagination, to speak of. I learned as time went on that he had learned his conjuring skill from an old performer, and had never expanded it or altered it by a jot. He had as little curiosity as any man I have ever known. But when we were riding on the train, in my very first week, he found that I must have a name, because the other performers, riding in the car reserved for the World of Wonders, were surprised to see a small boy in their midst, for whom no credentials were offered. Who was I?

"When the question was put directly to him by the wife of Joe Dark the Knife Thrower, Willard hesitated a moment, looked out of the window, and said: 'Oh, this is young Cass, a kind of relative of mine; Cass Fletcher.' Then he went off into one of his very rare fits of laughter.

"As soon as he could catch Charlie, who wandered up and down the car as it travelled through the flatlands of Western Ontario, and gossiped with everybody, Willard told him his great joke. 'Em Dark wanted to know the kid's name, see, and I was thinking who the hell is he, when I looked outa the window at one of these barns with a big sign saying FLETCHER'S CASTORIA, CHILDREN CRY FOR IT; and quick as a wink I says Cass Fletcher, that's his name. Pretty smart way to name a kid, eh?' I was offended at being named from a sign on a barn, but I was not consulted, and a general impression spread that I was Willard's nephew.

"At least, that was the story that was agreed on. As time went on I heart whispers between Molza the Fire Eater and Sonny Sonnenfels the Strong Man that Willard was something they called an arse-bandit—an expression I did not understand—and that the kid was probably more to him than just a nephew and the gaff for Abdullah.

"Gaff. That was a word I had to learn at once, in all its refinements. The gaff was the element of deception in an exhibition, and though all the Talent would have admitted you couldn't manage without it, there was a moral stigma attaching to it. Sonnenfels was not gaffed at all; he really was a strong man who picked up big bar-bells and tore up telephone books with his hands and lifted anybody who would volunteer to sit in a chair, which Sonny then heaved aloft with one hand. There are tricks to being a strong man, but no gaff; anybody was welcome to heft the bar-bells if they wanted to. Frank Molza the Fire Eater and Sword Swallower was partly gaffed, because his swords weren't as sharp as he pretended, and eating fire is a complicated chemical trick which usually proves bad for the health. But Professor Spencer, who had been born without arms—really he had two pathetic little flippers but he did not show them—was wholly free of gaff; he wrote with his feet, on a blackboard and, if you wanted to pay twenty-five cents, in an elegant script on twelve visiting cards, where your name would be handsomely displayed. Joe Dark and his wife Emily were not gaffed at all; Joe threw knives at Emily with such accuracy that he outlined her form on the soft board against which she stood; it was skill, and the only skill poor Joe possessed, for he was certainly the dullest man in the World of Wonders. Nor could you say there was any gaff about Heinie Bayer and his educated monkey Rango; it was an honest monkey, as monkeys go, and its tricks were on the level. The Midget Juggler, Piccino Zovene, was honest as a juggler, but as crooked as a corkscrew in any human dealings; he wasn't much of a juggler, and might have been improved by a little gaff.

"Gaff may have been said to begin with Zitta the Jungle Queen, whose snakes were kept quiet by various means, especially her sluggish old cobra who was over-fed and drugged. Snakes don't live long in the sort of life Zitta gave them; they can't stand constant mauling and dragging about; she was always wiring a supplier in Texas for new rattlers. I judged that a snake lived about a month to six weeks when once Zitta had got hold of it; they were nasty things, and I never felt much sympathy for them. Zitta was a nasty thing, too, but she was too stupid to give her nastiness serious play. Andro the Hermaphrodite was all gaff. He was a man, of a kind, and besottedly in love with himself. The left side of his body was supposed to be the female half, and he spent a lot of time on it with depilatories and skin creams; when he attached a pretty good left breast to it, and combed out the long, curly hair he allowed to grow on one side of his head, he was an interesting sight. His right side he exercised strenuously, so that he had big leg and arm muscles which he touched up with some fancy shadowing. I never became used to finding him using the men's bucket in the donniker—which was the word used on the show for the primitive sanitary conveniences in the small back dressing tent. He was a show-off; in show business you get used to vanity, but Andro was a very special case.

"Of course Abdullah was one hundred per cent gaff. I don't think anybody would have cared greatly, if they had not been stirred up to it by the one very remarkable Talent I haven't yet mentioned. She was Happy Hannah the Fat Lady.

"A Fat Lady, or a Fat Man, is almost a necessity for a show like Wanless's. Just as the public is fascinated by automata, it is unappeasable in its demand for fat people. A Human Skeleton is hardly worth having if he can't do something else—grow hair to his feet, or eat glass or otherwise distinguish himself. But a Fat Lady merely has to be fat. Happy Hannah weighed 487 pounds; all she needed to do was to show herself sitting in a large chair, and her living was assured. But that wasn't her style at all; she was an interferer, a tireless asserter of opinions, and—worst of all—a determined Moral Influence. It was this quality in her which made it a matter of interest whether she was gaffed or not.

"Willard was her enemy, and Willard said she was gaffed. For one thing, she wore a wig, a very youthful chestnut affair, curly and flirtatious; a kiss-curl coiled like a watchspring in front of each rosy ear. The rosy effect was gaffed, too, for Hannah was thickly made up. But these things were simple showmanship. Willard's insistence that the Fat Lady was gaffed rose from an occupational disability of Fat Ladies; this is copious sweating, which results, in a person whose bodily creases may be twelve inches deep, in troublesome chafing. Three or four times a day Hannah had to retire to the women's part of the dressing tent, and there Gus stripped her down and powdered her in these difficult areas with cornstarch. Very early in my experience on the show I peeped through a gap in the lacing of the canvas partition that divided the men's dressing-room from the women's, and was much amazed by what I saw; Hannah, who looked fairly jolly sitting on her platform, in a suit of pink cotton rompers, was a sorry mass of blubber when she was bent forward, her hands on the back of a chair; she had collops of fat on her flanks, like the wicked man in the Book of Job; her monstrous abdomen hung almost to her knees, the smart wig concealed an iron-grey crewcut, and her breasts hung like great half-filled wallets of suet far down on her belly. I have seen nothing like her since, except for an effigy of Smet Smet, the Hippopotamus Goddess, in an exhibition of African art Liesl made me attend a few years ago. The gaffing consisted of two large bath-towels, which were rolled and tucked under her breasts, giving them what was, in comparison with the reality, a buxom contour. These towels were great matters of contention between Hannah and Willard, for she insisted that they were sanitary necessities, and he said they were gross impostures on the public. He cared nothing about gaffing; it was Hannah who made it a moral issue and drew a sharp line between gaffed Talent, like Abdullah, and honest Talent, like Fat Ladies.

"They wrangled about it a good deal. Hannah was voluble and she had a quality of shrewishness that came strangely from one whose professional personality depended on an impression of sunny good nature. She would nag about it for half an hour at a stretch, as we travelled on the train, until at last the usually taciturn Willard would say, in a low, ugly voice: 'Listen, Miz Hannah, you shut your goddam trap or next time we got a big crowd I'm gonna tell 'em about those gaffed tits of yours. See? Now shut up, I tell ya!'

"He would never have done it, of course. It would have been unforgivable professional conduct, and even Charlie would not have been able to keep Gus from throwing him off the show. But the menace in his voice would silence Hannah for a few hours.

"I was entranced by the World of Wonders during those early weeks and I had plenty of time to study it, for it was part of the agreement under which I lived that I must never be seen during working hours, except when real necessity demanded a quick journey to the donniker, between tricks. I often ate in the seclusion of Abdullah. The hours of the show were from eleven in the morning until eleven at night, and so I ate as big a breakfast as I could get, and depended on a hot dog or something of the sort being brought to me at noon and toward evening. Willard was supposed to attend to it, but he often forgot, and it was good-hearted Emily Dark who saw that I did not starve. Willard never ate much, and like so many people he could not believe that anyone wanted more than himself. There was an agreement of some sort between Willard and Gus as to what my status was; I know he got extra money for me, but I never saw any of it; I know Gus made him promise he would look after me and treat me well, but I don't think he had any idea of what such words meant, and from time to time Gus would give him a dressing down about the condition I was in; for years I never had any clothes except those Gus bought me, stopping the money out of Willard's pay, but Gus had no idea of how to dress a child, and always bought everything too big, so that I would have lots of room to grow into it. Not that I needed many clothes; inside Abdullah I wore nothing but cotton shorts. I see now that it was a miserable life, and it is a wonder it didn't kill me; but at the time I accepted it as children must accept the world made for them by their guardians.

"At the beginning I was beglamoured by the show, and peeped at it out of Abdullah's bosom with unresting excitement. There was one full show an hour, and the whole of it was known as a trick. The trick began outside the tent on a platform beside the ticket-seller's box, and this part of it was called the bally. Not ballyhoo, which was an expression I had heard in the carnival world in my time. Gus usually sold the tickets, though there was someone to spell her when she had other business to attend to. Charlie was the outside talker, not a barker, which is another expression I did not hear until a movie or a play made it popular. He roared through a megaphone to tell the crowd about what was to be seen inside the tent. Charlie was a flashy dresser and handsome in a flashy way, and he did his job well, most of the time.

"High outside the tent hung the banners, which were the big painted signs advertising the Talent; each performer had to pay for his own banner, though Gus ordered them from the artist and assured that there would be a pleasing similarity of style. As well as the banners, some of the Talent had to appear on the bally, and this boring job usually fell to the lesser artistes; Molza ate a little fire, Sonny heaved a few weights, the Professor would lie on his back and write 'Pumpkin Centre, Agricultural Capital of Pumpkin County' on a huge piece of paper with his feet, and this piece of paper was thrown into the crowd, for whoever could grab it; Zovene the Midget Juggler did a few stunts, and now and then if business was slow Zitta would take out a few snakes, and the Darks would have to show themselves. But the essence of the bally was to create an appetite for what was inside the tent, not to give away entertainment, and Charlie pushed the purchase of tickets as hard as he could.

"After Abdullah was put on the show, which was as soon as we could get a fine banner sent up from New York, Willard did not have to take a turn on the bally.

"The bally and the sale of tickets took about twenty minutes, after which a lesser outside talker than Charlie did what he could to collect a crowd, and Charlie hurried inside, carrying a little cane he used as a pointer. Once in the tent he took on another role, which was called the lecturer, because everything in the World of Wonders was supposed to be improving and educational; Charlie's style underwent a change, too, for outside he was a great joker, whereas inside he was professorial, as he understood the word.

"I was much impressed by the fact that almost all the Talent spoke two versions of English—whatever was most comfortable when they were off duty, and a gaudy, begemmed, and gilded rhetoric when they were before the public. Charlie was a master of the impressive introduction when he presented the Talent to an audience.

"As spectators bought their tickets they were permitted into the tent, where they walked around and stared until the show began. Sometimes they asked questions, especially of Happy Hannah. 'You will assuredly hear everything in due season,' she would reply. The show was not supposed to begin without Charlie. When he pranced into the tent—he had an exaggeratedly youthful, high-stepping gait—he would summon the crowd around him and begin by introducing *Sonny, the Strongest Man you have ever seen, ladies and gentlemen, and the best-natured giant in the known world.* Poor old Sonny wasn't allowed to speak, because he had a strong German accent, and Germans were not popular characters in rural Canada in the late summer of 1918. Sonny was not allowed to linger over his demonstration, either, because Charlie was hustling the crowd toward Molza the Human Salamander, who thrust a lighted torch into his mouth, and then blew out a jet of flame which ignited a piece of newspaper Charlie held in his hand; Molza then swallowed swords until he had four of them stuck in his gullet. When I came to know him I got him to show me how to do it, and I can still swallow a paper-knife, or anything not too sharp. But swallowing swords and eating fire are hard ways to get a living, and dangerous after a few years. Then Professor Spencer wrote with his feet, having first demonstrated with some soap and a safety-razor with no blade in it how he shaved himself every day; the Professor would write the name of anybody who wished it; with his right foot he would write from left to right, and at the same time, underneath it and with his left foot, he would write the name from right to left. He wrote with great speed in a beautiful hand—or foot, I should say. It was quite a showy act, but the Professor never had his full due, I thought, because people were rather embarrassed by him. Then the Darks did their knife-throwing act.

"It was a very good act, and if only Joe had possessed some instinct of showmanship it would have been much better. But Joe was a very simple soul, a decent, honest fellow who ought to have been a workman of some sort. His talent for throwing knives was one of those freakish things that are sometimes found in people who are otherwise utterly unremarkable. His wife, Emily, was ambitious for him; she wanted him to be a veterinary, and when we were on the train she kept him pegging away at a correspondence course which would, when it was completed, bring him a diploma from some cut-rate college deep in the States. But it was obvious to everybody but Emily that it would never be completed, because Joe couldn't get anything into his head from a printed page. He could throw knives, and that was that. They both wore tacky home-made costumes, which bunched unbecomingly in the wrong places, and Emily stood in front of a pine board while Joe outlined her pleasant figure in knives. Nice people: minor Talent.

"By this time the audience had climbed the ladder of marvels to Rango the Missing Link, exhibited by Heinie Bayer. Rango was an orang-outang, who could walk a tightrope carrying a parasol; at the mid-point, he would suddenly swing downward, clinging to the rope with his toes, and reflectively eat bananas; then he would whirl upright, throw away the skin, and complete his journey. After that he sat at a table, and rang a bell, and Heinie, dressed as a clown waiter, served him a meal, which Rango ate with affected elegance, until he was displeased with a badly prepared dish, and pelted Heinie with food. Rango was surefire. Everybody loved him, and I was of their number until I tried to make friends with him and Rango spat some chewed-up nuts in my face. It was part of Heinie's deal with the management that Rango had to share a berth with him in our Pullman; although he was house-trained he was a nuisance because he was a bad sleeper, and likely to stick his hand into your berth in the night and pinch you—a very mean, twisting pinch. It was uncanny to poke your head out of your berth and see Rango swinging along the car, holding on to the tops of the green curtains, as if they were part of his native jungle.

"After Rango came Zitta the Jungle Queen. Snake acts are all the same. She pulled the snakes around her neck, wound them around her arms, and as a topper she knelt down and charmed her cobra *by no other power than that of the unaided human eye, with which she exerts hypnotic dominance over this most dreaded of jungle monsters,* as Charlie said, and ended by kissing it on its ugly snout.

"This was good showmanship. First the sunny side of nature, then the ominous side of nature. The trick, I learned, was that Zitta leaned down to the cobra from above its head; cobras cannot strike upwards. It was a thrill, and Zitta had to know her business. As I grew older and more cynical I sometimes wondered what it would be like if Zitta exercised her hypnotic powers on Rango, and kissed him, for a change. I don't think Rango was a lady's man.

"This left only Willard, Andro the Hermaphrodite, and Happy Hannah to complete the show; Zovene the Midget Juggler was only useful to get the audience out of the tent. On the basis of public attraction it was acknowledged that Willard must have the place of honour once Abdullah was on display. Charlie was in favour of giving Andro the place just before Abdullah but Happy Hannah would have none of it. She was clamorous. If a natural, educational wonder like herself, without any gaff about her, didn't take precedence over a gaffed monsterosity she was prepared to leave carnival life and despair of the human race. She made herself so unpleasant that she won the argument; Andro became very shrewish when he was under attack, but he lacked Hannah's large, embracing, Biblical flow of condemnation. When he had said that Hannah was a fat, loud-mouthed old bitch his store of abuse was exhausted; but she sailed into him with all guns firing.

"'Don't think I hold it against you personally, Andro. No, I know you for what you are. I know the rock from whence ye are hewn— that no-good bunch o' Boston Greek fish-peddlers and small-time thieves; and I likewise know the hole of the Pit whence ye are digged—offering yourself to stand bare-naked in front of artists, some of 'em women, at fifty cents an hour. So know it isn't really you that's speaking against me; it's the spirit of an unclean devil inside of you, crying with a loud voice; and rebuke it just as our dear Lord did; I'm sitting right here, crying, "Hold thy peace and come out of him!"'

"This was Hannah's strength. All her immense bulk was crammed with Bible knowledge and quotations and it oozed out of her like currant-juice oozing out of a jelly-bag. She offered herself to the public as a biblical marvel, a sort of she-Leviathan. She would not allow Charlie to speak for her. As soon as he had given her a lead— *And now, ladies and gentlemen, I present Happy Hannah, four hundred and eighty-seven pounds of good humour and chuckles*—she would burst in, 'Yes friends, and I'm the living proof of how fat a person can get and still bear it gladly in the Lord's name. I hope every person here knows his Bible and if they do, they know the comforting message of Proverbs eleven, twenty-five: *The liberal soul shall be made fat*. Yes friends, I am here not as a curiosity and certainly not as a monsterosity but to attest in my daily life and my public career to the Lord's abounding grace. I don't hafta be here; many offers from missionary societies and the biggest evangelists have been turned down in order that I may get around this whole continent and talk to the biggest possible audience of the real people, God's own folks, and attest to the Faith. Portraits of me as you see me now, each one individually autographed by my own hand, may be purchased at twenty-five cents apiece, and for another mere quarter I will include a priceless treasure, this copy of the New Testament which fits in the pocket and in which each and every word uttered by our Lord Jesus Christ during his earthly ministry is printed in RED. No Testament sold except with a portrait. Don't miss this great offer which is made by me at a financial sacrifice in order that the Lord's will may be done more abundantly here in Pumpkin Centre. Don't hang back folks; grab what I'm giving to you; I been made fat and when you possess this portrait of me as you see me now and this New Testament you'll hafta admit that I'm certainly the Liberal Soul. Come on, now, who's gonna be the first?'

"Hannah was able to hawk her pictures and her Testaments because of an arrangement written into every artiste's contract that they should be allowed to sell something at every show. They made their offer, or Charlie made it for them, as the crowd was about to move on to the next Wonder. The price was always twenty-five cents. Sonny had a book on body-building; Molza had only a picture of himself with his throat full of swords—a very slow item in terms of sales; Professor Spencer offered his personally written visiting cards, which were a nuisance because they took quite a while to prepare; Em Dark sold throwing knives Joe made in his spare time out of small files—a throwing knife has no edge, only a point; Heinie sold pictures of Rango; Zitta offered belts and bracelets which she made out of the skins of the snakes she had mauled to death—though Charlie didn't put it quite like that; Andro was another seller of pictures; Willard sold a pamphlet called *Secrets of Gamblers Revealed,* which was offered by Charlie as an infallible protection against dishonest card-players you might meet on trains; a lot of people bought them who didn't look like great travellers, and I judged they wanted to know the secrets of gamblers for some purpose of their own. I read it several times, and it was a stupefyingly uncommunicative little book, written at least thirty years before 1918. The agreement was that each Wonder offered his picture or whatever it might be after he had been exhibited, and that when the show had been completed, except for the Midget Juggler, Charlie would invite the audience once again not to leave without one of *these valuable mementoes of a unique and unforgettable personal experience and educational benefit.*

"From being an extremely innocent little boy it did not take me long to become a very knowing little boy. I picked up a great deal as we travelled from village to village on the train, for our Pullman was an educational benefit and certainly, for me, an unforgettable personal experience. I had an upper berth at the very end of the car, at some distance from Willard, whose importance in the show secured him a lower in the area where the shock of the frequent shuntings and accordion-like contractions of the train were least felt. I came to know who had bottles of liquor, and also who was gener-ous with it and who kept it for his own use. I knew that neither Joe nor Em Dark drank, because it would have been a ruinous indul-gence for a knife-thrower. The Darks, however, were young and vigorous, and sometimes the noises from their berth were enough to raise comment from the other Talent. I remember one night when Heinie, who shared his bottle with Rango, put Rango up to opening the curtains of the Darks' upper; Em screamed, and Joe grabbed Rango and threw him down into the aisle so hard that Rango screamed; Heinie offered to fight Joe, and Joe, stark naked and very angry, chased Heinie back to his berth and pummelled him. It took a full hour to soothe Rango; Heinie assured us that Rango was used to love and could not bear rough usage; Rango had to have at least two strong swigs of straight rye before he could sleep. But in the rough-and-tumble I had had a good look at Em Dark naked, and it was very different from Happy Hannah, I can assure you. All sorts of things that I had never heard of began, within a month, to whirl and surge and combine in my mind.

"A weekly event of some significance in our Pullman was Hannah's Saturday-night bath. She lived in continual hope of manag-ing it without attracting attention, but that was ridiculous. First Gus would bustle down the aisle with a large tarpaulin and an armful of towels. Then Hannah, in an orange mobcap and a red dressing-gown, would lurch and stumble down the car; she was too big to fall into anybody's berth, but she sometimes came near to dragging down the green curtains when we were going around a bend. We all knew what happened in the Ladies' Retiring Room; Gus spread the tarpaulin, Hannah stood on it hanging onto the wash-basin, and Gus swabbed her down with a large sponge. It was for this service of Christian charity that she was called Elephant Gus when she was out of earshot. Drying Hannah took a long time, because there were large portions of her that she could not reach herself, and Gus used to towel her down, making a hissing noise between her teeth, like a groom.

"Sometimes Charlie and Heinie and Willard would be sitting up having a game of poker, and while the bath was in progress they would sing a hymn, 'Wash me and I shall be whiter than snow'. If they were high they had another version—

> Wash me in the water
> That you washed the baby in,
> And I shall be whiter
> Than the whitewash on the wall.

This infuriated Hannah, and on her return trip she would favour them with a few Biblical admonitions; she had a good deal to say about lasciviousness, lusts, excess of wine, revellings, banquetings, games of hazard, and abominable idolatries, out of First Peter. But she hocussed the text. There is no mention of 'games of hazard' or gambling anywhere in the Bible. She put that in for her own particular satisfaction. I knew it, and I soon recognized Hannah as my first hypocrite. A boy's first recognition of hypocrisy is, or ought to be, more significant than the onset of puberty. By the time Gus had stowed her into her special lower, which was supported from beneath with a few fence-posts, she was so refreshed by anger that she fell asleep at once, and snored so that she could be heard above the noise of the train.

"Very soon I became aware that the World of Wonders which had been a revelation to me, and I suppose to countless other country village people, was a weary bore to the Talent. This is the gnawing canker of carnival life: it is monstrously boring.

"Consider. We did ten complete shows a day; we had an hour off for midday food and another hour between six and seven; otherwise it was unremitting. We played an average of five days a week, which means fifty shows. We began our season as early as we could, but nothing much was stirring in the outdoor carnival line till mid-May, and after that we traipsed across country playing anywhere and everywhere—I soon stopped trying to know the name of the towns, and called them all Pumpkin Centre, like Willard—until late October. That makes something over a thousand shows. No wonder the Talent was bored. No wonder Charlie's talks began to sound as if he was thinking about something else.

"The only person who wasn't bored was Professor Spencer. He was a decent man, and couldn't give way to boredom, because his affliction meant perpetual improvisation in the details of his life. For instance, he had to get somebody to help him in the donniker, which most of us were ready to do, but wouldn't have done if he had not always been cheerful and fresh. He offered to teach me some lessons, because he said it was shame for a boy to leave school as early as I had done. So he taught me writing, and arithmetic, and an astonishing amount of geography. He was the one man on the show who had to know where we were, what the population of the town was, the name of the mayor, and other things that he wrote on his blackboard as part of his show. He was a good friend to me, was Professor Spencer. Indeed, it was he who persuaded Willard to teach me magic.

"Willard had not been interested in doing that, or indeed anything, for me. I was necessary, but I was a nuisance. I have never met anyone in my life who was so bleakly and unconsciously selfish as Willard, and for one whose life has been spent in the theatre and carnival world that is a strong statement. But Professor Spencer nagged him into it—you could not shame or bully or cajole Willard into anything, but he was open to nagging—and he began to show me a few things with cards and coins. As my years with the World of Wonders wore on, I think what he taught me saved my reason. Certainly it is at the root of anything I can do now.

"Whoever taught Willard did it very well. He never gave names to the things he taught me, and I am sure he didn't know them. But since that time I have found that he taught me all there is to know about shuffling, forcing, and passing cards, and palming, ruffling, changing, and bridging, and the wonders of the *biseauté* pack, which is really the only trick pack worth having. With coins he taught me all the basic work of palming and passing, the French drop, *La Pincette*,

La Coulée, and all the other really good ones. His ideal among magicians was Nelson Downs, whose great act, The Miser's Dream, he had seen at the Palace Theatre, New York, which was the paradise of his limited imagination. Indeed, it was a very much debased version of The Miser's Dream that he had been doing when I first saw him. He now did little conjuring in the World of Wonders, because of the ease of managing Abdullah.

"Inside Abdullah I was busy for perhaps five minutes in every hour. My movement was greatly restricted; I could not make a noise. What was I to do? I practised my magic, and for hours on end I palmed coins and developed my hands in the dark, and that is how I gained the technique which has earned me the compliment of this film you gentlemen are making. I recommend the method to young magicians; get yourself into a close-fitting prison for ten hours a day, and do nothing but manipulate cards and coins; keep that up for a few years and, unless you are constitutionally incapable, like poor Ramsay here, you should develop some adroitness, and you will at least have no chance to acquire the principal fault of the bad magician, which is looking at your hands as you work. That was how I avoided boredom: constant practice, and entranced observation, through Abdullah's bosom, of the public and the Talent of the World of Wonders.

"Boredom is rich soil for every kind of rancour and ugliness. In my first months on the show this attached almost entirely to the fortunes of the War. I knew nothing about the War, although as a schoolchild I had been urged to bring all my family's peachstones to school, where they were collected for some war-like purpose. Knowing boys said that a terrible poison gas was made from them. Every morning in prayers our teacher mentioned the Allied Forces, and especially the Canadians. Once again knowing boys said you could always tell where her brother Jim was by the prayer, which was likely to contain a special reference to 'our boys at the Front', and later, 'our boys in the rest camps', and later still, 'our boys in the hospitals'. The War hung over my life like the clouds in the sky, and I heeded it as little. Once I saw Ramsay in the street, in what I later realized was the uniform of a recruit, but at the time I couldn't understand why he was wearing such queer clothes. I saw men in the streets with black bands on their arms, and asked my father why they wore them, but I can't remember what he answered.

"In the World of Wonders the War seemed likely at times to tear the show to pieces. The only music on the fairgrounds where we appeared came from the merry-go-round; tunes were fed into its calliope by the agency of large steel discs, perforated with rectangular holes; they worked on the same principle as the roll of a player-piano, but were much more durable, and rotated instead of uncoiling. Most of the music was of the variety we associate with merry-go-rounds. Who wrote it? Italians, I suspect, for it always had a gentle, quaintly melodious quality, except for one new tune which Steve, who ran the machine, had bought to give the show a modern air. It was the American war song—by that noisy fellow Cohan, was it?—called 'Over There!' It was less than warlike on a calliope, played at merry-go-round tempo, but everybody recognized it, and now and then some Canadian wag would sing loudly, to the final phrase—

And we won't be over
Till it's over
Over there!

If Hannah heard this, she became furious, for she was an inflamed American patriot and the War, for her, had begun when the Americans entered it in 1917. The Darks were Canadians, and not as tactful as Canadians usually are when dealing with their American cousins. I remember Em Dark, who was a most unlikely person to tell a joke, saying one midday, in September of 1918, when the Talent was in the dressing tent, eating its hasty picnic: 'I heard a good one yesterday. This fellow says, Say, why are the American troops called Doughboys? And the other fellow says, Gee, I dunno; why? And the first fellow says, It's because they were needed in 1914 but they didn't rise till 1917. Do you get it? Needed, you see, like kneading bread, and—' But Em wasn't able to continue with her explanation of the joke because Hannah threw a sandwich at her and told her to knead that, and she was sick and tired of ingratitude from the folks in a little, two-bit backwoods country where they still had to pay taxes to the English King, and hadn't Em heard about the Argonne and the American blood that was being shed there by the bucketful, and how did Em think they would make the Hun say Uncle anyways with a lot of fat-headed Englishmen and Frenchmen messing it all up, and what they needed over there was American efficiency and American spunk?

"Em didn't have a chance to reply, because Hannah was immediately in trouble with Sonnenfels and Heinie Bayer, who smouldered under a conviction that Germany was hideously wronged and that everybody was piling on the Fatherland without any cause at all, and though they were just as good Americans as anybody they were damn well sick of it and hoped the German troops would show Pershing something new about efficiency. Charlie tried to quiet them down by saying that everybody knew the War was a put-up job and nobody was getting anything out of it but the Big Interests. This was a mistake, because Sonny and Heinie turned on him and told him that they knew why he was so glad to be in Canada, and if they were younger men they'd be in the scrap and they weren't going to say which side they'd be on, neither, but if they met anything like Charlie on the battlefield they'd just put a chain on him and show him off beside Rango.

"The battle went on for weeks, during which Joe Dark suffered the humiliation of having Em tell everybody that he wasn't in the Canadian Army because he had flat feet, and Hannah replying that you didn't need feet to fly a plane, but you sure needed brains. The only reasonable voice was that of Professor Spencer, who was a great reader of the papers, and an independent thinker; he was all for an immediate armistice and a peace conference. But as nobody wanted to listen to him, he lectured me, instead, so that I still have a very confused idea of the causes of that War, and the way it was fought. Hannah got a Stars and Stripes from somewhere, and stuck it up on her little platform. She said it made her feel good just to have it there.

"It all came about because of boredom. Boredom and stupidity and patriotism, especially when combined, are three of the greatest evils of the world we live in. But a worse and more lasting source of trouble was the final show in each village, which was called the Last Trick.

"It was agreed that the Last Trick ought to be livelier than the other nine shows of the day. The fair was at its end, the serious matters like the judging of animals and fancy-work had been completed, and most of the old folks had gone home, leaving young men and their girls, and the village cutups on the fairground. It was then that the true, age-old Spirit of Carnival descended on Wanless's World of Wonders, but of course it didn't affect everybody in the same way. Outside, the calliope was playing its favourite tune, 'The Poor Butterfly Waltz'; supposedly unknown to Gus, the man who ran the cat-rack had slipped in the gaff, so that the eager suitor who was trying to win a kewpie doll for the girl of his heart by throwing baseballs found that the stuffed pussy-cats wouldn't be knocked down. It was a sleazier, crookeder fair altogether than the one the local Fair Board had planned, but there was always a young crowd that liked it that way.

"On the bally, Charlie allowed his wit a freer play. As Zovene juggled with his spangled Indian clubs, Charlie would say, in a pretended undertone which carried well beyond his audience: 'Pretty good, eh? He isn't big, but he's good. Anyways, how big would you be if you'd been strained through a silk handkerchief?' The young bloods would guffaw at this, and their girls would clamour to have it explained to them. And when Zitta showed her snakes, she would drag the old cobra suggestively between her legs and up her front, while Charlie whispered, 'Boys-oh-boys, who wouldn't be a snake?'

"Inside the tent Charlie urged the young men to model themselves on Sonnenfels, so that all the girls would be after them, and they'd be up to the job. And when he came to Andro he would ogle his hearers and say, 'He's the only guy in the world who's glad to wake up in the morning and find he's beside himself.' He particularly delighted in tormenting Hannah. She did her own talking, but as she shrieked her devotion to the Lord Jesus, Charlie would lean down low, and say, in a carrying whisper, 'She hasn't seen her ace o' spades in twenty years.' The burst of laughter made Hannah furious, though she never caught what was said. She knew, however, that it was something dirty. However often she complained to Gus, and however often Gus harangued Charlie, the Spirit of Carnival was always too much for him. Nor was Gus whole-hearted in her complaints; what pleased the crowd was what Gus liked.

"Hannah attempted to fight fire with fire. She often made it known, in the Pullman, that in her opinion these modern kids weren't bad kids, and if you gave them a chance they didn't want this Sex and all like that. Sure, they wanted fun, and she knew how to give 'em fun. She was just as fond of fun as anybody, but she didn't see the fun in all this Smut and Filth. So she gave 'em fun.

"'Lots o' fun in your Bible, boys and girls,' she would shout. 'Didn't you know that? Didya think the Good Book was all serious? You just haven't read it with the Liberal Heart, that's all. Come on now! Come on now, all of you! Who can tell me why you wouldn't dare to take a drink outa the first river in Eden? Come on, I bet ya know. Sure ya know. You're just too shy to say. Why wouldn't ya take a drink outa the first river in Eden?—Because it was Pison, that's why! If you don't believe me, look in Genesis two, eleven.' Then she would go off into a burst of wheezing laughter.

"Or she would point—and with an arm like hers, pointing was no trifling effort—at Zovene, shouting: 'You call him small? Say, he's a regular Goliath compared with the shortest man in the Bible. Who was he? Come on, who was he?—He was Bildad the Shu-hite, Job two, eleven. See, the Liberal Heart can even get a laugh outa one of Job's Comforters. I betcha never thought of that, eh?' And again, one of her terrible bursts of laughter.

"Hannah understood nothing of the art of the comedian. It is dangerous to laugh at your own jokes, but if you must, it is great mistake to laugh first. Fat people, when laughing, are awesome sights, enough to strike gravity into the onlooker. But Hannah was a whole World of Wonders in herself when she laughed. She forced her laughter, for after all, when you have told people for weeks that the only man in the Bible with no parents was Joshua, the son of Nun, the joke loses some of its savour. So she pushed laughter out of herself in wheezing, whooping cries, and her face became unpleasantly marbled with dabs of a darker red under the rouge she wore. Her collops wobbled uncontrollably, her vast belly heaved and trembled as she sucked breath, and sometimes she attempted to slap her thigh, producing a wet splat of sound. Fat Ladies ought not to tell jokes; their mirth is of the flesh, not of the mind. Fat Ladies ought not to laugh; a chuckle is all they can manage without putting a dangerous strain on their breathing and circulatory system. But Hannah would not listen to reason. She was determined to drive Smut back into its loathsome den with assaults of Clean Fun, and if she damaged herself in the battle, her wounds would be honourable.

"Sometimes she had an encouraging measure of success. Quite often there would be in the crowd some young man who was of a serious, religious turn of mind, and usually he was accompanied by a girl who had preacher's daughter written all over her. They had been embarrassed by Charlie's jokes when they understood them. They had been even more embarrassed when Rango, at a secret signal from Heinie, left his pretended restaurant table and urinated in a corner, while Heinie pantomimed a waiter's dismay. But with that camaraderie which exists among religious people just as it does among tinhorns and crooks, they recognized Hannah as a benign influence, and laughed with her, and urged her on to greater flights. She gave them her best. 'What eight fellas in the Bible milked a bear? *You* know! You musta read it a dozen times. D'ya give it up? Well, listen carefully: Huz, Buz, Kemuel, Chesed, Hazo, Pildash, Jidlaph, and Bethuel—*these eight did Milcah bear to Nahor, Abraham's brother.* Didya never think of it that way? Eh? Didn't ya? Well, it's in Genesis twenty-two.'

"When one of these obviously sanctified couples appeared, it was Hannah's pleasure to single them out and hold them up to the rest of the crowd as great cutups. 'Oh, I see ya,' she would shout; 'it's the garden of Eden all over again; the trouble isn't with the apple in the tree, it's with that pair on the ground.' And she would point at them, and they would blush and laugh and be grateful to be given a reputation for wickedness without having to do anything to acquire it.

"All of this cost Hannah dearly. After a big Saturday night, when she had exhausted her store of Bible riddles, she was almost too used up for her ritual bath. But she had worked herself up into a shocking sweat, and sometimes the smell of wet cornstarch from her sopping body spread a smell like a gigantic nursery pudding through the whole of the tent, and bathed she had to be, or there would be trouble with chafing.

"Her performance on these occasions made Willard deeply, cruelly angry. He would stand beside Abdullah and I could hear him swearing, repetitively but with growing menace, as she carried on. The worst of it was, if she secured any sort of success, she was not willing to stop; even when the crowd had passed on to see Abdullah, she would continue, at somewhat lesser pitch, with a few lingerers, who hoped for more Bible fun. In the Last Trick it was Willard's custom to have three people cut the cards for the automaton, instead of the usual one, and he wanted the undivided attention of the crowd. He hated Hannah, and from my advantageous peephole I was not long in coming to the conclusion that Hannah hated him.

"There were plenty of places in southern Ontario at that time where religious young people were numerous, and in these communities Hannah did not scruple to give a short speech in which she looked forward to seeing them next year, and implored them to join her in a parting hymn. 'God be with you till we meet again', she would strike up, in her thin, piercing voice, like a violin string played unskilfully and without a vibrato, and there were always those who, from religious zeal or just because they liked to sing, would join her. Nor was one verse enough. Charlie would strike in, as boldly as he could: *And now, ladies and gentlemen, our Master Marvel of the World of Wonders—Willard the Wizard and his Card-Playing Automaton, Abdullah, as soon to be exhibited on the stage of the Palace Theatre, New York*—but Hannah would simply put on more steam, and slow down, and nearly everybody in the tent would be wailing—

> God be with you till we meet again!
> Keep love's banner floating o'er you,
> Smite death's threatening wave before you:
> God be with you till we meet again!

And then the whole dismal chorus. It was a hymn of hate, and Willard met it with such hate as I have rarely seen.

"As for me, I was only a child, and my experience of hatred was slight, but so far as I could, and with what intensity of spirit I could muster, I hated them both. Hate and bitterness were becoming the elements in which I lived."

Eisengrim had a fine feeling for a good exit-line, and at this point he rose to go to bed. We rose, as well, and he went solemnly around the circle, shaking hands with us all in the European manner. Lind and Kinghovn even bowed as they did so, and when Magnus turned at the door to give us a final nod, they bowed again.

"Now why do you suppose we accord these royal courtesies to a man who has declared that he was Nobody for so many years," said Ingestree, when we had sat down again. "Because it is so very plain that he is not Nobody now. He is almost oppressively Somebody. Are we rising, and grinning, and even bowing out of pity? Are we trying to make it up to a man who suffered a dreadful denial of personality by assuring him that now we are quite certain he is a real person, just like us? Decidedly not. We defer to him, and hop around like courtiers because we can't help it. Why? Ramsay, do you know why?"

"No," said I; "I don't, and it doesn't trouble me much. I rather enjoy Magnus's lordly airs. He can come off his perch when he thinks proper. Perhaps we do it because we know he doesn't take it seriously; it's part of a game. If he insisted, we'd rebel."

"And when you rebelled, you would see a very different side of his nature," said Liesl.

"You play the game with him, I observe," said Ingestree. "You stand up when His Supreme Self-Assurance leaves the company. Yet you are mistress here, and we are your guests. Now why is that?"

"Because I am not quite sure who he is," said Liesl.

"You don't believe this story he's telling us?"

"Yes. I think that he has come to the time of his life when he feels the urge to tell. Many people feel it. It is the impulse behind a hundred bad autobiographies every year. I think he is being as honest as he can. I hope that when he finishes his story—if he does finish it—I shall know rather more. But I may not have my answer then."

"I don't follow; you hope to hear his story out, but you don't think it certain that you will know who he is even then, although you think he is being honest. What is this mystery?"

"Who is anybody? For me, he is whatever he is to me. Biographical facts may be of help, but they don't explain that. Are you married, Mr. Ingestree?"

"Well, no, actually, I'm not."

"The way you phrase your reply speaks volumes. But suppose you were married; do you think that your wife would be to you precisely what she was to her women friends, her men friends, her doctor, lawyer, and hairdresser? Of course not. To you she would be something special, and to you that would be the reality of her. I have not yet found out what Magnus is to me, although we have been business associates and friendly intimates for a long time. If I had been the sort of person who is somebody's mistress, I would have been his mistress, but I've never cared for the mistress role. I am too rich for it. Mistresses have incomes, and valuable possessions, but not fortunes. Nor can I say we have been lovers, because that is a messy expression people use when they are having sexual intercourse on fairly regular terms, without getting married. But I have had many a jolly night with Magnus, and many an exciting day with him. I still have to decide what he is to me. If humouring his foible for royal treatment helps me to come to a conclusion, I have no objection."

"Well, what about you, Ramsay? He keeps referring to you as his first teacher of magic. You knew him from childhood, then? You could surely say who he was?"

"I was almost present at his birth. But does that mean anything? An infant is a seed. Is it an oak seed or a cabbage seed? Who knows? All mothers think their children are oaks, but the world never lacks for cabbages. I would be the last man to pretend that knowing somebody as a child gave any real clue to who he is as a man. I can tell you this: he jokes about the lessons I gave him when he was a child, but he didn't think them funny then; he had a great gift for something I couldn't do at all, or could do with absurd effort. He was deadly serious during our lessons, and for a good reason. I could read the books and he couldn't. I think that may throw some light on what we have been hearing about the World of Wonders, which he presents as a kind of joke. I am perfectly certain it wasn't a joke at the time."

"I am sure he wasn't joking when he spoke of hatred," said Lind. "He was funny, or ironic, or whatever you want to call it, about the World of Wonders. We all know why people talk in that way; if we are amusing about our trials in the past, it is as if we say, 'See what I over-came—now I treat it as a joke—see how strong I have been and ask yourself if you could have overcome what I overcame?' But when he spoke of hatred, there was no joking."

"I don't agree," said Ingestree. "I think joking about the past is a way of suggesting that it wasn't really important. A way of veiling its horror, perhaps. We shudder when we hear of yesterday's plane accident, in which seventy people were killed; but we become increasingly philosophical about horrors that are further away. What is the Charge of the Light Brigade now? We remember it as a military blunder and we use it as a stick to beat military commanders, who are all popularly supposed to be blunderers. It has become a poem by Tennyson that embarrasses us by its exaltation of unthinking obedi-ence. We joke about the historical fact and the poetic artifact. But how many people ever think of the young men who charged? Who takes five minutes to summon up in his mind what they felt as they rushed to death? It is the fate of the past to be fuel for humour."

"Have you put your finger on it?" said Lind. "Perhaps you have. Jokes dissemble horrors and make them seem unimportant. And why? Is it in order that more horrors may come? In order that we may never learn anything from experience? I have never been very fond of jokes. I begin to wonder if they are not evil."

"Oh rubbish, Jurgen," said Ingestree. "I was only talking about one aspect of humour. It's absolutely vital to life. It's one of the marks of civilization. Mankind wouldn't be mankind without it."

"I know that the English set a special value on humour," said Lind. "They have a very fine sense of humour and sometimes they think theirs the best in the world, like their marmalade. Which reminds me that during the First World War some of the English troops used to go over the top shouting, 'Marmalade!' in humorously chivalrous voices, as if it were a heroic battle-cry. The Germans could never get used to it. They puzzled tirelessly to solve the mystery. Because a German cannot conceive that a man in battle would want to be funny, you see. But I think the English were dissembling the horror of their situation so that they would not notice how close they were to Death. Again, humour was essentially evil. If they had thought of the truth of their situation, they might not have gone over the top. And that might have been a good thing."

"Let's not theorize about humour, Jurgen," said Ingestree; "it's utterly fruitless and makes the very dullest kind of conversation."

"Now it's my turn to disagree," I said. "This notion that nobody can explain humour, or even talk sensibly about it, is one of humour's greatest cover-ups. I've been thinking a great deal about the Devil lately, and I have been wondering if humour isn't one of the most brilliant inventions of the Devil. What have you just been saying about it? It diminishes the horrors of the past, and it veils the horrors of the present, and therefore it prevents us from seeing straight, and perhaps from learning things we ought to know. Who profits from that? Not mankind, certainly. Only the Devil could devise such a subtle agency and persuade mankind to value it."

"No, no, no, Ramsay," said Liesl. "You are in one of your theological moods. I've watched you for days, and you have been moping as you do only when you are grinding one of your home-made theological axes. Humour is quite as often the pointer to truth as it is a cloud over truth. Have you never heard the Jewish legend—it's in the Talmud, isn't it?—that at the time of Creation the Creator displayed his masterwork, Man, to the Heavenly Host, and only the Devil was so tactless as to make a joke about it. And that was why he was thrown out of Heaven, with all the angels who had been unable to suppress their laughter. So they set up Hell as a kind of jokers' club, and thereby complicated the universe in a way that must often embarrass God."

"No," I said; "I've never heard that and as legends are my speciality I don't believe it. Talmud my foot! I suspect you made that legend up here and now."

Liesl laughed loud and long, and pushed the brandy bottle toward me. "You are almost as clever as I am, and I love you, Dunstan Ramsay," she said.

"New or old, it's a very good legend," said Ingestree. "Because that's always one of the puzzles of religion—no humour. Not a scrap. What is the basis of our faith, when we have a faith? The Bible. The Bible contains precisely one joke, and that is a school-masterish pun attributed to Christ when he told Peter that he was the rock on which the Church was founded. Very probably a later interpolation by some Church Father who thought it was a real rib-binder. But monotheism leaves no room for jokes, and I've thought for a long time that is what is wrong with it. Monotheism is too po-faced for the sort of world we find ourselves in. What have we heard tonight? A great deal about how Happy Hannah tried to squeeze jokes out of the Bible in the hope of catching a few young people who were brimming with life. Frightful puns; the kind of bricks you make without straw. Whereas the Devil, when he is represented in literature, is full of excellent jokes, and we can't resist him because he and his jokes make so much sense. To twist an old saying, if the Devil had not existed, we should have had to invent him. He is the only explanation of the appalling ambiguities of life. I give you the Devil!"

He raised his glass, but only he and Liesl drank the toast. Kinghovn, who had been getting into the brandy very heavily, was almost asleep. Lind was musing, and no sign of amusement appeared on his long face. I couldn't possibly have drunk such a toast, offered in such a spirit. Ingestree was annoyed.

"You don't drink," said he.

"Perhaps I shall do so later, when I have had time to think it over," said Lind. "Private toasts are out of fashion in the English-speaking world; you only drink them on formal occasions, as part of the decorum of stupidity. But we Scandinavians have still one foot in Odin's realm, and when we drink a toast we mean something quite serious. When I drink to the Devil I shall want to be quite serious."

"I hesitate to say so, Roland," I said, "but I wish you hadn't done that. I quite agree that the Devil is a great joker, but don't think it is particularly jolly to be the butt of one of his jokes. You have called his attention to you in what I must call a frivolous way—damned silly, to be really frank. I wish you hadn't done that."

"You mean he'll do something to me? You mean that from hence-forth I'm a Fated Man? You know, I've always fancied the role of

Fated Man. What do you think it'll be? Car accident? Loss of job? Even a nasty death?"

"Who am I to probe the mind of a World Spirit?" I said. "But if I were the Devil—which, God be thanked, I am not—I might throw a joke or two in your direction that would test your sense of humour. I don't suppose you're a Fated Man."

"You mean I'm too small fry for that?" said Ingestree. He was smiling, but he didn't like my serious tone and was inviting me to insult him. Luckily Kinghovn woke up, slightly slurred in speech but full of opinion.

"You're all out of your heads," he shouted. "No humour in the Bible. All right. Scrub out the Bible. Use the script Eisengrim has given us. Film the subtext. Then I'll show you some humour: that Fat Woman—let me give you a peep-shot of her groaning in the donniker, or being swilled down by Gus; let me show her shrieking her bloody-awful jokes while the Last Trick gets dirtier and dirtier. Then you'll hear some laughter. You're all mad for words. Words are just farts from a lot of fools who have swallowed too many books. Give me things! Give me the appearance of a thing, and I'll show you the way to photograph it so the reality comes right out in front of your eyes. The Devil? Balls! God? Balls! Get me that Fat Woman and I'll photograph her one way and you'll know the Devil made her, then I'll photograph her another way and you'll swear you see the work of God! Light! That's the whole secret. Light! And who understands it? I do!"

Lind and Ingestree decided it was time to take him to his bed. As they manhandled him down the long entry-steps of Sorgenfrei he was shouting, "Light! Let there be light! Who said that? I said it!"

(8)

The film-makers were drawing near the end of their work. All but a few special scenes of *Un Hommage à Robert-Houdin* were "in the can"; what remained was to arrange backstage shots of Eisengrim being put into his "gaffed" conjuror's evening coat by the actor who played the conjuror's son and assistant; of assistants working quietly and deftly while the great magician produced astonishing effects on the stage; of Mme Robert-Houdin putting the special padded covers over the precious and delicate automata; of the son-assistant gently loading a dozen doves, or three rabbits, or even a couple of ducks into a space which seemed incapable of holding them; of all the splendidly efficient organization which was needed to produce the effect of the illogical and incredible. That night, therefore, Eisengrim moved his narrative along a little faster.

"You don't want a chronological account of my seven years as the mechanism of Abdullah," he said, "and indeed it would be impossible for me to give you one. Something was happening all the time, but only two or three matters were of any importance. We were continually travelling and seeing new places, but in fact we saw nothing. We brought excitement and perhaps a whisper of magic into thousands of rural Canadian lives, but our own lives were vast unbroken prairies of boredom. We were continually on the alert, sizing up the Rubes and trying to match what we gave to what they wanted, but no serious level of our minds was ever put to work.

"For Sonnenfels, Molza, and poor old Professor Spencer it was the only life they knew or could expect to have; the first two kept themselves going by nursing some elaborate, inexhaustible, ill-defined personal grievance which they shared; Spencer fed himself on complex, unworkable economic theories, and he would jaw you half to death about bimetallism, or Social Credit, if you gave him a chance. The Fat Woman had her untiring crusade against smut and irreligion; she could not reconcile herself to being simply fat, and I suppose this suggests some kind of mental or spiritual life in her. I saw hope dying in poor Em Dark, as Joe proved his incapacity to learn anything that would get them out of carnival life. Zitta was continually on the lookout for somebody to marry; she couldn't make any money, because she had to spend so much on new, doctored snakes; but how do you get a sucker to the altar if you are always on the move? She would have snatched at Charlie, but Charlie liked something fresher, and anyhow Gus was vigilant to save Charlie from designing women. Zovene was locked in the misery of dwarfdom; he wasn't really a midget, because a midget has to be perfectly formed, and he had a small but unmistakable hump; he was a sour little fellow, and deeply unhappy, I'm sure. Heinie Bayer had lived so long with Rango that he was more like Rango than like a man; they did not bring out the best in each other.

"Like a lot of monkeys Rango was a great masturbator, and when Happy Hannah complained about it Heinie would snicker and say, 'It's natural, ain't it?' and encourage Rango to do it during the Last Trick, where the young people would see him. Then Hannah would shout across the tent, 'Whoso shall offend one of these little ones which believe in me, it were better for him that a millstone were hanged about his neck, and that he were drowned in the depth of the sea.' But the youngsters can't have been believers in the sense of the text, for they hung around Rango, some snickering, some ashamedly curious, and some of the girls obviously unable to understand what was happening. Gus tried to put a stop to this, but even Gus had no power over Rango, except to put him off the show, and he was too solid a draw for that. Hannah decided that Rango was a type of natural, unredeemed man, and held forth at length on that theme. She predicted that Rango would go mad, if he had any brains to go mad with. But Rango died unredeemed.

"So far as I was concerned, the whole of Wanless's World of Wonders was unredeemed. Did Christ die for these, I asked myself, hidden in the shell of Abdullah. I decided that He didn't. I now think I was mistaken, but you must remember that I began these reflections when I was ten years old, and deep in misery. I was in a world which seemed to me to be filthy in every way; I had grown up in a world where there was little love, but much concern about goodness. Here I could see no goodness, and felt no goodness."

Lind intervened. "Excuse me if I am prying," he said, "but you have been very frank with us, and my question is one of deep concern, not simple curiosity. You were swept into the carnival because Willard had raped you; was there any more of that?"

"Yes, much more of it. I cannot pretend to explain Willard, and I think such people must be rare. I know very well that homosexuality includes love of all sorts, but in Willard it was just a perverse drive, untouched by affection or any concern at all, except for himself. At least once every week we repeated that first act. Places had to be found, and when it happened it was quick and usually done in silence except for occasional whimpers from me and—this was very strange—something very like whimpers from Willard."

"And you never complained, or told anybody?"

"I was a child. I knew in my bones that what Willard did to me was very wrong, and he was careful to let me know that it was my fault. If I said a word to anybody, he told me, I would at once find myself in the hands of the law. And what would the law do to a boy who did what I did? Terrible things. When I dared to ask what the law would do to him, he said the law couldn't touch him; he knew highly placed people everywhere."

"How can you have continued to believe that?"

"Oh, you people who are so fortunately born, so well placed, so sure the policeman is your friend! Do you remember my home, Ramsay?"

"Very well."

"An abode of love, was it?"

"Your mother loved you very much."

"My mother was a madwoman. Why? Ramsay has very fine theories about her; he had a special touch with her. But to me she was a perpetual reproach because I knew that her madness was my fault. My father told me that she had gone mad at the time of my birth, and because of it. I was born in 1908, when all sorts of extraordinary things were still believed about childbirth, especially in places like Deptford. Those were the sunset days of the great legend of motherhood. When your mother bore you, she went down in her anguish to the very gates of Death, in order that you might have life. Nothing that you could do subsequently would work off your birth-debt to her. No degree of obedience, no unfailing love, could put the account straight. Your guilt toward her was a burden you carried all your life. Christ, I can hear Charlie now, standing on the stage of a thousand rotten little vaude houses, giving out that message in a tremulous voice, while the pianist played 'In a Monastery Garden'—

M is for the million smiles she gave me;
O means only that she's growing old;
T is for the times she prayed to save me;
H is for her heart, of purest gold;
E is every wrong that she forgave me;
R is right—and Right she'll always be!
   Put them all together, they spell MOTHER—
    A word that means the world to me!

That was the accepted attitude toward mothers, at that time, in the world I belonged to. Well? Imagine what it was like to grow up with a mother who had to be tied up every morning before my father could go off to his work as an accountant at the planing-mill; he was a parson no longer because her disgrace had made it impossible for him to continue his ministry. What was her disgrace? Something that made my schoolmates shout 'Hoor!' when they passed our house. Something that made them call out filthy jokes about hoors when they saw me. So there you have it. A disgraced and ruined home, and for what reason? Because I was born into it. That was the reason.

"That wasn't all. I said that when Willard used me he whimpered. Sometimes he spoke in his whimpering, and what he said then was, 'You goddam little hoor!' And when it was over, more than once he slapped me mercilessly around the head, saying, 'Hoor! You're nothing but a hoor!' It wasn't really condemnation; it seemed to be part of his fulfilment, his ecstasy. Don't you understand? 'Hoor' was what my mother was, and what had brought our family down because of my birth. 'Hoor' was what I was. I was the filthiest thing alive. And I was Nobody. Now do you ask me why I didn't complain to someone about ill usage? What rights had I? I hadn't even a conception of what 'rights' were."

"Could this go on without anybody knowing, or at least suspecting?" Lind was pale; he was taking this hard; I had not thought of him as having so much compassionate feeling.

"Of course they knew. But Willard was crafty and they had no proof. They'd have had to be very simple not to know that something was going on, and carnival people weren't ignorant about perversion.

They hinted, and sometimes they were nasty, especially Sonnenfels and Molza. Heinie and Zovene thought it was a great joke. Em Dark had spells of being sorry for me, but Joe didn't want her to mix herself up in anything that concerned Willard, because Willard was a power in the World of Wonders. He and Charlie were very thick, and if Charlie turned against any of the Talent, there were all kinds of ways he could reduce their importance in the show, and then Gus might get the idea that some new Talent was wanted.

"Furthermore, I was thought to be bad luck by most of the Talent, and show people are greatly involved with the idea of luck. Early in my time on the show I got into awful trouble with Molza because I inadvertently shifted his trunk a few inches in the dressing tent. It was on a bit of board I wanted to use in my writing-lesson with Professor Spencer. Suddenly Molza was on me, storming incomprehensibly, and Spencer had trouble quieting him down. Then Spencer warned me against ever moving a trunk, which is very bad luck indeed; when the handlers bring it in from the baggage wagon they put it where it ought to go, and there it stays until they take it back to the train. I had to go through a complicated ceremony to ward off the bad luck, and Molza fussed all day.

"The idea of the Jonah is strong with show people. A bringer of ill luck can blight a show. Some of the Talent were sure I was a Jonah, which was just a way of focussing their detestation of what I represented, and of Willard, whom they all hated.

"Only the Fat Woman ever spoke to me directly about who and what I was. I forget exactly when it was, but it was fairly early in my experience on the show. It might have been during my second or third year, when I was twelve or thereabouts. One morning before the first trick, and even before the calliope began its toot-up, which was the signal that the World of Wonders and its adjuncts were opening for business, she was sitting on her throne and I was doing something to Abdullah, which I checked carefully every day for possible trouble.

"'Come here, kid,' she said. 'I wanta talk to you. And I wanta talk mouth to mouth, even apparently, and not in dark speeches. Them words mean anything to you?'

"'That's from Numbers,' I said.

"'Numbers is right; Numbers twelve, verse eight. How do you know that?'

"'I just know it.'

"'No, you don't just know it. You been taught it. And you been taught it by somebody who cared for your soul's salvation. Was it your Ma?'

"'My Pa,' I said.

"'Then did he ever teach you Deuteronomy twenty-three, verse ten?'

"'Is that about uncleanness in the night?'

"'That's it. You been well taught. Did he ever teach you Genesis thirteen, verse thirteen? That's one of the unluckiest verses in the Bible.'

"'I don't remember.'

"'Not that the men of Sodom were wicked and sinners before the Lord exceedingly?'

"'I don't remember.'

"'I bet you remember Leviticus twenty, thirteen.'

"'I don't remember.'

"'You do so remember! If a man also lie with mankind as he lieth with a woman, both of them have committed an abomination; they shall surely be put to death; their blood shall be upon them.'

"I said nothing, but I am sure my face gave me away. It was one of Willard's most terrible threats that if I were caught I should certainly be hanged. But I was mute before the Fat Woman.

"'You know what that means, dontcha?'

"Oh, I knew what it meant. In my time on the show I had already learned a great deal about mankind lying with women, because Charlie talked about little else when he sat on the train with Willard. It was a very dark matter, for all I knew about it was the parody of this act which I was compelled to go through with Willard, and I assumed that the two must be equally horrible. But I clung to the child's refuge: silence.

"'You know where that leads, dontcha? Right slap to Hell, where the worm dieth not and the fire is not quenched.'

"From me, nothing but silence.

"'You're in a place where no kid ought to be. I don't mean the show, naturally. The show contains a lotta what's good. But that Abdullah! That's an idol, and that Willard and Charlie encourage the good folks that come in here for an honest show to bow down and worship almost before it, and they won't be held guiltless. No sirree! Nor you, neither, because you're the works of an idol and just as guilty as they are.'

"'I just do what I'm told,' I managed to say.

"'That's what many a sinner's said, right up to the time when it's no good saying it any longer. And those tricks. You're learning tricks, aren't you? What do you want tricks for?'

"I had a happy inspiration. I looked her straight in the eye. 'I count them but dung, that I may win Christ,' I said.

"'That's the right way to look at it, boy. Put first things first. If that's the way you feel, maybe there's some hope for you still.' She sat a little forward in her chair, which was all she could manage, and put her podgy hands on her great knees, which were shown off to advantage by her pink rompers. 'I'll tell you what I always say,' she continued; 'there's two things you got to be ready to do in this world, and that's fight for what's right, and read your Bible every day. I'm a fighter. Always have been. A mighty warrior for the Lord. And you've seen me on the train, reading my old Bible that's so worn and thumbed that people say to me, "that's a disgrace; why don't you get yourself a decent copy of the Lord's Word?" And I reply, "I hang on to this old Bible because it's seen me through thick and thin, and what looks like dirt to you is the wear of love and reverence on every page." A clean sword and a dirty Bible! That's my war-cry in my daily crusade for the Lord: a clean sword and a dirty Bible! Now, you remember that. And you ponder on Leviticus twenty, thirteen, and cut out all that fornication and Sodom abomination before it's too late, if it isn't too late already.'

"I got away, and hid myself in Abdullah and thought a lot about what Happy Hannah had said. My thoughts were like those of many a convicted sinner. I was pleased with my cleverness in thinking up that text that had averted her attack. I sniggered that I had even been able to use a forbidden word like 'dung' in a sanctified sense. I was frightened by Leviticus twenty, thirteen, and—you see how much a child of the superstitious carnival I had already become—by the double thirteen verse from Genesis. Double thirteen! What could be more ominous! I knew I ought to repent, and I did, but I knew I could not leave off my sin, or Willard might kill me, and not only was I afraid to die, I quite simply didn't want to die. And such is the resilience of childhood that when the first trick advanced as far as Abdullah, I was pleased to defeat a particularly obnoxious Rube.

"After that I had many a conversation with Hannah in which we matched texts. Was I a hypocrite? I don't think so. I had simply acquired the habit of adapting myself to my audience. Anyhow, my readiness with the Bible seemed to convince her that I was not utterly damned. I had no such assurance, but I was getting used to living with damnation.

"I had a Bible. I stole it from a hotel. It was one of those sturdy copies the Gideons spread about so freely in hotel rooms. I snitched one at the first opportunity, and as Professor Spencer was teaching me to read very capably I spent many an hour with it. I felt no compunction about the theft, because theft was part of the life I lived. Willard was as good a pickpocket as I have ever known, and one of the marks of his professionalism was that he was not greedy or slapdash in his methods.

"He had an agreement with Charlie. At a point about the middle of the bally, during one of the night shows, Charlie would interrupt his description of the World of Wonders to say, very seriously, *Ladies and gentlemen, I think I ought to warn you, on behalf of the management, that pickpockets may be at work at this fair. I give you my assurance that nothing is farther from the spirit of amusement and education represented by our exhibition than the utterly indefensible practice of theft. But as you know, we cannot control everything that may happen in the vicinity of our show. And therefore I urge you, as your friend and as a member of the Wanless organization which holds nothing dearer than its reputation for unimpeachable honesty, that you should keep a sharp eye, and perhaps also a hand, on your wallets. And if there should be any loss—which the Wanless organization most sincerely hopes may not be the case—we beg you to report it to us, and to your excellent local police force, so that the thief may be appre-hended if that should prove to be possible.* The gaff here was that when he spoke of thieves, Rubes who had a full wallet were likely to put a hand on it. Willard spotted them from the back of the crowd, and during the rest of Charlie's pious spiel he would gently lift one from a promising Rube. It had to be very quick work. Then, when he had taken the money, he substituted a wad of newspaper of the appropriate size, and either during the bally, or when the Rube came into the tent, he would put the wallet back in place. Rubes generally carried their wallets on the left hip, and as their pants were often a tight fit, a light hand was necessary.

"Willard was never caught. If the Rube came to complain that he had been robbed, Charlie put on a show for him, shook his head sadly, and said that this was one of the problems that confronted honest show folks. Willard never pinched more than one bankroll in a town, and never robbed in the same town two years running. Willard liked best to steal from the local cop, but as cops rarely had much money this was a larcenous foppery which he did not often allow himself.

"Gus never caught on. Gus was a strangely innocent woman in everything that pertained to Charlie and his doings. Of course Charlie got a fifty per cent cut of what Willard stole.

"Willard knew I stole the Bible, and he was angry. Theft, he gave me to understand, was serious business and not for kids. Get caught stealing some piece of junk, and how were you to get back to serious theft again? Never steal anything trivial. This was perhaps the only moral precept Willard ever impressed on me.

"Anyhow, I had a hotel Bible, and I read it constantly, in many another hotel. The carnival business is a fair-weather business, and in winter it could not be pursued and the carnival had to be put to bed.

"That did not mean a cessation of work. The brother who never travelled with the carnival, but who did all our booking, was Jerry Wanless, and he handled the other side of the business, which was vaudeville booking. As soon as the carnival season was over, Willard and Abdullah were booked into countless miserable little vaudeville theatres throughout the American and Canadian Middle West.

"It was an era of vaudeville and there were thousands of acts to fill thousands of spots all over the continent. There was a hierarchy of performance, beginning with the Big Time, which was composed of top acts that played in the big theatres of big cities for a week or more at a stretch. After it came the Small Big Time, which was pretty good and played lesser houses in big and middle-sized cities. Then came the Small Time, which played smaller towns in the sticks and was confined to split weeks. Below that was a rabble of acts that nobody wanted very much, which played for rotten pay in the worst vaude houses. Nobody ever gave it a name, and those who belonged to it always referred to it as Small Time, but it was really Very Small Time. That was where Jerry Wanless booked incompetent dog acts, jugglers who were on the booze, dirty comedians, Single Women without charm or wit, singers with nodes on their vocal chords, conjurors who dropped things, quick-change artistes who looked the same in all their impersonations, and a crowd of carnies like Willard and some of the other Talent from the World of Wonders.

"It was the hardest kind of entertainment work, and we did it in theatres that seemed never to have been swept, for audiences that seemed never to have been washed. We did continuous vaudeville: six acts followed by a 'feature' movie, round and round and round from one o'clock in the afternoon until midnight. The audience was invited to come when it liked and stay as long as it liked. In fact, it changed completely almost every show, because there was always an act called a 'chaser' which was reckoned to be so awful that even the people who came to our theatres couldn't stand it. Quite often during my years in vaudeville Zovene the Midget Juggler filled this ignominious spot. Poor old Zovene wasn't really as awful as he appeared, but he was pretty bad and he was wholly out of fashion. He dressed in a spangled costume that was rather like the outfit worn by Mr Punch—a doublet and tight knee-breeches, with striped stockings and little pumps. He had only one outfit, and he had shed spangles for so long that he looked very shabby. There was still a wistful prettiness about him as he skipped nimbly to 'Funiculi funicula' and tossed coloured Indian clubs in the air. But it was a prettiness that would appeal only to an antiquarian of the theatre, and we had no such rarities in our audiences.

"There is rank and precedence everywhere, and here, on the bottom shelf of vaudeville, Willard was a headliner. He had the place of honour, just before Zovene came on to empty the house. The 'professor' at the piano would thump out an Oriental theme from *Chu Chin Chow* and the curtain would rise to reveal Abdullah, bathed in whatever passed for an eerie light in that particular house. Behind Abdullah might be a backdrop representing anything—a room in a palace, a rural glade, or one of those improbable Italian gardens, filled with bulbous balustrades and giant urns, which nobody has ever seen except a scene-painter.

"Willard would enter in evening dress, wearing a cape, which he doffed with an air, and held extended briefly at his right side; when he folded it, a shabby little table with his cards and necessaries had appeared behind it. Applause? Never! The audiences we played to rarely applauded and they expected a magician to be magical. If they were not asleep, or drunk, or pawing the woman in the next seat, they received all Willard's tricks with cards and coins stolidly.

"They liked it better when he did a little hypnotism, asking for members of the audience to come to the stage to form a 'committee' which would watch his act at close quarters, and assure the rest of the audience that there was no deception. He did the conventional hypnotist's tricks, making men saw wood that wasn't there, fish in streams that had no existence, and sweat in sunlight that had never penetrated into that dismal theatre. Finally he would cause two of the men to start a fight, which he would stop. The fight always brought applause. Then, when the committee had gone back to their seats, came the topper of his act, Abdullah the Wonder Automaton of the Age. It was the same old business; three members of the audience chose cards, and three times Abdullah chose a higher one. Applause. Real applause, this time. Then the front-drop—the one with advertisements painted on it— came down and poor old Zovene went into his hapless act.

"The only other Talent from the World of Wonders that was booked into the places where we played were Charlie, who did a monologue, and Andro.

"Andro was becoming the worst possible kind of nuisance. He was showing real talent, and to hear Charlie and Willard talk about it you would think he was a traitor to everything that was good and pure in the world of show business. But I was interested in Andro, and watched him rehearse. He never talked to me, and probably regarded me as a company spy. There were such things, and they reported back to Jerry in Chicago what Talent was complaining about money, or slacking on the job, or black-mouthing the management. But Andro was the nearest thing to real Talent I had met with up to that time, and he fascinated me. He was a serious, unrelenting worker and perfectionist.

"Imitators of his act have been common in night-clubs for many years, and I don't suppose he was the first to do it, but certainly he was the best of the lot. He played in the dark, except for a single spot-light, and he waltzed with himself. That is to say, on his female side he wore a red evening gown, cut very low in the back, and showing lots of his female leg in a red stocking; on his masculine side he wore only half a pair of black satin knee-breeches, a black stocking and a pump with a phoney diamond buckle. When he wrapped himself in his own arms, we saw a beautiful woman in the arms of a half-naked muscular man, whirling rhythmically around the stage in a rapturous embrace. He worked up all sorts of illusions, kissing his own hand, pressing closer what looked like two bodies, and finally whirling offstage for what must undoubtedly be further romance. He was a novelty, and even our audiences were roused from their lethargy by him. He improved every week.

"Willard and Charlie couldn't stand it. Charlie wrote to Jerry and I heard what he said, for Charlie liked his own prose and read it aloud to Willard. Charlie deplored 'the unseemly eroticism' of the act, he said. It would get Jerry a bad name to book such an act into houses that catered to a family trade. Jerry wrote back telling Charlie to shut up and leave the booking business to him. He suggested that Charlie clean up his own act, of which he had received bad reports. Obviously some stool-pigeon had it in for Charlie.

"As a monologist, Charlie possessed little but the self-assurance necessary for the job. Such fellows used to appear before the audi-ence, flashily dressed, with the air of a relative who has made good in the big city and come home to amuse the folks. 'Friends, just before the show I went into one of your local restaurants and looked down the menoo for something tasty. I said to the waiter, Say, have you got frogs' legs? No sir, says he, I walk like this because I got corns. You know, one of the troubles today is Prohibition. Any disagreement? No. I didn't think there would be. But the other day I stepped into a blind pig not a thousand miles from this spot, and I said to the waiter, Bring me a couple of glasses of beer. So he did. So I drank one. Then I got up to leave, and the waiter comes running. Hey, you didn't pay for those two glasses of beer, he said. That's all right, I said, I drank one and left the other to settle. Then I went to keep a date with a pretty schoolteacher. She's the kind of schoolteacher I like best—lots of class and no principle. I get on better with schoolteachers now than I did when I was a kid. My education was completed early. One day in school I put up my hand and the teacher said, What is it, and I said, Please may I leave the room? No, she says, you stay here and fill the inkwells. So I did, and she screamed, and the principal expelled me,...' And so on, for ten or twelve minutes, and then he would say, 'But seriously folks—' and go into a rhapsody about his Irish mother, and a recitation of that tribute to motherhood. Then he would run off the stage quickly, laughing as if he had been enjoying himself too much to hold it in. Sometimes he got a spatter of applause. Now and then there would be dead silence, and some sighing. Vaudeville audiences in those places could give the loudest sighs I have ever heard. Prisoners in the Bastille couldn't have touched them.

"In the monologues of people like Charlie there were endless jokes about minorities—Jews, Dutch, Squareheads, Negroes, Irish, everybody. I never heard of anybody resenting it. The sharpest jokes about Jews and Negroes were the ones we heard from Jewish and Negro comedians. Nowadays I understand that a comedian doesn't dare to make a joke about anyone but himself, and if he does too much of that he is likely to be tagged as a masochist, playing for sympathy because he is so mean to himself. The old vaude jokes were sometimes cruel, but they were fairly funny and they were lightning-rods for the ill-will of audiences like ours, who had a plentiful supply of ill-will. We played to people who had not been generously used by life, and I suppose we reflected their state of mind.

"I spent my winters from 1918 until 1928 in vaudeville houses of the humblest kind. As I sat inside Abdullah and peeped out through the spy-hole in his bosom I learned to love these dreadful theatres. However wretched they were, they appealed to me powerfully. It was not until much later in my life that I learned what it was that spoke to me of something fine, even when the language was garbled. It was Liesl, indeed, who showed me that all theatres of that sort—the proscenium theatres that are out of favour with modern architects— took their essential form and style from the ball-rooms of great palaces, which were the theatres of the seventeenth and eighteenth centuries. All the gold, and stucco ornamentation, the cartouches of pan-pipes and tambourines, the masks of Comedy, and the uphol-stery in garnet plush were democratic stabs at palatial luxury; these were the palaces of the people. Unless they were Catholics, and spent some time each week in a gaudy church, this was the finest place our audiences could enter. It was heart-breaking that they should be so tasteless and run-down and smelly, but their ancestry was a noble one. And of course the great movie and vaudeville houses where Charlie and Willard would never play, or enter except as paying customers, were real palaces of the people, built in what their owners and customers believed to be a regal mode.

"There was nothing regal about the accommodation for the Talent. The dressing-rooms were few and seemed never to be cleaned; when there were windows they were filthy, and high in the walls, and were protected on the outside by wire mesh which caught paper, leaves, and filth; as I remember them now most of the rooms had a dado of deep brown to a height of about four feet from the floor, above which the walls were painted horrible green. There were wash-basins in these rooms, but there was never more than one donniker, usually in a pitiful state of exhaustion, sighing and wheezing the hours away at the end of a corridor. But there was always a star painted on the door of one of these dismal holes, and it was in the star dressing-room that Willard, and Charlie (as a relative of the management) changed their clothes, and where I was tolerated as a dresser and helper.

"It was as a dresser that I travelled, officially. Dresser, and assistant to Willard. It was never admitted that I was the effective part of

Abdullah, and we carried a screen which was set up to conceal the back of the automaton, so that the stagehands never saw me climbing into my place. They knew, of course, but they were not supposed to know, and such is the curious loyalty and discipline of even these rotten little theatres that I never heard of anyone telling the secret. Everybody backstage closed ranks against the audience, just as in the carnival we were all in league against the Rubes.

"I spent all day in the theatre, because the only alternative was the room I shared with Willard in some cheap hotel, and he didn't want me there. My way of life could hardly have been more in contradiction of what is thought to be a proper environment for a growing boy. I saw little sunlight, and I breathed an exhausted and dusty air. My food was bad, because Willard kept me on a very small allowance of money, and as there was nobody to make me eat what I should, I ate what I liked, which was cheap pastry, candy, and soft drinks. I was not a fanatical washer, but as I shared a bed with Willard he sometimes insisted that I take a bath. By every rule of hygiene I should have died of several terrible diseases complicated with malnutrition, but I didn't. In a special and thoroughly unsuitable way, I was happy. I even contrived to learn one or two things which were invaluable to me.

"Except for his dexterity as a conjuror, pickpocket, and card-sharp, Willard did nothing with his hands. As I told you, Abdullah had some mechanism in his base, and when Willard moved the handle that set it in motion, it was supposed to enable Abdullah to do clever things with cards. The mechanism was a fake only in so far as it related to Abdullah's skill; otherwise it was genuine enough. But it was always breaking down, and this was embarrassing when we were on show. Early in my time with Willard I explored those wheels and springs and cogs, and very soon discovered how to set them right when they stuck. The secret was very simple; Willard never oiled the wheels, and if somebody else oiled them for him, he allowed the oil to grow thick and dirty so that it clogged the works. Quite soon I took over the care of Abdullah's fake mechanism, and though I still did not really understand it I was capable enough at maintaining it.

"I suppose I was thirteen or so when a property man at one of the theatres where we played saw me cleaning and oiling these gaffs, and we struck up a conversation. He was interested in Abdullah, and I was nervous about letting him probe the works, fearing that he would find out that they were fakes, but I need not have worried. He knew that at a glance. 'Funny that anybody'd take the trouble to put this class of work into an old piece of junk like this,' he said. 'D'you know who made it?' I didn't. 'Well, I'll bet anything you like a clock-maker made it,' said he. 'Lookit; I'll show you.' And he proceeded to give me a lecture that lasted for almost an hour about the essentials of clock-work, which is a wonderful complexity of mechanism that is, at base, quite simple and founded on a handful of principles. I won't pretend that everybody would have understood him as well as I did, but I am not telling you this story to gain a reputation for modesty. I took to it with all the enthusiasm of a curious boy who had nothing else in the world to occupy his mind. I pestered the property man whenever he had a moment of spare time, demanding more explanation and demonstration. He had been trained as a clock- and watch-maker as a boy—I think he was a Dutchman but I never bothered to learn his name except that it was Henry—and he was a kindly fellow. The third day, which was our last stay in that town, he opened his own watch, took out the movement, and showed me how it could be taken to pieces. I felt as if Heaven had opened. My hands were by this time entirely at my command because of my hundreds of hours of prac-tice in the deeps of Abdullah, and I begged him to let me reassemble the watch. He wouldn't do that; he prized his watch, and though I showed some promise he was not ready to take risks. But that night, after the last show, he called me to him and handed me a watch—a big, old-fashioned turnip with a German-silver case—and told me to try my luck with that. 'When you come back this way,' he said, 'let's see how you've got on.'

"I got on wonderfully. During the next year I took that watch apart and reassembled it time after time. I tinkered and cleaned and oiled and fiddled with the old-fashioned regulator until it was as accurate a timepiece as its age and essential character allowed. I longed for greater knowledge, and one day when opportunity served I stole a wrist-watch—they were novelties still at that time—and discovered to my astonishment that it was pretty much the same inside as my old turnip, but not such good workmanship. This was the foundation of my mechanical knowledge. I soon had the gaffed works of Abdullah going like a charm, and even introduced a few improvements and replaced some worn parts. I persuaded Willard that the wheels and springs of Abdullah should be on view at all times, and not merely during his preliminary lecture; I put my own control handle inside where I could reach it and cause Abdullah's wheels to change speed when he was about to do his clever trick. Willard didn't like it. He disapproved of changes, and he didn't want me to get ideas above my station.

"However, that is precisely what I did. I began to understand that Willard had serious limitations, and that perhaps his power over me was not so absolute as he pretended. But I was still much too young and frightened to challenge him in anything serious. Like all great revolutions, mine was a long time preparing. Furthermore, the sexual subjection in which I lived still had more power over me than the occasional moments of happiness I enjoyed, and which even the most miserable slaves enjoy.

"From the example of Willard and Charlie I learned a cynicism about mankind which it would be foolish to call deep, but certainly it was complete. Humanity was divided into two groups, the Wise Guys and the Rubes, the Suckers, the Patsys. The only Wise Guys within my range were Willard and Charlie. It was the law of nature that they should prey on the others.

"Their contempt for everyone else was complete, but whereas Charlie was good-natured and pleased with himself when he got the better of a Sucker, Willard merely hated the Sucker. The sourness of his nature did not display itself in harsh judgements or wisecracks; he possessed no wit at all—not even the borrowed wit with which Charlie decked his act and his private conversation. Willard simply thought that everybody but himself was a fool, and his contempt was absolute.

"Charlie wasted a good deal of time, in Willard's opinion, chasing girls. Charlie fancied himself as a seducer, and waitresses and chambermaids and girls around the theatre were all weighed by him in terms of whether or not he would be able to 'slip it to them'. That was his term. I don't think he was especially successful, but he worked at his hobby and I suppose he had a measure of success. 'Did you notice that kid in the Dancing Hallorans?' he would ask Willard. 'She's got round heels. I can always tell. What do you wanta bet I slip it to her before we get outa here?' Willard never wanted to bet about that; he liked to bet on certainties.

"The Rubes who wanted to play cards with Abdullah in the vaude houses were of a different stamp from those we met in the carnival world. The towns were bigger than the villages which supported country fairs, and in every one there were a few gamblers. They would turn up at an evening show, and it was not hard to spot them; a gambler looks like anyone else when he is not gambling, but when he takes the cards or the dice in his hands he reveals himself. They were piqued by their defeat at the hands of an automaton and wanted revenge. It was Charlie who sought them out and suggested a friendly game after the theatre was closed.

"The friendly game always began with another attempt to defeat Abdullah, and sometimes money was laid on it. After a sufficient number of defeats—three was usually enough—Willard would say, 'You're not going to get anywhere with the Old Boy here, and I don't want to take your money. But how about a hand or two of Red Dog?' He always started with Red Dog, but in the end they played whatever game the Suckers chose. There they would sit, in a corner of the stage, with a table if they could find one, or else playing on top of a box, and it would be three or four in the morning before they rose, and Willard and Charlie were always the winners.

"Willard was an accomplished card-sharp. He never bothered with any of the mechanical aids some crooks use—hold-outs, sleeve pockets, and such things—because he thought them crude and likely to be discovered, as they often are. He always played with his coat off and his sleeves rolled up, which had an honest look; he depended on his ability as a shuffler and dealer, and of course he used marked cards. Sometimes the Rubes brought their own cards, which he would not allow them to use with Abdullah—he explained that Abdullah used a sensitized deck—but which he was perfectly willing to play with in the game. If they were marked he knew it at once, and after a game or two he would say, in a quiet but firm voice, that he thought a change of deck would be pleasant, and produced a new deck fresh from a sealed package, calling attention to the fact that the cards were not marked and could not be.

"They did not remain unmarked for long, however. Willard had a left thumbnail which soon put the little bumps in the tops and sides of the cards that told him all he needed to know. He let the Rubes win for an hour or so, and then their luck changed, and sometimes big money came into Willard's hands at the end of the game. He was the best marker of cards I have ever known except myself. Some gamblers hack their cards so that you could almost see the marks across a room, but Willard had sensitive hands and he nicked them so cleverly that a man with a magnifying glass might have missed it. Nor was he a flashy dealer; he left that to the Rubes who wanted to show off. He dealt rather slowly, but I never saw him deal from the bottom of the deck, although he certainly did so in every game. He and Charlie would sometimes move out of a town with five or six hundred dollars to split between them, Charlie being paid off as the steerer who brought in the Rubes, and Willard as the expert with the cards. Charlie sometimes appeared to be one of the losers in these games, though never so much so that it looked suspicious. The Rubes had a real Rube conviction that show folks and travelling men ought to be better at cards than the opponents they usually met.

"I watched all of this from the interior of Abdullah, because after the initial trials against the automaton it was impossible for me to escape. I was warned against falling asleep, lest I might make some sound that would give away the secret. So, heavy-eyed, but not unaware, I saw everything that was done, saw the greed on the faces of the Rubes, and saw the quiet way in which Willard dealt with the occasional quarrels. And of course I saw how much money changed hands.

"What happened to all that money? Charlie, I knew, was being paid seventy-five dollars a week for his rotten monologues, which would have been good pay if he had not had to spend so much of it on travel; part of Jerry's arrangement was that all Talent paid for its own tickets from town to town, as well as costs of room and board.

Very often we had long hops from one stand to another, and travel was a big expense. And of course Charlie spent a good deal on bootleg liquor and the girls he chased.

"Willard was paid a hundred a week, as a headliner, and because the transport of Abdullah, and myself at half-fare, cost him a good deal. But Willard never showed any sign of having much money, and this puzzled me for two or three years. But then I became aware that Willard had an expensive habit. It was morphine. This of course was before heroin became the vogue.

"Sharing a bedroom with him I could not miss the fact that he gave himself injections of something at least once a day, and he told me that it was a medicine that kept him in trim for his demanding work. Taking dope was a much more secret thing in those days than it has become since, and I had never heard of it, so I paid no attention. But I did notice that Willard was much pleasanter after he had taken his medicine than he was at other times, and it was then that he would sometimes give me a brief lesson in sleight-of-hand.

"Occasionally he would give himself a little extra treat, and then, before he fell asleep, he might talk for a while about what the future held. 'It'll be up to Albee,' he might say; 'he'll have to make his decision. I'll tell him—E.F., you want me at the Palace? Okay, you know my figure. And don't tell me I have to arrange it with Martin Beck. You talk to Beck. You paid that French dame, that Bernhardt, $7,000 a week at the Palace. I'm not going to up the ante on you. That figure'll do for me. So any time you want me, you just have to let me know, and I promise you I'll drop everything else to oblige you—' Even in my ignorant ears this sounded unlikely. Once I asked him if he would take Abdullah to the Palace, and he gave one of his rare, snorting laughs. 'When I go to the Palace, I'll go alone,' he said; 'the day I get the high sign from Albee, you're on your own.' But he didn't hear from Albee, or any manager but Jerry Wanless.

"He began to hear fairly often from Jerry, whose stool-pigeons were reporting that Willard was sometimes vague on the stage, mistimed a trick now and then, and even dropped things, which is something a headline magician, even on Jerry's circuit, was not supposed to do. I thought these misadventures came from not eating enough, and used to urge Willard to get himself a square meal, but he had never cared much for food, and as the years wore on he ate less and less. I thought this was why he so rarely needed to go to the donniker, and why he was so angry with me when I was compelled to do so, and it was not until years later that I learned that constipation is a symptom of Willard's indulgence. He was usually better in health and sharper on the job when we were with the carnival, because he was in the open air, even though he worked in a tent, but during the winters he was sometimes so dozy—that was Charlie's word for it—that Charlie was worried.

"Charlie had reason to be worried. He was Willard's source of supply. Charlie was a wonder at discovering a doctor in every town who could be squared, because he was always on the lookout for abortionists. Not that he needed abortionists very often, but he belonged to a class of man who regards such knowledge as one of the hallmarks of the Wise Guy. An abortionist might also provide what Willard wanted, for a price, and if he didn't, he knew someone else who would do so. Thus, without, I think, being malignant or even a very serious drug pusher, Charlie was Willard's supplier, and a large part of Willard's winnings in the night-long card games stuck to Charlie for expenses and recompense for the risks he took. When Willard began to be dozy, Charlie saw danger to his own income, and he tried to keep Willard's habit within reason. But Willard was resistant to Charlie's arguments, and became in time even thinner than he had been when first I saw him, and he was apt to be twitchy if he had not had enough. A twitchy conjuror is useless; his hands tremble, his speech is hard to understand, and he makes disturbing faces. The only way to keep Willard functioning efficiently, both as an entertainer and as a card-sharp, was to see that he had the dose he needed, and if his need increased, that was his business, according to Charlie.

"When Willard felt himself denied, it was I who had to put up with his ill temper and spite. There was only one advantage in the gradual decline of Willard so far as I was concerned, and that was that as morphine became his chief craze, his sexual approaches to me became fewer. Sharing a bed with him when he was restless was nervous work, and I usually preferred to sneak one of his blankets and lie on the floor. If the itching took him, his wriggling and scratching were dreadful, and went on until he was exhausted and fell into a stupor rather than a sleep. Sometimes he had periods of extreme sweating, which were very hard on a man who was already almost a skeleton. More than once I have had to rouse Charlie in the middle of the night, and tell him that Willard had to have some of his medicine, or he might go mad. It was always called 'his medicine' by me and by Charlie when he talked to me. For of course I was included in the all-embracing cynicism of these two. They assumed that I was stupid, and this was only one of their serious mistakes.

"I too became cynical, with the whole-hearted, all-inclusive vigour of the very young. Why not? Was I not shut off from mankind and any chance to gain an understanding of the diversity of human temperament by the life I led and the people who dominated me? Yet I saw people, and I saw them very greatly to their disadvantage. As I sat inside Abdullah, I saw them without being seen, while they gaped at the curiosities of the World of Wonders. What I saw in most of those faces was contempt and patronage for the show folks, who got an easy living by exploiting their oddities, or doing tricks with snakes or fire. They wanted us; they needed us to mix a little leaven in their doughy lives, but they did not like us. We were outsiders, holiday people, untrustworthy, and the money they spent to see us was foolish money. But how much they revealed as they stared! When the Pharisees saw us they marvelled, but it seemed to me that their inward parts were full of ravening and wickedness. Day after day, year after year, they believed that somehow they could get the better of Abdullah, and their greed and stupidity and cunning drove them on to try their hands at it. Day after day, year after year, I defeated them, and scorned them because they could not grasp the very simple fact that if Abdullah could be defeated, Abdullah would cease to be. Those who tried their luck I despised rather less than those who hung back and let somebody else try his. The change in their loyalty was always the same; they were on the side of the daring one until he was defeated, and then they laughed at him, and sided with the idol.

"In those years I formed a very low idea of crowds. And of all those who pressed near me the ones I hated most, and wished the worst luck, were the young, the lovers, who were free and happy. Sex to me meant terrible bouts with Willard and the grubby seductions of Charlie. I did not believe in the happiness or the innocence or the goodwill of the couples who came to the fair for a good time. My reasoning was simple, and of a very common kind: if I were a hoor and a crook, were not whoredom and dishonesty the foundations on which humanity rested? If I were at the outs with God—and God never ceased to trouble my mind—was anyone else near Him? If they were, they must be cheating. I very soon came to forget that it was I who was the prisoner: I was the one who saw clearly and saw the truth because I saw without being seen. Abdullah was the face I presented to the world, and I knew that Abdullah, the undefeated, was worth no more than I.

"Suppose that Abdullah were to make a mistake? Suppose when Uncle Zeke or Swifty Dealer turned up a ten of clubs, Abdullah were to reply with a three of hearts? What would Willard say? How would he get out of his predicament? He was not a man of quick wit and as the years wore on I understood that his place in the world was even shakier than my own. I could destroy Willard.

"Of course I didn't do it. The consequences would have been terrible. I was greatly afraid of Willard, afraid of Charlie, of Gus, and most afraid of the world into which such an insubordinate act would certainly throw me. But do we not all play, in our minds, with terrible thoughts which we would never dare to put into action? Could we live without some hidden instincts of revolt, of some protest against our fate in life, however enviable it may seem to those who do not have to bear it? I have been, for twenty years past, admittedly the greatest magician in the world. I have held my place with such style and flourish that I have raised what is really a very petty achievement to the dignity of art. Do you imagine that in my best moments when I have had very distinguished audiences—crowned heads, as all magicians love to boast—that I have not thought fleetingly of producing a full chamber-pot out of a hat, and throwing it into the royal box, just to show that it can be done? But we all hug our chains. There are no free men.

"As I sat in the belly of Abdullah, I thought often of Jonah in the belly of the great fish. Jonah, it seemed to me, had an easy time of it.

'Out of the belly of hell cried I, and thou heardest my voice'; that was what Jonah said. But I cried out of the belly of hell, and nothing whatever happened. Indeed, the belly of hell grew worse and worse, for the stink of the dwarf gave place to the stink of Cass Fletcher, who was not a clean boy and ate a bad diet; we can all stand a good deal of our own stink, and there are some earthy old sayings which prove it, but after a few years Abdullah was a very nasty coffin, even for me. Jonah was a mere three days in his fish. After three years I was just beginning my sentence. What did Jonah say? 'When my soul fainted within me I remembered the Lord.' So did I. Such was the power of my early training that I never became cynical about the Lord—only about his creation. Sometimes I thought the Lord hated me; sometimes I thought he was punishing me for—for just about everything that had ever happened to me, beginning with my birth; sometimes I thought he had forgotten me, but that thought was blasphemy, and I chased it away as fast as I could. I was an odd boy, I can tell you.

"Odd, but—what is truly remarkable—not consciously unhappy. Unhappiness of the kind that is recognized and examined and brooded over is a spiritual luxury. Certainly it was a luxury beyond my means at that time. The desolation of the spirit in which I lived was in the grain of my life, and to admit its full horror would have destroyed me. Deep in my heart I knew that. Somehow I had to keep from falling into despair. So I seized upon, and treasured, every lightening of the atmosphere, everything that looked like kindness, every joke that interrupted the bleak damnation of the World of Wonders. I was a cynic about the world, but I did not dare to become a cynic about myself. Who does? Certainly not Willard or Charlie. If one becomes a cynic about oneself the next step is the physical suicide which is the other half of that form of self-destruction.

"This was the life I lived, from that ill-fated thirtieth of August in 1918 until ten years had passed. Many things happened, but the pattern was invariable; the World of Wonders from the middle of May until the middle of October, and the rest of the time in the smallest of small-time vaudeville. I ranged over all of central Canada, and just about every town of medium size in the middle of the U.S. west of Chicago. When I say that many things happened I am not talking about events of world consequence; in the carnival and the vaude houses we were isolated from the world, and this was part of the paradox of our existence. We seemed to bring a breath of something larger into country fairs and third-rate theatres, but we were little touched by the changing world. The automobile was linking the villages with towns, and the towns with cities, but we hardly noticed. In the vaude houses we knew about the League of Nations and the changing procession of American Presidents because these things provided the jokes of people like Charlie. The splendour of motherhood was losing some of its gloss, and something called the Jazz Age was upon us. So Charlie dropped mother, and substituted a recitation that was a parody of 'Gunga Din', which older vaudevillians were still reciting.

> Though I've belted you and flayed you
> By the Henry Ford that made you
> You're a better car than Packard
> Hunka Tin!

—he concluded, and quite often the audience laughed. As we traipsed around the middle of the Great Republic we hardly noticed that the movies were getting longer and longer, and that Hollywood was planning something that would put us all out of work. Who were the Rubes? I think we were the Rubes.

"My education continued its haphazard progress. I would do almost anything to fight the boredom of my life and the sense of doom that I had to suppress or be destroyed by it. I hung around the property-shops of theatres that possessed such things, and learned a great deal from the old men there who had been compelled, in their day, to produce anything from a workable elephant to a fake diamond ring, against time. I sometimes haunted watch-repair shops, and pestered busy men to know what they were doing; I even picked up their trick of looking through a jeweller's *loupe* with one eye while surveying the world fishily through the other. I learned some not very choice Italian from Zovene, some Munich German from Sonny, and rather a lot of pretty good French from a little man who came on the show when Molza's mouth finally became so painful that he took the extraordinary step of visiting a doctor, and came back to the World of Wonders with a very grey face, and packed up his traps. This Frenchman, whose name was Duparc, was an India Rubber Wonder, a contortionist and an uncommonly cheerful fellow. He became my teacher, so far as I had one; Professor Spencer was becoming queerer and queerer and gave up selling the visiting cards which he wrote with his feet; instead he tried to persuade the public to buy a book he had written and printed at his own expense, about monetary reform. He was, I believe, one of the last of the Single Tax men. In spite of the appearance of Duparc, and the disappearance of Andro, who had left the very small time and was now a top-liner on the Orpheum Circuit, we had all been together in the World of Wonders for too many years. But Gus was too tender-hearted to throw anybody off the show, and Jerry got us cheap, and such is the professional vanity of performers of all kinds that we didn't notice that the little towns were growing tired of us.

"Duparc taught me French, and I knew I was learning, but I had another teacher from whom I learned without knowing. Almost everything of great value I have learned in life has been taught me by women. The woman who taught me the realities of hypnotism was Mrs Constantinescu, a strange old girl who travelled around with our show for a few years, running a mitt-camp.

"It was not part of the World of Wonders; it was a concession which Jerry rented, as he rented the right to run a hot-dog stand, a Wheel of Fortune, the cat-rack and, of course, the merry-go-round. The mitt-camp was a fortune-telling tent, with a gaudy banner outside with the signs of the zodiac on it, and an announcement that inside Zingara would reveal the Secrets of Fate. Mrs Constantinescu was Zingara, and for all I know she may have been a real gypsy, as she claimed; certainly she was a good fortune-teller. Not that she would ever admit such a thing. Fortune-telling is against the law in just about every part of Canada and the U.S. When her customers came in she would sell them a copy of *Zadkiel's Dream Book* for ten cents, and offer a personal interpretation for a further fifteen cents, and a full-scale investigation of your destiny for fifty cents, *Zadkiel* included. Thus it was possible for her to say that she was simply selling a book, if any nosey cop interfered with her. They very rarely did so, because it was the job of our advance man to square the cops with money, bootleg hooch, or whatever their fancy might be. Her customers never complained. Zingara knew how to deliver the goods.

"She liked me, and that was a novelty. She was sorry for me, and except for Professor Spencer, nobody had been sorry for me in a very long time. But what made her really unusual in the World of Wonders was that she was interested in people; the Talent regarded the public as Rubes, to be exploited, and whether it was Willard's kind of exploitation or Happy Hannah's, it came to the same thing. But Zingara never tired of humanity or found it a nuisance. She enjoyed telling fortunes and truly thought that she did good by it.

"'Most people have nobody to talk to,' she said to me many times. 'Wives and husbands don't talk; friends don't really talk because people don't want to get mixed up in anything that might cost them something in the end. Nobody truly wants to hear anybody else's worries and troubles. But everybody has worries and troubles and they don't cover a big range of subjects. People are much more like one another than they are unlike. Did you ever think of that?

"'Well? So I am somebody to talk to. I'll talk, and I'll be gone in the morning, and everything I know goes away with me. I don't look like the neighbours. I don't look like the doctor or the preacher, always judging, always tired. I've got mystery, and that's what everybody wants. Maybe they're church-goers, the people in these little dumps, but what does the church give them? Just sermons from some poor sap who doesn't understand life any more than they do; they know him, and his salary, and his wife, and they know he's no great magician. They want to talk, and they want the old mystery, and that's what I give 'em. A good bargain.'

"Clearly they did want it, for though there was never any crowd around Zingara's tent she took in twenty to twenty-five dollars a day, and after fifty a week had been paid to Jerry, that left her with more money than most of the Talent in the World of Wonders.

"'You have to learn to look at people. Hardly anybody does that. They stare into people's faces, but you have to look at the whole person. Fat or thin? Where is the fat? What about the feet? Do the feet show vanity or trouble? Does she stick out her breast or curl her shoulders to hide it? Does he stick out his chest or his stomach? Does he lean forward and peer, or backward and sneer? Hardly anybody stands straight. Knees bent, or shoved back? The bum tight or drooping? In men, look at the lump in the crotch; big or small? How tall is he when he sits down? Don't miss hands. The face comes last. Happy? Probably not. What kind of unhappy? Worry? Failure? Where are the wrinkles? You have to look good, and quick. And you have to let them see that you're looking. Most people aren't used to being looked at except by the doctor, and he's looking for something special.

"'You take their hand. Hot or cold? Dry or wet? What rings? Has a woman taken off her wedding-ring before she came in? That's always a sign she's worried about a man, probably not the husband. A man—big Masonic or K. of C. ring? Take your time. Tell them pretty soon that they're worried. Of course they're worried; why else would they come to a mitt-camp at a fair? Feel around, and give them chances to talk; you know as soon as you touch the sore spot. Tell them you have to feel around because you're trying to find the way into their lives, but they're not ordinary and so it takes time.

"'Who are they? A young woman—it's a boy, or two boys, or no boy at all. If she's a good girl—you know by the hair-do—probably her mother is eating her. Or her father is jealous about boys. An older woman—why isn't my husband as romantic as I thought he was; is he tired of me; why haven't I got a husband; is my best friend sincere; when are we going to have more money; my son or daughter is disobedient, or saucy, or wild; have I had all the best that life is going to give me?

"'Suppose it's a man; lots of men come, usually after dark. He wants money; he's worried about his girl; his mother is eating him; he's two-timing and can't get rid of his mistress; his sex is wearing out and he thinks it's the end; his business is in trouble; is this all life holds for me?

"'It's an old person. They're worried about death; will it come soon and will it hurt? Have I got cancer? Did I invest my money right? Are my grandchildren going to make out? Have I had all life holds for me?

"'Sure you get smart-alecs. Sometimes they tell you most. Flatter them. Laugh at the world with them. Say they can't be deceived. Warn them not to let their cleverness make them hard, because they're really very fine people and will make a big mark in the world. Look to see what they are showing to the world, then tell them they are the exact opposite. That works for almost everybody.

"'Flatter everybody. Is it crooked? Most people are starved to death for a kind word. Warn everybody against something, usually something they will be let in for because they are too honest, or too good-natured. Warn against enemies; everybody's got an enemy. Say things will take a turn for the better soon, because they will; talking to you will make things better because it takes a load off their minds.

"'But not everybody can do it. You have to know how to get people to talk. That's the big secret. That Willard! He calls himself a hypnotist, so what does he do? He stands up a half-dozen Rubes and says, I'm going to hypnotize you! Then he bugs his eyes and waves his hands and after a while they're hypnotized. But the real hypnotism is something very different. It's part kindness and part making them feel they're perfectly safe with you. That you're their friend even though they never saw you until a minute ago. You got to lull them, like you'd lull a child. That's the real art. You mustn't overdo it. No saying, you're safe with me, or anything like that. You have to give it out, and they have to take it in, without a lot of direct talk. Of course you look at them hard, but not domineering-hard like vaude hypnotists. You got to look at them as if they was all you had on your mind at the moment, and you couldn't think of anything you'd rather do. You got to look at them as if it was a long time since you met an equal. But don't push; don't shove it. You got to be wide open to them, or else they won't be wide open to you.'

"Of course I wanted to have my fortune told by Mrs Constantinescu, but it was against the etiquette of carnival. We never dreamed of asking Sonnenfels to lift anything heavy, or treated the Fat Woman as if she was inconvenient company. But of course Zingara knew what I thought, and she teased me about it. 'You want to know your future, but you don't want to ask me? That's right; don't put your faith in sideshow gypsies. Crooks, the whole lot of them. What do they know about the modern world? They belong to the past. They got no place in North America.' But one day, when I suppose I was looking blue, she did tell me a few things.

"'You got an easy fortune to tell, boy. You'll go far. How do I know? Because life is goosing you so hard you'll never stop climbing. You'll rise very high and you'll make people treat you like a king. How do I know? Because you're dirt right now, and it grinds your gizzard to be dirt. What makes me think you've got the stuff to make the world admire you? Because you couldn't have survived the life you're leading if you hadn't got lots of sand. You don't eat right and you got filthy hair and I'll bet you've been lousy more than once. If it hasn't killed you, nothing will.'

"Mrs Constantinescu was the only person who had ever talked to me about what Willard was still doing to me. The Fat Woman muttered now and then about 'abominations' and Sonny was sometimes very nasty to me, but nobody came right out and said anything unmistakable. But old Zingara said 'You're his bumboy, eh? Well, it's not good, but it could be worse. I've known men who liked goats best. It gives you a notion what women got to put up with. The stories I hear! If he calls you "hoor" just think what that means. I've known plenty of hoors who made it a ladder to something very good. But if you don't like it, do something about it. Get your hair cut. Keep yourself clean. Stop wiping your nose on your sleeve. If you got no money, here's five dollars. Now you start out with a good Turkish bath. Build yourself up. If you gotta be a hoor, be a clean hoor. If you don't want to be a hoor, don't look like a lousy bum.'

"At that time, which was the early twenties, a favourite film star was Jackie Coogan; he played charming waifs, often with Charlie Chaplin. But I was a real waif, and sometimes when a Coogan picture was showing in the vaude houses where Willard and I appeared, I was humiliated by how far I fell short of the Coogan ideal.

"I tried a more thorough style of washing, and I got a haircut, a terrible one from a barber who wanted to make everybody look like Rudolph Valentino. I bought some pomade for my hair from him, and the whole World of Wonders laughed at me. But Mrs Constantinescu encouraged me. Later, when I was with Willard on the vaude circuit, we had three days in a town where there was a Turkish bath, and I spent a dollar and a half on one. The masseur worked on me for half an hour, and then said: 'You know what? I never seen a dirtier guy. Jeeze, there's still grey stuff comin' outa ya! Look at these towels! What you do for a living, kid? Sweep chimneys?' I developed quite a taste for Turkish baths, and stole money regularly from Willard to pay for them. I'm sure he knew I stole, but he preferred that to having me ask him for money. He was growing very careless about money, anyhow.

"I was emboldened to steal enough, over a period of a few weeks, to buy a suit. It was a dreadful suit, God knows, but I had been wearing Willard's cast-offs, cheaply cut down, and it was a royal robe to me. Willard raised his eyebrows when he saw it, but he said nothing. He was losing his grip on the world, and losing his grip on me, and like many people who are losing their grip, he mistook it for the coming of a new wisdom in himself. But when summer came, and Mrs Constantinescu saw me, she was pleased.

"'You're doing fine,' she said. 'You got to get yourself ready to make a break. This carnival is running downhill. Gus is getting tired. Charlie is getting too big a boy for her to handle. He's drunk on the show now, and she don't even bawl him out. Bad luck is coming. How do I know? What else could be coming to a stale tent-show like this? Bad luck. You watch out. Their bad luck will be your good luck, if you're smart. Keep your eyes open.'

"I mustn't give the impression that Mrs Constantinescu was always at my elbow uttering gypsy warnings. I didn't understand much of what she said, and I mistrusted some of what I understood. That business about looking at people as if you were interested in nothing else, for instance; when I tried it, I suppose I looked foolish, and Happy Hannah made a loud fuss in the Pullman one day, declaring that I was trying to learn the Evil Eye, and she knew who was teaching me. Mrs Constantinescu was very high on her list of abominations. She urged me to search Deuteronomy to learn what happened to people who had the Evil Eye; plagues wonderful, and plagues of my seed, even great plagues of long continuance, and sore sickness; that was what was in store for me unless I stopped bugging my eyes at folks who had put on the whole armour of God, that they might stand against the wiles of the Devil. Like every young person, I was abashed at the apparent power of older people to see through me. I suppose I was pitifully transparent, and Happy Hannah's inveterate malignancy gave her extraordinary penetration. Indeed, I was inclined to think at that time that Mrs Constantinescu was a nut, but she was an interesting nut, and willing to talk. It wasn't until years later that I realized how much good sense was in what she said.

"Of course she was right about bad luck coming to the show. It happened suddenly.

"Em Dark was a nice woman, and she tried to fight down her growing disappointment with Joe by doing everything she could for him, which included making herself attractive. She was small, and rather plump, and dressed well, making all her clothes. Joe was very proud of her appearance, and I think poor Joe was beginning to be aware that the best thing about him was his wife. So he was completely thrown off base one day, as the Pullman was carrying us from one village to another, to see a horrible caricature of Em walk past him and down the aisle toward Heinie and Sonny, who were laughing their heads off in the door of the smoking-room. It was Rango, dressed in Em's latest and best, with a *cloche* hat on his head, and one of Em's purses in his hairy hand. There is no doubt that Heinie and Sonny meant to get Joe's goat, and to spatter the image of Em, because that was the kind of men they were, and that was what they thought funny. Joe looked like a man who has seen a ghost. He was working, as he so often was, on one of the throwing knives he sold as part of his act, and I think before he knew what he had done, he threw it, and got Rango right between the shoulders. Rango turned, with a look of dreadful pathos on his face, and fell in the aisle. The whole thing took less than thirty seconds.

"You can imagine the uproar. Heinie rushed to Rango, coddled him in his arms, wept, swore, screamed, and became hysterical. But Rango was dead. Sonny stormed and accused Joe in German; he was the kind of man who jabs with his forefinger when he is angry. Gus and Professor Spencer tried to restore order, but nobody wanted order; the excitement was the most refreshing thing that had happened to the World of Wonders in years. Everybody had a good deal to say on one side or the other, but mostly against Joe. The love between Joe and Em concentrated the malignancy of those unhappy people, but this was the first time they had been given a chance to attack it directly. Happy Hannah was seized with a determination to stop the train. What good that would have done nobody knew, but she felt that a big calamity demanded the uttermost in drama.

"I did not at first understand the full enormity of what Joe had done. To kill Rango was certainly a serious injury to Heinie, whose livelihood he was. To buy and train another orang-outang would be months of work. It was Zovene, busily crossing himself, who put the worst of the horror in words: it is a well-known fact in the carnival and circus world that if anybody kills a monkey, three people will die. Heinie wanted Joe to be first on the list, but Gus held him back; luckily for him, because in a fight Joe could have murdered anybody on the show, not excluding Sonny.

"What do you do with a dead monkey? First of all Rango had to be disentangled from Em Dark's best outfit, which Em quite understandably didn't want and threw off the back of the car with Rango's blood on it. (What do you suppose the finder made of that?) Then the body had to be stowed somewhere, and Heinie would have it nowhere except in his berth, which Rango customarily shared with him. You can't make a dead monkey look dignified, and Rango was not an impressive corpse. His eyes wouldn't shut; one stared and the other eyelid drooped, and soon both eyes took on a bluish film; his yellow teeth showed. The Darks felt miserable, because of what Joe had done, and because their love had been held up to mockery in the naked passion and hatred of the hour after Rango's death. Heinie had not scrupled to say that Rango was a lot more use on the show and a lot better person, even though not human, than a little floozie who just stood up and let a dummkopf of a husband throw knives at her; if Joe was so good at hitting Rango, how come he never hit that bitch of a wife of his? This led to more trouble, and it was Em who had to prevent Joe from battering Heinie. I must say that Heinie took the fullest advantage of the old notion that a man is not responsible for what he does in his grief. He got very drunk that night, and wailed and grieved all up and down the car.

"Indeed, the World of Wonders got drunk. Private bottles appeared from everywhere, and were private no more. Professor Spencer accepted a large drink, and it went a very long way with him, for he was not used to it. Indeed, even Happy Hannah took a drink, and quite shortly everyone wished she hadn't. It had been her custom for some years to drink a lot of cider vinegar; she said it kept her blood from thickening, to the great danger of her life, and she got away with so much vinegar that she always smelled of it. Her unhappy inspiration was to spike her evening slug of vinegar with a considerable shot of bootleg hooch which Gus pressed on her, and it was hardly down before it was up again. A nauseated Fat Woman is a calamity on a monumental scale, and poor Gus had a bad night of it with Happy Hannah. Only Willard kept out of the general saturnalia; he crept into his berth, injected himself with his favourite solace, and was out of that world of sorrow, over which the corpse of Rango spread an increasing influence.

"From time to time the Talent would gather around Heinie's berth, and toast the remains. Professor Spencer made a speech, sitting on the edge of the upper berth opposite the one which had become Rango's bier; in this comfortable position he was able to hold his glass with a device he possessed, attached to one foot. He was drunkenly eloquent, and talked touchingly if incoherently about the link between Man and the Lesser Creation, which was nowhere so strong or so truly understood as in circuses and carnivals; had we not, through the years, come to esteem Rango as one of ourselves, a delightful Child of Nature who spoke not with the tongue of man, but through a thousand merry tricks, which now, alas, had been brought to an untimely end? ('Rango'd of been twenty next April,' sobbed Heinie; 'twenty-two, more likely, but I always dated him from when I bought him.') Professor Spencer did not want to say that Rango had been struck down by a murderer's hand. No, that wasn't the way he looked at it. He would speak of it more as a Cream Passional, brought on by the infinite complexity of human relationships. The Professor rambled on until he lost his audience, who took affairs into their own hands, and drank toasts to Rango as long as the booze held out, with simple cries of 'Good luck and good-bye, Rango old pal.'

"At last Rango's wake was over. The Darks had lain unseen in their berth ever since it had been possible to go to bed, but it was half past three when Heinie crawled in beside Rango and wept himself to sleep with the dead monkey in his arms. By now Rango was firmly advanced in *rigor mortis* and his tail stuck from between the curtains of the berth like a poker. But Heinie's devotion was much admired; Gus said it warmed the cuckolds of her heart.

"Next morning, at the fairground, our first business was to bury Rango. 'Let him lay where his life was spent for others,' was what Heinie said. Professor Spencer, badly hung over, asked God to receive Rango. The Darks came, and brought a few flowers, which Heinie ostentatiously spurned from the grave. All Rango's possessions—his cups and plates, the umbrella with which he coquetted on the tightrope—were buried with him.

"Was Zingara tactless, or mischievous, when she said loudly, as we broke up to go about our work: 'Well, how long do we wait to see who's first?' The calliope began the toot-up—it was 'The Poor Butterfly Waltz'—and we got ready for the first trick which, without Rango, put extra work on all of us.

"As the days passed we realized just how much extra work the absence of Rango did mean. There was nothing Heinie could do without him, and five minutes of performance time had somehow to be made up at each trick. Sonnenfels volunteered to add a minute to his act, and so did Duparc; Happy Hannah was always glad to extend the time during which she harassed her audience about religion, and it was simple for Willard to extend the doings of Abdullah for another minute; so it seemed easy. But an additional ten minutes every day was not so easy for Sonnenfels as for the others; as Strong Men go, he was growing old. Less than a fortnight after the death of Rango, at the three o'clock trick, he hoisted his heaviest bar-bell to his knee, then level with his shoulders, then dropped it with a crash and fell forward. There was a doctor on the fairground, and it was less than three minutes before he was with Sonny, but even at that he came too late. Sonny was dead.

"It is much easier to dispose of a Strong Man than it is of a monkey. Sonny had no family, but he had quite a lot of money in a belt he wore at all times, and we were able to bury him in style. He had been a stupid, evil-speaking, bad-tempered man—quite the opposite of the genial giant described by Charlie in his introduction—and no one but Heinie regretted him deeply. But he left another hole in the show, and it was only because Duparc could do a few tricks on the tightrope that the gap could be filled without making the World of Wonders seem skimpy. Heinie mourned Sonny as uproariously as he had mourned Rango, but this time his grief was not so well received by the Talent.

"Sonny's death was proof positive that the curse of a dead monkey was a fact. Zingara was not slow to point out how short a time had been needed to set the bad luck to work. The Talent turned against Heinie with just as much extravagance of sentimentality as they had shown in pitying him. They were inclined to blame him for Sonny's death. He was still hanging around the show, and he was still drawing a salary, because he had a contract which said nothing about the loss of his monkey by murder. He was on the booze. Gus and Charlie resented him because he cost money without bringing anything in. His presence was a perpetual reminder of bad luck, and soon he was suffering the cold shoulder that had been my lot when Happy Hannah first decided I was a Jonah. Heinie was a proven Jonah, and to look at him was to be reminded that somebody was next on the list of the three who must atone for Rango. Heinie had ceased to be Talent; his reason for being was buried with Rango. He was an outsider, and in the carnival world an outsider is very far outside indeed.

"We were near the end of the autumn season, and no more deaths occurred before we broke up for winter, some of us to our vaudeville work, and others, like Happy Hannah, to a quiet time in dime museums and Grand Congresses of Strange People in the holiday grounds of the warm south. Zingara was not the only one to remark that poor Gus was looking very yellow. Happy Hannah thought Gus must be moving into The Change, but Zingara said The Change didn't make you belch a lot, and go off your victuals, like Gus, and whispered a word of fear. When we assembled again the following May, Gus was not with us.

"There the deaths seemed to stop, for those who were less perceptive than Zingara, and myself. But something happened during the winter season that was surely a death of a special kind.

"It was in Dodge City. Willard was fairly reliable during our act, but sometimes during the day he was perceptibly under the influence of morphine, and at other and much worse times he was feeling the want of it. I did not know how prolonged addiction works on the imagination; I was simply glad that his sexual demands on me had dropped almost to nothing. Therefore I did not know what to make of it when he seized me one afternoon in the wings of the vaude house, and accused me violently of sexual unfaithfulness to him. I was 'at it', he said, with a member of a Japanese acrobatic troupe on the bill, and he wasn't going to stand for that. I was a hoor right enough, but by God I wasn't going to be anybody else's hoor. He cuffed me, and ordered me to get into Abdullah, and stay there, so he would know where I was; and I wasn't to get out of the automaton any more, ever. He hadn't kept me all these years to be cheated by any such scum as I was.

"All of this was said in a low voice, because although he was irrational, he wasn't so far gone that he wanted the stage manager to drop on him, and perhaps fine him, for making a row in the wings during the show. I was seventeen or eighteen, I suppose—I had long ago forgotten my birthday, which had never been a festival in our house anyhow—and although I was still small I had some spirit, and it all rushed to my head when he struck me over the ear. Abdullah was standing in the wings in the place where the image was stored between shows, and I was beside it. I picked up a stage-brace, and lopped off Abdullah's head with one strong swipe; then I took after Willard. The stage manager was soon upon us, and we scampered off to the dressing-room, where Willard and I had such a quarrel as neither of us had ever known before. It was short, but decisive, and when it ended Willard was whining to me to show him the kind of consideration he deserved, as one who had been more than a father to me, and taught me an art that would be a fortune to me; I had declared that I was going to leave him then and there.

"I did nothing of the kind. These sudden transformations of character belong to fiction, not to fact, and certainly not to the world of dependence and subservience that I had known for so many years. I was quite simply scared to leave Willard. What could I do without him? I found out very quickly.

"The stage manager had told the manager about the brief outburst in the wings, and the manager came to set us right as to what he would allow in his house. But with the manager came Charlie, who carried great weight because he was the brother of Jerry, who booked the Talent for that house. It was agreed that—just this once—the matter would be overlooked.

"Willard could not be overlooked a couple of hours later, when he was so far down in whatever world his drug took him to that it was impossible for him to go on the stage. There was all the excitement and loud talk you might expect, and the upshot was that I was ordered to take Willard's place at the next show, and do his act as well as I could, without Abdullah. And that is what I did. I was in a rattle of nerves, because I had never appeared on a stage before, except when I was safely concealed in the body of the automaton. I didn't know how to address an audience, how to time my tricks, or how to arrange an act. The hypnotism was beyond me, and Abdullah was a wreck. I suppose I must have been dreadful, but somehow I filled in the time, and when I had done all I could the spatter of applause was only a little less encouraging than it had been for Willard for several months past.

"When Willard recovered enough to know what had happened he was furious, but his fury simply persuaded him to seek relief from the pain of a rotten world with the needle. This was what precipitated the crisis that delivered me from Abdullah forever; Jerry was on the long-distance telephone, wrangling with Charlie, and the upshot of Charlie's best persuasion was that Willard could finish his season if Charlie would keep him in condition to appear on the stage, and that if Willard didn't appear, I was to do so, and I was to be made to perform a proper, well-planned act. I see now that this was very decent of Jerry, who had all the problems of an agent to trouble him. He must have been fond of Charlie. But it

seemed a dreadful sentence at the time. Beginners in the entertainment world are all supposed to be panting for a chance to rush
before an audience and prove themselves; I was frightened of
Willard, frightened of Jerry, and most frightened of all of failure.

"As is usually the case with understudies I neither failed nor
succeeded greatly. In a short time I had worked out a version of The
Miser's Dream that was certainly better than Willard's, and on
Charlie's strong advice I did it as a mute act. I had very little voice,
and what I had was a thin, ugly croak; I had no vocabulary of the kind
that a magician needs; my conversation was conducted in illiterate
carnival slang, varied now and then with some Biblical turn of speech
that had clung to me. So I simply appeared on the stage and did my
stuff without sound, while the pianist played whatever he thought
appropriate. My greatest difficulty was in learning how to perform
slowly enough. In my development of a technique while I was
concealed in Abdullah I had become so fast and so slick that my work
was incomprehensible; the quickness of the hand should certainly
deceive the eye, but not so fast the eye doesn't realize that it is being
deceived.

"Abdullah simply dropped out of use. We lugged him around for
a few weeks, but his transport was costly, and as I would not get inside
him now he was useless baggage. So one morning, on a railway
siding, Charlie and I burned him, while Willard moaned and grieved
that we were destroying the greatest thing in his life, and an irre-
placeable source of income.

"That was the end of Abdullah, and the happiest moment of my
life up to then was when I saw the flames engulf that ugliest of images.

"In their strange way Charlie and Willard were friends, and
Charlie thought the moment had come for him to reform Willard.
He set about it with his usual enthusiasm, conditioned by a very
simple mind. Willard must break the morphine habit. He was to cut
the stuff out, at a stroke, and with no thought of looking back. Of
course this meant that in a very few days Willard was a raving
lunatic, rolling on the floor, the sweating, shrieking victim of crawl-
ing demons. Charlie was frightened out of his wits, brought in one
of his ambiguous doctors, bought Willard a syringe to replace the

one he had dramatically thrown away, and loaded him up to keep him quiet. There was no more talk of abstinence. Charlie kept assuring me that 'somehow we've got to see him through it.' But there was no way through it. Willard was a gone goose.

"I speak of this lightly now, but at the time I was just as frightened and puzzled as Charlie. I was alarmed to find how dependent on Willard I had become. I had lived with him in dreadful servitude for almost half my life, and now I didn't know what I should do without him. Furthermore, he had been jolted by his attempt at reform into one of those dramatic changes of character which are so astonishing to people who find themselves responsible for a drug addict. He who had been domineering and ugly became embarrassingly fawning and frightened. His great dread was that Charlie and I would put him in a hospital. All he wanted was to be cared for, and supplied with enough morphine to keep him comfortable. A simple demand, wasn't it? But somehow we managed it, and one consequence was that I became involved in the nuisance of finding suppliers of the drug, making approaches to them, and paying the substantial prices they demanded.

"By the time it was the season for rejoining the World of Wonders, I had taken over completely the job of filling Willard's place in the vaude programmes, and Willard was an invalid who had to be dragged from date to date. It was a greatly changed carnival that season. Gus was gone, and the new manager was a tough little carnie who knew how to manage the show, but had none of Gus's pride in it; he took his tone from Charlie, as the real representative of the owners. Charlie had finally wakened up to the fact that the day of such shows was passing, and that fair dates were harder to get. That was when he decided to add a blow-off to the World of Wonders, and as well to set up in a little business of his own, unknown to Jerry.

"A blow-off is an annex to a carnival show. Sometimes it is well-advertised, if it is a speciality that does not quite fit into the show proper, like Australian stock-whip performers, or a man and a girl who do tricks with lariats, in cowboy costume. But it can also be a part of the show that is very quietly introduced, and that is not necessarily seen during every performance. Charlie's blow-off was of this latter kind, and the only attractions in it were Zitta and Willard.

"Zitta was now too fat and too ugly to hold a place in the main tent, but in the blow-off, which occupied a smaller tent entered through the World of Wonders, she could still do a dirty act with some snakes, a logical development from the stunts she had formerly done during the Last Trick. But it was Willard's role that startled me. Charlie had decided to exhibit him as a Wild Man. Willard sat in ragged shirt and pants, his feet bare, in the dust. After he had gone for a few weeks without shaving he looked convincingly wild. His skin had by this time taken on the bluish tinge of the morphine addict, and his eyes, with their habitually contracted pupils, looked terrifying enough to the rural spectators. Charlie's explanation was that Zitta and Willard came from the Deep South, and were sad evidence of what happened when fine old families, reduced from plantation splendour, became inbred. The suggestion was that Willard was the outcome of a variety of incestuous matings. I doubt if many of the people who came to see Willard believed it, but the appetite for marvels and monsters is insatiable, and he was a good eyeful for the curious. The Shame of the Old South, as the blow-off was called, did pretty good business.

"As for Charlie's enterprise, he had become a morphine-pusher. 'Cut out the middle man,' he said to me by way of explanation; he now bought the stuff from even bigger pushers, and sold it at a substantial price to those who wanted it. The medical profession, he said to me, was intolerably greedy, and he didn't see why he should always be on the paying end of a profitable trade.

"I am sorry to say that I shared Charlie's opinion at that time, and for a while I was his junior in the business. I offer no excuses. I had become fond of the things money can buy, and keeping Willard stoked with what he wanted was very costly. So I became a supplier, rather than a purchaser, and did pretty well by it. But I never put all my eggs in one basket. I was still primarily a conjuror, and the World of Wonders, even in its reduced circumstances, paid me sixty-five dollars a week to do my version of The Miser's Dream for five minutes an hour, twelve hours a day.

"I am going to ask you to excuse me from a detailed account of what followed during the next couple of years. It was inevitable, I suppose, that a simpleton like Charlie, with a greenhorn like myself as his lieutenant, should be caught in one of the periodic crackdowns on drug trafficking. The F.B.I. in the States and the R.C.M.P. in Canada began to pick up some of the small fry like ourselves, as leads to the bigger fish who were more important in the trade. I do not pretend that I behaved particularly well, and the upshot was that Charlie was nabbed and I was not, and that I made my escape by ship with a passport that cost me a great deal of money; I have it still, and it is a beautiful job, but it is not as official as it looks. My problem when the trouble came was what I was going to do with Willard. My solution still surprises me. When every consideration of good sense and self-preservation said that I should ditch him, and let the police find him, I decided instead to take him with me. Explain it as you will, by saying that my conscience overcame my prudence, or that there had grown up a real affection between us during all those years when I was his slave and the secret source of his professional reputation, but I decided that I must take Willard where I was going. Willard was always reminding me that he had never abandoned me when it would have been convenient to do so. So, one pleasant Friday morning in 1927, Jules LeGrand and his invalid uncle, Aristide LeGrand, sailed from Montreal on a C.P.R. ship bound for Cherbourg, and somewhat later Charlie Wanless stood trial in his native state of New York and received a substantial sentence.

"The passports and the steamship passages just about cleaned me out, but I think Willard saved me from being caught. He made a very convincing invalid in his wheelchair, and although I know the ship was watched we had no trouble. But when we arrived in France, what was to be done? Thanks to Duparc I could speak French pretty well, though I could neither read nor write the language. I was a capable conjuror, but the French theatrical world did not have the kind of third-class variety theatre into which I could make my way. However, there were small circuses, and eventually I got a place in *Le grand Cirque forain de St Vite* after some rough adventures during which I was compelled to exhibit Willard as a geek.

"You know what a geek is, Ramsay, but perhaps these gentlemen are not so well versed in the humbler forms of carnival performance. You let it be known that you have, concealed perhaps in a stable at the back of a village inn, a man who eats strange food. When the crowd comes—and not too much of a crowd, because the police don't like such shows—you lecture for a while on the yearning of the geek for raw flesh and particularly for blood; you explain that it is something the medical profession knows about, but keeps quiet so that the relatives of people thus afflicted will not be put to shame. Then, if you can get a chicken, you give the geek a chicken, and he growls and gives a display of animal passion, and finally bites the chicken in the neck, and seems to drink some of its blood. If you are reduced to the point where you can't afford even a superannuated chicken, you find a grass snake or two, or perhaps a rabbit. I was the lecturer, and Willard was the geek. It raised enough money to keep us from starvation, and to keep Willard supplied with just enough of his fancy to prevent a total breakdown.

"You discovered us under the banner of St Vite, Ramsay, when we were travelling in the Tyrol. I suppose it looked very humble to you, but it was a step on an upward path for us. I appeared, you remember, as Faustus LeGrand, the conjuror; I thought Faustus sounded well for a magician; poor old Willard was *Le Solitaire des forêts,* which was certainly an improvement on geeking and sounds much more elegant than Wild Man."

"I remember it very well," said I, "and I remember that you were not at all anxious to recognize me."

"I wasn't anxious to see anybody from Canada. I hadn't seen you for—surely it must have been fourteen years. How was I to know that you had enlisted in the R.C.M.P.—possibly become the pride of the Narcotics Squad? But let that go. I was in a confused state of mind at the time. Do you know what I mean? Something is taking all your attention—something inward—and the outer world is not very real, and you deal with it hastily and badly. I was still battling in my conscience about Willard. By this time I thoroughly hated him. He was an expensive nuisance, yet I couldn't make up my mind to get rid of him. Besides, he might just have enough energy, prompted by anger, to betray me to the police, even at the cost of his own destruction. Still, his life lay in my power. A smallish extra injection some day would have disposed of him.

"But I couldn't do it. Or rather—I've said so much, and put myself so thoroughly to the bad, that I might just as well go all the way—I didn't really want to do it because I got a special sort of satisfaction from his presence. This confused old wreck had been my master, my oppressor, the man who let me live hungry and dirty, who used my body shamefully and never let me lift my head above the shame. Now he was utterly mine; he was my thing. That was how it was now between me and Willard. I had the upper hand, and I admit frankly that it gave me a delicious satisfaction to have the upper hand. Willard had just enough sense of reality left to understand without any question of a mistake who was master. Not that I stressed it coarsely. No, no. If thine enemy be hungry, give him bread to eat; and if he be thirsty, give him water to drink; for thou shalt heap coals of fire on his head, and the Lord shall reward thee. Indeed so. The Lord rewarded me richly, and it seemed to me the Lord's face was dark and gleeful as he did so.

"This was Revenge, which we have all been told is a very grave sin, and in our time psychologists and sociologists have made it seem rather lower class, and unevolved, as well. Even the State, which retains so many primitive privileges that are denied to its citizens, shrinks from Revenge. If it catches a criminal the State is eager to make it clear that whatever it chooses to do is for the possible reform of that criminal, or at the very most for his restraint. Who would be so crass as to suggest that the criminal might be used as he has used his fellow man? We don't admit the power of the Golden Rule when it seems to be working in reverse gear. Do unto others as society says they should do unto you, even when they have done something quite different. We're all sweetness and light now, in our professions of belief. We have shut our minds against the Christ who cursed the fig-tree. Revenge—horrors! So there it was: I was revenging myself on Willard, and I'm not going to pretend to you that when he crunched into a grass snake to give a thrill to a stable filled with dull peasants, who despised him for doing it, I didn't have a warm sense of satisfaction. The Lord was rewarding me. Under the banner of St Vite, the man who had once been Mephistopheles in my life was now just a tremulous, disgusting Wild Man, and if anybody was playing

Mephistopheles, the role was mine. Blessed be the name of the Lord, who forgettest not his servant.

"Don't ask me if I would do it now. I don't suppose for a moment that I would. But I did it then. Now I am famous and rich and have delightful friends like Liesl and Ramsay; charming people like yourselves come from the B.B.C. to ask me to pretend to be Robert-Houdin. But in those days I was Paul Dempster, who had been made to forget it and take a name from the side of a barn, and be the pathic of a perverted drug-taker. Do you think I have forgotten that even now? I have a lifelong reminder. I am a sufferer from a tiresome little complaint called *proctalgia fugax*. Do you know it? It is a cramping pain in the anus that wakes you out of a sound sleep and gives you five minutes or so of great unease. For years I thought that Willard, by his nasty use of me, had somehow injured me irreparably. It took a little courage to go to a doctor and find out that it was quite harmless, though I suppose it has some psychogenic origin. It is useless to ask Magnus Eisengrim if he would exert himself to torment a worm like Willard the Wizard; he has the magnanimity that comes so easily to the rich and powerful. But if you had put the question to Faustus LeGrand in 1929 his answer would have been the one I have just given you.

"Yes, gentlemen, it was Revenge, and it was sweet. If I am to be damned for a sin, I expect that will be the one. Shall I tell you the cream of it—or the worst of it, according to your point of view? There came a time when Willard could stand no more. Jaunting around southern France, and the Tyrol and parts of Switzerland, even when he had absorbed the minimum dose I allowed him, was a weariness that he could no longer endure. He wanted to die, and begged me for death. 'Just gimme a little too much, kid,' was what he said. He was never eloquent but he managed to put a really heartbreaking yearning into those words. What did I reply? 'I couldn't do it, Willard. Really I couldn't. I'd have your life on my conscience. You know we're forbidden by every moral law to take life. If I do what you ask, not only am I a murderer, but you are a suicide. Can you face the world to come with that against you?' Then he would curse and call me every foul name he could think of. And next day it would be the same. I didn't kill him. Instead I withheld death from him, and it was balm to my spirit to be able to do it.

"Of course it came at last. From various evidence I judge that he was between forty and forty-five, but he looked far worse than men I have seen who were ninety. You know how such people die. He had been blue before, but for a few hours before the end he was a leaden colour, and as his mouth was open it was possible to see that it was almost black inside. His teeth were in very bad condition from geeking, and he looked like one of those terrible drawings by Daumier of a pauper corpse. The pupils of his eyes were barely perceptible. His breath was very faint, but what there was of it stank horribly. Till quite near the end he was begging for a shot of his fancy. The only other person with us was a member of the St Vite troupe, a bearded lady—you remember her, don't you, Ramsay?— but as Willard spoke no French she didn't know what he was saying, or if she did she gave no sign. Then a surprising thing happened; a short time before he died his pupils dilated extraordinarily, and that, with his wide-stretched mouth and his colour, gave him the look of a man dying of terror. Indeed, perhaps it was so. Was he aware of the lake which burneth with fire and brimstone, where he would join the unbelieving and the abominable, the whore-mongers, sorcerers, and idolaters? I had seen Abdullah go into the fire. Was it so also with Willard?

"But he was dead, and I was free. Had I not been free for years? Free since I struck the head off Abdullah? No; freedom does not come suddenly. One has to grow into it. But now that Willard was dead, I felt truly free, and I hoped that I might throw off some of the unpleasant characteristics I had taken upon myself but not, I hoped, forever taken within myself.

"I finished my season with *Le grand Cirque* because I did not want to attract attention by leaving as soon as Willard was out of the way. Without his luxury to pay for I was able to give up occasional pocket-picking, and save a little money. I knew what I wanted to do. I wanted to get to England; I knew there were vaude houses or variety shows of some kind in England, and I thought I could get a job there.

"I remember that I took stock of myself, as cold-bloodedly as I could, but not, I think, unjustly. The Deptford parson's son, the madwoman's son, had become a pretty widely experienced young tough; I could pick pockets, I could push dope. I could fight with a broken bottle and I had picked up the French knack of boxing with my feet. I could now speak and read French, and a little German and Italian, and I could speak a terrible patois of English, in which I sounded like the worst of Willard and Charlie combined.

"What was there on the credit side? I was an expert conjuror, and I was beginning to have some inkling of what Mrs Constantinescu meant when she talked about real hypnotism as opposed to the sideshow kind. I was a deft mechanic, could mend anybody's watch, and humour an old calliope. Although I had been the passive partner in countless acts of sodomy I was still, so far as my own sexual activity was concerned, a virgin, and likely to remain one, because I knew nothing about women other than Fat Ladies, Bearded Ladies, Snake Women, and mitt-camp gypsies; on the whole I liked women, but I had no wish to do to anybody I liked what Willard had done to me—and although of course I knew that the two acts differed I supposed they were pretty much the same to the recipient. I had none of Charlie's unresting desire to 'slip it' to anybody. As you see, I was a muddle of toughness and innocence.

"Of course I didn't think of myself as innocent. What young man ever does? I thought I was the toughest thing going. A verse from the Book of Psalms kept running through my head that seemed to me to describe my state perfectly. 'I am become like a bottle in the smoke.' It's a verse that puzzles people who think it means a glass bottle, but my father would never have allowed me to be so ignorant as that. It means one of those old wineskins the Hebrews used; it means a goatskin that has been scraped out, and tanned, and blown up, and hung over the fire till it was as hard as a warrior's boot. That was how I saw myself.

"I was twenty-two, so far as I could reckon, and a bottle that had been thoroughly smoked. What was life going to pour into the bottle? I didn't know, but I was off to England to find out.

"And you are off to England in the morning gentlemen. Forgive me for holding you so long. I'll say good-night."

And for the last time at Sorgenfrei we went through that curious little pageant of bidding our ceremonious good-night to Magnus Eisengrim, who said his farewells with unusual geniality.

Of course the film-makers didn't go back to their inn. They poured themselves another round of drinks and made themselves comfortable by the fire.

"What I can't decide," said Ingestree, "is how much of what we have heard we are to take as fact. It's the inescapable problem of the autobiography: how much is left out, how much has been genuinely forgotten, how much has been touched up to throw the subject into striking relief? That stuff about Revenge, for instance. Can he have been as horrible as he makes out? He doesn't seem a cruel man now. We must never forget that he's a conjuror by profession; his lifelong pose has been demonic. I think he'd like us to believe he played the demon in reality, as well."

"I take it seriously," said Lind. "You are English, Roly, and the English have a temperamental pull toward cheerfulness; they don't really believe in evil. If the Gulf Stream ever deserted their western coast, they'd think differently. Americans are supposed to be the great optimists, but the English are much more truly optimistic. I think he has done all he says he has done. I think he killed his enemy slowly and cruelly. And I think it happens oftener than is supposed by people who habitually avert their minds from evil."

"Oh, I'm not afraid of evil," said Ingestree. "Glad to look on the dark side any time it seems necessary. But I think people dramatize themselves when they have a chance."

"Of course you are afraid of evil," said Lind. "You'd be a fool if you weren't. People talk about evil frivolously, just as Eisengrim says they do; it's a way of diminishing its power, or seeming to do so. To talk about evil as if it were just waywardness or naughtiness is very stupid and trivial. Evil is the reality of at least half the world."

"You're always philosophizing," said Kinghovn; "and that's the dope of the Northern mind. What's evil? You don't know. But when you want an atmosphere of evil in your films you tell me and I arrange lowering skies and funny light and find a good camera angle;

if I took the same thing in blazing sunlight, from another place, it'd look like comedy."

"You're always playing the tough guy, the realist," said Lind, "and that's wonderful. I like you for it, Harry. But you're not an artist except in your limited field, so you leave it to me to decide what's evil and what's comedy on the screen. That's something that goes beyond appearances. Right now we're talking about a man's life."

Liesl had said very little at any of these evening sessions, and I think the film-makers had made the mistake of supposing she had nothing to say. She struck in now.

"Which man's life are you talking about?" she said. "That's another of the problems of biography and autobiography, Ingestree, my dear. It can't be managed except by casting one person as the star of the drama, and arranging everybody else as supporting players. Look at what politicians write about themselves! Churchill and Hitler and all the rest of them seem suddenly to be secondary figures surrounding Sir Numskull Poop, who is always in the limelight. Magnus is no stranger to the egotism of the successful performing artist. Time after time he has reminded us that he is the greatest creature of his kind in the world. He does it without shame. He is not held back by any middle-class notion that it would be nicer if we said it instead of himself. He knows we're not going to say it, because nothing so destroys the sense of equality on which all pleasant social life depends as perpetual reminders that one member of the company out-ranks all the rest. When it is so, it is considered good manners for the pre-eminent one to keep quiet about it. Because Magnus has been talking for a couple of hours we have assumed that his emphasis is the only emphasis.

"This business of the death of Willard: if we listen to Magnus we take it for granted that Magnus killed Willard after painfully humiliating him for quite a long time. The tragedy of Willard's death is the spirit in which Faustus LeGrand regarded it. But isn't Willard somebody, too? As Willard lay dying, who did he think was the star of the scene? Not Magnus, I'll bet you. And look at it from God's point of view, or if that strains you uncomfortably, suppose that you have to make a movie of the life and death of Willard. You need Magnus, but he is not the star. He is the necessary agent who brings Willard to the end. Everybody's life is his Passion, you know, and you can't have much of a Passion if you haven't got a good strong Judas. Somebody has to play Judas, and it is generally acknowledged to be a fine, meaty role. There's a pride in being cast for it. You recall the Last Supper? Christ said that he would be betrayed by one of those who sat at the table with him. The disciples called out, Lord, is it I? And when Judas asked, Christ said it was he.

"Has it never occurred to you that there might have been just the tiniest feeling in the bosom of one of the lesser apostles— Lebbaeus, for instance, whom tradition represents as a fat man— that Judas was thrusting himself forward again? Christ died on the Cross, and Judas also had his Passion, but can anybody tell me what became of Lebbaeus? Yet he too was a man, and if he had written an autobiography do you suppose that Christ would have had the central position? There seems to have been a Bearded Lady at the deathbed of Willard, and I would like to know her point of view. Being a woman, she probably had too much intelligence to think that she was the central figure, but would she have awarded that role to Willard or to Magnus?"

"Either would do," said Kinghovn; "but you need a point of focus, you know. Otherwise you get this *cinéma vérité* stuff, which is some-times interesting but it damn well isn't *vérité* because it fails utterly to convince. It's like those shots of war you see on TV; you can't believe anything serious is happening. If you want your film to look like truth you need somebody like Jurgen to decide what truth is, and somebody like me to shoot it so it never occurs to you that it could appear any other way. Of course what you get is not truth, but it's probably a lot better in more ways than just the cinematic way. If you want the death of Willard shot from the point of view of the Bearded Lady I can certainly do it. And simply because I can do it to order I don't know how you can pretend it has any special superior-ity as truth."

"I suppose it's part of that human condition silly-clever people are always grizzling about," said Liesl. "If you want truth, I suppose you must shoot the film from God's point of view and with God's point of focus, whatever it may be. And I'll bet the result won't look much like *cinéma vérité*. But I don't think either you or Jurgen are up to that job, Harry."

"There is no God," said Kinghovn; "and I've never felt the least necessity to invent one."

"Probably that is why you have spent your life as a technician; a very fine one, but a technician," said Lind. "It's only by inventing a few gods that we get that uneasy sense that something is laughing at us which is one of the paths to faith."

"Eisengrim talks a lot about God," said Ingestree, "and God seems still to be a tremendous reality to him. But there's no question of God laughing. The bottle in the smoke—that's what he was. I really must read the Bible some time; there are such marvellous goodies in it, just waiting to be picked up. But even these Bibles Designed to be Read as Literature are so bloody thick! I suppose one could browse, but when I browse I never seem to find anything except tiresome stud-book stuff about Aminadab begetting Jonadab and that kind of thing."

"We've only had part of the story," I said. "Magnus has carefully pointed out to us that he is looking backward on his early life as a man who has changed decisively in the last forty years. What's his point of focus?"

"Nobody changes so decisively that they lose all sense of the reality of their youth," Lind said. "The days of childhood are always the most vivid. He has let us think that his childhood made him a villain. So I think we must assume that he is a villain now. A quiescent villain, but not an extinct one."

"I think that's a lot of romantic crap," said Kinghovn. "I'm sick of all the twaddle about childhood. You should have seen me as a child; a flaxen-haired little darling playing in my mother's garden in Aalborg. Where is he now? Here I sit, a very well-smoked bottle like our friend who has gone to bed. If I met that flaxen-haired child now I would probably give him a good clout over the ear. I've never much liked kids. Which was the greater use in the world? That child, so sweet and pure, or me, as I am now, not sweet and damned well not pure?"

"That's a dangerous question for a man who doesn't believe in God," I said, "because there is no answer to it without God. I could answer it for you, if I thought you were open to anything but drink and photography, Harry, but I'm not going to waste precious argument. What I want is to defend Eisengrim against the charge of being a villain, now or at any other time. You must look at his history in the light of myth—"

"Aha, I thought we should get to myth in time," said Liesl.

"Well, myth explains much that is otherwise inexplicable, just because myth is a boiling down of universal experience. Eisengrim's story of his childhood and youth is as new to me as it is to you, although I knew him when he was very young—"

"Yes, and you were an influence in making him what he is," said Liesl.

"Because you taught him conjuring?" said Lind.

"No, no; Ramsay was personally responsible for the premature birth of little Paul Dempster, and responsible also for Paul's mother's madness, which marked him so terribly," said Liesl.

I gaped at her in astonishment. "This is what comes of confiding in women! Not only can they not keep a secret; they re-tell it in an utterly false way! I must put this matter right. It is true that Paul Dempster was born prematurely because his mother was hit on the head by a snowball. It is true that the snowball was meant to hit me, and it hit her instead because I dodged it. It is true that the blow on the head and the birth of the child seemed to precipitate an instability that sometimes amounted to madness. And it is true that I felt some responsibility in the matter. But that was long ago and far away, in a country which you would scarcely recognize as modern Canada. Liesl, I blush for you!"

"What a lovely old-fashioned thing to say, dear Ramsay. Thank you very much for blushing for me, because I long ago lost the trick of blushing for myself. But I didn't spill the beans about you just to make you jump. I wanted to make the point that you are a figure in this story, too. A very strange figure, just as odd as any in your legends. You precipitated, by a single action—and who could think you guilty just because you jumped out of the way of a snowball (who, that is, but a grim Calvinist like yourself, Ramsay)— everything that we have been hearing from Magnus during these nights past. Are you a precipitating figure in Magnus's story, or he in yours? Who could comb it all out? But get on with your myth, dear man. I want to hear what lovely twist you will give to what Magnus has told us."

"It is not a twist, but an explication. Magnus has made it amply clear that he was brought up in a strict, unrelenting form of puritanism. In consequence he still blames himself whenever he can, and because he knows the dramatic quality of the role, he likes to play the villain. But as for his keeping Willard as a sort of hateful pet, in order to jeer at him, I simply don't believe it was like that at all. What is the mythical element in his story? Simply the very old tale of the man who is in search of his soul, and who must struggle with a monster to secure it. All myth and Christianity—which has never been able to avoid the mythical pull of human experience—are full of similar instances, and people all around us are living out this basic human pattern every day. In the study of hagiography—"

"I knew you'd get to saints before long," said Liesl.

"In the study of hagiography we have legends and all those splendid pictures of saints who killed dragons, and it doesn't take much penetration to know that the dragons represent not simply evil in the world but their personal evil, as well. Of course, being saints, they are said to have killed their dragons, but we know that dragons are not killed; at best they are tamed, and kept on the chain. In the pictures we see St George, and my special favourite, St Catherine, triumphing over the horrid beast, who lies with his tongue out, looking as if he thoroughly regretted his mistaken course in life. But I am strongly of the opinion that St George and St Catherine did not kill those dragons, for then they would have been wholly good, and inhuman, and useless and probably great sources of mischief, as one-sided people always are. No, they kept the dragons as pets. Because they were Christians, and because Christianity enjoins us to seek only the good and to have nothing whatever to do with evil, they doubtless rubbed it into the dragons that it was uncommonly broadminded and decent of them to let the dragons live at all. They may even have given the dragon occasional treats: you may breathe a little fire, they might say, or you may leer desirously at that virgin yonder, but if you make one false move you'll wish you hadn't. You must be a thoroughly submissive dragon, and remember who's boss. That's the Christian way of doing things, and that's what Magnus did with Willard. He didn't kill Willard. The essence of Willard lives with him today. But he got the better of Willard. Didn't you notice how he was laughing as he said good-night?"

"I certainly did," said Ingestree. "I didn't understand it at all. It wasn't just the genial laughter of a man saying farewell to some guests. And certainly he didn't seem to be laughing at us. I thought perhaps it was relief at having got something off his chest."

"The laugh troubled me," said Lind. "I am not good at humour, and I like to be perfectly sure what people are laughing at. Do you know what it was, Ramsay?"

"Yes," I said, "I think I do. That was Merlin's Laugh."

"I don't know about that," said Lind.

"If Liesl will allow it, I must be mythological again. The magician Merlin had a strange laugh, and it was heard when nobody else was laughing. He laughed at the beggar who was bewailing his fate as he lay stretched on a dunghill; he laughed at the foppish young man who was making a great fuss about choosing a pair of shoes. He laughed because he knew that deep in the dunghill was a golden cup that would have made the beggar a rich man; he laughed because he knew that the pernickety young man would be stabbed in a quarrel before the soles of his new shoes were soiled. He laughed because he knew what was coming next."

"And of course our friend knows what is coming next in his own story," said Lind.

"Are we to take it then that there was some striking reversal of fortune awaiting him when he went to England?" said Ingestree.

"I know no more than you," said I. "I do not hear Merlin's Laugh very often, though I think I am more sensitive to its sound than most people. But he spoke of finding out what wine would be poured into the well-smoked bottled that he had become. I don't know what it was."

Ingestree was more excited than the rest. "But are we never to know? How can we find out?"

"Surely that's up to you," said Lind. "Aren't you going to ask Eisengrim to come to London to see the rushes of this film we have been making? Isn't that owing to him? Get him in London and ask him to continue."

Ingestree looked doubtful. "Can it be squeezed out of the budget?" he said. "The corporation doesn't like frivolous expenses. Of course I'd love to ask him, but if we run very much over budget, well, it would be as good as my place is worth, as servants used to say in the day when they knew they were servants."

"Nonsense, you can rig it," said Kinghovn. But Ingestree still looked like a worried, rather withered baby.

"I know what is worrying Roly," said Liesl. "He thinks that he could squeeze Eisengrim's expenses in London out of the B.B.C., but he knows he can't lug in Ramsay and me, and he's too nice a fellow to suggest that Magnus travel without us. Isn't that it, Roly?"

Ingestree looked at her, "Bang on the head," he said.

"Don't worry about it," said Liesl. "I'll pay my own way, and even this grinding old miser Ramsay might unchain a few pennies for himself. Just let us know when to come."

And so, at last, they went. As we came back into the large, gloomy, nineteenth-century Gothic hall of Sorgenfrei, I said to Liesl: "It was nice of you to think of Lebbaeus, tonight. People don't mention him very often. But you're wrong, you know, saying that there is no record of what he did after the Crucifixion. There is a non-canonical Acts of Thaddaeus—Thaddaeus was his surname, you recall—that tells all about him. It didn't get into the Bible, but it exists."

"What's it like?"

"A great tale of marvels. Real Arabian Nights stuff. Puts him dead at the centre of affairs."

"Didn't I say so! Just like a man. I'll bet he wrote it himself."

2

Merlin's Laugh

(1)

Because of Jurgen Lind's slow methods of work, it took longer to get *Un Hommage à Robert-Houdin* into a final form than we had expected, and it was nearly three months later when Eisengrim, Liesl, and I journeyed to London to see what it looked like. The polite invitation suggested that criticism would be welcome. Eisengrim was the star, and Liesl had put up a good deal of the money for the venture, expecting to get it back over the next two or three years, with substantial gains, but I think we all knew that criticism of Lind would not be gratefully received. A decent pretence was to be kept up, all the same.

We three rarely travelled together; when we did there was always a good deal of haggling about where we should stay. I favoured small, modest hotels; Liesl felt a Swiss nationalist pull toward any hotel, anywhere, that was called the Ritz; Eisengrim wanted to stop at the Savoy.

The suite we occupied at the Savoy was precisely to his taste. It had been decorated in the twenties, and not changed since; the rooms were large, and the walls were in that most dismal of decorators' colours, "off-white"; below the ceiling of the drawing-room was a nine-inch border of looking-glass; there was an Art Moderne fireplace with an electric fire in it which, when in use, gave off a heavy smell of roasted dust and reminiscences of mice; the furniture was big, and clumsy in the twenties mode. The windows looked out on what I called an alley, and what even Liesl called "a mean street", but to our amazement Magnus came up with the comment that nobody who called himself a gentleman ever looked out of the window. (What did he know about the fine points of upper-class behaviour?) There was a master bedroom of astonishing size, and Magnus grabbed it for himself, saying that Liesl might have the other bed in it. My room, not quite so large but still a big room, was nearer the bathroom. That chamber was gorgeous in a style long forgotten, with what seemed to be Roman tiling, a sunken bath, and a giantess's bidet. The daily rate for this grandeur startled me even when I had divided it by three, but I held my peace, and hoped we would not stay long. I am not a stingy man, but I think a decent prudence becoming even in the very rich, like Liesl. Also, I knew enough about the very rich to understand that I should not be let off with a penny less than my full third of whatever was spent.

Magnus was taking his new position as a film star—even though it was only as the star of a television "special"—with a seriousness that seemed to me absurd. The very first night he insisted on having Lind and his gang join us for what he called a snack in our drawing-room. Snack! Solomon and the Queen of Sheba would have been happy with such a snack; when I saw it laid out by the waiters I was so oppressed by the thought of what a third of it would come to that I wondered if I should be able to touch a morsel. But the others ate and drank hugely, and almost as soon as they entered the room began hinting that Magnus should continue the story he had begun at Sorgenfrei. That was what I wanted, too, and as it was plain that I was going to pay dear to hear it, I overcame my scruple and made sure of my share of the feast.

The showing of *Hommage* had been arranged for the following afternoon at three o'clock. "Good," said Magnus; "that will allow me the morning to make a little sentimental pilgrimage I have in mind."

Polite interest from Ingestree, and delicately inquisitive probings as to what this pilgrimage might be.

"Something associated with a turning-point in my life," said Magnus. "I feel that one should not be neglectful of such observances."

Was it anything with which the B.B.C. could be helpful, Ingestree asked.

"No, not at all," said Magnus. "I simply want to lay some flowers at the foot of a monument."

Surely, Ingestree persisted, Magnus would permit somebody from the publicity department, or from a newspaper, to get a picture of this charming moment? It could be so helpful later, when it was necessary to work up enthusiasm for the film.

Magnus was coy. He would prefer not to make public a private act of gratitude and respect. But he was willing to admit, among friends, that what he meant to do was part of the subtext of the film; an act related to his own career; something he did whenever he found himself in London.

He had now gone so far that it was plain he wanted to be coaxed, and Ingestree coaxed him with a mixture of affection and respect that was worthy of admiration. It was plain to be seen how Ingestree had not merely survived, but thriven, in the desperate world of television. It was not long before Magnus yielded, as I suppose he meant to do from the beginning.

"It's nothing in the least extraordinary. I'm going to lay a few yellow roses—I hope I can get yellow ones—at the foot of the monument to Henry Irving behind the National Portrait Gallery. You know it. It's one of the best-known monuments in London. Irving, splendid and gracious, in his academical robes, looking up Charing Cross Road. I promised Milady I'd do that, in her name and my own, if I ever came to the point in life where I could afford such gestures. And I have. And so I shall."

"Now you really mustn't tease us any more," said Ingestree. "We must be told. Who is Milady?"

"Lady Tresize," said Magnus, and there was no hint of banter in his voice any longer. He was solemn. But Ingestree hooted with laughter.

"My God!" he said, "You don't mean Old Mother Tresize? Old Nan? You knew her?"

"Better than you apparently did," said Magnus. "She was a dear friend of mine, and very good to me when I needed a friend. She was one of Irving's protégées, and in her name I do honour to his memory."

"Well—I apologize. I apologize profoundly. I never knew her well, though I saw something of her. You'll admit she was rather a joke as an actress."

"Perhaps. Though I saw her give some remarkable performances. She didn't always get parts that were suited to her."

"I can't imagine what parts could ever have suited her. It's usually admitted she held the old man back. Dragged him down, in fact. He really may have been good, once. If he'd had a decent leading lady he mightn't have ended up as he did."

"I didn't know that he had ended up badly. Indeed I know for a fact that he had quite a happy retirement, and was happier because he shared it with her. Are we talking about the same people?"

"I suppose it depends on how one looks at it. I'd better shut up."

"No, no," said Lind. "This is just the time to keep on. Who are these people called Tresize? Theatre people, I suppose?"

"Sir John Tresize was one of the most popular romantic actors of his day," said Magnus.

"But in an absolutely appalling repertoire," said Ingestree, who seemed unable to hold his tongue. "He went on into the twenties acting stuff that was moth-eaten when Irving died. You should have seen it, Jurgen! *The Lyons Mail, The Corsican Brothers*, and that inter-minable *Master of Ballantrae;* seeing him in repertory was a peep into the dark backward and abysm of time, let me tell you!"

"That's not true," said Magnus, and I knew how hot he was by the coolness with which he spoke. "He did some fine things, if you would take the trouble to find out. Some admired Shakespearean performances; a notable Hamlet. The money he made on *The Master of Ballantrae* he spent on introducing the work of Maeterlinck to England."

"Maeterlinck's frightfully old hat," said Ingestree.

"Now, perhaps. But fashions change. And when Sir John Tresize introduced Maeterlinck to England he was an innovator. Have you no charity toward the past?"

"Not a scrap."

"I think less of you for it."

"Oh, come off it! You're an immensely accomplished actor your-self. You know how the theatre is. Of all the arts it has least patience with bygones."

"You have said several times that I am a good actor, because I can put up a decent show as Robert-Houdin. I'm glad you think so. Have you ever asked yourself where I learned to do that? One of the things that has given my work a special flavour is that I give my audiences something to look at apart from good tricks. They like the way I act the part of a conjuror. They say it has romantic flair. What they really mean is that it is projected with a skilled nineteenth-century technique. And where did I learn that?"

"Well, obviously you're going to tell me you learned it from old Tresize. But it isn't the same, you know. I mean, I remember him. He was lousy."

"Depends on the point of view, I suppose. Perhaps you had some reason not to like him."

"Not at all."

"You said you knew him."

"Oh, very slightly."

"Then you missed a chance to know him better. I had that chance and I took it. Probably I needed it more than you did. I took it, and I paid for it, because knowing Sir John didn't come cheap. And Milady was a great woman. So tomorrow morning—yellow roses."

"You'll let us send a photographer?"

"Not after what you've been saying. I don't pretend to an overwhelming delicacy, but I have some. So keep away, please, and if you disobey me I won't finish the few shots you still have to make on *Hommage*. Is that clear?"

It was clear, and after lingering a few minutes, just to show that they could not be easily dismissed, Ingestree, and Jurgen Lind, and Kinghovn left us.

(2)

Both Liesl and I went with Magnus the following morning on his sentimental expedition. Liesl wanted to know who Milady was; her curiosity was aroused by the tenderness and reverence with which he spoke of the woman who appeared to Ingestree to be a figure of fun. I was curious about everything concerning him. After all, I had my document to consider. So we both went with him to buy the roses. Liesl protested when he bought an expensive bunch of two dozen. "If you leave them in the street, somebody will steal them," she said; "the gesture is the same whether it's one rose or a bundle. Don't waste your money." Once again I had occasion to be surprised at the way very rich people think about money; a costly apartment at the Savoy, and a haggle about a few roses! But Eisengrim was not to be changed from his purpose. "Nobody will steal them, and you'll find out why," said he. So off we went on foot along the Strand, because Magnus felt that taking a taxi would lessen the solemnity of his pilgrimage.

The Irving monument stands in quite a large piece of open pavement; near by a pavement artist was chalking busily on the flagstones. Beside the monument itself a street performer was unpacking some ropes and chains, and a woman was helping him to get ready for his performance. Magnus took off his hat, laid the flowers at the foot of the statue, arranged them to suit himself, stepped back, looked up at the statue, smiled, and said something under his breath. Then he said to the street performer: "Going to do a few escapes, are you?"

"Right you are," said the man.

"Will you be here long?"

"Long as anybody wants to watch me."

"I'd like you to keep an eye on those flowers. They're for the Guvnor, you see. Here's a pound. I'll be back before lunch, and if they're still there, and if you're still here, I'll have another pound for you. I want them to stay where they are for at least three hours; after that anybody who wants them can have them. Now let's see your show."

The busker and the woman went to work. She rattled a tambourine, and he shook the chains and defied the passers-by to tie him up so that he couldn't escape. A few loungers gathered, but none of them seemed anxious to oblige the escape-artist by tying him up. At last Magnus did it himself.

I didn't know what he had in mind, and I wondered if he meant to humiliate the poor fellow by tying him up and leaving him to struggle; after all, Magnus had been a distinguished escape-artist himself in his time, and as he was a man of scornful mind such a trick would not have been outside his range. He made a thorough job of it, and before he had done there was a crowd of fifteen or twenty people gathered to see the fun. It is not every day that one of these shabby street performers has a beautifully dressed and distinguished person as an assistant. I saw a policeman halt at the back of the crowd, and began to worry. My philosophical indifference to human suffering is not as complete as I wish it were. If Magnus tied up the poor wretch and left him, what should I do? Interfere, or run away? Or would I simply hang around and see what happened?

At last Magnus was contented with his work, and stepped away from the busker, who was now a bundle of chains and ropes. The man dropped to the ground, writhed and grovelled for a few seconds, worked himself up on his knees, bent his head and tried to get at one of the ropes with his teeth, and in doing so fell forward and seemed to hurt himself badly. The crowd murmured sympathetically, and pressed a bit nearer. Then, suddenly, the busker gave a triumphant cry, and leapt to his feet, as chains and ropes fell in a tangle on the pavement.

Magnus led the applause. The woman passed the tattered cap that served as a collection bag. Some copper and a few silver coins were dropped in it. Liesl contributed a fifty-penny piece, and I found another. It was a good round for the busker; astonishingly good, I imagine, for the first show of the day.

When the crowd had dispersed, the busker said softly to Magnus: "Pro, ain't yer?"

"Yes, I'm a pro."

"Knew it. You couldn't of done them ties without bein' a pro. You playin' in town?"

"No, but I have done. Years ago, I used to give a show right where we're standing now."

"You did! Christ, you've done well."

"Yes. And I started here under the Guvnor's statue. You'll keep an eye on his flowers, won't you?"

"Too right I will! And thanks!"

We walked away, Magnus smiling and big with mystery. He knew how much we wanted to know what lay behind what we had just seen, and was determined to make us beg. Liesl, who has less pride about such things than I, spoke before we had passed the pornography shops into Leicester Square.

"Come along, Magnus. Enough of this. We want to know and you want to tell. I can feel it. When did you ever perform in the London streets?"

"After I got away from France, and the travelling circus, and the shadow of Willard. I came to London, which was dangerous with the kind of passport I carried, but I managed it. What was I to do? You don't get jobs in variety theatres just by hanging around the stage doors. It's a matter of agents, and having press cuttings, and being known to somebody. And I was down and out. I hadn't a penny. No, that's not quite true; I had forty-two shillings and that was just enough to buy a few old ropes and chains. So I took a look around the West End, and soon found out that the choice position for open-air shows was the place we've just visited. But even that wasn't free; street-artists of long standing had first call on the space. I tried to do my little act when they weren't busy, and three of them took me up an alley and convinced me that I had been tactless. Nevertheless, with a black eye I managed to show them a little magic that persuaded one of them to let me add something to his own show, and for that I got a very small daily sum. Still, I was seen, and it wasn't more than a few days before I was taken to Milady, and after that everything was glorious."

"Why should Milady want to see you? Really, Magnus, you are intolerable. You are going to tell us, so why don't you do it without making me corkscrew every word out of you?"

"If I tell you now, in the street, don't you think I am being rather unfair to Lind? He wants to know too, you know."

"Last night you virtually ordered Lind and his friends out of the hotel. Do you mean you are going to change your mind about that?"

"I was annoyed with Ingestree."

"Yes, I know that. But what's so bad about Ingestree? He doesn't agree with you about Milady. Is the man to have no mind of his own? Must everybody agree with you? Ingestree isn't a bad fellow."

"Not a bad fellow. A fool perhaps."

"Since when is it a criminal offence to be a fool? You're rather a fool yourself, especially about women. I insist on knowing whatever there is to know about Milady."

"And so you shall, my dear Liesl. So you shall. You have only to wait until this evening. I guarantee that when we go back to the Savoy we shall find that Lind has called, that Ingestree is ready to apologize, and that we are all three asked to dinner tonight so that I may very graciously go on with my subtext to *Hommage*. Which I am perfectly willing to do. And Ramsay will be pleased, because the free dinner he gets tonight will somewhat offset the cost of the dinner he had to share in giving last night. You see, all things work together for good to them that love God."

"Sometimes I wish I were a professing Christian, so that I would have the right to tell you how much your blasphemous quoting of Scripture annoys me. And you mustn't torment Ramsay. He hasn't had your advantages. He's never been really poor, and that is a terrible drawback to a man.—Will you promise to be decent to Ingestree?"

An unwonted sound: Eisengrim laughed aloud: Merlin's laugh, if ever I heard it.

(3)

Magnus was having one of his tiresome spells, during which he was right about everything. We were indeed asked to dine as Lind's guests after the showing of *Hommage*. What we saw in the poky little viewing-room was a version of the film that was almost complete; everything that was to be cut out had been removed, but a few shots—close-ups of Magnus—had still to be taken and incorporated. It was a source of astonishment, for I saw nothing that I had not seen while it was being filmed; but the skill of the cutting, and the juxtapositions, and the varieties of pace that had been achieved, were marvels to me. Clearly much of what had been done owed its power to the art of Harry Kinghovn, but the unmistakable impress of Lind's mind was on it, as well. His films possessed a weight of

implication—in St Paul's phrase, "the evidence of things not seen"—
that was entirely his own.

The greatest surprise was the way in which Eisengrim emerged.
His unique skill as a conjuror was there, of course, but somehow
magic is not so impressive on the screen as it is in direct experience,
just as he had said himself at Sorgenfrei. No, it was as an actor that he
seemed like a new person. I suppose I had grown used to him over the
years, and had seen too much of his backstage personality, which was
that of the theatre martinet, the watchful, scolding, impatient star of
the *Soirée of Illusions*. The distinguished, high-bred, romantic figure I
saw on the screen was someone I felt I did not know. The waif I had
known when we were boys in Deptford, the carnival charlatan I had
seen in Austria as Faustus LeGrand in *Le grand Cirque forain de St
Vite,* the successful stage performer, and the amusing but testy and
incalculable permanent guest at Sorgenfrei could not be reconciled
with this fascinating creature, and it couldn't all be the art of Lind
and Kinghovn. I must know more. My document demanded it.

Liesl, too, was impressed, and I am sure she was as curious as I. So
far as I knew, she had at some time met Magnus, admired him,
befriended him, and financed him. They had toured the world
together with their *Soirée of Illusions,* combining his art as a public
performer with her skill as a technician, a contriver of magical apparatus, and her artistic taste, which was far beyond his own. If he was
indeed the greatest conjuror of his time, or of any time, she was
responsible for at least half of whatever had made him so. Moreover,
she had educated him, in so far as he was formally educated, and had
transformed him from a tough little carnie into someone who could
put up a show of cultivation. Or was that the whole truth? She
seemed as surprised by his new persona on the screen as I was.

This was clearly one of Magnus's great days. The film people were
delighted with him, as entrepreneurs always are with anybody who
looks as if he could draw in money, and at dinner he was clearly the
guest of honour.

We went to the Café Royal, where a table had been reserved in the
old room with the red plush benches against the wall, and the lush
girls with naked breasts holding up the ceiling, and the flattering

looking-glasses. We ate and drank like people who were darlings of Fortune. Ingestree was on his best behaviour, and it was not until we had arrived at brandy and cigars that he said—

"I passed the Irving statue this afternoon. Quite by chance. Nothing premeditated. But I saw your flowers. And I want to repeat how sorry I am to have spoken slightingly about your old friend Lady Tresize. May we toast her now?"

"Here's to Milady," said Magnus, and emptied his glass.

"Why was she called that?" said Liesl. "It sounds terribly pretentious if she was simply the wife of a theatrical knight. Or it sounds frowsily romantic, like a Dumas novel. Or it sounds as if you were making fun of her. Or was she a cult figure in the theatre? The Madonna of the Greasepaint? You might tell us, Magnus."

"I suppose it was all of those things. Some people thought her pretentious, and some thought the romance that surrounded her was frowsy, and people always made a certain amount of fun of her, and she was a cult figure as well. In addition she was a wonderfully kind, wise, courageous person who was not easy to understand. I've been thinking a lot about her today. I told you that I was a busker beside the Irving statue when I came to London. It was there Holroyd picked me up and took me to Milady. She decided I should have a job, and made Sir John give me one, which he didn't want to do."

"Magnus, do please, I implore you, stop being mysterious. You know very well you mean to tell us all about it. You want to, and furthermore, you must. Do it to please me." Liesl was laying herself out to be irresistible, and I have never known a woman who was better at the work.

"Do it for the sake of the subtext," said Ingestree, who was also making himself charming, like a naughty boy who has been forgiven.

"All right. So I shall. My show under the shadow of Irving was not extensive. The buskers I was working with wouldn't give me much of a chance, but they allowed me to draw a crowd by making some showy passes with cards. It was stuff I had learned long ago with Willard—shooting a deck into the air and making it slide back into my hand like a beautiful waterfall, and that sort of thing. It can be done with a deck that is mounted on a rubber string, but I could do it with any deck. It's simply a matter of hours of practice, and confidence that you can do it. I don't call it conjuring. More like juggling. But it makes people gape.

"One day, a week or two after I had begun in this underpaid, miserable work, I noticed a man hanging around at the back of the crowd, watching me very closely. He wore a long overcoat, though it wasn't a day for such a coat, and he had a pipe stuck in his mouth as if it had grown there. He worried me because, as you know, my passport wasn't all it should have been. I thought he might be a detective. So as soon as I had done my short trick, I made for a near-by alley. He was right behind me. 'Hi!' he shouted, 'I want a word with you.' There was no getting away, so I faced him. 'Are you interested in a better job than that?' he asked. I said I was. 'Can you do a bit of juggling?' said he. Yes, I could do juggling, though I wouldn't call myself a juggler. 'Any experience walking a tightrope?' Because of the work I had done with Duparc I was able to say I could. 'Then you come to this address tomorrow morning at twelve,' said he, and gave me a card on which was his name—James Holroyd—and he had scribbled a direction on it.

"Of course I was there, next day at noon. The place was a pub called The Crown and Two Chairmen, and when I asked for Mr Holroyd I was directed upstairs to a big room, in which there were a few people. Holroyd was one of them, and he nodded to me to wait.

"Queer room. Just an empty space, with some chairs piled in a corner, and a few odds and ends of pillars, and obelisks and altar-like boxes, which I knew were Masonic paraphernalia, also stacked against a wall. It was one of those rooms common enough in London, where lodges met, and little clubs had their gatherings, and which theatrical people rented by the day for rehearsal space.

"The people who were there were grouped around a man who was plainly the boss. He was short, but by God he had presence; you would have noticed him anywhere. He wore a hat, but not as I had ever seen a hat worn before. Willard and Charlie were hat men, but somehow their hats always looked sharp and dishonest—you know, too much down on one side? Holroyd wore a hat, a hard hat of the kind that Winston Churchill made famous later; a sort of top hat that had lost courage and hadn't grown the last three inches, or acquired any gloss. As I came to know Holroyd I sometimes wondered if he had been born in that hat and overcoat, because I hardly ever saw him without both. But this little man's hat looked as if it should have had a plume in it. It was a perfectly ordinary, expensive felt hat, but he gave it an air of costume, and when he looked from under the brim you felt he was sizing up your costume, too. And that was what he was doing. He took a look at me and said, in a kind of mumble, 'That's your find, eh? Doesn't look much, does he, mph? Not quite as if he might pass for your humble, what? Eh, Holroyd? Mph?'

"'That's for you to say, of course,' said Holroyd.

"'Then I say no. Must look again. Must be something better than that, eh?'

"'Won't you see him do a few tricks?'

"'Need I? Surely the appearance is everything, mph?'

"'Not everything, Guvnor. The tricks are pretty important. At least the way you've laid it out makes the tricks very important. And the tightrope, too. He'd look quite different dressed up.'

"'Of course. But I don't think he'll do. Look again, eh, like a good chap?'

"'Whatever you say, Guvnor. But I'd have bet money on this one. Let him flash a trick or two, just to see.'

"The little man wasn't anxious to waste time on me, but I didn't mean to waste time either. I threw a couple of decks in the air, made them do a fancy twirl, and let them slip back into my hands. Then I twirled on my toes, and made the decks do it again, in a spiral, which looks harder than it is. There was clapping from a corner—the kind of soft clapping women produce by clapping in gloves they don't want to split. I bowed toward the corner, and that was the first time I saw Milady.

"It was a time when women's clothes were plain; the line of the silhouette was supposed to be simple. There was nothing plain or simple about Milady's clothes. Drapes and swags and swishes, and scraps of fur everywhere, and the colours and fabrics were more like upholstery than garments. She had a hat, like a witch's, but with more style to it, and some soft stuff wrapped around the crown dangled

over the brim to one shoulder. She was heavily made up—really she
wore an extraordinary amount of make-up—in colours that were too
emphatic for daylight. But neither she nor the little man seemed to be
meant for daylight; I didn't realize it at the time, but they always
looked as if they were ready to step on the stage. Their clothes, and
manner and demeanour all spoke of the stage."

"The Crummles touch," said Ingestree. "They were about the last
to have it."

"I don't know who Crummles was," said Magnus. "Ramsay will tell
me later. But I must make it clear that these two didn't look in the
least funny to me. Odd, certainly, and unlike anything I had ever seen,
but not funny. In fact, ten years later I still didn't think them funny,
though I know lots of people laughed. But those people didn't know
them as I did. And as I've told you I first saw Milady when she was
applauding my tricks with the cards, so she looked very good to me.

"'Let him show what he can do, Jack,' she said. And then to me,
with great politeness, 'You do juggling, don't you? Let us see you
juggle.'

"I had nothing to juggle with, but I didn't mean to be beaten. And
I wanted to prove to the lady that I was worth her kindness. So with
speed and I hope a reasonable amount of politeness I took her
umbrella, and the little man's wonderful hat, and Holroyd's hat and
the soft cap I was wearing myself, and balanced the brolly on my nose
and juggled the three hats in an arch over it. Not easy, let me tell you,
for all the hats were of different sizes and weights, and Holroyd's
hefted like iron. But I did it, and the lady clapped again. Then she
whispered to the little man she called Jack.

"'I see what you mean, Nan,' he said, 'but there must be some sort
of resemblance. I hope I'm not vain, but I can't persuade myself we
can manage a resemblance, mphm?'

"I put on a little more steam. I did some clown juggling, pretending every time the circle went round that I was about to drop
Holroyd's hat, and recovering it with a swoop, and at last keeping that
one in the air with my right foot. That made the little man laugh, and
I knew I had had a lucky inspiration. Obviously Holroyd's hat was
rather a joke among them. 'Come here, m'boy,' said the boss. 'Stand

back to back with me.' So I did, and we were exactly of a height. 'Extraordinary,' said the boss; 'I'd have sworn he was shorter.'

"'He's a little shorter, Guvnor,' said Holroyd, 'but we can put him in lifts.'

"'Aha, but what will you do about the face?' said the boss. 'Can you get away with the face?'

"'I'll show him what to do about the face,' said the lady. 'Give him his chance, Jack. I'm sure he's lucky for us and I'm never wrong. After all, where did Holroyd find him?'

"So I got the job, though I hadn't any idea what the job was, and nobody thought to tell me. But the boss said I was to come to rehearsal the following Monday, which was five days away. In the meantime, he said, I was to give up my present job, and keep out of sight. I would have accepted that, but again the lady interfered.

"'You can't ask him to do that, Jack,' she said. 'What's he to live on in the meantime?'

"'Holroyd will attend to it,' said the little man. Then he offered the lady his arm, and put his hat back on his head (after Holroyd had dusted it, quite needlessly) and they swept out of that grubby assembly room in the Crown and Two Chairmen as if it were a palace.

"I said to Holroyd, 'What's this about lifts? I'm as tall as he is; perhaps a bit taller.'

"'If you want this job, m'boy, you'll be shorter and stay shorter,' said Holroyd. Then he gave me thirty shillings, explaining that it was an advance on salary. He also asked for a pledge in return, just so that I wouldn't make off with the thirty shillings; I gave him my old silver watch. I respected Holroyd for that; he belonged to my world. It was clear that it was time for me to go, but I still didn't know what the job was, or what I was letting myself in for. That was obviously the style around there. Nobody explained anything. You were supposed to know.

"So, not being a fool, I set to work to find out. I discovered downstairs in the bar that Sir John Tresize and his company were rehearsing above, which left me not much wiser, except that it was some sort of theatricals. But when I went back to the buskers and told them I was quitting, and why, they were impressed, but not pleased.

"'You gone legit on us,' said the boss of the group, who was an escape-man, like the one we saw this morning. 'You and your Sir John-bloody-Tresize. Amlet and Oh Thello and the like of them. If you want my opinion, you've got above yourself, and when they find out, don't come whinin' back to me, that's all. Don't come whinin' bloody back here.' Then he kicked me pretty hard in the backside, and that was the end of my engagement as an open-air entertainer.

"I didn't bother to resent the kick. I had a feeling something important had happened to me, and I celebrated by taking a vacation. Living for five days on thirty shillings was luxury to me at that time. I thought of augmenting my money by doing a bit of pocket-picking, but I rejected the idea for a reason that will show you what had happened to me; I thought such behaviour would be unsuitable to one who had been given a job because of the interference of a richly-dressed lady with an eye for talent.

"The image of the woman called Nan by Sir John Tresize dominated my mind. Her umbrella, as I balanced it on my nose, gave forth an expensive smell of perfume, and I could recall it even in the petrol stink of London streets. I was like a boy who is in love for the first time. But I wasn't a boy; it was 1930, so I must have been twenty-two, and I was a thorough young tough—side-show performer, vaudeville rat, pick-pocket, dope-pusher, a forger in a modest way, and for a good many years the despised utensil of an arse-bandit. Women, to me, were members of a race who were either old and tougher than the men who work in carnivals, or the flabby, pallid strumpets I had occasionally seen in Charlie's room when I went to rouse him to come to the aid of Willard. But so far as any sexual association with a woman went, I was a virgin. Yes, ladies and gentlemen, I was a hoor from the back and a virgin from the front, and so far as romance was concerned I was as pure as the lily in the dell. And there I was, over my ears in love with Lady Tresize, professionally known as Miss Annette de la Borderie, who cannot have been far off sixty and was, as Ingestree is eager to tell you, not a beauty. But she had been kind to me and said she would show me what to do about my face—whatever that meant—and I loved her.

"What do I mean? That I was constantly aware of her, and what I believed to be her spirit transfigured everything around me. I held wonderful mental conversations with her, and although they didn't make much sense they gave me a new attitude toward myself. I told you I put aside any notion of picking a pocket in order to refresh my exchequer because of her. What was stranger was that I felt in quite a different way about the poor slut that helped the escape-artist who kicked me; he was rough with her, I knew, and I pitied her, though I had taken no notice of her before then. It was the dawn of chivalry in me, coming rather late in life. Most men, unless they are assembled on the lowest, turnip-like principle, have a spell of chivalry at some time in their lives. Usually it comes at about sixteen. I understand boys quite often wish they had a chance to die for the one they love, to show that their devotion stops at nothing. Dying wasn't my line; a good religious start in life had given me too much respect for death to permit any extravagance of that sort. But I wanted to live for Lady Tresize, and I was overjoyed by the notion that, if I could do whatever Holroyd and Sir John wanted, I might be able to manage it.

"It wasn't lunacy. She had that effect, in lesser measure, on a lot of people, as I found out when I joined the Tresize Company. Everybody called Sir John 'Guvnor', because that was his style; lots of heads of theatrical companies were called Guvnor. But they called Lady Tresize 'Milady'. It would have been reasonable enough for her maid to do that, but everybody did it, and it was respectful, and affectionately mocking at the same time. She understood both the affection and the mockery, because Milady was no fool.

"Five days is a long time to be cut off from Paradise, and I had nothing to occupy my time. I suppose I walked close to a hundred miles through the London streets. What else was there to do? I bummed around the Victoria and Albert Museum quite a lot, looking at the clocks and watches, but I wasn't dressed for it and I suppose a young tough who hung around for hours made the guards nervous. I looked like a ruffian, and I suppose I was one, and I held no grudge when I was politely warned away. I saw a few free sights—churches and the like—but they meant little to me. I liked the streets best, so I walked and stared, and slept in a Salvation Army hostel for indigents. But I was no indigent; I was rich in feeling, and that was a luxury I had rarely known.

"As the Monday drew near when I was to present myself again I worried a lot about my clothes. All I owned was what I stood up in, and my very poor things were a good protective covering in the streets, where I looked like a thousand others, but they weren't what I needed for a great step upward in the theatrical world. There was nothing to be done, and with my experience I knew my best plan was to present an appearance of honest poverty, so I spent some money on a bath, and washed the handkerchief I wore around my throat in the bathwater, and got a street shoeshine boy to do what he could with my dreadful shoes, which were almost falling apart.

"When the day came, I was well ahead of time, and had my first taste of a theatrical rehearsal. Milady didn't appear at it, and that was a heavy disappointment, but there was plenty to take in, all the same.

"It was education by observation. Nobody paid any heed to me. Holroyd nodded when I went into the room, and told me to keep out of the way, so I sat on a windowsill and watched. Men and women appeared very promptly to time, and a stage manager set out a few chairs to mark entrances and limits to the stage on the bare floor. Bang on the stroke of ten Sir John came in, and sat down in a chair behind a table, tapped twice with a silver pencil, and they went to work.

"You know what early rehearsals are like. You would never guess they were getting up a play. People wandered on and off the stage area, reading from sheets of paper that were bound up in brown covers; they mumbled and made mistakes as if they had never seen print before. Sir John mumbled worse than anyone. He had a way of talking that I could hardly believe belonged to a human being, because almost everything he said was cast in an interrogative tone, and was muddled up with a lot of 'Eh?' and 'Mphm?' and a queer noise he made high up in the back of his nose that sounded like 'Quonk?' But the actors seemed used to it and amid all the muttering and quonking a good deal of work seemed to be done. Now and then Sir John himself would appear in a scene, and then the muttering sank almost to inaudibility. Very soon I was bored.

"It was not my plan to be bored, so I looked for something to do. I was a handy fellow, and a lot younger than the stage manager, so when the chairs had to be arranged in a different pattern I nipped forward and gave him a hand, which he allowed me to do without comment. Before the rehearsal was finished I was an established chair lifter, and that was how I became an assistant stage manager. My immediate boss was a man called Macgregor, whose feet hurt; he had those solid feet that seem to be all in one piece, encased in heavy boots; he was glad enough to have somebody who would run around for him. It was from him, during a break in the work, that I found out what we were doing.

"'It's the new piece,' he explained. 'Scaramouche. From the novel by Rafael Sabatini. You'll have heard of Rafael Sabatini? You haven't? Well, keep your lugs open and you'll get the drift of it. Verra romantic, of course.'

"'What am I to do, Mr Macgregor?' I asked.

"'Nobody's told me,' he said. 'But from the cut of your jib I'd imagine you were the Double.'

"'Double what?'

"'The Double in Two, two,' he said, in a very Scotch way. I learned long ago, from you, Ramsay, that it's no use asking questions of a Scot when he speaks like that—dry as an old soda biscuit. So I held my peace.

"I picked up a little information by listening and asking an occasional question when some of the lesser actors went downstairs to the bar for a modest lunch. After three or four days I knew that Scaramouche was laid in the period of the French Revolution, though when that was I did not know. I had never heard that the French had a revolution. I knew the Americans had had one, but so far as detail went it could have been because George Washington shot Lincoln. I was pretty strong on the kings of Israel; later history was closed to me. But the story of the play leaked out in dribbles. Sir John was a young Frenchman who was 'born with a gift of laughter and a sense that the world was mad'; that was what one of the other actors said about him. The astonishing thing was that nobody thought it strange that Sir John was so far into middle age that he was very near to emerging from the far side of it. This young Frenchman got himself into trouble with the nobility because he had advanced notions. To conceal himself he joined a troupe of travelling actors, but his revolutionary zeal was so great that he could not hold his tongue, and denounced the aristocracy from the stage, to the scandal of everyone. When the Revolution came, which it did right on time when it was needed, he became a revolutionary leader, and was about to revenge himself on the nobleman who had vilely slain his best friend and nabbed his girl, when an elderly noblewoman was forced to declare that she was his mother and then, much against her will, further compelled to tell him that his deadly enemy whom he held at the sword's point was—his father!

"Verra romantic, as Macgregor said, but not so foolish as I have perhaps led you to think. I give it to you as it appeared to me on early acquaintance. I was only interested in what I was supposed to do to earn my salary. Because I now had a salary—or half a salary, because that was the pay for the rehearsal period. Holroyd had presented me with a couple of pages of wretchedly typed stuff, which was my contract. I signed it Jules LeGrand, so that it agreed with my passport. Holroyd looked a little askew at the name, and asked me if I spoke French. I was glad that I could say yes, but he gave me a pretty strong hint that I might consider finding some less foreign name for use on the stage. I couldn't imagine why that should be, but I found out when we reached Act Two, scene two.

"We had approached this critical point—critical for me, that's to say—two or three times during the first week of rehearsal, and Sir John had asked the actors to 'walk through' it, without doing more than find their places on the stage. It was a scene in which the young revolutionary lawyer, whose name was André-Louis, was appearing on the stage with the travelling actors. They were a troupe of Italian Comedians, all of whom played strongly marked characters such as Polichinelle the old father, Climene the beautiful leading lady, Rhodomont the braggart, Leandre the lover, Pasquariel, and other figures from the Commedia dell' Arte. I didn't know what that was, but picked up the general idea, and it wasn't so far away from vaudeville as you might suppose. Indeed, some of it reminded me of poor Zovene, the wretched juggler. André-Louis (that was Sir John) had assumed the role of Scaramouche, a dashing, witty scoundrel.

"In Act Two, scene two, the Italian Comedians were giving a performance, and at the very beginning of it Scaramouche had to do some flashy juggling tricks. Later, he seized his chance to make a revolutionary speech which was not in the play as the Comedians had rehearsed it; when his great enemy and some aristocratic chums stormed the stage to punish him, he escaped by walking across the stage on a tightrope, far above their heads, making jeering gestures as he did so. Very showy. And clearly not for Sir John. So I was to appear in a costume exactly like his, do the tricks, get out of the way so Sir John could make his revolutionary speech, and take over again when it was time to walk the tightrope.

"This would take some neat managing. When Macgregor said, 'Curtain up,' I leapt onto the stage area from the audience's right, and danced toward the left, juggling some plates; when Polichinelle broke the plates with his stick, causing a lot of clatter and uproar, I pretended to dodge behind his cloak, and Sir John popped into sight immediately afterward. Sounds simple, but as we had to pretend to have the plates, and the cloak, and everything else, I found it confusing. The tightrope trick was 'walked' in the same way; Sir John was always talking about 'walking' something when we weren't ready to do it in reality. At the critical moment when the aristocrats rushed the stage, Sir John retreated slowly toward the left side, keeping them off with a stick; then he hopped backward onto a chair—which I must say he did with astonishing spryness—and there was a flurry of cloaks, during which he got out of the way and I emerged above on the tightrope, having stepped out on it from the wings. Easy, you would say, for an old carnival hand? But it wasn't easy at all, and after a few days it looked as if I would lose my job. Even when we were 'walking', I couldn't satisfy Sir John.

"As usual, nobody said anything to me, but I knew what was up one morning when Holroyd appeared with a fellow who was obviously an acrobat and Sir John talked with him. I hung around, officiously helping Macgregor, and heard what was said, or enough of it. The acrobat seemed to be very set on something he wanted, and it wasn't long before he was on his way, and Sir John was in an exceedingly bad temper. All through the rehearsal he bullied everybody. He bullied Miss Adele Chesterton, the pretty girl who played the second romantic interest; she was new to the stage and a natural focus for temper. He bullied old Frank Moore, who played Polichinelle, and was a very old hand and an extraordinarily nice person. He was crusty with Holroyd and chivvied Macgregor. He didn't shout or swear, but he was impatient and exacting, and his annoyance was so thick it cut down the visibility in the room to about half, like dark smoke. When the time came to rehearse Two, two, he said he would leave it out for that day, and he brought the rehearsal to an early close. Holroyd asked me to wait after the others had gone, but not to hang around. So I kept out of the way near the door while Sir John, Holroyd, and Milady held a summit conference at the farther end of the room.

"I couldn't hear much of what they said, but it was about me, and it was hottish. Holroyd kept saying things like, 'You won't get a real pro to agree to leaving his name off the bills,' and 'It's not as easy to get a fair resemblance as you might suppose—not under the conditions.' Milady had a real stage voice, and when she spoke her lowest it was still as clear as a bell at my end of the room, and her talk was all variations on 'Give the poor fellow chance, Jack—everybody must have at least one chance.' But of Sir John I could hear nothing. He had a stage voice, too, and knew how far it could be heard, so when he was being confidential he mumbled on purpose and threw in a lot of Eh and Quonk, which seemed to convey meaning to people who knew him.

"After ten minutes Milady said, so loudly that there could be no pretence that I was not to hear, 'Trust me, Jack. He's lucky for us. He has a lucky face. I'm never wrong. And if I can't get him right, we'll say no more about it.' Then she swept down the room to me, using the umbrella, with more style than you'd think possible, as a walking-stick, and said, 'Come with me, my dear boy; we must have a very intimate talk.' Then something struck her, and she turned to the two men; 'I haven't a penny,' she said, and from the way both Sir John and Holroyd jumped forward to press pound notes on her you could tell they were both devoted to her. That made me feel warmly toward them, even though they had been talking about sacking me a minute before.

ROBERTSON DAVIES

"Milady led the way, and I tagged behind. We went downstairs, where she poked her head into the Public Bar, which was just opening and said, in a surprisingly genial voice, considering that she was Lady Tresize talking to a barman, 'Do you think I could have Rab Noolas for a private talk, for about half an hour, Joey?', and the barman shouted back, 'Whatever you say, Milady', and she led me into a gloomy pen, surrounded on three sides by dingy etched glass, with Saloon Bar on the door. When I closed the door behind us this appeared in reverse and I understood that we were now in Rab Noolas. The barman came behind the counter on our fourth side and asked us what it would be. 'A pink gin, Joey', said Milady, and I said I'd have the same, not knowing what it was. Joey produced them, and we sat down, and from the way Milady did so I knew it was a big moment. Fraught, as they say, with consequence.

"'Let us be very frank. And I'll be frank first, because I'm the oldest. You simply have no notion of the wonderful opportunity you have in *Scaramouche*. Such a superb little cameo. I say to all beginners: they aren't tiny parts, they're little cameos, and the way you carve them is the sign of what your whole career will be. Show me a young player who can give a superb cameo in a small part, and I'll show you a star of the future. And yours is one of the very finest opportunities I have ever seen in my life in the theatre, because you must be so marvellous that nobody—not the sharpest-eyed critic or the most adoring fan—can distinguish you from my husband. Suddenly, before their very eyes, stands Sir John, juggling marvellously, and of course they adore him. Then, a few minutes later, they see Sir John walking the tightrope, and they see half a dozen of his little special tricks of gesture and turns of the head, and they are thunderstruck because they can't believe that he has learned to walk the tightrope. And the marvel of it, you see, is that it's you, all the time! You must use your imagination, my dear boy. You must see what a stunning effect it is. And what makes it possible? You do!'

"'Oh I do see all that, Milady', I said. 'But Sir John isn't pleased. I wish I knew why. I'm honestly doing the very best I can, considering that we haven't anything to juggle with, or any tightrope. How can I do better?'

160

"'Ah, but you've put your finger on it, dear boy. I knew from the moment I saw you that you had great, great understanding—not to speak of a lucky face. You have said it yourself. You're doing the best *you* can. But that's not what's wanted, you see. You must do the best Sir John can.'

"'But—Sir John can't do anything,' I said. 'He can't juggle and he can't walk rope. Otherwise why would he want me?'

"'No, no; you haven't understood. Sir John can, and will, do something absolutely extraordinary: he will make the public—the great audiences of people who come to see him in everything—believe he is doing those splendid, skilful things. He can make them want to believe he can do anything. They will quite happily accept you as him, if you can get the right rhythm.'

"'But I still don't understand. People aren't as stupid as that. They'll guess it's a trick.'

"'A few, perhaps. But most of them will prefer to believe it's a reality. That's what the theatre's about, you see. People want to believe that what they see is true, even if only for the time they're in the playhouse. That's what theatre is, don't you understand? Showing people what they wish were true.'

"Then I began to get the idea. I had seen that look in the faces of the people who watched Abdullah, and who saw Willard swallow needles and thread and pull it out of his mouth with the needles all dangling from the thread. I nervously asked Milady if she would like another pink gin. She said she certainly would, and gave me a pound note to pay for it. When I demurred she said, 'No, no; you must let me pay. I've got more money than you, and I won't presume on your gallantry—though I value it, my dear, don't imagine I don't value it.'

"When the gins came, she continued: 'Let us be very, very frank. Your marvellous cameo must be a great secret. If we tell everybody, we stifle some of their pleasure. You saw that young man who came this morning, and argued so tiresomely? He could juggle and he could walk the rope, quite as well as you, I expect, but he was no use whatever, because he had the spirit of a circus person; he wanted his name on the program, and he wanted featured billing. Wanted his name to come at the bottom of the bills, you see, after all the cast had been listed, "AND

Trebelli". An absurd request. Everybody would want to know who Trebelli was and they would see at once that he was the juggler and rope-walker. And Romance would fly right up the chimney. Besides which I could see that he would never deceive anyone for an instant that he was Sir John. He had a brassy, horrid personality. Now you, my dear, have the splendid qualification of having very little personality. One hardly notices you. You are almost a *tabula rasa*.'

"'Excuse me, Milady, but I don't know what that is.'

"'No? Well, it's a—it's a common expression. I've never really had to define it. It's a sort of charming nothing; a dear, sweet little zero, in which one can paint any face one chooses. An invaluable possession, don't you see? One says it of children when one's going to teach them something perfectly splendid. They're wide open for teaching.'

"'I want to be taught. What do you want me to learn?'

"'I knew you were quite extraordinarily intelligent. More than intelligent, really. Intelligent people are so often thoroughly horrid. You are truly sensitive. I want you to learn to be exactly like Sir John.'

"'Imitate him, you mean?'

"'Imitations are no good. There have been people on the music-halls who have imitated him. No: if the thing is to work as we all want it to work, you must quite simply *be* him.'

"'How, if I don't imitate him?'

"'It's a very deep thing. Of course you must imitate him, but be careful he doesn't catch you at it, because he doesn't like it. Nobody does, do they? What I mean is—oh, dear, it's so dreadfully difficult to say what one really means—you must catch his walk, and his turn of the head, and his gestures and all of that, but the vital thing is that you must catch his rhythm.'

"'How would I start to do that?'

"'Model yourself on him. Make yourself like a marvellously sensitive telegraph wire that takes messages from him. Or perhaps like wireless, that picks up things out of the air. Do what he did with the Guvnor.'

"'I thought he was the Guvnor.'

"'He is now, of course. But when we both worked under the dear old Guvnor at the Lyceum Sir John absolutely adored him, and laid himself open to him like Danae to the shower of gold—you know about that, of course?—and became astonishingly like him in a lot of ways. Of course Sir John is not so tall as the Guvnor; but you're not tall either, are you? It was the Guvnor's romantic splendour he caught. Which is what you must do. So that when you dance out before the audience juggling those plates they don't feel as if the electricity had suddenly been cut off. Another pink gin, if you please.'

"I didn't greatly like pink gin. In those days I couldn't afford to drink anything, and pink gin is a bad start. But I would have drunk hot fat to prolong this conversation. So we had another one each, and Milady dealt with hers much better than I did. A pink gin later—call it ten minutes—I was thoroughly confused, except that I wanted to please her, and must find out somehow what she was talking about.

"When she wanted to leave I rushed to call her a taxi, but Holroyd was ahead of me, and in much better condition. He must have been in the Public Bar. We both bowed her into the cab—I seem to remember having one foot in the gutter and the other on the pavement and wondering what had happened to my legs—and when she drove off he took me by the arm and steered me back into the Public Bar, where we tucked into a corner with old Frank Moore.

"'She's been giving him advice and pink gin,' said Holroyd.

"'Better give him a good honest pint of half-and-half to straighten him out,' said Frank, and signalled to the barman.

"They seemed to know what Milady had been up to, and were ready to put it in language that I could understand, which was kind of them. They made it seem very simple: I was to imitate Sir John, but I was to do it with more style than I had been showing. I was supposed to be imitating a great actor who was imitating an eighteenth-century gentleman who was imitating a Commedia dell' Arte comedian—that's how simple it was. And I was doing everything too bloody fast, and slick and cheap, so I was to drop that and catch Sir John's rhythm.

"'But I don't get it about all this rhythm,' I said. 'I guess I know about rhythm in juggling; it's getting everything under control so you don't have to worry about dropping things because the things are behaving properly. But what the hell's all this human rhythm? You mean like dancing?'

"'Not like any dancing I suppose you know,' said Holroyd. 'But yes—a bit like dancing. Not like this Charleston and all that jerky stuff. More a fine kind of complicated—well, rhythm.'

"'I don't get it at all,' I said. 'I've got to get Sir John's rhythm. Sir John got his rhythm from somebody called the Guvnor. What Guvnor? Is the whole theatre full of Guvnors?'

"'Ah, now we're getting to it,' said old Frank. 'Milady talked about the Guvnor, did she? The Guvnor was Irving, you muggins. You've heard of Irving?'

"'Never,' I said.

"Old Frank looked wonderingly at Holroyd. 'Never heard of Irving. He's quite a case, isn't he?'

"'Not such a case as you might think, Frank,' said Holroyd. 'These kids today have never heard of anybody. And I suppose we've got to remember that Irving's been dead for twenty-five years. You remember him. You played with him. I just remember him. But what's he got to do with a lad like this?—Well, now just hold on a minute. Milady thinks there's a connection. You know how she goes on. Like a loony, sometimes. But just when you can't stand it any more she proves to be right, and righter than any of us. You remember where I found you?' he said to me.

"'In the street. I was doing a few passes with the cards.'

"'Yes, but don't you remember where? I do. I saw you and I came back to rehearsal and said to Sir John, I think I've got what we want. Found him under the Guvnor's statue, picking up a few pennies as a conjuror. And that was when Milady pricked up her ears. Oh Jack, she said, it's a lucky sign! Let's see him at once. And when Sir John wanted to ask perfectly reasonable questions about whether you would do for height, and whether a resemblance could be contrived between you and him, she kept nattering on about how you must be a lucky find because I saw you, as she put it, working the streets under Irving's protection. You know how the Guvnor stood up for all the little people of the theatre, Jack, she said. I'm sure this boy is a lucky find. Do let's have him. And she's stood up for you ever since, though I don't suppose you'll be surprised to hear that Sir John wants to get rid of you.'

"The pint of half-and-half had found its way to the four pink gins, and I was having something like a French Revolution in my innards. I was feeling sorry for myself. 'Why does he hate me so,' I said, snivelling a bit. 'I'm doing everything I know to please him.'

"'You'd better have it straight,' said Holroyd. 'The resemblance is a bit too good. You look too much like him.'

"'Just what I said when I first set eyes on you,' said old Frank. 'My God, I said, what a Double! You might have been spit out of his mouth.'

"'Well, isn't that what they want?' I said.

"'You have to look at it reasonable,' said Holroyd. 'Put it like this: you're a famous actor, getting maybe just the tiniest bit past your prime—though still a top-notcher, mind you—and for thirty years everybody's said how distinguished you are, and what a beautiful expressive face you have, and how Maeterlinck damn near threw up his lunch when you walked on the stage in one of his plays, and said to the papers that you had stolen his soul, you were so good—meaning spiritual, romantic, poetic, and generally gorgeous. You still get lots of fan letters from people who find some kind of ideal in you. You've had all the devotion—a bit cracked some of it, but mostly very real and touching—that a great actor inspires in people, most of whom have had some kind of short-change experience in life. So: you want a Double. And when the Double comes—and such a Double that you can't deny him—he's a seedy little carnie, with the shifty eyes of a pickpocket and the breath of somebody that eats the cheapest food, and you wouldn't trust him with sixpenn'orth of copper, and every time you look at him you heave. He looks like everything inside yourself that you've choked off and shut out in order to be what you are now. And he looks at you all the time—you do this, you know—as if he knew something about you you didn't know yourself. Now: fair's fair. Wouldn't you want to get rid of him? Yet here's your wife, who's stood by you through thick and thin, and held you up when you were ready to sink under debts and bad luck, and whom you love so much everybody can see it, and thinks you're marvellous because

ROBERTSON DAVIES

of it, and what does she say? She says this nasty mess of a Double is lucky, and has to be given his chance. You follow me? Try to be objective. I don't want to say hard things about you, but truth's truth and must be served. You're not anybody's first pick for a Double, but there you are. Sir John's dead spit, as Frank here says.'

"Very soon I was going to have to leave them. My stomach was heaving. But I was still determined to find out whatever I could to keep my job. I wanted it now more desperately than before. 'So what do I do?' I asked.

"Holroyd puffed at his pipe, groping for an answer, and it was old Frank who spoke. He spoke very kindly. 'You just keep on keeping on,' he said. 'Try to find the rhythm. Try to get inside Sir John.'

"These were fatal words. I rushed out into the street, and threw up noisily and copiously in the gutter. Try to get inside Sir John! Was this to be another Abdullah?

"It was, but in a way I could not have foreseen. Experience never repeats itself in quite the same way. I was beginning another servitude, much more dangerous and potentially ruinous, but far removed from the squalor of my experience with Willard. I had entered upon a long apprenticeship to an egoism.

"Please notice that I say egoism, not egotism, and I am prepared to be pernickety about the distinction. An egotist is a self-absorbed creature, delighted with himself and ready to tell the world about his enthralling love affair. But an egoist, like Sir John, is a much more serious being, who makes himself, his instincts, yearnings, and tastes the touchstone of every experience. The world, truly, is his creation. Outwardly he may be courteous, modest, and charming—and certainly when you knew him Sir John was all of these—but beneath the velvet is the steel; if anything comes along that will not yield to the steel, the steel will retreat from it and ignore its existence. The egotist is all surface; underneath is a pulpy mess and a lot of self-doubt. But the egoist may be yielding and even deferential in things he doesn't consider important; in anything that touches his core he is remorseless.

"Many of us have some touch of egoism. We who sit at this table are no strangers to it. You, I should think, Jurgen, are a substantial

166

egoist, and so are you, Harry. About Ingestree I can't say. But Liesl is certainly an egoist and you, Ramsay, are a ferocious egoist battling with your demon because you would like to be a saint. But none of you begins to approach the egoism of Sir John. His egoism was fed by the devotion of his wife, and the applause he could call forth in the theatre. I have never known anyone who came near him in the truly absorbing and damning sin of egoism."

"Damning?" I leapt on the word.

"We were both brought up to believe in damnation, Dunny," said Eisengrim, and he was deeply serious. "What does it mean? Does it mean shut off from the promptings of compassion; untouched by the feelings of others except in so far as they can serve us; blind and deaf to anything that is not grist to our mill? If that is what it means, and if that is a form of damnation, I have used the word rightly.

"Don't misunderstand. Sir John wasn't cruel, or dishonourable or overreaching in common ways; but he was all of these things where his own interest as an artist was concerned; within that broad realm he was without bowels. He didn't make Adele Chesterton cry at every rehearsal because he was a brute. He hadn't brought Holroyd—who was a tough nut in every other way—to a condition of total subjection to his will because he liked to domineer over a fellow-being. He hadn't turned Milady into a kind of human oilcan who went about cooling wheels he had worn red-hot because he didn't know that she was a woman of rare spirit and fine sensitivity. He did these things and a thousand others because he was wholly devoted to an ideal of theatrical art that was contained—so far as he was concerned—within himself. I think he knew perfectly well what he did, and he thought it worth the doing. It served his art, and his art demanded a remorseless egoism.

"He was one of the last of a kind that has now vanished. He was an actor-manager. There was no Arts Council to keep him afloat when he failed, or pick up the bill for an artistic experiment or act of daring. He had to find the money for his ventures, and if the money was lost on one production he had to get it back from another, or he would soon appeal to investors in vain. Part of him was a financier. He asked people to invest in his craft and skill and sense of business.

Beyond that, he asked people to invest in his personality and charm, and the formidable technique he had acquired to make personality and charm vivid to hundreds of thousands of people who bought theatre seats. In justice it must be said that he had a particular sort of taste and flair that lifted him above the top level of actors to the very small group of stars with an assured following. He wasn't personally greedy, though he liked to live well. He did what he did for art. His egoism lay in his belief that art, as he embodied it, was worth any sacrifice on his part and on the part of people who worked with him.

"When I became part of his company the fight against time had begun. Not simply the fight against the approach of age, because he was not deluded about that. It was the fight against the change in the times, the fight to maintain a nineteenth-century idea of theatre in the twentieth century. He believed devoutly in what he did; he believed in Romance, and he couldn't understand that the concept of Romance was changing.

"Romance changes all the time. His plays, in which a well-graced hero moved through a succession of splendid adventures and came out on top—even when that meant dying for some noble cause—were becoming old hat. Romance at that time meant *Private Lives*, which was brand-new. It didn't look to its audiences like Romance, but that was what it was. Our notion of Romance, which is so often exploration of squalor and degradation, will become old hat, too. Romance is a mode of feeling that puts enormous emphasis—but not quite a tragic emphasis—on individual experience. Tragedy puts something above humanity; so does Comedy; Romance puts humanity first. The people who liked Sir John's kind of Romance were middle-aged, or old. Oh, lots of young people came to see him, but they weren't the most interesting kind of young people. Perhaps they weren't really young. The interesting young people were going to see a different sort of play. They were flocking to *Private Lives*. You couldn't expect Sir John to understand. His ideal of Romance was far from that, and he had shaped a formidable egoism to serve his ideal."

"It's the peril of the actor," said Ingestree. "Do you remember what Aldous Huxley said? 'Acting inflames the ego in a way which few other professions do. For the sake of enjoying regular emotional self-abuse, our societies condemn a considerable class of men and women to a perpetual inability to achieve non-attachment. It seems a high price to pay for our amusements.' A profound comment. I used to be deeply influenced by Huxley."

"I gather you got over it," said Eisengrim, "or you wouldn't be talking about non-attachment over the ruins of a tremendous meal and a huge cigar you have been sucking like a child at its mother's breast."

"I thought you had forgiven me," said Ingestree, being as winsome as his age and appearance allowed. "I don't pretend to have set aside the delights of this world; I tried that and it was no good. But I have my intellectual fopperies, and they pop out now and then. Do go on about Sir John and his egoism."

"So I shall," said Magnus, "but at another time. The waiters are hovering and I perceive the delicate fluttering of paper in the hands of the chief bandit yonder."

I watched with envy as Ingestree signed the bill without batting an eyelash. I suppose it was company money he was spending. We went out into the London rain and called for cabs.

(4)

In the days that followed, Magnus was busy filming the last scraps of *Hommage* in a studio near London; these were close-ups, chiefly of his hands, as he did intricate things with cards and coins, but he insisted on wearing full costume and make-up. There was also a time-taking quarrel with a fashionable photographer who was to provide publicity pictures, and who kept assuring Magnus that he wanted to catch "the real you". But Magnus didn't want candid pictures of himself, and he was rather personal in his insistence that the photographer, a bearded fanatic who wore sandals, was not likely to capture with his camera something he had taken pains to conceal for more than thirty years. So we went to a very famous photographer who was celebrated for his pictures of royalty, and he and Magnus plotted some portraits, taken in a splendid old theatre, that satisfied both of them. All of this took time, until there was no longer any reason for us to stay in London. But Lind and Ingestree, and to a lesser degree Kinghovn, were determined to hear the remainder of Magnus's story, and after a good deal of teasing and protesting that there was really nothing to it, and that he was tired of talking about himself, it was agreed that they should spend our last day in London with us, and have their way.

"I'm doing it for Ingestree, really," said Magnus, and I thought it an odd remark, as he and Roly had not been on the best of terms since they first met at Sorgenfrei. Inquisitive, as always, I found a time to mention this to Roly, who was puzzled and flattered. "Can't imagine why he said that," was his comment; "but there's something about him that rouses more than ordinary curiosity in me. He's terribly like someone I've known, but I can't say who it is. And I'm fascinated by his crusty defence of old Tresize and his wife. I know a bit about Sir John that puts him in a very different light from the rosy glow Magnus spreads over his memories. These recollections of old actors, you know—awful old hams, most of them. It's the most perishable of the arts. Have you ever had the experience of seeing a film you saw thirty or even forty years ago and thought wonderful? Avoid it, I urge you. Appallingly disillusioning. One remembers something that never had any reality. No, old actors should be let die."

"What about old conjurors?" I said; "why *Hommage*? Why don't you leave Robert-Houdin in his grave?"

"That's precisely where he is. You don't think this film we're making is really anything like the old boy, do you? With every modern technique at our command, and Jurgen Lind sifting every shot through his own marvellously contemporary concept of magic—no, no, if you could be whisked back in time and see Robert-Houdin you'd see something terribly tacky in comparison with what we're offering. He's just a peg on which Jurgen is hanging a fine modern creation. We need all the research and reconstruction and whatnot to produce something inescapably contemporary; a paradox, but that's how it is."

"Then you believe that there is no time but the present moment, and that everything in the past is diminished by the simple fact that it is irrecoverable? I suppose there's a name for that point of view, but at present I can't put my tongue to it."

"Yes, that's pretty much what I believe. Eisengrim's raptures about Sir John and Milady interest me as a phenomenon of the present; I'm fascinated that he should think as he does at this moment, and put so much feeling into expressing what he feels. I can't be persuaded for an instant that those two old spooks were anything very special."

"You realize, of course, that you condemn yourself to the same treatment? You've done some work that people have admired and admire still. Are you agreed that it should be judged as you judge Magnus's idols?"

"Of course. Let it all go! I'll have my whack and that'll be the end of me. I don't expect any yellow roses on my monument. Nor a monument, as a matter of fact. But I'm keenly interested in other monument-worshippers. Magnus loves the past simply because it feeds his present, and that's all there is to it. It's the piety and ancestor-worship of a chap who, as he's told us, had a nasty family and a horrid childhood and has had to dig up a better one. Before he's finished he'll tell us the Tresizes were his real parents, or his parents in art, or something of that sort. Want to bet?"

I never bet, and I wouldn't have risked money on that, because I thought that Ingestree was probably right.

(5)

Our last day was a Saturday, and the three film-makers appeared in time for lunch at the Savoy. Liesl had arranged that we should have one of the good tables looking out over the Embankment, and it was a splendid autumn day. The light, as it fell on our table, could not have been improved on by Kinghovn himself. Magnus never ate very much, and today he confined himself to some cold beef and a dish of rice pudding. It gave him a perverse pleasure to order these nursery dishes in restaurants where other people gorged on luxuries, and he insisted that the Savoy served the best rice pudding in London. The others ate heartily, Ingestree with naked and rather touching relish, Kinghovn like a man who has not seen food for a week, and Lind with a curious detachment, as though he were eating to oblige somebody else, and did not mean to disappoint them. Liesl was in one of her ogress moods and ordered steak tartare, which seemed to me no better than raw meat. I had the set lunch; excellent value.

"You spoke of Tresize's egoism when last we dealt with the subtext," said Lind, champing his great jaws on a lamb chop.

"I did, and I may have misled you. Shortly after I had my talk with Milady, we stopped rehearsing at the Crown and Two Chairmen, and moved into the theatre where *Scaramouche* was to appear. It was the Globe. We needed a theatre with plenty of backstage room because it was a pretty elaborate show. Sir John still held to the custom of opening in London with a new piece; no out-of-town tour to get things shaken down. It was an eye-opener to me to walk into a theatre that was better than the decrepit vaudeville houses where I had appeared with Willard; there was a discipline and a formality I had never met with. I was hired as an assistant stage manager (with a proviso that I should act 'as cast' if required) and I had everything to learn about the job. Luckily old Macgregor was a patient and thorough teacher. I had lots to do. That was before the time when the stage-hands' union was strict about people who were not members moving and arranging things, and some of my work was heavy. I was on good terms with the stage crew at once, and I quickly found out that this put a barrier between me and the actors, although I had to become a member of Actors' Equity. But I was 'crew', and although everybody was friendly I was not quite on the level of 'company'. What was I? I was necessary, and even important, to the play, but I found out that my name was to appear on the programme simply as Macgregor's assistant. I had no place in the list of the cast.

"Yet I was rehearsed carefully, and it seemed to me that I was doing well. I was trying to capture Sir John's rhythm, and now, to my surprise, he was helping me. We spent quite a lot of time on Two, two. I did my juggling with my back to the audience, but as I was to wear a costume identical with Sir John's, the audience would assume that was who I was, if I could bring off another sort of resemblance.

"That was an eye-opener. I was vaudeville trained, and my one idea of stage deportment was to be fast and gaudy. That wasn't Sir John's way at all. 'Deliberately: deliberately,' he would say, over and over again. 'Let them see what you're doing. Don't be flashy and confusing. Do it like this.' And then he would caper across the stage, making motions like a man juggling plates, but at a pace I thought impossibly slow. 'It's not keeping the plates in the air that's important,' he would say. 'Of course you can do that. It's being Scaramouche that's important. It's the character you must get across. Eh? You understand the character, don't you? Eh? Have you looked at the Callots?'

"No, I hadn't looked at the Callots, and didn't know what they were. 'Here m'boy; look here,' he said, showing me some funny little pictures of people dressed as Scaramouche, and Polichinelle and other Commedia characters. 'Get it like that! Make that real! You must be a Callot in motion!'

"It was new and hard work for me to catch the idea of making myself like a picture, but I was falling under Sir John's spell and was ready to give it a try. So I capered and pointed my toes, and struck exaggerated postures like the little pictures, and did my best.

"'Hands! Hands!' he would shout, warningly, when I had my work cut out to make the plates dance. 'Not like hooks, m'boy, like this! See! Keep 'em like this!' And then he would demonstrate what he wanted, which was a queer trick for a juggler, because he wanted me to hold my hands with the little finger and the forefinger extended, and the two middle fingers held together. It looked fine as he did it, but it wasn't my style at all. And all the time he kept me dancing with my toes stuck out and my heels lifted, and he wanted me to get into positions which even I could see were picturesque, but couldn't copy.

"'Sorry, Sir John,' I said one day. 'It's just that it feels a bit loony.'

"'Aha, you're getting it at last!' he shouted, and for the first time he smiled at me. 'That's what I want! I want it a bit loony. Like Scaramouche, you see. Like a charlatan in a travelling show.'

"I could have told him a few things about charlatans in travelling shows, and the way their looniness takes them, but it wouldn't have done. I see now that it was Romance he was after, not realism, but it was all a mystery to me then. I don't think I was a slow learner, and in our second rehearsal in the theatre, where we had the plates, and the cloaks, and the tightrope to walk, I got my first real inkling of what it was all about, and where I was wrong and Sir John—in terms of Romance—was right.

"I told you I had to caper across the tightrope, as Scaramouche escaping from the angry aristocrats. I was high above their heads, and as I had only about thirty feet to go, at the farthest, I had to take quite a while over it while pretending to be quick. Sir John wanted the rope—it was a wire, really—to be slackish, so that it rocked and swayed. Apparently that was the Callot style. For balance I carried a long stick that I was supposed to have snatched from Polichinelle. I was doing it circus-fashion, making it look as hard as possible, but that wouldn't do: I was to rock on the wire, and be very much at ease, and when I was halfway across the stage I was to thumb my nose at the Marquis de la Tour d'Azyr, my chief enemy. I could thumb my nose. Not the least trouble. But the way I did it didn't please Sir John. 'Like this,' he would say, and put an elegant thumb to his long, elegant nose, and twiddle the fingers. I did it several times, and he shook his head. Then an idea seemed to strike him.

"'M'boy, what does that gesture mean to you?' he asked, fixing me with a lustrous brown eye.

"'Kiss my arse, Sir John,' said I, bashfully: I wasn't sure he would know such a rude word. He looked grave, and shook his head slowly from side to side three or four times.

"'You have the essence of it, but only in the sense that the snail on the garden wall is the essence of *Escargots à la Niçoise*. What you convey by that gesture is all too plainly the grossly derisive invitation expressed by your phrase, Kiss my arse; it doesn't even get as far as *Baisez mon cul*. What I want is a Rabelaisian splendour of contempt linked with a Callotesque elegance of grotesquerie. What it boils down to is that you're not thinking it right. You're thinking Kiss my arse with a strong American accent, when what you ought to be thinking is—' and suddenly, though he was standing on the stage, he swayed perilously and confidently as though he were on the wire, and raised one eyebrow and opened his mouth in a grin like a leering wolf, and allowed no more than the tip of a very sharp red tongue to loll out on his lips and there it was! Kiss my arse *with class,* and God knows how many years of actor's technique and a vivid memory of Henry Irving all backing it up.

"'I think I get it,' I said, and had a try. He was pleased. Again. Better pleased. 'You're getting close,' he said; 'now, tell me what you're thinking when you do that? Mph? Kiss my arse, quonk? But what kind of Kiss my arse? Quonk? Quonk?'

"I didn't know what to tell him, but I couldn't be silent. 'Not Kiss my arse at all,' I said.

"'What then? What are you thinking? Eh? You must be thinking something, because you're getting what I want. Tell me what it is?'

"Better be truthful, I thought. He sees right into me and he'll spot a lie at once. I took my courage in my hand. 'I was thinking that I must be born again,' I said. 'Quite right, m'boy; born again and born different, as Mrs Poyser very wisely said,' was Sir John's comment. (Who was Mrs Poyser? I suppose it's the kind of thing Ramsay knows.)

"Born again! I'd always thought of it, when I thought about it at all, as a spiritual thing; you went through a conversion, or you found Christ, or whatever it was, and from that time you were different and never looked back. But to get inside Sir John I had to be born again physically, and if the spiritual trick is harder than that, Heaven must be thinly populated. I spent hours capering about in quiet places offstage, whenever Macgregor didn't need me, trying to be like Sir John, trying to get style even into Kiss my arse. What was the result? Next time we rehearsed Two, two, I was awful. I nearly dropped a plate, and for a juggler that's a shattering experience. (Don't laugh! I don't mean it as a joke.) But worse was to come. At the right moment I stepped out on the swaying wire, capered toward middle stage, thumbed my nose at Gordon Barnard, who was playing the Marquis, lost my balance, and fell off; Duparc's training stood by me, and I caught the wire with my hands, swung in mid-air for a couple of seconds, and then heaved myself back up and got my footing, and scampered to the opposite side. The actors who were rehearsing that day applauded, but I was destroyed with shame, and Sir John was grinning exactly like Scaramouche, with an inch of red tongue between his lips.

"'Don't think they'll quite accept you as me if you do that, m'boy,' said he. 'Eh, Holroyd? Eh, Barnard? Quonk? Try it again.'

"I tried it again, and didn't fall, but I knew was I hopeless; I hadn't found Sir John's style and I was losing my own. After another bad try Sir John moved on to another scene, but Milady beckoned me away into a box, from which she was watching the rehearsal. I was full of apologies.

"'Of course you fell,' she said. 'But it was a good fall. Laudable pus, I call it. You're learning.'

"Laudable pus! What in God's name did she mean! I thought I would never get used to Milady's lingo. But she saw the bewilderment in my face, and explained.

"'It's a medical expression. Out of fashion now, I expect. But my grandfather was rather a distinguished physician and he used it often. In those days, you know, when someone had a wound, they couldn't heal it as quickly as they do now; they dressed it and probed it every few days to see how it was getting on. If it was healing well, from the bottom, there was a lot of nasty stuff near the surface, and that was evidence of proper healing. They called it laudable pus. I know you're trying your very best to please Sir John, and it means a sharp wound to your own personality. As the wound heals, you will be nearer what we all want. But meanwhile there's laudable pus, and it shows itself in clumsiness and falls. When you get your new style, you'll understand what I mean.'

"Had I time to get a new style before the play opened? I was worried sick, and I suppose it showed, because when he had a chance old Frank Moore had a word with me.

"'You're trying to catch the Guvnor's manner and you aren't making a bad fist of it, but there are one or two things you haven't noticed. You're an acrobat, good enough to walk the slackwire, but you're tight as a drum. Look at the Guvnor: he hasn't a taut muscle in his body, nor a slack one, either. He's in easy control all the time. Have you noticed him standing still? When he listens to another actor, have you seen how still he is? Look at you now, listening to me; you bob about and twist and turn and nod your head with enough energy to turn a windmill. But it's all waste, y'see. If we were in a scene, you'd be killing half the value of what I say with all that movement. Just try to sit still. Yes, there you go; you're not still at all, you're frozen. Stillness isn't looking as if you were full of coiled springs. It's repose. Intelligent repose. That's what the Guvnor has. What I have, too, as a matter of fact. What Barnard has. What Milady has. I suppose you think repose means asleep, or dead.

"'Now look, my lad, and try to see how it's done. It's mostly your back. Got to have a good strong back, and let it do ninety per cent of the work. Forget legs. Look at the Guvnor hopping around when he's being Scaramouche. He's nippier on his pins than you are. Look at me. I'm real old, but I bet I can dance a hornpipe better than you can. Look at this! Can you do a double shuffle like that? That's legs, to look at, but it's back in reality. Strong back. Don't pound down into the floor at every step. Forget legs.

"'How do you get a strong back? Well, it's hard to describe it, but once you get the feel of it you'll see what I'm talking about. The main thing is to trust your back and forget you have a front; don't stick out your chest or your belly; let 'em look after themselves. Trust your back and lead from your back. And just let your head float on top of your neck. You're all made of whipcord and wire. Loosen it up and take it easy. But not slump, mind! Easy.'

"Suddenly the old man grabbed me by the neck and seemed about to throttle me. I jerked away, and he laughed. 'Just as I said, you're all wire. When I touch your neck you tighten up like a spring. Now you try to strangle me.' I seized him by the neck, and I thought his poor old head would come off in my hands; he sank to the floor, moaning, 'Nay, spare m' life!' Then he laughed like an old loony, because I suppose I looked horrified. 'D'you see? I just let myself go and trusted to my back. You work on that for a while and bob's your uncle; you'll be fit to act with the Guvnor.'

"'How long do you think it will take?' I said. 'Oh, ten or fifteen years should see you right,' said old Frank, and walked away, still chuckling at the trick he had played on me.

"I had no ten or fifteen years. I had a week, and much of that was spent slaving for Macgregor, who kept me busy with lesser jobs while he and Holroyd fussed about the scenery and trappings for

Scaramouche. I had never seen such scenery as the stage crew began to rig from the theatre grid; the vaudeville junk I was used to didn't belong in the same world with it. The production had all been painted by the Harker Brothers, from designs by a painter who knew exactly what Sir John wanted. It was a revelation to me then, but now I understand that it owed much to prints and paintings of France during the Revolutionary period, and a quality of late-eighteenth-century detail had been used in it, apparently in a careless and half-hidden spirit, but adding up to pictures that supported and explained the play just as did the handsome costumes. People are supposed not to like scenery now, but it could be heart-stirring stuff when it was done with love by real theatre artists.

"The first act setting was in the yard of an inn, and when it was all in place I swear you could smell the horses, and the sweet air from the fields. Nowadays they fuss a lot about light in the theatre, and even stick a lot of lamps in plain sight of the audience, so you won't miss how artistic they are being; but Sir John didn't trouble about light in that way—the subtle effects of light were painted on the scenery, so you knew at once what time of day it was by the way the shadows fell, and what the electricians did was to illuminate the actors, and Sir John in particular.

"During all the years I worked with Sir John there was one standing direction for the electricians that was so well understood Macgregor hardly had to mention it: when the play began all lights were set at two-thirds of their power, and when Sir John was about to make his entrance they were gradually raised to full power, so that as soon as he came on the stage the audience had the sensation of seeing—and therefore understanding—much more clearly than before. Egoism, I suppose, and a little hard on the supporting actors, but Sir John's audiences wanted him to be wonderful and he did whatever was necessary to make sure that he damned well was wonderful.

"Ah, that scenery! In the last act, which was in the salon of a great aristocratic house in Paris, there were large windows at the back, and outside those windows you saw a panorama of Paris at the time of the Revolution that conveyed, by means I don't pretend to understand, the spirit of a great and beautiful city under appalling stress. The Harkers did it with colour; it was mostly in reddish browns highlighted with rose, and shadowed in a grey that was almost black. Busy as I was, I still found time to gape at that scenery as it was assembled.

"Costumes, too. Everybody had been fitted weeks before, but when the clothes were all assembled, and the wig-man had done his work, and the actors began to appear in carefully arranged ensembles in front of that scenery, things became clear that I had missed completely at rehearsals: things like the relation of one character to another, and of one class to another, and the Callot spirit of the travelling actors against the apparently everyday clothes of inn-servants and other minor people, and the superiority and unquestioned rank of the aristocrats. Above all, of the unquestioned supremacy of Sir John, because, though his clothes were not gorgeous, like those of Barnard as the Marquis, they had a quality of style that I did not understand until I had tried them on myself. Because, you see, as his double, I had to have a costume exactly like his when he appeared as the charlatan Scaramouche, and the first time I put it on I thought there must be some mistake, because it didn't seem to fit at all. Sir John showed me what to do about that.

"'Don't try to drag your sleeves down m'boy; they're intended to be short, to show your hands to advantage, mphm? Keep 'em up, like this, and if you use your hands the way I showed you, everything will fit, eh? And your hat—it's not meant to keep off the rain, m'boy, but to show your face against the inside of the brim, quonk? Your breeches aren't too tight; they're not to sit down in—I don't pay you to sit down in costume—but to stand up in, and show off your legs. Never shown your legs off before, have you? I thought as much. Well, learn to show 'em off now, and not like a bloody chorus-girl either, but like a man. Use 'em in masculine postures, but not like a butcher boy either, and if you aren't proud of your legs they're going to look damned stupid, eh, when you're walking across the stage on that rope.'

"I was green as grass. Naive, though I didn't know the word at that time. It was very good for me to feel green. I had begun to think I knew all there was about the world, and particularly the performing world, because I had won in the struggle to keep alive in Wanless's World of Wonders, and in *Le grand Cirque forain de St Vite*. I had even dared in my heart to think I knew more about the world of travelling shows than Sir John. Of course I was right, because I knew a scrap of the reality. But he knew something very different, which was what the public wants to think the world of travelling shows is like. I possessed a few hard-won facts, but he had artistic imagination. My job was somehow to find my way into his world, and take a humble, responsible part in it.

"Little by little it dawned on me that I was important to *Scaramouche;* my two short moments, when I juggled the plates, and walked the wire and thumbed my nose at the Marquis, added a cubit to the stature of the character Sir John was creating. I had also to swallow the fact that I was to do that without anybody knowing it. Of course the public would tumble to the fact that Sir John, who was getting on for sixty, had not learned juggling and wire-walking since last they saw him, but they wouldn't understand it until they had been thrilled by the spectacle, apparently, of the great man doing exactly those things. I was anonymous and at the same time conspicuous.

"I had to have a name. Posters with the names of the actors were already in place outside the theatre, but in the programme I must appear as Macgregor's assistant, and I must be called something. Holroyd mentioned it now and again. My name at that time, Jules LeGrand, wouldn't do. Too fancy and, said Holroyd, a too obvious fake.

"Here again I was puzzled. Jules LeGrand an obvious fake? What about the names of some of the other members of the company? What about Eugene Fitzwarren, who had false teeth and a wig and, I would bet any money, a name that he had not been born to? What about C. Pengelly Spickernell, a withered, middle-aged fruit, whose eyes sometimes rested warmly on my legs, when Sir John was talking about them. Had any parents, drunk or sober, with such a surname as Spickernell, ever christened a child Cuthbert Pengelly? And if it came to fancy sounds, what about Milady's stage name? Annette de la Borderie? Macgregor assured me that it was indeed her own, and that she came from the Channel Islands, but why was it credible when Jules LeGrand was not?

"Of course I was too green to know that I did not stand on the same footing as the other actors. I was just a trick, a piece of animated scenery, when I was on the stage. Otherwise I was Macgregor's assistant, and none too experienced at the job, and a grand name did not befit my humble station. What was I to be called?

"The question was brought to a head by Holroyd, who approached, not me, but Macgregor, in a break between an afternoon and evening rehearsal during the final week of preparation. I was at hand, but obviously not important to the discussion. 'What are you going to call your assistant, Mac?' said Holroyd. 'Time's up. He's got to have a name.' Macgregor looked solemn. 'I've given it careful thought,' he said, 'and I think I've found the verra word for him. Y'see, what's he to the play? He's Sir John's double. That and no more. A shadow, you might say. But can you call him Shadow? Nunno: absurd! And takes the eye, which is just what we don't want to do. So where do we turn—' Holroyd broke in here, because he was apt to be impatient when Macgregor had one of his explanatory fits. 'Why not call him Double? Dick Double! Now there's a good, simple name that nobody's going to notice.' 'Hut!' said Macgregor; 'that's a foolish name. Dick Double! It sounds like some fella in a pantomime!' But Holroyd was not inclined to give up his flight of fancy. 'Nothing wrong with Double,' he persisted. 'There's a Double in Shakespeare. *Henry IV,* Part Two, don't you remember? Is Old Double dead? So there must have been somebody called Double. The more I think of it the better I like it. I'll put him down as Richard Double.' But Macgregor wouldn't have it. 'Nay, nay, you'll make the lad a figure of fun,' he said. 'Now listen to me, because I've worked it out verra carefully. He's a double. And what's a double? Well, in Scotland, when I was a boy, we had a name for such things. If a man met a creature like himself in a lane, or in town, maybe, in the dark, it was a sure sign of ill luck or even death. Not that I suggest anything of that kind here. Nunno; as I've often said Airt has her own rules, and they're not the rules of common life. Now: such an uncanny creature was called a fetch. And this lad's a fetch, and we can do no better than to name him Fetch.' By this time old Frank Moore joined the group, and he liked the sound of Fetch. 'But what first name will you tack on to it?'

he said. 'I suppose he's got to be something Fetch? Can't be just naked, unaccommodated Fetch.' Macgregor closed his eyes and raised a fat hand. 'I've thought of that, also,' he said. 'Fetch being a Scots name, he'd do well to carry a Scots given name, for added authority. Now I've always had a fancy for the name Mungo. In my ear it has a verra firm sound. Mungo Fetch. Can we do better?' He looked around, for applause. But Holroyd was not inclined to agree; I think he was still hankering after Double. 'Sounds barbaric to me. A sort of cannibal-king name, to my way of thinking. If you want a Scotch name why don't you call him Jock?' Macgregor looked disgusted. 'Because Jock is not a name, but a diminutive, as everybody knows well. It is the diminutive of John. And John is not a Scots name. The Scots form of that name is Ian. If you want to call him Ian Fetch, I shall say no more. Though I consider Mungo a much superior solution to the problem.'

"Holroyd nodded at me, as if he and Macgregor and Frank Moore had been generously expending their time to do me a great favour. 'Mungo Fetch it's to be then, is it?' he said, and went about his business before I had time to collect my wits and say anything at all.

"That was my trouble. I was like someone living in a dream. I was active and occupied and heard what was said to me and responded reasonably, but nevertheless I seemed to be in a lowered state of consciousness. Otherwise, how could I have put up with a casual conversation that saddled me with a new name—and a name nobody in his right mind would want to possess? But not since my first days in Wanless's World of Wonders had I been so little in command of myself, so little aware of what fate was doing to me. It was as if I were being thrust toward something I did not know by something I could not see. Part of it was love, for I was beglamoured by Milady and barely had sense enough to understand that my state was as hopeless as it could possibly be, and that my passion was in every way absurd. Part of it must have been physical, because I was getting a pretty good regular wage, and could eat better than I had done for several months. Part of it was just astonishment at the complex business of getting a play on the stage, which presented me with some new marvel every day.

"As Macgregor's assistant I had to be everywhere and consequently I saw everything. Because of my mechanical bent I took pleasure in all the mechanism of a fine theatre, and wanted to know how the flymen and scene-shifters organized their work, how the electrician contrived his magic, and how Macgregor controlled it all with signal-lights from his little cubby-hole on the left-hand side of the stage, just inside the proscenium. I had to make up the call-lists, so that the call-boy—who was no boy but older than myself—could warn the actors when they were wanted on stage five minutes before each entrance. I watched Macgregor prepare his Prompt Book, which was an interleaved copy of the play, with every cue for light, sound, and action entered into it; he was proud of his books, and marked them in a fine round hand, in inks of different colours, and every night the book was carefully locked in a safe in his little office. I helped the property-man prepare his lists of everything that was needed in the play, so that a mass of materials from snuffboxes to hay-forks could be organized on the property-tables in the wings; my capacity to make or mend fiddling little bits of mechanism made me a favourite with him. Indeed the property-man and I worked up a neat little performance as a flock of hens who were heard clucking in the wings when the curtain rose on the inn scene. It was my job to hand C. Pengelly Spickernell the trumpet on which he sounded a fanfare just before the travelling-cart of the Commedia dell' Arte players made its entrance into the inn-yard; to hand it to him and recover it later, and shake C. Pengelly's spit out of it before putting it back on the property-table. There seemed to be no end to my duties.

"I had also to learn to make up my face for my brief appearance. Vaudevillian that I was, I had been accustomed to colour my face a vivid shade of salmon, and touch up my eyebrows; I had never made up my neck or my hands in my life. I quickly learned that something more subtle was expected by Sir John; his make-up was elaborate, to disguise some signs of age but even more to throw his best features into prominence. Eric Foss, a very decent fellow in the company, showed me what to do, and it was from him I learned that Sir John's hands were always coloured an ivory shade, and that his ears were liberally touched up with carmine. Why red ears, I wanted to know.

'The Guvnor thinks it gives an appearance of health,' said Foss, 'and make sure you touch up the insides of your nostrils with the same colour, because it makes your eyes look bright.' I didn't understand it, but I did as I was told.

"Make-up was a subject on which every actor had strong personal opinions. Gordon Barnard took almost an hour to put on his face, transforming himself from a rather ordinary-looking chap into a strikingly handsome man. Reginald Charlton, on the other hand, was of the modern school and used as little make-up as possible, because he said it made the face into a mask, and inexpressive. Grover Paskin, our comedian, put on paint almost with a trowel, and worked like a Royal Academician building up warts and nobbles and tufts of hair on his rubbery old mug. Eugene Fitzwarren strove for youth, and took enormous pains making his eyes big and lustrous, and putting white stuff on his false teeth so that they would flash to his liking.

"Old Frank Moore was the most surprising of the lot, because he had become an actor when water colours were used for make-up instead of the modern greasepaints. He washed his face with care, powdered it dead white, and then applied artist's paints out of a large Reeves' box, with fine brushes, until he had the effect he wanted. In the wings he looked as if his face were made of china, but under the lights the effect was splendid. I particularly marvelled at the way he put shadows where he wanted them by drawing the back of a lead spoon over the the hollows of his eyes and cheeks. It wasn't good for his skin, and he had a hide like an alligator in private life, but it was certainly good for the stage, and he was immensely proud of the fact that Irving, who made up in the same way, had once complimented him on his art.

"So, working fourteen hours a day, but nevertheless in a dream, I made my way through the week of the final dress rehearsal, and something happened there that changed my life. I did my stage manager's work in costume, but with a long white coat over it, to keep it clean, and when Two, two came I had to whip it off, pop on my hat, take a final look in the full-length mirror just offstage in the corridor, and dash back to the wings to be ready for my plate-juggling moment. That went as rehearsed, but when it was time for my second appearance, walking the rope, I forgot something. During the scene when André-Louis made his revolutionary speech, he began by taking off his hat, and thrusting his Scaramouche mask up on his forehead. It was a half-mask, coming down to the mouth only; it was coloured a rosy red, and had a very long nose, just as Callot would have drawn it. When Sir John thrust it up on his brow, revealing his handsome, intent revolutionary's face, extremely picturesque, it was a fine accent of colour, and the long nose seemed to add to his height. But when I appeared on the rope I was to have the mask pulled down, and when I made my contemptuous gesture toward the Marquis it was the long red nose of the mask I was to thumb.

"I managed very well till it came to the nose-thumbing bit, when I realized with horror that it was my own nose flesh I was thumbing. I had forgotten the mask! Unforgivable! So as soon as I could get away from Macgregor during the interval for the scene-change, I rushed to find Sir John and make my apologies. He had gone out into the stalls of the theatre, and was surrounded by a group of friends, who were congratulating him in lively tones, and I didn't need to listen for long to find out that it was his performance on the rope they were talking about. So I crept away, and waited till he came backstage again. Then I approached him and said my humble say.

"Milady was with him and she said, 'Jack, you'd be mad to throw it away. It's a gift from God. If it fooled Reynolds and Lucy Bellamy it will fool anyone. They've known you for years, and it deceived them completely. You must let him do it.' But Sir John was not a man to excuse anything, even a happy accident, and he fixed me with a stern eye. 'Do you swear that was by accident? You weren't presuming? Because I won't put up with any presumption from a member of my company.' 'Sir John, I swear on the soul of my mother it was a mistake,' I said. (Odd that I should have said that, but it was a very serious oath of Zovene's, and I needed something serious at that moment; actually, at the time I spoke, my mother was living and whatever Ramsay says to the contrary, her soul was in bad repair.) 'Very well,' said Sir John, 'we'll keep it in. In future, when you walk the rope, wear your mask up on your head, as I do mine. And you'd better come to me for a lesson in make-up. You look like Guy Fawkes. And bear in mind that this is not to be a precedent. Any other clever ideas that come to you you'd be wise to suppress. I don't encourage original thought in my productions.' He looked angry as he walked away. I wanted to thank Milady for intervening on my behalf, but she was off to make a costume change.

"When I went back to Macgregor I thought he looked at me very queerly. 'You're a lucky laddie, Mungo Fetch,' said he, 'but don't press your luck too hard. Many a small talent has come to grief that way.' I asked him what he meant, but he just made his Scotch noise—'Hut'—and went on with his work.

"I don't think I would have dared to carry the matter any further if Holroyd and Frank Moore had not borne down on Macgregor after the last act. 'What do you think of your Mungo now?' said Frank, and once again they began to talk exactly as if I were not standing beside them, busy with a time-sheet. 'I think it would have been better to give him another name,' said Macgregor; 'a fetch is an uncanny thing, and I don't want anything uncanny in any theatre where I am in a place of responsibility.' But Holroyd was as near buoyant as I ever saw him. 'Uncanny, my eye,' he said; 'it's the cherry on the top of the cake. The Guvnor's close friends were deceived. *Coup de théâtre* they called it; that's French for a bloody good wheeze.' 'You don't need to tell me it's French,' said Macgregor. 'I've no use for last-minute inspirations and unrehearsed effects. Amateurism, that's what that comes to.'

"I couldn't be quiet. 'Mr. Macgregor, I didn't mean to do it,' I said; 'I swear it on the soul of my mother.' 'All right, all right, I believe you without your Papist oaths,' said Macgregor, 'and I'm just telling you not to presume on the resemblance any further, or you'll be getting a word from me.' 'What resemblance?' I said. 'Don't talk to us as if we're fools, m'boy,' said old Frank. 'You know damned well you're the living image of the Guvnor in that outfit. Or the living image of him when I first knew him, I'd better say. Don't you hear what's said to you? Didn't I tell you a fortnight ago? You're as like the Guvnor as if you were spit out of his mouth. You're his fetch, right enough.' 'Dinna say that,' shouted Macgregor, becoming very broad in his Scots; 'haven't I told you it's uncanny?' But I began to understand, and I was as horrified as Macgregor. The impudence of it! Me, looking like the

Guvnor! 'What'd I better do?' I said, and Holroyd and old Frank laughed like a couple of loonies. 'Just be tactful, that's all,' said Holroyd. 'It's very useful. You're the best double the Guvnor's ever had, and it'll be a livelihood to you for quite a while, I dare say. But be tactful.'

"Easy to tell me to be tactful. When your soul is blasted by a sudden uprush of pride, it's cruel hard work to be tactful. Within an hour my sense of terrible impertinence in daring to look like the Guvnor had given way to a bloating vanity. Sir John was handsome, right enough, but thousands of men are handsome. He was something far beyond that. He had a glowing splendour that made him unike anybody else—except me, it appeared, when the circumstances were right. I won't say he had distinction, because the word has been chewed to death to describe all kinds of people who simply look frozen. Take almost any politician and put a special cravat on him and stick a monocle in his eye and he becomes the distinguished Sir Nincome Poop, M.P. Sir John wasn't frozen and his air of splendour had nothing to do with oddity. I suppose living and breathing Romance through a long career had a great deal to do with it, but it can't have been the whole thing. And I was his fetch! I hadn't really understood it when Moore and Holroyd had told me in the Crown and Two Chairmen that I looked like him. I knew I was of the same height, and we were built much the same—shorter than anybody wants to be, but with a length of leg that made the difference between being small and being stumpy. In my terrible clothes and with my flash, carnie's ways—outward evidence of the life I had led and the kind of thinking it begot in me—I never thought the resemblance went beyond a reasonable facsimile. But when Sir John and I were on equal terms—dressed and wigged alike, against the same scenery and under the same lights, and lifted into the high sweet air of Romance—his friends had been deceived by the likeness. That was a stupefying drink for Paul Dempster, alias Cass Fletcher, alias Jules LeGrand—cheap people, every one of them. Ask me to be tactful in the face of that! Ask the Prince of Wales to call you a taxi!

"With the first night at hand my new vanity would not have been noticed, even if I had been free to display it. Our opening was exciting, but orderly. Macgregor, splendid in a dinner jacket, was a perfect field officer and everything happened smartly on cue. Sir John's first entrance brought the expected welcome from the audience, and in my new role as a great gentleman of the theatre I watched carefully while he accepted it. He did it in the old style, though I didn't know that at the time: as he walked swiftly down the steps from the inn, calling for the ostler, he paused as though surprised at the burst of clapping; 'My dear friends, is this generosity truly for me?' he seemed to be saying, and then, as the applause reached its peak, he gave the least perceptible bow, not looking toward the house, but keeping within the character of André-Louis Moreau, and began calling once more, which brought silence. Easy to describe, but no small thing to do, as I learned when my time came to do it myself. Only the most accomplished actors know how to manage applause, and I was lucky to learn it from a great master.

"Milady was welcomed in the same way, but her entrance was showy, as his was not—except, of course, for that little vanity of the lighting, which was a great help. She came on with the troupe of strolling players, and it couldn't have failed. There was C. Pengelly Spickernell on the trumpet, to begin with, and a lot of excited shouting from the inn-servants, and then further shouting from the Italian Comedians, as they strutted onstage with their travelling-wagon; Grover Paskin led on the horse that pulled the cart, and it was heaped high with drums and gaudy trunks, baskets and rolls of flags, and on the top of the heap sat Milady, making more racket than anybody as she waved a banner in the air. It would have brought a round from a Presbyterian General Assembly. The horse alone was a sure card, because an animal on the stage gives an air of opulence to a play no audience can resist, and this stage horse was famous Old Betsy, who did not perhaps remember Garrick but who had been in so many shows that she was an admired veteran. My heart grew big inside me at the wonder of it, as I watched from the wings, and my eyes moistened with love.

"They were not too moist to notice one or two things that followed. The other women in the troupe of players walked on foot. How slim they looked, and I saw that Milady, with every aid of costume, was not slim. How fresh and pretty they looked, and Milady, though extraordinary, was not fresh nor pretty. When Eugene Fitzwarren gave her his arm to descend from the cart I could not help seeing that she came down on the stage heavily, with an audible plop that she tried to cover with laughter, and the ankles she showed were undeniably thick. All right, I thought, in my fierce loyalty, what of it? She could act rings around any of them, and did it. But she was not young, and if I had been driven to the last extreme of honesty I should have had to admit that she was like nothing in the heavens above, nor in the earth beneath, nor in the waters under the earth. I only loved her the more, and yearned for her to show how marvellous she was, though—it had to be faced—too old for Climene. She was supposed to be the daughter of old Frank Moore as Polichinelle, but I fear she looked more like his frivolous sister.

"It was not until I read the book, years later, that I found out what sort of woman Sabatini meant Climene to be. She was a child just on the verge of love whose ambition was to find a rich protector and make the best bargain for her beauty. That wasn't in Milady's range, physically or temperamentally, for there was nothing calculating or cheap about her. So, by patient re-writing of the lines during rehearsals, she became a witty, large-hearted actress, as young as the audience would believe her to be, but certainly no child, and no beauty. Or should I say that? She had a beauty all her own, of that rare kind that only great comic actresses have; she had beauty of voice, boundless charm of manner, and she made you feel that merely pretty women were lesser creatures. She had also I cannot tell how many decades of technique behind her, because she had begun her career when she really was a child, in Irving's Lyceum, and she could make even an ordinary line sound like wit.

"I saw all of that, and felt it through and through me like the conviction of religion, but still, alas, I saw that she was old, and eccentric, and there was a courageous pathos about what she was doing.

"I was bursting with loyalty—a new and disturbing emotion for me—and Two, two went just as Sir John wanted it. My reward was that when I appeared on the tightrope there was an audible gasp from the house, and the curtain came down to great applause and even a few cries of Bravo. They were for Sir John; of course I knew that and wished it to be so. But I was aware that without me that climax would have been a lesser achievement.

"The play went on, it seemed to me, from triumph to triumph, and the last act, in Madame de Plougastel's salon, shook me as it had never done in rehearsal. When André-Louis Moreau, now a leader in the Revolution, was told by the tearful Madame de Plougastel that she was his mother and that his evil genius, the Marquis de la Tour d'Azyr, was his father—this revelation drawn from her only when Moreau had his enemy at the sword's point—it seemed to me drama could go no higher. The look that came over Sir John's face of disillusion and defeat, before he burst into Scaramouche's mocking laugh, I thought the perfection of acting. And so it was. It wouldn't do now—quite out of fashion—but if you're going to act that kind of thing, that's the way to do it.

"Lots of curtain calls. Flowers for Milady and some for Adele Chesterton, who had not been very good but who was so pretty you wanted to eat her with a silver spoon. Sir John's speech, which I came to know very well, in which he declared himself and Milady to be the audience's 'most obedient, most devoted, and most humble servants'. Then the realities of covering the furniture with dust-sheets, covering the tables of properties, checking the time-sheet with Macgregor, and watching him hobble off to put the prompt-copy to bed in the safe. Then taking off my own paint, with a feeling of exaltation and desolation combined, as if I had never been so happy before, and would certainly never be so happy again.

"It was never the custom in that company to sit up and wait to see what the newspapers said; I think that was always more New York's style than London's. But when I went to the theatre the following afternoon to attend to some duties, all the reports were in but those of the great Sunday thunderers, which were very important indeed. Most of the papers said kind things, but even I sensed something about these criticisms that I could have wished otherwise expressed, or not said at all. 'Unabashed romanticism ... proof positive that the Old School is still vital ... dear, familiar situations, resolved in the manner hallowed by romance ... Sir John's perfect command shows no sign of diminution with the years ... Lady Tresize brings a wealth of experience to a role which, in younger hands, might have seemed contrived ... Sabatini is a gift to players who require the full-flavoured melodrama of an earlier day ... where do we look today for acting of this scope and authority?'

"Among the notices there had been one, in the *News-Chronicle*, where a clever new young man was on the job, which was downright bad. PITCHER GOES TOO OFTEN TO WELL, it was headed, and it said flatly that the Tresizes were old-fashioned and hammy, and should give way to the newer theatre.

"When the Sunday papers came, the *Observer* took the same line as the dailies, as though they had been looking at something very fine, but through the wrong end of the binoculars; it made *Scaramouche* seem small and very far away. James Agate, in the *Sunday Times*, condemned the play, which he likened to clockwork, and used Sir John and Milady as sticks to beat modern actors who did not know how to speak or move, and were ill bred and brittle.

"'Nothing there to pull 'em in,' I heard Holroyd saying to Macgregor.

"Nevertheless, we did pull 'em in for nearly ten weeks. Business was slack at the beginning of each week, and grew from Wednesday onward; matinees were usually sold out, chiefly to women from the suburbs, in town for a look at the shops and a play. But I knew from the gossip that business like that, in a London theatre, was covering running costs at best, and the expenses of production were still on the Guvnor's overdraft. He seemed cheerful, and I soon found out why. He was going to do the old actor-manager's trick and play *Scaramouche* as long as it would last and then replace it 'by popular request' with a few weeks of his old war-horse, *The Master of Ballantrae*.'

"Oh my God!" said Ingestree, and it seemed to me that he turned a little white.

"You remember this play?" said Lind.

"Vividly," said Roly.

"A very bad play?"

"I don't want to hurt the feelings of our friend here, who feels so strong about the Tresizes," said Ingestree. "It's just that *The Master of*

Ballantrae coincided with rather a low point in my own career. I was finding my feet in the theatre, and it wasn't really the kind of thing I was looking for."

"Perhaps you would like me to pass over it," said Magnus, and although he was pretending to be solicitous I knew he was enjoying himself.

"Is it vital to your subtext?" said Ingestree, and he too was half joking.

"It is, really. But I don't want to give pain, my dear fellow."

"Don't mind me. Worse things have happened since."

"Perhaps I can be discreet," said Magnus. "You may rely on me to be as tactful as possible."

"For God's sake don't do that," said Ingestree. "In my experience tact is usually worse than the brutalities of truth. Anyhow, my recollections of that play can't be the same as yours. My troubles were mostly private."

"Then I shall go ahead. But please feel free to intervene whenever you feel like it. Put me right on matters of fact. Even on shades of opinion. I make no pretence of being an exact historian."

"Shoot the works," said Ingestree. "I'll be as still as a mouse. I promise."

"As you wish. Well—*The Master of Ballantrae* was another of the Guvnor's romantic specials. It too was from a novel, by somebody-or-other—"

"By Robert Louis Stevenson," said Ingestree, in an undertone, "though you wouldn't have guessed it from what appeared on the stage. These adaptations! Butcheries would be a better word—"

"Shut up, Roly," said Kinghovn. "You said you'd be quiet."

"I'm no judge of what kind of adaptation it was," said Magnus, "because I haven't read the book and I don't suppose I ever will. But it was a good, tight, well-caulked melodrama, and people had been eating it up since the Guvnor first brought it out, which I gathered was something like thirty years before the time I'm talking about. I told you he was an experimenter and an innovator, in his day. Well, whenever he had lost a packet on Maeterlinck, or something new by Stephen Phillips, he would pull *The Master* out of the storehouse and fill up the bank-account again. He could go to Birmingham, and Manchester, and Newcastle, and Glasgow, and Edinburgh or any big provincial town—and those towns had big theatres, not like the little pill-boxes in London—and pack 'em in with the *The Master*. Especially Edinburgh, because they seemed to take the play for their own. Macgregor told me, '*The Master*'s been a mighty get-penny for Sir John.' When you saw him in it you knew why it was so. It was made for him."

"It certainly was," said Ingestree. "Made for him out of the blood and bones of poor old Stevenson. I have no special affection for Stevenson, but he didn't deserve that."

"As you can see, it was a play that called forth strong feeling," said Magnus. "I never read it, myself, because Macgregor always held the prompt-copy and did the prompting himself, if anybody was so absurd as to need prompting. But of course I picked up the story as we rehearsed.

"It had a nice meaty plot. Took place in Scotland around the middle of the eighteenth century. There had been some sort of trouble—I don't know the details—and Scottish noblemen were divided in allegiance between Bonny Prince Charlie and the King of England. The play was about a family called Durie; the old Lord of Durrisdeer had two sons, the first-born being called the Master of Ballantrae and the younger being simply Mr Henry Durie. The old Lord decided on a sneaky compromise when the trouble came, and sent the Master off to fight for Bonny Charlie, while Mr Henry remained at home to be loyal to King George. On those terms, you see, the family couldn't lose, whichever way the cat jumped.

"The Master was a dashing, adventurous fellow, but essentially a crook, and he became a spy in Prince Charlie's camp, leaking information to the English: Mr Henry was a scholarly, poetic sort of chap, and he stayed at home and mooned after Miss Alison Graeme; she was the old Lord's ward, and of course she loved the dashing Master. When news came from the wars that the Master had been killed, she consented to marry Mr Henry as a matter of duty and to provide Durrisdeer with an heir. 'But ye ken she never really likit the fella,' as Macgregor explained it to me; her heart was always with the Master, alive or dead. But the Master wasn't dead; he wasn't the dying kind: he slipped away from the battle and became a pirate—not one of your low-living dirty-faced pirates, but a very classy privateer and spy. And so, when the troubles had died down and Bonny Charlie was out of the way, the Master came back to claim Miss Alison, and found that she was Mrs Henry, and the mother of a fine young laird.

"The Master tried to lure Miss Alison away from her husband: Mr Henry was noble about it, and he nobly kept mum about the Master having turned spy during the war. 'A verra strong situation,' as Macgregor said. Consequence, a lot of taunting talk from the Master, and an equal amount of noble endurance from Mr Henry, and at last a really good scene, of the kind Roly hates, but our audiences loved.

"The Master had picked up in his travels an Indian servant, called Secundra Dass; he knew a lot of those Eastern secrets that Western people believe in so religiously. When Mr Henry could bear things no longer, he had a fight with the Master, and seemed to kill him; but as I told you, the Master wasn't the dying kind. So he allowed himself to be buried, having swallowed his tongue (he'd learned that from Secundra Dass) and, as it said in the play, 'so subdued his vital forces that the spark of life, though burning low, was not wholly extinguished.' Mr Henry, tortured by guilt, confessed his crime to his wife and the old Lord, and led them to the grove of trees where the body was buried. When the servants dug up the corpse, it was no corpse at all, but the Master, in very bad shape; the tongue-trick hadn't worked quite as he expected—something to do with the chill of the Scottish climate, I expect—and he came to life only to cry, 'Murderer, Henry—false, false!' and drop dead, but not before Mr Henry shot himself. Thereupon the curtain came down to universal satisfaction.

"I haven't described it very respectfully. I feel irreverent vibrations coming to me from Roly, the way mediums do when there is an unbeliever at a seance. But I assure you that as the Guvnor acted it, the play compelled belief and shook you up pretty bad. The beauty of the old piece, from the Guvnor's point of view, was that it provided him with what actors used to call 'a dual role'. He played both the Master and

Mr Henry, to the huge delight of his audiences; his fine discrimination between the two characters gave extraordinary interest to the play.

"It also meant some neat work behind the scenes, because there were times when Mr Henry had barely left the stage before the Master came swaggering on through another door. Sir John's dresser was an expert at getting him out of one coat, waistcoat, boots, and wig and into another in a matter of seconds, and his characterization of the two men was so sharply differentiated that it was art of a very special kind.

"Twice, a double was needed, simply for a fleeting moment of illusion, and in the brief last scene the double was of uttermost importance, because it was he who stood with his back to the audience, as Mr Henry, while the Guvnor, as the Master, was being dug up and making his terrible accusation. Then—doubles don't usually get such opportunities—it was the double's job to put the gun to his head, fire it, and fall at the feet of Miss Alison, under the Master's baleful eye. And I say with satisfaction that as I was an unusually successful double—or dead spit, as old Frank Moore insisted on saying—I was allowed to fall so that the audience could see something of my face, instead of dying under suspicion of being somebody else.

"Rehearsals went like silk, because some of the cast were old hands, and simply had to brush up their parts. Frank Moore had played the old Lord of Durrisdeer scores of times, and Eugene Fitzwarren was a seasoned Secundra Dass; Gordon Barnard had played Burke, the Irishman, and built it up into a very good thing; C. Pengelly Spickernell fancied himself as Fond Barnie, a loony Scot who sang scraps of song, and Grover Paskin had a good funny part as a drunken butler; Emilia Pauncefort, who played Madame de Plougastel in *Scaramouche,* loved herself as a Scots witch who uttered the dire Curse of Durrisdeer—

> Twa Duries in Durrisdeer,
>   Ane to bide and ane to ride;
> An ill day for the groom,
>   And a waur day for the bride.

And of course the role of Alison, the unhappy bride of Mr Henry and the pining adorer of the Master, had been played by Milady since the play was new.

"That was where the difficulty lay. Sir John was still great as the Master, and looked surprisingly like himself in his earliest photographs in that part, taken thirty years before; time had been rougher with Milady. Furthermore, she had developed an emphatic style of acting which was not unacceptable in a part like Climene but which could become a little strong as a high-bred Scots lady.

"There were murmurs among the younger members of the company. Why couldn't Milady play Auld Cursin' Jennie instead of Emilia Pauncefort? There was a self-assertive girl in the company named Audrey Sevenhowes who let it be known that she would be ideally cast as Alison. But there were others, Holroyd and Macgregor among them, who would not hear a word against Milady. I would have been one of them too, if anybody had asked my opinion, but nobody did. Indeed, I began to feel that the company thought I was rather more than an actor who doubled for Sir John; I was a double indeed, and a company spy, so that any disloyal conversation stopped as soon as I appeared. Of course there was lots of talk; all theatrical companies chatter incessantly. On the rehearsals went, and as Sir John and Milady didn't bother to rehearse their scenes together, nobody grasped how extreme the problem had become.

"There was another circumstance about those early rehearsals that caused some curiosity and disquiet for a while; a stranger had appeared among us whose purpose nobody seemed to know, but who sat in the stalls making notes busily, and now and then exclaiming audibly in a tone of disapproval. He was sometimes seen talking with Sir John. What could he be up to? He wasn't an actor, certainly. He was young, and had lots of hair, but he wasn't dressed in a way that suggested the stage. His sloppy grey flannels and tweed coat, his dark blue shirt and tie like a piece of old rope—hand-woven, I suppose— and his scuffed suede shoes made him look even younger than he was. 'University man,' whispered Audrey Sevenhowes, who recognized the uniform. 'Cambridge,' she whispered, a day later. Then came the great revelation—'Writing a play!' Of course she didn't confide these things to me, but they leaked from her close friends all through the company.

"Writing a play! Rumour was busily at work. It was to be a grand new piece for Sir John's company, and great opportunities might be secured by buttering up the playwright. Reginald Charlton and Leonard Woulds, who hadn't much to do in *Scaramouche* and rather less in *The Master,* began standing the university genius drinks; Audrey Sevenhowes didn't speak to him, but was frequently quite near him, laughing a silvery laugh and making herself fascinating. Old Emilia Pauncefort passed him frequently, and gave him a stately nod every time. Grover Paskin told him jokes. The genius liked it all, and in a few days was on good terms with everybody of any importance, and the secret was out. Sir John wanted a stage version of Dr Jekyll and Mr Hyde, and the genius was to write it. But as he had never written a play before, and had never had stage experience except with the Cambridge Marlowe Society, he was attending rehearsals, as he said to 'get the feel of the thing'.

"The genius was free with his opinions. He thought little of *The Master of Ballantrae.* 'Fustian' was the word he used to describe it, and he made it clear that the era of fustian was over. Audiences simply wouldn't stand it any more. A new day had dawned in the theatre, and he was a particularly bright beam from the rising sun.

"He was modest, however. There were brighter beams than he, and the brightest, most blinding beam in the literature of the time was somebody called Aldous Huxley. No, Huxley didn't write plays. It was his outlook—wry, brilliantly witty, rooted in tremendous scholarship, and drenched in the Ironic Spirit—that the genius admired, and was about to transfer to the stage. In no time he had a tiny court, in which Charlton and Woulds and Audrey Sevenhowes were the leaders, and after rehearsals they were always to be seen in the nearest pub, laughing a great deal. With my very long ears it wasn't long before I knew they were laughing at Milady and Frank Moore and Emilia Pauncefort, who were the very warp and woof of fustian, and who couldn't possibly be worked into the kind of play the genius had in mind. No, he hadn't begun writing yet, but he had a Concept, and though he hated the word 'metaphysical' he didn't mind using it to give a rough idea of how the Concept would take shape.

"Sir John didn't know about the Concept as yet, but when it was explained to him he would get a surprise. The genius was hanging around *The Master of Ballantrae* because it was from a novel by the same chap that had written *Jekyll and Hyde*. But this chap—Roly says his name was Stevenson, and I'm sure he knows—had never fully shouldered the burden of his own creative gift. This was something the genius would have to do for him. Stevenson, when he had thought of *Jekyll and Hyde*, had seized upon a theme that was Dostoyevskian, but he had worked it out in terms of what some people might call Romance, but the genius regretfully had to use the word fustian. The only thing the genius could do, in order to be true to his Concept, was to rework the Stevenson material in such a way that its full implications—the ones Stevenson had approached, and run away from in fright—were revealed.

"He thought it could be done with masks. The genius confessed, with a laugh at his own determination, that he would not attempt the thing at all unless he was given a completely free hand to use masks in every possible way. Not only would Jekyll and Hyde wear masks, but the whole company would wear them, and sometimes there would be eight or ten Jekylls on the stage, all wearing masks showing different aspects of that character, and we would see them exchange the masks of Jekyll—because there was to be no nonsense about realism, or pretending to the audience that what they saw had any relationship to what they foolishly thought of as real life—for masks of Hyde. There would be dialogue, of course, but mostly in the form of soliloquies, and a lot of the action would be carried out in mime—a word which the genius liked to pronounce 'meem', to give it the flavour he thought it needed.

"Charlton and Woulds and Audrey Sevenhowes thought this sounded wonderful, though they had some reservations, politely expressed, about the masks. They thought stylized make-up might do just as well. But the genius was rock-like in his insistence that it would be masks or he would throw up the whole project.

"When this news leaked through to the other members of the company they were disgusted. They talked about other versions of

Jekyll and Hyde they had seen, which did very well without any nonsense about masks. Old Frank Moore had played with Henry Irving's son 'H.B.' in a Jekyll and Hyde play where H.B. had made the transformation from the humane doctor to the villainous Hyde before the eyes of the audience, simply by ruffling up his hair and distorting his body. Old Frank showed us how he did it: first he assumed the air of a man who is about to be wafted off the ground by his own moral grandeur, then he drank the dreadful potion out of his own pot of old-and-mild, and then, with an extraordinary display of snarling and gnawing the air, he crumpled up into a hideous gnome. He did this one day in the pub and some strangers, who weren't used to actors, left hurriedly and the landlord asked Frank, as a personal favour, not to do it again. Frank had an extraordinarily gripping quality as an actor.

"Nevertheless, as I admired his snorting and chomping depiction of evil, I was conscious that I had seen even more convincing evil in the face of Willard the Wizard, and that there it had been as immovable and calm as stone.

"Suddenly, one day at rehearsal, the genius lost stature. Sir John called to him, 'Come along, you may as well fit in here, mphm? Give you practical experience of the stage, quonk?', and before we knew what was happening he had the genius acting the part of one of the menservants in Lord Durrisdeer's household. He wasn't bad at all, and I suppose he had learned a few things in his amateur days at Cambridge. But at a critical moment Sir John said, 'Clear away your master's chair, m'boy; when he comes downstage to Miss Alison you take the chair back to the upstage side of the fireplace.' Which the genius did, but not to Sir John's liking; he put one hand under the front of the seat, and the other on the back of the armchair, and hefted it to where he had been told. Sir John said, 'Not like that, m'boy; lift it by the arms.' But the genius smiled and said, 'Oh no, Sir John, that's not the way to handle a chair; you must always put one hand under its apron, so as not to put a strain on its back.' Sir John went rather cool, as he did when he was displeased, and said, 'That may have been all very well in your father's shop, m'boy, but it won't do on my stage. Lift it as *I* tell you.' And the genius turned exceedingly red, and began to argue. At which Sir John said to the other extra, 'You do it, and show him how.' And he ignored the genius until the end of the scene.

"Seems a trivial thing, but it rocked the genius to his foundations; after that he never seemed to be able to do anything right. And the people who had been all over him before were much cooler after that slight incident. It was the mention of the word 'shop'. I don't think actors are particularly snobbish, but I suppose Audrey Sevenhowes and the others had seen him as a gilded undergraduate; all of a sudden he was just a clumsy actor who had come from some sort of shop, and he never quite regained his former lustre. When we dress-rehearsed *The Master* it was apparent that he knew nothing about make-up; he appeared with a horrible red face and a huge pair of false red eyebrows. 'Good God, m'boy,' Sir John called from the front of the house, when this spook appeared, 'what have you been doing to your face?' The genius walked to the footlights—inexcusable, he should have spoken from his place on the stage—and began to explain that as he was playing a Scots servant he thought he should have a very fresh complexion to suggest a peasant ancestry, a childhood spent on the moors, and a good deal more along the same lines. Sir John shut him up, and told Darton Flesher, a good, useful actor, to show the boy how to put on a decent, unobtrusive face, suited to chair-lifting.

"The genius was huffy, backstage, and talked about throwing up the whole business of Jekyll and Hyde and leaving Sir John to stew in his own juice. But Audrey Sevenhowes said, 'Oh, don't be so silly; everybody has to learn,' and that cooled him down. Audrey also threw him a kind word about how she couldn't spare him because he was going to write a lovely part for her in the new play, and gave him a smile that would have melted—well, I mustn't be extreme—that would have melted a lad down from Cambridge whose self-esteem had been wounded. It wouldn't have melted me; I had taken Miss Sevenhowes' number long before. But then, I was a hard case.

"Not so hard that I hadn't a little sympathy for Adele Chesterton, whose nose was out of joint. She was still playing in *Scaramouche*, but she had not been cast in *The Master;* an actress called Felicity Larcombe had been brought in for the second leading female role in that. She was one of the most beautiful women I have ever seen anywhere: very dark brown hair, splendid eyes, a superb slim figure, and that air of enduring a secret sorrow bravely which so many men find irresistible. What was more, she could act, which poor Adele Chesterton, who was the Persian-kitten type, could only do by fits and starts. But she was a decent kid, and I was sorry for her, because the company, without meaning it unkindly, neglected her. You know how theatre companies are: if you're working with them, you're real, and if you aren't, you have only a half-life in their estimation. Adele was the waning, and Felicity the waxing, moon.

"As usual, Audrey Sevenhowes had a comment. 'Nobody to blame but herself,' said she; 'made a Horlicks—an utter Horlicks—of her part. I could have shown them, but—' Her shrug showed what she thought of the management's taste. 'Horlicks' was a word she used a lot; it suggested 'ballocks' but avoided a direct indecency. Charlton and Woulds loved to hear her say it; it seemed delightfully daring, and sexy, and knowing. It was my first encounter with this sort of allurement, and I disliked it.

"I mentioned to Macgregor that Miss Larcombe seemed a very good, and probably expensive, actress for her small part in *The Master*. 'Ah, she'll have a great deal to do on the tour,' he replied, and I pricked up my ears. But there was nothing more to be got out of him about the tour.

"It was all clear before we opened *The Master*, however; Sir John was engaging a company to make a longish winter tour in Canada, with a repertoire of some of his most successful old pieces, and *Scaramouche* as a novelty. Holroyd was asking people to drop into his office and talk about contracts.

"Of course the company buzzed about it. For the established actors a decision had to be made: would they absent themselves from London for the best part of a winter season? All actors under a certain age are hoping for some wonderful chance that will carry them into the front rank of their profession, and a tour in Sir John's repertoire wasn't exactly it. On the other hand, a tour of Canada could be a lark, because Sir John was known to be a great favourite there and they would play to big audiences, and see a new country while they did it.

"For the middle-aged actors it was attractive. Jim Hailey and his wife Gwenda Lewis jumped at it, because they had a boy to educate and it was important to them to keep in work. Frank Moore was an enthusiastic sightseer and traveller, and had toured Australia and South Africa but had not been to Canada since 1924. Grover Paskin and C. Pengelly Spickernell were old standbys of Sir John's, and would cheerfully have toured Hell with him. Emilia Pauncefort wasn't likely to get other offers, because stately old women and picturesque hags were not frequent in West End shows that season, and the Old Vic, where she had staked out quite a little claim in cursing queens, had a new director who didn't fancy her.

"But why Gordon Barnard, who was a very good leading man, or Felicity Larcombe, who was certain to go to the top of the profession? Macgregor explained to me that Barnard hadn't the ambition that should have gone with his talent, and Miss Larcombe, wise girl, wanted to get as much varied experience as she could before descending on the West End and making it hers forever. There was no trouble at all in recruiting a good company, and I was glad to sign my own contract, to be assisttant to Mac and play doubles without having my name on the programme. And to everybody's astonishment, the genius was offered a job on the tour, and took it. So eighteen actors were recruited, not counting Sir John and Milady, and with Holroyd and some necessary technical staff, the final number of the company was to be twenty-eight.

"The work was unrelenting. We opened *The Master of Ballantrae,* and although the other critics were not warm about it Agate gave it a push and we played a successful six weeks in London. God, what audiences! People came out of the woodwork to see it, and it seemed they had all seen it before and couldn't get enough of it. 'It's like peeping into the dark backward and abysm of time,' the genius said, and even I felt that in some way the theatre had been put back thirty years when we appeared in that powerful, thrilling, but strangely antique piece.

"Every day we were called for rehearsal, in order to get the plays ready for the tour. And what plays they were! *The Lyons Mail* and *The Corsican Brothers,* in both of which I doubled for Sir John, and

Rosemary, a small play with a minimum of scenery, which was needed to round out a repertoire in which all the other plays were big ones, with cartloads of scenery and dozens of costumes. I liked *Rosemary* especially, because I didn't double in it but I had a showy appearance as a stilt walker. How we sweated! It was rough on the younger people, who had to learn several new parts during days when they were working a full eight hours, but Moore and Spickernell and Paskin and Miss Pauncefort seemed to have been playing these melo-dramas for years, and the lines rolled off their tongues like grave old music. As for Sir John and Milady, they couldn't have been happier, and there is nothing so indestructibly demanding and tireless as a happy actor.

"Did I say we worked eight hours? Holroyd and Macgregor, with me as their slave, worked much longer than that, because the three plays we were adding to *Scaramouche* and *The Master* had to be retrieved from storage and brushed up and made smart for the tour. But it was all done at last, and we closed in London one Saturday night, with everything finished that would make it possible for us to sail for Canada the following Tuesday.

"A small matter must be mentioned. The genius's mother turned up for one of the last performances of *The Master,* and it fell to me to show her to Sir John's dressing-room. She was a nice little woman, but not what one expects of the mother of such a splendid creature, and when I showed her through the great man's door she looked as if she might faint from the marvel of it all. I felt sorry for her; it must be frightening when one mothers such a prodigy, and she had the humble look of somebody who can't believe her luck."

It was here that Roland Ingestree, who had been decidedly out of sorts for the past half-hour, intervened.

"Magnus, I don't much mind you taking the mickey out of me, if that's how you get your fun, but I think you might leave poor old Mum out of it."

Magnus pretended astonishment. "But my dear fellow, I don't see how I can. I've done my best to afford you the decency of obscurity. I'd hoped to finish my narrative without letting the others in on our secret. I could have gone on calling you 'the genius', though you had other names in the company. There were some who called you 'the Cantab' because of your degree from Cambridge, and there were others who called you 'One' because you had that mock-modest trick of referring to yourself as One when in your heart you were crying, 'Me, me, glorious ME!' But I can't leave you out, and I don't see how I can leave your Mum out, because she threw so much light on you, and therefore lent a special flavour to the whole story of Sir John's touring company."

"All right, Magnus; I was a silly young ass, and I freely admit it. But isn't one permitted to be an ass for a year or two, when one is young, and the whole world appears to be open to one, and waiting for one? Because you had a rotten childhood, don't suppose that everybody else who had better luck was utterly a fool. Have you any idea what *you* looked like in those days?"

"No, I haven't, really, but I see you are dying to tell me. Do please go ahead."

"I shall. You were disliked and distrusted because everybody thought you were a sneak, as you've said yourself. But you haven't told us that you *were* a sneak, and blabbed to Macgregor about every trivial breach of company discipline—who came into the theatre after the half-hour call, and who might happen to have a friend in the dressing-room during the show, and who watched Sir John from the wings when he had said they weren't to, and anything else you could find out by pussy-footing and snooping. Even that might have passed as your job, if you hadn't had such a nasty personality—always smiling like a pantomime demon—always stinking of some sort of cheap hair oil—always running like a rabbit to open doors for Milady—and vain as a peacock about your tuppenny-ha'penny juggling and wire-walking. You were a thoroughly nasty little piece of work, let me tell you."

"I suppose I was. But you make the mistake of thinking I was pleased with myself. Not a bit of it. I was trying to learn the ropes of another mode of life—"

"Indeed you were! You were trying to be Sir John off the stage as well as on. And what a caricature you made of it! Walking like Spring-Heeled Jack because Frank Moore had tried to show you something about deportment, and parting your greasy long hair in the middle because Sir John was the last actor on God's earth to do so, and wearing clothes that would make a cat laugh because Sir John wore eccentric duds that looked as if he'd had 'em since Mafeking Night."

"Do you think I'd have been better off to model myself on you?"

"I was no prize as an actor. Don't think I don't know it. But at least I was living in 1932, and you were aping a man who was still living in 1902, and if there hadn't been a very strong uncanny whiff about you you'd have been a total freak."

"Ah, but there was an uncanny whiff about me. I was Mungo Fetch, don't forget. We fetches can't help being uncanny."

Lind intervened. "Dear friends," he said, being very much the courtly Swede, "let us not have a quarrel about these grievances which are so long dead. You are both different men now. Think, Roly, of your achievements as a novelist and broadcaster; One, and the Genius and the Cantab are surely buried under that? And you, my dear Eisengrim, what reason have you to be bitter toward anyone? What have you desired that life has not given you? Including what I now see is a very great achievement; you modelled yourself on a fine actor of the old school, and you have put all you learned at the service of your own art, where it has flourished wonderfully. Roly, you sought to be a literary man, and you are one; Magnus, you wanted to be Sir John, and it looks very much as if you had succeeded, in so far as anyone can succeed—"

"Just a little more than most people succeed," said Ingestree, who was still hot; "you ate poor old Sir John. You ate him down to the core. We could see it happening, right from the beginning of that tour."

"Did I really?" said Magnus, apparently pleased. "I didn't know it showed so plainly. But now you are being melodramatic, Roly. I simply wanted to be like him. I told you, I apprenticed myself to an egoism, because I saw how invaluable that egoism was. Nobody can steal another man's ego, but he can learn from it, and I learned. You didn't have the wits to learn."

"I'd have been ashamed to toady as you did, whatever it brought me."

"Toady? Now that's an unpleasant word. You didn't learn what there was to be learned in that company, Ingestree. You were at every rehearsal and every performance of *The Master of Ballantrae* that I was. Don't you remember the splendid moment when Sir John, as Mr Henry, said to his father: 'There are double words for everything: the word that swells and the word that belittles; my brother cannot fight me with a word.' Your word for my relationship to Sir John is toadying, but mine is emulation, and I think mine is the better word."

"Yours is the dishonest word. Your emulation, as you call it, sucked the pith out of that poor old ham, and gobbled it up and made it part of yourself. It was a very nasty process."

"Roly, I idolized him."

"Yes, and to be idolized by you, as you were then, was a terrible, vampire-like feeding on his personality and his spirit—because his personality as an actor was all there was of his spirit. You were a double, right enough, and such a double as Poe and Dostoyevsky would have understood. When we first met at Sorgenfrei I thought there was something familiar about you, and the minute you began to act I sensed what it was; you were the fetch of Sir John. But I swear it wasn't until today, as we sat at this table, that I realized you really were Mungo Fetch."

"Extraordinary! I recognized you the minute I set eyes on you, in spite of the rather Pickwickian guise you have acquired during the past forty years."

"And you were waiting for a chance to knife me?"

"Knife! Knife! Always these belittling words! Have you no sense of humour, my dear man?"

"Humour is a poisoned dagger in the hands of a man like you. People talk of humour as if it were all jolly, always the lump of sugar in the coffee of life. A man's humour takes its quality from what a man is, and your humour is like the scratch of a rusty nail."

"Oh, balls," said Kinghovn. Ingestree turned on him, very white in the face.

"What the hell do you mean by interfering?" he said.

"I mean what I say. Balls! You people who are so clever with words never allow yourselves or anybody else a moment's peace. What is this all about? You two knew each other when you were young and you didn't hit it off. So now we have all this gaudy abuse about vampires and rusty nails from Roly, and Magnus is leading him on to make a fool of himself and cause a fight. I'm enjoying myself. I like this subtext and I want the rest of it. We had just got to where Roly's Mum was paying a visit to Sir John backstage. I want to know about that. I can see it in my mind's eye. Colour, angle of camera, quality of light—the whole thing. Get on with it and let's forget all this subjective stuff; it has no reality except what somebody like me can provide for it, and at the moment I'm not interested in subjective rubbish. I want the story. Enter Roly's Mum; what next?"

"Since Roly's Mum is such a hot potato, perhaps Roly had better tell you," said Eisengrim.

"So I will. My Mum was a very decent body, though at the time I was silly enough to underrate her; as Magnus has made clear I was a little above myself in those days. University does it, you know. It's such a protected life for a young man, and he so easily loses his frail hold on reality.

"My people weren't grand, at all. My father had an antique shop in Norwich, and he was happy about that because he had risen above his father, who had combined a small furniture shop with an undertaking business. Both my parents had adored Sir John, and ages before the time we are talking about—before the First Great War, in fact—they did rather a queer thing that brought them to his attention. They loved *The Master of Ballantrae;* it was just their meat, full of antiquery and romance; they liked selling antiques because it seemed romantic, I truly believe. They saw *The Master* fully ten times when they were young, and loved it so that they wrote out the whole play from memory—I don't suppose it was very accurate, but they did—and sent it to Sir John with an adoring letter. Sort of tribute from playgoers whose life he had illumined, you know. I could hardly believe it when I was young, but I know better now; fans get up to the queerest things in order to associate themselves with their idols.

"Sir John wrote them a nice letter, and when next he was near Norwich, he came to the shop. He loved antiques, and bought them all over the place, and I honestly think his interest in them was simply romantic, like my parents'. They never tired of telling about how he came into the shop, and inquired about a couple of old chairs, and finally asked if they were the people who had sent him the manuscript. That was a glory-day for them, I can tell you. And afterward, whenever they had anything that was in his line, they wrote to him, and quite often he bought whatever it was. That was why it was so bloody-minded of him to take it out of me about the proper way to handle a chair, and to make that crack about the shop. He knew it would hurt.

"Anyhow, my mother was out of her mind with joy when she wangled me a job with his company; thought he was going to be my great patron, I suppose. My father had died, and the shop could keep her, but certainly not me, and anyhow I was set on being a writer. I admit I was pleased to be asked to do a literary job for him; it wasn't quite as grand as I may have pretended to Audrey Sevenhowes, but who hasn't been a fool in his time? If I'd been shrewd enough to resist a pretty girl I'd have been a sharp little piece of glass like Mungo Fetch, instead of a soft boy who had got a swelled head at Cambridge, and knew nothing about the world.

"When my Mum knew I was going to Canada with the company she came to London to say good-bye—I'm ashamed to say I had told her there was no chance of my going to Norwich, though I suppose I could have made it—and she wanted to see Sir John. She'd brought him a gift, the loveliest little wax portrait relievo of Garrick you ever saw; I don't know where she picked it up, but it was worth eighty pounds if it was worth a ha'penny, and she gave it to him. And she asked him, in terms that made me blush, to take good care of me while I was abroad. I must say the old boy was decent, and said very kindly that he was sure I didn't need supervision, but that he would always be glad to talk with me if anything came up that worried me."

"Audrey Sevenhowes put it about that your Mum had asked Milady to see that you didn't forget your bedsocks in the Arctic wildernesses of Canada," said Eisengrim.

"You don't surprise me. Audrey Sevenhowes was a bitch, and she made a fool of me. But I don't care. I'd rather be a fool than a tough any day. But I assure you there was no mention of bedsocks; my Mum was not a complex woman, but she wasn't stupid, either."

"Ah, there you have the advantage of me," said Magnus, with a smile of great charm. "My mother, I fear, was very much more than stupid, as I have already told you. She was mad. So perhaps we can be friends again, Roly?"

He put out his hand across the table. It was not a gesture an Englishman would have made, and I couldn't quite make up my mind whether he was sincere or not. But Ingestree took his hand, and it was perfectly plain that he meant to make up the quarrel.

The waiters were beginning to look at us meaningly, so we adjourned upstairs to our expensive apartment, where everybody had a chance to use the loo. The film-makers were not to be shaken. They wanted the story to the end. So, after the interval—not unlike an interval at the theatre—we reassembled in our large sitting-room, and it now seemed to be understood, without anybody having said so, that Roly and Magnus were going to continue the story as a duet.

I was pleased, as I was pleased by anything that gave me a new light or a new crumb of information about my old friend, who had become Magnus Eisengrim. I was puzzled, however, by the silence of Liesl, who had sat through the narration at the lunch table without saying a word. Her silence was not of the unobtrusive kind; the less she said the more conscious one became of her presence. I knew her well enough to bide my time. Though she said nothing, she was big with feeling, and I knew that she would have something to say when she felt the right moment had come. After all, Magnus was in a very real sense her property: did he not live in her house, treat it as his own, share her bed, and accept the homage of her extraordinary courtesy, yet always understanding who was the real ruler of Sorgenfrei? What did Liesl think about Magnus undressing himself, inch by inch, in front of the film-makers? Particularly now that it was clear that there was an old, unsettled hostility between him and Roland Ingestree, what did she think?

What did I think, as I carefully wiped my newly scrubbed dentures on one of the Savoy's plentiful linen hand-towels, before slipping them back over my gums? I thought I wanted all I could get of this vicarious life. I wanted to be off to Canada with Sir John Tresize. I knew what Canada meant to me: what had it meant to him?

(6)

When I returned to our drawing-room Roly was already aboard ship.

"One of my embarrassments—how susceptible the young are to embarrassment—was that my dear Mum had outfitted me with a vast woolly steamer-rug in a gaudy design. The company kept pestering Macgregor to know what tartan it was, and he thought it looked like Hunting Cohen, so The Hunting Cohen it was from that time forth. I didn't need it, God knows, because the C.P.R. ship was fiercely hot inside, and it was too late in the season for anyone to sit on deck in any sort of comfort.

"My Mum was so solicitous in seeing me off that the company pretended to think I needed a lot of looking after, and made a great game of it. Not unkind (except for Charlton and Woulds, who were bullies) but very joky and hard to bear, especially when I wanted to be glorious in the eyes of Audrey Sevenhowes. But my Mum had also provided me with a *Baedeker's Canada,* the edition of 1922, which had somehow found its way into the shop, and although it was certainly out of date a surprising number of people asked for a loan of it, and informed themselves that the Government of Canada issued a four-dollar bill, and that the coloured porters on the sleeping-cars expected a minimum tip of twenty-five cents a day, and that a guard's van was called a caboose on Canadian railways, and similar useful facts.

"The Co. may have thought me funny, but they were a quaint sight themselves when they assembled on deck for a publicity picture before we left Liverpool. There were plenty of these company pictures taken through the whole length of the tour, and in every one of them Emilia Pauncefort's extraordinary travelling coat (called behind her back the Coat of Many Colours) and the fearful man's cap that Gwenda Lewis fastened to her head with a hatpin, so that she would be ready for all New World hardships, and the fur cap C. Pengelly Spickernell wore, assuring everybody that a skin cap with earflaps was absolutely *de rigueur* in the Canadian winter, Grover Paskin's huge pipe, with a bowl about the size of a brandy-glass, and Eugene Fitzwarren's saucy Homburg and coat with velvet collar, in the

Edwardian manner—all these strange habiliments figured prominently. Even though the gaudy days of the Victorian mummers had
long gone, these actors somehow got themselves up so that they
couldn't have been taken for anything else on God's earth but actors.

"It was invariable, too, that when Holroyd had mustered us for
one of these obligatory pictures, Sir John and Milady always appeared
last, smiling in surprise, as if a picture were the one thing in the world
they hadn't expected, and as if they were joining in simply to humour
the rest of us. Sir John was an old hand at travelling in Canada, and
he wore an overcoat of Raglan cut and reasonable weight, but of an
amplitude that spoke of the stage—and, as our friend has told us, the
sleeves were always a bit short so that his hands showed to advantage.
Milady wore fur, as befitted the consort of an actor-knight; what fur
it was nobody knew, but it was very furry indeed, and soft, and
smelled like money. She topped herself with one of those *cloche* hats
that were fashionable then, in a hairy purple felt; not the happiest
choice, because it almost obscured her eyes, and threw her long
duck's-bill nose into prominence.

"But never—never, I assure you—in any of these pictures would
you find Mungo Fetch. Who can have warned him off? Whose decision was it that a youthful Sir John, in clothes that were always too
tight and sharply cut, wouldn't have done in one of these pictures
which always appeared in Canadian papers with a caption that read:
'Sir John Tresize and his London company, including Miss Annette
de la Borderie (Lady Tresize), who are touring Canada after a
triumphant season in the West End.'"

"It was a decision of common sense," said Magnus. "It never
worried me. I knew my place, which is more than you did, Roly."

"Quite right. I fully admit it. I didn't know my place. I was under
the impression that a university man was acceptable everywhere, and
inferior to no one. I hadn't twigged that in a theatrical company—or
any artistic organization, for that matter—the hierarchy is decided by
talent, and that art is the most rigorously aristocratic thing in our
democratic wodd. So I always pushed in as close to Audrey
Sevenhowes as I could, and I even picked up the trick from Charlton
of standing a bit sideways, to show my profile, which I realize now

would have been better kept a mystery. I was an ass. Oh, indeed I was a very fine and ostentatious ass, and don't think I haven't blushed for it since."

"Stop telling us what an ass you were," said Kinghovn. "Even I recognize that as an English trick to pull the teeth of our contempt. 'Oh, I say, what a jolly good chap: says he's an ass, don't yer know; he couldn't possibly say that if he was really an ass.' But I'm a tough-minded European; I think you really were an ass. If I had a time-machine, I'd whisk myself back into 1932 and give you a good boot in the arse for it. But as I can't, tell me why you were included on the tour. Apparently you were a bad actor and an arguing nuisance as a chair-lifter. Why would anybody pay you money, and take you on a jaunt to Canada?"

"You need a drink, Harry. You are speaking from the deep surliness of the deprived boozer. Don't fuss; it'll be the canonical, appointed cocktail hour quite soon, and then you'll regain your temper. I was taken as Sir John's secretary. The idea was that I'd write letters to fans that he could sign, and do general dog's-body work, and also get on with Jekyll-and-Hyde.

"That was where the canker gnawed, to use an appropriately melodramatic expression. I had thought, you see, that I was to write a dramatization of Stevenson's story, and as Magnus has told you I was full of great ideas about Dostoyevsky and masks. I used to quote Stevenson at Sir John: 'I hazard the guess that man will be ultimately known for a mere polity of multifarious, incongruous, and independent denizens,' I would say, and entreat him to let me put the incongruous denizens on the stage, in masks. He merely shook his head and said, 'No good, m'boy; my public wouldn't like it.' Then I would have at him with another quotation, in which Jekyll tells of 'those appetites I had long secretly indulged, and had of late begun to pamper'. Once he asked me what I had in mind. I had lots of Freudian capers in mind: masochism, and sadism, and rough-stuff with girls. That rubbed his Victorianism the wrong way. 'Unwholesome rubbish,' was all he would say.

"In the very early days of our association I was even so daring as to ask him to scrap Jekyll-and-Hyde and let me do a version of

Dorian Gray for him. That really tore it! 'Don't ever mention that man to me again,' he said; 'Oscar Wilde dragged his God-given genius in unspeakable mire, and the greatest kindness we can do is to forget his name. Besides, my public wouldn't hear of it.' So I was stuck with Jekyll-and-Hyde.

"Stuck even worse than I had at first supposed. Ages and ages before, at the beginning of their career together, Sir John and Milady had concocted *The Master of Ballantrae* themselves, with their own innocent pencils. They made the scenario, down to the last detail, then found some hack to supply dialogue. This, I discovered to my horror, was what they had done again. They had made a scheme for Jekyll-and-Hyde, and they expected me to write some words for it, and he had the gall to say they would *polish*. Those two mountebanks *polish* my stuff! I was no hack; hadn't I got a meritorious second in Eng. Lit. at Cambridge? And it would have been a first, if I had been content to crawl and stick to the party line about everything on the syllabus from Beowulf on down! Don't laugh, you people. I was young and I had pride."

"But no stage experience," said Lind.

"Perhaps not, but I wasn't a fool. And you should have seen the scenario Sir John and Milady had cobbled up between them. Stevenson must have turned in his grave. Do you know *The Strange Case of Dr Jekyll and Mr Hyde*? It's tremendously a *written* book. Do you know what I mean? Its quality is so much in the narrative manner; extract the mere story from it and it's just a tale of bugaboo. Chap drinking a frothy liquid that changes from clear to purple and then to green—*green* if you can imagine anything so corny—and he shrinks into his wicked *alter ego*. I set myself to work to discover a way of getting the heart of the literary quality into a stage version.

"Masks would have helped enormously. But those two had seized on what was, for them, the principal defect of the original, which was that there was no part for a woman in it. Well, imagine! What would the fans of Miss Annette de la Borderie say to that? So they had fudged up a tale in which Dr Jekyll had a secret sorrow; it was that a boyhood friend had married the girl he truly loved, who discovered after the marriage that she truly loved Jekyll. So he adored her honourably, while her husband went to the bad through drink. The big Renunciation ploy, you see, which was such a telling card in *The Master*.

"To keep his mind off his thwarted love, Dr Jekyll took to mucking with chemicals, and discovered the Fateful Potion. Then the husband of the True Love died of booze, and Jekyll and she were free to marry. But by that time he was addicted to the Fateful Potion. Had taken so much of it that he was likely to give a shriek and dwindle into Hyde at any inconvenient moment. So he couldn't marry his True Love and couldn't tell her why. Great final scene, where he is locked in his laboratory, changed into Hyde, and quite unable to change back, because he's run out of the ingredients of the F.P.; True Love, suspecting something's up, storms the door with the aid of a butler and footman who break it in; as the blows on the door send him into the trembles, Jekyll, with one last superhuman clutching at his Better Self, realizes that there is only one honourable way out; he takes poison, and hops the twig just as True Love bursts in; she holds the body of Hyde in her arms, weeping piteously, and the power of her love is so great that he turns slowly back into the beautiful Dr Jekyll, redeemed at the very moment of death."

"A strong curtain," said I. "I don't know what you're complaining about. I should like to have seen that play. I remember Tresize well; he could have done it magnificently."

"You must be pulling my leg," said Ingestree, looking at me in reproach.

"Not a bit of it. Good, gutsy melodrama. You've described it in larky terms, because you want us to laugh. But I think it would have worked. Didn't you ever try?"

"Oh yes, I tried. I tried all through that Canadian tour. I would slave away whenever I got a chance, and then show my homework to Sir John, and he would mark it up in his own spidery handwriting. Kept saying I had no notion of how to make words effective, and wrote three sentences where one would do.

"I tried everything I knew. I remember saying to myself one night, as I lay in my berth in a stiflingly hot Canadian train, What would Aldous Huxley do, in my position? And it came to me that Aldous would have used what we call a distancing-technique—you know, he would have written it all apparently straight, but with a choice of vocabulary that gave it all an ironic edge, so that the perceptive listener would realize that the whole play was ambiguous, and could be taken as a hilarious send-up. So I tried a scene or two like that, and I don't believe Sir John even twigged; he just sliced out all the telling adjectives, and there it was, melodrama again. I never met a man with such a deficient literary sense."

"Did it ever occur to you that perhaps he knew his job?" said Lind. "I've never found that audiences liked ambiguity very much. I've got all my best effects by straight statement."

"Dead right," said Kinghovn. "When Jurgen wants ambiguity he tips me the wink and I film the scene a bit skew-whiff, or occasionally going out of focus, and that does the trick."

"You're telling me this now," said Ingestree, "and I expect you're right, in your unliterary way. But there was nobody to tell me anything then, except Sir John, and I could see him becoming more and more stagily patient with me, and letting whatever invisible audience he acted to in his offstage moments admire the way in which the well-graced actor endured the imbecilities of the dimwitted boy. But I swear there was something to be said on my side, as well. But as I say I was an ass. Am I never to be forgiven for being an ass?"

"That's a very pretty theological point," I said. "'In the law of God there is no statute of limitations.'"

"My God! Do you remember that one?" said Ingestree.

"Oh yes; I've read Stevenson too, you know, and that chilly remark comes in *Jekyll and Hyde,* so you are certainly familiar with it. Are we ever forgiven for the follies even of our earliest years? That's something that torments me often."

"Bugger theology!" said Kinghovn. "Get on with the story."

"High time Harry had a drink," said Liesl. "I'll call for some things to be sent up. And we might as well have dinner here, don't you think? I'll choose."

When she had gone into the bedroom to use the telephone Magnus looked calculatingly at Ingestree, as if at some curious creature he had not observed before. "You describe the Canadian tour simply as a personal Gethsemane, but it was really quite an elaborate affair," he said. "I suppose one of your big problems was trying to fit a part into Jekyll-and-Hyde for the chaste and lovely Sevenhowes. Couldn't you have made her a confidential maid to the True Love, with stirring lines like, 'Ee, madam, Dr Jekyll 'e do look sadly mazy-like these latter days, madam'? That would have been about her speed. A rotten actress. Do you know what became of her? Neither do I. What becomes of all those pretty girls with a teaspoonful of talent who seem to drift off the stage before they are thirty? But really, my dear Roly, there was a great deal going on. I was working like a galley-slave."

"I'm sure you were," said Ingestree; "toadying to Milady, as I said earlier. I use the word without malice. Your approach was not describable as courtier-like, nor did it quite sink to the level of fawning; therefore I think toadying is the appropriate expression."

"Call it toadying if it suits your keen literary sense. I have said several times that I loved her, but you choose not to attach any importance to that. Loved her not in the sense of desiring her, which would have been grotesque, and never entered my head, but simply in the sense of wishing to serve her and do anything that was in my power to make her happy. Why I felt that way about a woman old enough to be my mother is for you dabblers in psychology to say, but nothing you can think of will give the real quality of my feeling; there is a pitiful want of resonance in so much psychological explanation of what lies behind things. If you had felt more, Roly, and been less remorselessly literary, you might have seen possibilities in the plan for the Jekyll and Hyde play. A man redeemed and purged of evil by a woman's love—now there's a really unfashionable theme for a play in our time! So unfashionable as to be utterly incredible. Yet Sir John and Milady seemed to know what such themes were all about. They were more devoted than any people I have ever known."

"Like a couple of old love-birds," said Ingestree.

"Well, what would you prefer? A couple of old scratching cats? Don't forget that Sir John was a symbol to countless people of romantic love in its most chivalrous expression. You know what Agate wrote about him once—'He touches women as if they were camellias.' Can you name an actor on the stage today who makes love like that? But there was never a word of scandal about them, because off the stage they were inseparables.

"I think I penetrated their secret: undoubtedly they began as lovers but they had long been particularly close friends. Is that common? I haven't seen much of it, if it is. They were sillies, of course. Sir John would never hear a word that suggested that Milady was unsuitably cast as a young woman, though I know he was aware of it. And she was a silly because she played up to him, and clung quite pitiably to some mannerisms of youth. I knew them for years, you know; you only knew them on that tour. But I remember much later, when a newspaper interviewer touched the delicate point, Sir John said with great dignity and simplicity, 'Ah, but you see, we always felt that our audiences were ready to make allowances if the physical aspect of a character was not ideally satisfied, because they knew that so many other fine things in our performances were made possible thereby.'

"He had a good point, you know. Look at some of the leading women in the Comédie Française; crone is not too hard a word when first you see them, but in ten minutes you are delighted with the art, and forget the appearance, which is only a kind of symbol, anyhow. Milady had extraordinary art, but alas, poor dear, she did run to fat. It's better for an actress to become a bag of bones, which can always be equated somehow with elegance. Fat's another thing. But what a gift of comedy she had, and how wonderfully it lit up a play like *Rosemary,* where she insisted on playing a character part instead of the heroine. Charity, Roly, charity."

"You're a queer one to be talking about charity. You ate Sir John. I've said it once and I'll say it again. You ate that poor old ham."

"That's one of your belittling words, like 'toady'. I've said it: I apprenticed myself to an egoism, and if in the course of time, because I was younger and had a career to make, the egoism became more mine than his, what about it? Destiny, m'boy? Inevitable, quonk?"

"Oh, God, don't do that, it's too horribly like him."

"Thank you. I thought so myself. And, as I tell you, I worked to achieve it!

"You had quite a jolly time on the voyage to Canada, as I recall. But don't you remember those rehearsals we held every day, in such holes and corners of the ship as the Purser could make available to us? Macgregor and I were too busy to be seasick, which was a luxury you didn't deny yourself. You were sick the night of the ship's concert. Those concerts are utterly a thing of the past. The Purser's assistant was busy almost before the ship left Liverpool, ferreting out what possible talent there might be on board—ladies who could sing 'The Rosary' or men who imitated Harry Lauder. A theatrical company was a godsend to the poor man. And in the upshot C. Pengelly Spickernell sang 'Melisande in the Wood' and 'The Floral Dance' (nicely contrasted material, was what he called it) and Grover Paskin told funny stories (insecurely cemented together with 'And that reminds me of the time—') and Sir John recited Clarence's Dream from *Richard III;* Milady made the speech hitting up the audience for money for the Seaman's Charities, and did it with so much charm and spirit that they got a record haul.

"But that's by the way. We worked on the voyage and after we'd docked at Montreal the work was even harder. We landed on a Friday, and opened on Monday at Her Majesty's for two weeks, one given wholly to *Scaramouche* and the second to *The Corsican Brothers* and *Rosemary*. We did first-rate business, and it was the beginning of what the old actors loved to call a triumphal tour. You wouldn't believe how we were welcomed, and how the audiences ate up those romantic plays—"

"I remember some fairly cool notices," said Roly.

"But not cool audiences. That's what counts. Provincial critics are always cool; they have to show they're not impressed by what comes from the big centres of culture. The audiences thought we were wonderful."

"Magnus, the audiences thought England was wonderful. The Tresize company came from England, and if the truth is to be told it came from a special England many of the people in those audiences cherished—the England they had left when they were young, or the England they had visited when they were young, and in many cases an England they simply imagined and wished were a reality.

"Even in 1932 all that melodrama was terribly old hat, but every audience had a core of people who were happy just to be listening to

English voices repeating noble sentiments. The notion that everybody wants the latest is a delusion of intellectuals; a lot of people want a warm, safe place where Time hardly moves at all, and to a lot of those Canadians that place was England. The theatre was almost the last stronghold of the old colonial Canada. You know very well it was more than twenty years since Sir John had dared to visit New York, because his sort of theatre was dead there. But it did very well in Canada because it wasn't simply theatre there—it was England, and they were sentimental about it.

"Don't you remember the smell of mothballs that used to sweep up onto the stage when the curtain rose, from all the bunny coats and ancient dress suits in the expensive seats? There were still people who dressed for the theatre, though I doubt if they dressed for anything else, except perhaps a regimental ball or something that also reminded them of England. Sir John was exploiting the remnants of colonialism. You liked it because you knew no better."

"I knew Canada," said Magnus. "At least, I knew the part of it that had responded to Wanless's World of Wonders and Happy Hannah's jokes. The Canada that came to see Sir John was different but not wholly different. We didn't tour the villages; we toured the cities with theatres that could accommodate our productions, but we rushed through many a village I knew as we jaunted all those thousands of miles on the trains. As we travelled, I began to think I knew Canada pretty well. But quite another thing was that I knew what entertains people, what charms the money out of their pockets, and feeds their imagination.

"The theatre to you was a kind of crude extension of Eng. Lit. at Cambridge, but the theatre I knew was the theatre that makes people forget some things and remember others, and refreshes dry places in the spirit. We were both ignorant young men, Roly. You were the kind that is so scared of life that you only know how to despise it, for fear you might be tricked into liking something that wasn't up to the standards of a handful of people you admired. I was the kind that knew very little that wasn't tawdry and tough and ugly, but I hadn't forgotten my Psalms, and I thirsted for something better as the hart pants for the water-brooks. So Sir John's plays, and the decent manners he insisted on in his company, and the regularity and honesty of the Friday treasury, when I got my pay without having to haggle or kick back any part of it to some petty crook, did very well for me."

"You're idealizing your youth, Magnus. Lots of the company just thought the tour was a lark."

"Yes, but even more of the company were honest players and did their best in the work they had at hand. You saw too much of Charlton and Woulds, who were no good and never made any mark in the profession. And you were under the thumb of Audrey Sevenhowes, who was another despiser, like yourself. Of course we had our ridiculous side. What theatrical troupe hasn't? But the effect we produced wasn't ridiculous. We had something people wanted, and we didn't give them short weight. Very different from my carnival days, when short weight was the essence of everything."

"So for you the Canadian tour was a time of spiritual growth," said Lind.

"It was a time when I was able to admit that honesty and some decency of life were luxuries within my grasp," said Magnus. "Can you imagine that? You people all have the flesh and finish of those who grew up feeling reasonably safe in the world. And you grew up as visible people. Don't forget that I had spent most of my serious hours inside Abdullah."

"Melodrama has eaten into your brain," said Roly. "When I knew you, you were inside Sir John, inside his body and inside his manner and voice and everything about him that a clever double could imitate. Was it really different?"

"Immeasurably different."

"I wish you two would stop clawing one another," said Kinghovn. "If it was all so different—and I'm quite ready to believe it was—how was it different? If it's possible to find out, of course. You two sound as if you had been on different tours."

"Not a bit of it. It was the same tour, right enough," said Magnus; "but I probably remember more of its details than Roly. I'm a detail man; it's the secret of being a good illusionist. Roly has the big, broad picture, as it would have appeared to someone of his temperament and education. He saw everything it was proper for the Cantab and

One to notice; I saw and tried to understand everything that passed before my eyes.

"Do you remember Morton W. Penfold, Roly? No, I didn't think you would. But he was one of the casters on which that tour rolled. He was our Advance.

"The tour was under the management of a syndicate of rich Canadians who wanted to encourage English theatre companies to visit Canada, partly because they wanted to stem what they felt was a too heavy American influence, partly in the hope that they might make a little money, partly because they felt the attraction of the theatre in the ignorant way rich businessmen sometimes do. When we arrived in Montreal some of them met the ship and bore Sir John and Milady away, and there was a great deal of wining and dining before we opened on Monday. Morton W. Penfold was their representative, and he went ahead of us like a trumpeter all across the country. Arranged about travel and saw that tickets for everybody were forthcoming whenever we mounted a train. Saw that trains were delayed when necessary, or that an improvised special helped us to make a difficult connection. Arranged that trucks and sometimes huge sleighs were ready to lug the scenery to and from the theatres. Arranged that there were enough stagehands for our heavy shows, and a rough approximation of the number of musicians we needed to play out music, and college boys or other creatures of the right height and bulk who were needed for the supers in *The Master* and *Scaramouche*. Saw that a horse of guaranteed good character and continence was hired to pull Climene's cart. Placed the advertisements in the local papers ahead of our appearance, and also tasty bits of publicity about Sir John and Milady; had a little anecdote ready for every paper that made it clear that the name Tresize was Cornish and that the emphasis came on the second syllable; also provided a little packet of favourable reviews from London, Montreal, and Toronto papers for the newspapers in small towns where there was no regular critic, and such material might prime the pump of a local reporter's invention. He also saw that the information was provided for the programmes, and warned local theatre managers that Madame de Plougastel's Salon was not a misprint for Madame de Plougastel's Saloon, which some of them were apt to think.

"Morton W. Penfold was a living marvel, and I learned a lot from him on the occasions when he was in the same town with us for a few days. He was more theatrical than all but the most theatrical of the actors; had a big square face with a blue jaw, a hypnotist's eyebrows, and a deceptive appearance of dignity and solemnity, because he was a fellow of infinite wry humour. He wore one of those black Homburg hats that politicians used to affect, but he never dinted the top of it, so that he had something of the air of a Mennonite about the head; wore a stiff choker collar and one of those black satin stocks that used to be called a dirty-shirt necktie, because it covered everything within the V of his waistcoat. Always wore a black suit, and had a dazzling ten-cent shoeshine every day of his life. His business office was contained in the pockets of his black overcoat; he could produce anything from them, including eight-by-ten-inch publicity pictures of the company.

"He was pre-eminently a great fixer. He seemed to know everybody, and have influence everywhere. In every town he had arranged for Sir John to address the Rotarians, or the Kiwanians, or whatever club was meeting on an appropriate day. Sir John always gave the same speech, which was about 'cementing the bonds of the British Commonwealth'; he could have given it in his sleep, but he was too good an actor not to make it seem tailor-made for every new club.

"If we were going to be in a town that had an Anglican Cathedral over a weekend it was Morton W. Penfold who persuaded the Dean that it was a God-given opportunity to have Sir John read the Second Lesson at the eleven o'clock service. His great speciality was getting Indian tribes to invest a visiting English actor as a Chief, and he had convinced the Blackfoot that Sir John should be re-christened Soksi-Poyina many years before the tour I am talking about.

"Furthermore, he knew the idiosyncrasies of the liquor laws in every Canadian province we visited, and made sure the company did not run dry; this was particularly important as Sir John and Milady had a taste for champagne, and liked it iced but not frozen, which was not always a simple requirement in that land of plentiful ice. And in every town we visited, Morton W. Penfold had made sure that our advertising sheets, full-size, half-size, and folio, were well displayed and that our little flyers, with pictures of Sir John in some of his most popular roles, were on the reception desks of all the good hotels.

"And speaking of hotels, it was Morton W. Penfold who took particulars of everybody's taste in accommodation on that first day in Montreal, and saw that wherever we went reservations had been made in the grand railway hotels, which were wonderful, or in the dumps where people like James Hailey and Gwenda Lewis stayed, for the sake of economy.

"Oh, those cheap hotels! I stayed in the cheapest, where one electric bulb hung from a string in the middle of the room, where the sheets were like cheesecloth, and where the mattresses—when they were revealed as they usually were after a night's restless sleep—were like maps of strange worlds, the continents being defined by unpleasing stains, doubtless traceable to the incontinent dreams of travelling salesmen, or the rapturous deflowerings of brides from the backwoods.

"Was he well paid for his innumerable labours? I don't know, but I hope so. He said very little that was personal, but Macgregor told me that Morton W. Penfold was born into show business, and that his wife was the granddaughter of the man whom Blondin the Magnificent had carried across Niagara Gorge on his shoulders in 1859. It was under his splendid and unfailing influence that we travelled thousands of miles across Canada and back again, and played a total of 148 performances in forty-one towns, ranging from places of about twenty thousand souls to big cities. I think I could recite the names of the theatres we played in now, though they showed no great daring in what they called themselves; there were innumerable Grands, and occasional Princesses or Victorias, but most of them were just called Somebody's Opera House."

"Frightful places," said Ingestree, doing a dramatic shudder.

"I've seen worse since," said Magnus. "You should try a tour in Central America, to balance your viewpoint. What was interesting about so many of the Canadian theatres, outside the big cities, was that they seemed to have been built with big ideas, and then abandoned before they were equipped. They had pretty good foyers and auditoriums with plush seats, and invariably eight boxes, four on each side of the stage, from which nobody could see very well. All of them had drop curtains with views of Venice or Rome on them, and a spy-hole through which so many actors had peeped that it was ringed with a black stain from their greasepaint. Quite a few had special curtains on which advertisements were printed for local merchants; Sir John didn't like those, and Holroyd had to do what he could to suppress them.

"Every one had a sunken pen for an orchestra, with a fancy balustrade to cut it off from the stalls, and nobody ever seemed to sweep in there. At performance time a handful of assassins would creep into the pen from a low door beneath the stage, and fiddle and thump and toot the music to which they were accustomed. C. Pengelly Spickernell used to say bitterly that these musicians were all recruited from the local manager's poor relations; it was his job to assemble as many of them as could get away from their regular work on a Monday morning and take them through the music that was to accompany our plays. Sir John was fussy about music, and always had a special overture for each of his productions, and usually an entr'acte as well.

"God knows it was not very distinguished music. When we heard it, it was a puzzle to know why 'Overture to *Scaramouche*' by Hugh Dunning did any more for the play that followed than if the orchestra had played 'Overture to *The Master of Ballantrae*' by Festyn Hughes. But there it was, and to Sir John and Milady these two lengths of mediocre music were as different as daylight and dark, and they used to sigh and raise their eyebrows at one another when they heard the miserable racket coming from the other side of the curtain, as if it were the ravishing of a masterpiece. In addition to this specially written music we carried a substantial body of stuff with such titles as 'Minuet d'Amour', 'Peasant Dance', and 'Gaelic Memories', which did for *Rosemary;* and for *The Corsican Brothers* Sir John insisted on an overture that had been written for Irving's production of *Robespierre* by somebody called Litolff. Another great standby was 'Suite: At the Play', by York Bowen. But except in the big towns the orchestra couldn't manage anything unfamiliar, so we generally ended up with 'Three Dances from *Henry VIII*', by Edward

German, which I suppose is known to every bad orchestra in the world. C. Pengelly Spickernell used to grieve about it whenever anybody would listen, but I honestly think the audiences liked that bad playing, which was familiar and had associations with a good time.

"Backstage there was nothing much to work with. No light, except for a few rows of red, white, and blue bulbs that hardly disturbed the darkness when they were full on. The arrangements for hanging and setting our scenery were primitive, and only in the big towns was there more than one stagehand with anything that could be called experience. The others were jobbed in as they were needed, and during the day they worked in factories or lumber-yards. Consequently we had to carry everything we needed with us, and now and then we had to do some rapid improvising. It wasn't as though these theatres weren't used; most of them were busy for at least a part of each week for seven or eight months every year. It was simply that the local magnate, having put up the shell of a theatre, saw no reason to go further. It made touring adventurous, I can tell you.

"The dressing-rooms were as ill equipped as the stages. I think they were worse than those in the vaude houses I had known, because those at least were in constant use and had a frowsy life to them. In many towns there were only two wash-basins backstage for a whole company, one behind a door marked M and the other behind a door marked F. These doors, through years of use, had ceased to close firmly, which at least meant that you didn't need to knock to find out if they were occupied. Sir John and Milady used small metal basins of their own, to which their dressers carried copper jugs of hot water—when there was any hot water.

"One thing that astonished me then, and still surprises me, is that the stage door, in nine towns out of ten, was up an unpaved alley, so that you had to pick your way through mud, or snow in the cold weather, to reach it. You knew where you were heading because the only light in the alley was one naked electric bulb, stuck laterally into a socket above the door, with a wire guard around it. It was not the placing of the stage door that surprised me, but the fact that, for me, that desolate and dirty entry was always cloaked in romance. I would rather go through one of those doors, even now, than walk up a garden path to be greeted by a queen."

"You were stage-struck," said Roly. "You rhapsodize. I remember those stage doors. Ghastly."

"I suppose you're right," said Magnus. "But I was very, very happy. I'd never been so well placed, or had so much fun in my life. How Macgregor and I used to labour to teach those stagehands their job! Do you remember how, in the last act of *The Corsican Brothers*, when the Forest of Fontainebleau was supposed to be covered in snow, we used to throw down coarse salt over the stage-cloth, so that when the duel took place Sir John could kick some of it aside to get a firm footing? Can you imagine trying to explain how that salt should be placed to some boob who had laboured all day in a planing-mill, and had no flair for romance? The snow was always a problem, though you'd think that Canadians, of all people, would understand snow. At the beginning of that act the forest is supposed to be seen in that dull but magical light that goes with snowfall. Old Boissec the wood-cutter—Grover Paskin in one of his distinguished cameos—enters singing a little song; he represents the world of everyday, drudging along regardless of the high romance which is shortly to burst upon the scene. Sir John wanted a powdering of snow to be falling as the curtain rose; just a few flakes, falling slowly so that they caught a little of the winter light. Nothing so coarse as bits of paper for us! It had to be fuller's earth, so that it would drift gently, and not be too fiercely white. Do you think we could get one of those stagehands on the road to grasp the importance of the speed at which that snow fell, and the necessity to get it exactly right? If we left it to them they threw great handfuls of snow bang on the centre of the stage, as if some damned great turkey with diarrhoea were roosting up in a tree. So it was my job to get up on the catwalk, if there was one, and on something that had been improvised and was usually dangerous if there wasn't, and see that the snow was just as Sir John wanted it. I suppose that's being stage-struck, but it was worth every scruple of the effort it took. As I said, I'm a detail man, and without the uttermost organization of detail there is no illusion, and consequently no romance. When I was in charge of the snow the audience was put in the right mood for the duel, and for the Ghost at the end of the play."

"You really can't blame me for despising it," said Roly. "I was one of the New Men; I was committed to a theatre of ideas."

"I don't suppose I've ever had more than half a dozen ideas in my life, and even those wouldn't have much appeal for a philosopher," said Magnus. "Sir John's theatre didn't deal in ideas, but in feelings. Chivalry, and loyalty and selfless love don't rank as ideas, but it was wonderful how they seized on our audiences; they loved such things, even if they had no intention of trying them out in their own lives. No use arguing about it, really. But people used to leave our performances smiling, which isn't always the case with a theatre of ideas."

"Art as soothing syrup, in fact."

"Perhaps. But it was very good soothing syrup. We never made the mistake of thinking it was a universal panacea."

"Soothing syrup in aid of a dying colonialism."

"I expect you're right. I don't care, really. It's true we thumped the good old English drum pretty loudly, but that was one of the things the syndicate wanted. When we visited Ottawa, Sir John and Milady were the Governor General's guests at Rideau Hall."

"Yes, and what a bloody nuisance that was! Actors ought never to stay in private houses or official residences. I had to scamper out there every morning with the letters, and get my orders for the day. Run the gamut of snotty aides who never seemed to know where Lady Tresize was to be found."

"Didn't she ever tell you any stories about that? Probably not. I don't think she liked you much better than you liked her. Certainly she told me that it was like living in a very pretty little court, and that all sorts of interesting people came to call. Don't you remember that the Governor General and his suite came to *Scaramouche* one night when we were playing in the old Russell Theatre? 'God Save the King' was played after they came in, and the audience was so frozen with etiquette that nobody dared to clap until the G.G. had been seen to do so. There were people who sucked in their breath when I thumbed my nose while walking the tightrope; they thought I was Sir John, you see, and they couldn't imagine a knight committing such an unspeakable rudery in the presence of an Earl. But Milady told me the Earl was away behind the times; he didn't know what it meant in Canadian terms, and thought it still meant something called 'fat bacon', which I suppose was Victorian. He guffawed and thumbed his nose and muttered, 'Fat bacon, what?' at the supper party afterward, at which Mr Mackenzie King was a guest; Mr King was so taken aback he could hardly eat his lobster. Apparently he got over it though, and Milady said she had never seen a man set about a lobster with such whole-souled enthusiasm. When he surfaced from the lobster he talked to her very seriously about dogs. Funny business, when you think of it—I mean all those grandees sitting at supper at midnight, after a play. That must have been romantic too, in its way, although there were no young people present—except the aides and one or two ladies-in-waiting, of course. In fact, I thought a lot of Canada was romantic."

"I didn't. I thought it was the rawest, roughest, crudest place I had ever set eyes on, and in the midst of that, all those vice-regal pretensions were ridiculous."

"I wonder if that's what you really thought, Roly? After all, what were you comparing it with? Norwich, and Cambridge, and a brief sniff at London. And you weren't in a condition to see anything except through the spectacles of a thwarted lover and playwright. You were being put through the mincer by the lovely Sevenhowes; you were her toy for the tour, and your agonies were the sport of her chums Charlton and Woulds. Whenever we were on one of those long train hops from city to city, we all saw it in the dining-car.

"Those dining-cars! There was romance for you! Rushing through the landscape; that fierce country north of Lake Superior, and the marvellous steppes of the prairies, in an elegant, rather too hot, curiously shaped dining-room, full of light, glittering with tablecloths and napkins so white they looked blue, shining silver (or something very close), and all those clean, courteous, friendly black waiters—if that wasn't romance you don't know the real thing when you see it! And the food! Nothing hotted up or melted out in those days, but splendid stuff that came on fresh at every big stop; cooked brilliantly

in the galley by a real chef; fresh fish, tremendous meat, real fruit—
don't you remember what their baked apples were like? With thick
cream! Where does one get thick cream now? I remember every
detail. The cube sugar was wrapped in pretty white paper with Castor
printed on it, and every time we put it in our coffee I suppose we
enriched our dear friend Boy Staunton, so clear in the memory of
Dunny and myself, because he came from our town, though I didn't
know that at the time...." (My ears pricked up: I swear my scalp
tingled. Magnus had mentioned Boy Staunton, the Canadian tycoon,
and also my lifelong friend, whom I was pretty sure Magnus had
murdered. Or, if not murdered, had given a good push on a path that
looked like suicide. This was what I wanted for my document. Had
Magnus, who withheld death cruelly from Willard, given it almost as
a benefaction to Boy Staunton? Would his present headlong, confessional mood carry him to the point where he would admit to murder,
or at least give a hint that I, who knew so much but not enough,
would be able to interpret?... But I must miss nothing, and Magnus
was still rhapsodizing about C.P.R. food as once it was.) "... And the
sauces, real sauces, made by the chef—exquisite!

"There were bottled sauces, too. Commercial stuff I learned to
hate because at every meal that dreary utility actor Jim Hailey asked
for Garton's; then he would wave it about saying, 'Anybody want any
of the Handkerchief?' because, as he laboriously pointed out, if you
spelled Garton's backward it came out Snotrag; poor Hailey was that
depressing creature, a man of one joke. Only his wife laughed and
blushed because he was being 'awful', and she never failed to tell
him so. But I suppose you didn't see because you always tried to sit
at the table with Sevenhowes and Charlton and Woulds; if she was
cruel and asked Eric Foss to sit with them instead, you sat as near as
you could and hankered and glowered as they laughed at jokes you
couldn't hear.

"Oh, the trains, the trains! I gloried in them because with Wanless's
I had done so much train travel and it was wretched. I began my train
travel, you remember, in darkness and fear, hungry, with my poor little
bum aching desperately. But here I was, unmistakably a first-class
passenger, in the full blaze of that piercing, enveloping, cleansing

Canadian light. I was quite content to sit at a table with some of the technical staff, or sometimes with old Mac and Holroyd, and now and then with that Scheherazade of the railways, Morton W. Penfold, when he was making a hop with us.

"Penfold knew all the railway staff; I think he knew all the waiters. There was one conductor we sometimes encountered on a transcontinental, who was a special delight to him, a gloomy man who carried a real railway watch—one of those gigantic nickel-plated turnips that kept very accurate time. Penfold would hail him: 'Lester, when do you think we'll be in Sault Ste Marie?' Then Lester would pull up the watch out of the well of his waistcoat, and look sadly at it, and say, 'Six fifty-two, Mort, *if we're spared.*' He was gloomy-religious, and everything was conditional on our being spared; he didn't seem to have much confidence in either God or the C.P.R.

"Penfold knew the men on the locomotives, too, and whenever we came to a long, straight stretch of track, he would say, 'I wonder if Fred is dipping his piles.' This was because one of the oldest and best of the engineers was a martyr to haemorrhoids, and Penfold swore that whenever we came to an easy piece of track, Fred drew off some warm water from the boiler into a basin, and sat in it for a few minutes, to ease himself. Penfold never laughed; he was a man of deep, private humour, and his solemn, hypnotist's face never softened, but the liquid on his lower eyelid glittered and occasionally spilled over, and his head shook; that was his laugh.

"Now and then, on long hauls, the train carried a private car for Sir John and Milady; these luxuries could not be hired—or only by the very rich—but sometimes a magnate who owned one, or a politician who had the use of one, would put it at the disposal of the Tresizes, who had armies of friends in Canada. Sir John, and Milady especially, were not mingy about their private car, and always asked a few of the company in, and now and then, on very long hauls, they asked us all in and we had a picnic meal from the dining-car. Now surely that was romance, Roly? Or didn't you find it so? All of us perched around one of those splendid old relics, most of which had been built not later than the reign of Edward the Seventh, full of marquetry woodwork (there was usually a little plaque somewhere that told you where all the woods came from) and filigree doodads around the ceiling, and armchairs with a fringe made of velvet bobbles everywhere that fringe could be imagined. In a sort of altar-like affair at one end of the drawing-room area were magazines in thick leather folders—and what magazines! Always the *Sketch* and the *Tatler* and *Punch* and the *Illustrated London News*—it was like a club on wheels. And lashings of drink for everybody—that was Penfold's craft at work—but it wasn't at all the thing for anybody to guzzle and get drunk, because Sir John and Milady didn't like that."

"He was a great one to talk," said Ingestree. "He could drink any amount without showing it, and it was believed everywhere that he drank a bottle of brandy a day just to keep his voice mellow."

"Believed, but simply not true. It's always believed that star actors drink heavily, or beat their wives, or deflower a virgin starlet every day to slake their lust. But Sir John drank pretty moderately. He had to. Gout. He never spoke about it, but he suffered a lot with it. I remember one of those parties when the train lurched and Felicity Larcombe stumbled and stepped on his gouty foot, and he turned dead white, but all he said was, 'Don't speak of it, my dear,' when she apologized."

"Yes, of course you'd have seen that. You saw everything. Obviously, or you couldn't tell us so much about it now. But we saw you seeing everything, you know. You weren't very good at disguising it, even if you tried. Audrey Sevenhowes and Charlton and Woulds had a name for you—the Phantom of the Opera. You were always somewhere with your back against a wall, looking intently at every-thing and everybody. 'There's the Phantom, at it again,' Audrey used to say. It wasn't a very nice kind of observation. It had what I can only call a wolfish quality about it, as if you were devouring everything. Especially devouring Sir John. I don't suppose he made a move without you following him with your eyes. No wonder you knew about the gout. None of the rest of us did."

"None of the rest of you cared, if you mean the little clique you travelled with. But the older members of the company knew, and certainly Morton W. Penfold knew, because it was one of his jobs to see that the same kind of special bottled water was always available for Sir John on every train and in every hotel. Gout's very serious for an actor. Any suggestion that a man who is playing the Master of Ballantrae is hobbling is bad for publicity. It was clear enough that Sir John wasn't young, but it was of the uttermost importance that on the stage he should seem young. To do that he had to be able to walk slowly; it's not too hard to seem youthful when you're leaping about the stage in a duel, but it's a very different thing to walk as slowly as he had to when he appeared as his own ghost at the end of *The Corsican Brothers*. Detail, my dear Roly; without detail there can be no illusion. And one of the odd things about Sir John's kind of illusion (and my own, when later on I became a master illusionist) is that the showiest things are quite simply arranged, but anything that looks like simplicity is extremely difficult.

"The gout wasn't precisely a secret, but it wasn't shouted from the housetops, either. Everybody knew that Sir John and Milady travelled a few fine things with them—a bronze that he particularly liked, and she always had a valuable little picture of the Virgin that she used for her private devotions, and a handsome case containing miniatures of their children—and that these things were set up in every hotel room they occupied, to give it some appearance of personal taste. But not everybody knew about the foot-bath that had to be carried for Sir John's twice-daily treatment of the gouty foot; a bathtub wouldn't do, because it was necessary that all of his body be at the temperature of the room, while the foot was in a very hot mineral solution.

"I've seen him sitting in his dressing-gown with the foot in that thing at six o'clock, and at half-past eight he was ready to step on the stage with the ease of a young man. I never thought it was the mineral bath that did the trick; I think it was more an apparatus for concentrating his will, and determination that the gout shouldn't get the better of him. If his will ever failed, he was a goner, and he knew it.

"I've often had reason to marvel at the heroism and spiritual valour that people put into causes that seem absurd to many observers. After all, would it have mattered if Sir John had thrown in the towel, admitted he was old, and retired to cherish his gout? Who would have been the loser? Who would have regretted *The Master of Ballantrae*? It's easy to say, No one at all, but I don't think that's true.

You never know who is gaining strength as a result of your own bitter struggle; you never know who sees *The Master of Ballantrae,* and quite improbably draws something from it that changes his life, or gives him a special bias for a lifetime.

"As I watched Sir John fighting against age—watched him wolfishly, I suppose Roly would say—I learned something without knowing it. Put simply it is this: no action is ever lost—nothing we do is without result. It's obvious, of course, but how many people ever really believe it, or act as if it were so?"

"You sound woefully like my dear old Mum," said Ingestree. "No good action is ever wholly lost, she would say."

"Ah, but I extend your Mum's wisdom," said Magnus. "No evil action is ever wholly lost, either."

"So you pick your way through life like a hog on ice, trying to do nothing but good actions? Oh, Magnus! What balls!"

"No, no, my dear Roly, I am not quite such a fool as that. We can't know the quality or the results of our actions except in the most limited way. All we can do is to try to be as sure as we can of what we are doing so far as it relates to ourselves. In fact, not to flail about and be the deluded victims of our passions. If you're going to do something that looks evil, don't smear it with icing and pretend it's good; just bloody well do it and keep your eyes peeled. That's all."

"You ought to publish that. *Reflections While Watching an Elderly Actor Bathing His Gouty Foot.* It might start a new vogue in morality."

"I was watching a little more than Sir John's gouty foot, I assure you. I watched him pumping up courage for Milady, who had special need of it. He wasn't a humorous man; I mean, life didn't appear to him as a succession of splendid jokes, big and small, as it did to Morton W. Penfold. Sir John's mode of perception was romantic, and romance isn't funny except in a gentle, incidental way. But on a tour like that, Sir John had to do things that had their funny side, and one of them was to make that succession of speeches, which Penfold arranged, at service clubs in the towns where we played. It was the heyday of service clubs, and they were hungrily looking for speakers, whose job it was to say something inspirational, in not more than fifteen minutes, at their weekly luncheon meetings. Sir John always cemented the bonds of the Commonwealth for them, and while he was waiting to do it they levied fines on one another for wearing loud neckties, and recited their extraordinary creeds, and sang songs they loved but which were as barbarous to him as the tribal chants of savages. So he would come back to Milady afterward, and teach her the songs, and there they would sit, in the drawing-room of some hotel suite, singing

Rotary Ann, she went out to get some clams,
Rotary Ann, she went out to get some clams,
Rotary Ann, she went out to get some clams,
But she didn't get a——clam!

—and at the appropriate moments they would clap their hands to substitute for the forbidden words 'God-damn', which good Rotarians knew, but wouldn't utter.

"I tell you it was eerie to see those two, so English, so Victorian, so theatrical, singing those utterly uncharacteristic words in their high-bred English accents, until they were laughing like loonies. Then Sir John would say something like 'Of course one shouldn't laugh at them, Nan, because they're really splendid fellows at heart, and do marvels for crippled children—or is it tuberculosis? I can never remember.' But the important thing was that Milady had been cheered up. She never showed her failing spirits—at least she thought she didn't—but he knew. And I knew.

"It was another of those secrets like Sir John's gout, which Mac and Holroyd and some of the older members of the company were perfectly well aware of but never discussed. Milady had cataracts, and however courageously she disguised it, the visible world was getting away from her. Some of the clumsiness on stage was owing to that, and much of the remarkable lustre of her glance—that bluish lustre I had noticed the first time I saw her—was the slow veiling of her eyes. There were days that were better than others, but as each month passed the account was further on the debit side. I never heard them mention it. Why would I? Certainly I wasn't the kind of person they would have confided in. But I was often present when all three of us knew what was in the air.

"I have you to thank for that, Roly. Ordinarily it would have been the secretary who would have helped Milady when something had to be read, or written, but you were never handily by, and when you were it was so clear that you were far too busy with literary things to be just a useful pair of eyes that it would have been impertinence to interrupt you. So that job fell to me, and Milady and I made a pretence about it that was invaluable to me.

"It was that she was teaching me to speak—to speak for the stage, that's to say. I had several modes of speech; one was the tough-guy language of Willard and Charlie, and another was a half-Cockney lingo I had picked up in London; I could speak French far more correctly than English, but I had a poor voice, with a thin, nasal tone. So Milady had me read to her, and as I read she helped me to place my voice differently, breathe better, and choose words and expressions that did not immediately mark me as an underling. Like so many people of deficient education, when I wanted to speak classy—that was what Charlie called it—I always used as many big words as I could. Big words, said Milady, were a great mistake in ordinary conversation, and she made me read the Bible to her to rid me of the big-word habit. Of course the Bible was familiar ground to me, and she noticed that when I read it I spoke better than otherwise, but as she pointed out, too fervently. That was a recollection of my father's Bible-reading voice. Milady said that with the Bible and Shakespeare it was better to be a little cool, rather than too hot; the meaning emerged more powerfully. 'Listen to Sir John,' she said, 'and you'll find that he never pushes a line as far as it will go.' That was how I learned about never doing your damnedest; your next-to-damnedest was far better.

"Sir John was her ideal, so I learned to speak like Sir John, and it was quite a long time before I got over it, if indeed I ever did completely get over it. It was a beautiful voice, and perhaps too beautiful for everybody's taste. He produced it in a special way, which I think he learned from Irving. His lower lip moved a lot, but his upper lip was almost motionless, and he never showed his upper teeth; completely loose lower jaw, lots of nasal resonance, and he usually spoke in his upper register, but sometimes he dropped into deep tones, with extraordinary effect. She insisted on careful phrasing, long breaths, and never accentuating possessive pronouns—she said that made almost anything sound petty.

"So I spent many an hour reading the Bible to her, and refreshing my memory of the Psalms. 'Consider and hear me, O Lord my God: lighten mine eyes, lest I sleep the sleep of death. Lest mine enemy say, I have prevailed against him; and those that trouble me rejoice when I am moved.' We had that almost every day. That, and 'Open thou mine eyes, that I may behold wondrous things out of thy law.' It was not long before I understood that Milady was praying, and I was helping her, and after the first surprise—I had been so long away from anybody who prayed, except for Happy Hannah, whose prayers were like curses—I was pleased and honoured to do it. But I didn't intrude upon her privacy; I was content to be a pair of eyes, and to learn to be a friendly voice. May I put in here that this was another side of apprenticeship to Sir John's egoism, and it was not something I had greedily sought. On the contrary it was something to which I seemed to be fated. If I stole something from the old man, the impulse for the theft was not wholly mine; I seemed to be pushed into it.

"One of the things that pushed me was that as Milady's sight grew dimmer, she liked to have somebody near to whom she could speak in French. As I've told you, she came from the Channel Islands, and from her name I judge that French was her cradle-tongue. So, under pretence of correcting my French pronunciation, we had many a long talk, and I read the Bible to her in French, as well as in English. That was a surprise for me! Like so many English-speaking people I could not conceive of the words of Christ in any language but my own, but as we worked through Le Nouveau Testament in her chunky old Geneva Bible, there they were, coloured quite differently. *Je suis le chemin, & la vérité, & la vie; nul ne vient au Père sinon par moi.* Sounded curiously frivolous, but nothing to *Bienheureux sont les débonnaires: car ils hériteront la terre.* I thought I concealed the surprise in my voice at that one, but Milady heard it (she heard every-thing) and explained that I must think of *débonnaire* as meaning *clément,* or perhaps *les doux.* But of course we all interpret Holy Writ to suit ourselves as much as we dare; I liked *les débonnaires,* because I was striving as hard as I could to be debonair myself, and I had an eye on at least a good-sized chunk of *la terre* for my inheritance. Learning to speak English and French with an upper-class accent— or at least a stage accent, which was a little more precise than merely upper class—was part of my campaign.

"As well as reading aloud, I listened to her as she rehearsed her lines. The old plays, like *The Master of Ballantrae,* were impressed on her memory forever, but she liked to go over her words for *Rosemary* and *Scaramouche* before every performance, and I read her cues for her. I learned a good deal from that, too, because she had a fine sense of comedy (something Sir John had only in a lesser degree), and I studied her manner of pointing up a line so that something more than just the joke—the juice in which the joke floated—was carried to the audience. She had a charming voice, with a laugh in it, and I noticed that clever Felicity Larcombe was learning that from her, as well as I.

"Indeed, I became a friend of Milady's, and rather less of an adorer. Except for old Zingara, who was a very different pair of shoes, she was the only woman I had ever known who seemed to like me, and think I was of any interest or value. She rubbed it into me about how lucky I was to be working with Sir John, and doing marvellous little cameos which enhanced the value of a whole production, but I had enough common sense to see that she was right, even though she exaggerated.

"One thing about me that she could not understand was that I had no knowledge of Shakespeare. None whatever. When I knew the Bible so well, how was it that I was in darkness about the other great classic of English? Had my parents never introduced me to Shakespeare? Of course Milady could have had no idea of the sort of people my parents were. I suppose my father must have heard of Shakespeare, but I am sure he rejected him as a fellow who had frittered away his time in the theatre, that Devil's domain where lies were made attractive to frivolous people.

"I have often been amazed at how well comfortable and even rich people understand the physical deprivations of the poor, without having any notion of their intellectual squalor, which is one of the things that makes them miserable. It's a squalor that is bred in the bone, and rarely can education do much to root it out if education is simply a matter of schooling. Milady had come of quite rich parents, who had daringly allowed her to go on the stage when she was no more than fourteen. In Sir Henry Irving's company, of course, which wasn't like kicking around from one stage door to another, and snatching for little jobs in pantomime. To be one of the Guvnor's people was to be one of the theatrically well-to-do, not simply in wages but in estate. And at the Lyceum she had taken in a lot of Shakespeare at the pores, and had whole plays by heart. How could anyone like that grasp the meagreness of the household in which I had been a child, and the remoteness of intellectual grace from the Deptford life? So I was a pauper in a part of life where she had always been wrapped in plenty.

"I was on friendly terms, with proper allowance for the disparity in our ages and importance to the company, by the time we had journeyed across Canada and played Vancouver over Christmas. We were playing two weeks at the Imperial; the holiday fell on the middle Sunday of our fortnight that year, and Sir John and Milady entertained the whole company to dinner at their hotel. It was the first time I had ever eaten a Christmas dinner, though during the previous twenty-three years I suppose I must have taken some sort of nourishment on the twenty-fifth of December, and it was the first time I had ever been in a private dining-room in a first-class hotel.

"It seemed elegant and splendid to me, and the surprise of the evening was that there was a Christmas gift for everybody. They were vanity things and manicure sets and scarves and whatnot for the girls, and the men had those big boxes of cigarettes that one never sees any more and notecases and all the range of impersonal but pleasant stuff you would expect. But I had a bulky parcel, and it was a complete Shakespeare—one of those copies illustrated with photographs of actors in their best roles; this one had a coloured frontispiece of Sir John as Hamlet, looking extremely like me, and across it he had written, 'A double blessing is a double grace—Christmas Greetings, John Tresize.' Everybody wanted to see it, and the company was about equally divided between those who thought Sir John was a darling to have done that for a humble member of his troupe, and those who thought I must be gaining a power that was above my station; the latter group did not say anything, but their feelings could be deduced from the perfection of their silence.

"I was in doubt about what I should do, because it was the first time in my life that anybody had ever given me anything; I had earned things, and stolen things, but I had never been given anything before and I was embarrassed, suspicious, and clumsy in my new role.

"Milady was behind it, of course, and perhaps she expected me to bury myself in the book that night, and emerge, transformed by poetry and drama, a wholly translated Mungo Fetch. The truth is that I had a nibble at it, and read a few pages of the first play in the book, which was *The Tempest,* and couldn't make head nor tail of it. There was a shipwreck, and then an old chap beefing to his daughter about some incomprehensible grievance in the past, and it was not my line at all, and I gave up.

"Milady was too well bred ever to question me about it, and when we were next alone I managed to say some words of gratitude, and I don't know whether she ever knew that Shakespeare and I had not hit it off. But the gift was very far from being a dead loss: in the first place it was a gift, and the first to come my way; in the second it was a sign of something much akin to love, even if the love went no further than the benevolence of two people with a high sense of obligation to their dependants and colleagues, down to the humblest. So the book became something more than an unreadable volume; it was a talisman, and I cherished it and gave it an importance among my belongings that was quite different from what it was meant to be. If it had been a book of spells, and I a sorcerer's apprentice who was afraid to use it, I could not have held it in greater reverence. It contained something that was of immeasurable value to the Tresizes, and I cherished it for that. I never learned anything about Shakespeare, and on the two or three occasions when I have seen Shakespearean plays in my life they have puzzled and bored me as much as *The Tempest,* but my superstitious veneration of that book has never failed, and I have it still.

"There's evidence, if you need it, that I am not really a theatre person. I am an illusionist, which is a different and probably a lesser creature. I proved it that night. After the dinner and the gifts, we had an impromptu entertainment, a very mixed bag. Audrey Sevenhowes danced the Charleston, and did it very well; C. Pengelly Spickernell sang two or three songs, vaguely related to Christmas, and Home, and England. Grover Paskin sang a comic song about an old man who had a fat sow, and we all joined in making pig-noises on cue. I did a few tricks, and was the success of the evening.

"Combined with the special gift, that put me even more to the bad with the members of the company who were always looking for hidden meanings and covert grabs for power. My top trick was when I borrowed Milady's Spanish shawl and produced from beneath it the large bouquet the company had clubbed together to give her; as I did it standing in the middle of the room, with no apparent place to conceal anything at all, not to speak of a thing the size of a rosebush, it was neatly done, but as sometimes happens with illusions, it won almost as much mistrust as applause. I know why. I had not at that time grasped the essential fact that an illusionist must never seem to be pleased with his own cleverness, and I suppose I strutted a bit. The Cantab and Sevenhowes and Charlton and Woulds sometimes spoke of me as The Outsider, and that is precisely what I was. I don't regret it now. I've lived an Outsider's life, though not in quite the way they meant; I was outside something beyond their comprehension.

"That was an ill-fated evening, as we discovered on the following day. There was champagne, and Morton W. Penfold, who was with us, gained heroic stature for finding it in what the English regarded as a desert. Everybody drank as much as they could get, and there were toasts, and these were Sir John's downfall. The Spartan regime of a gouty man was always a burden to him, and he didn't see why he should drink whisky when everybody else was drinking the wine he loved best. He proposed a toast to The Profession, and told stories about Irving; it called for several glasses, though not really a lot, and before morning he was very ill. A doctor came, and saw that there was more than gout wrong with him. It was an inflamed appendix, and it had to come out at once.

"Not a great calamity for most people, even though such an operation wasn't as simple then as it is now, but it was serious for a star actor, half-way through a long tour. He would be off the stage for not less than three weeks.

"Sir John's illness brought out the best and the worst in his company. All the old hands, and the people with a thoroughly professional attitude, rallied round at once, with all their abilities at top force. Holroyd called a rehearsal for ten o'clock Monday morning, and Gordon Barnard, who was our second lead, sailed through *Scaramouche* brilliantly; he was very different from Sir John, as a six-foot-two actor of the twentieth century must be different from a five-foot-two actor who is still in the nineteenth, but there was no worry whatever about him. Darton Flesher, who had to step into Barnard's part, needed a good deal of help, solid man though he was. But then somebody had to fill in for Flesher, and that was your friend Leonard Woulds, Roly, who proved not to know the lines which, as an understudy, he should have had cold. So it was a busy day.

"Busy for Morton W. Penfold, who had to tell the papers what had happened, and get the news on the Canadian Press wire, and generally turn a misfortune into some semblance of publicity. Busy for Felicity Larscombe, who showed herself a first-rate person as well as a first-rate actress; she undertook to keep an eye on Milady, so far as anyone could, because Milady was in a state. Busy also for Gwenda Lewis, who was a dull actress and silly about her dull husband, Jim Hailey; but Gwenda had been a nurse before she went on the stage, and she helped Felicity to keep Milady in trim to act that evening. Busy for old Frank Moore and Macgregor, who both spread calm and assurance through the company—you know how easily a company can be rattled—and lent courage where it was wanted.

"The consequence was that that night we played *Scaramouche* very well, to a capacity audience, and did excellent business until it was time for us to leave Vancouver. The only hitch, which both the papers mentioned humorously, was that when Scaramouche walked the tightrope, it looked as if Sir John had mischievously broken out of the hospital and taken the stage. But there was nothing anybody could do about that, though I did what I could by wearing my red mask.

"It seemed as though the public were determined to help us through our troubles, because we played to full houses all week. Whenever Milady made her first entrance, there was warm applause, and this was a change indeed, because usually Morton W. Penfold had to arrange for the local theatre manager to be in the house at that time to start the obligatory round when she came on. Indeed, by the end of the week, Penfold was able to circulate a funny story to the papers that Sir John had announced from his hospital bed that it was obvious that the most profitable thing a visiting star could do was to go to bed and send his understudy on in his place. Dangerous publicity, but it worked.

"So everything appeared to be in good order, except that we had to defer polishing up *The Lyons Mail,* which we had intended to put into the repertory instead of *The Corsican Brothers* for our return journey across Canada.

"Not everything was satisfactory, however, because the Sevenhowes, Charlton, and Woulds faction were making mischief. Not very serious mischief in the theatre, because Holroyd would not have put up with that, but personal mischief in the company was much more difficult to check. They tried sucking up to Gordon Barnard, who was now the leading man, telling him how much easier it was to act with him than with Sir John. Barnard wouldn't have any of that, because he was a decent fellow, and he knew his own shortcomings. One of these was that in *The Master* and *Scaramouche* we used a certain number of extras, and these inexperienced people tended to look wooden on the stage unless they were jollied, or harried, into more activity than they could generate by themselves; Sir John was an expert jollier and harrier—as I understand Irving also was—and he had his own ways of hissing remarks and encouragement to these inexperienced people that kept them up to the mark; Barnard couldn't manage it, because when he hissed the extras immediately froze in their places, and looked at him in terror. Just a question of personality, but there it was; he was a good actor, but a poor inspirer. When this happened, Charlton and Woulds laughed, sometimes so that the audience could see them, and Macgregor had to speak to them about it.

"They also made life hard for poor old C. Pengelly Spickernell, in ways that only actors understand; when they were on stage with him, they would contrive to be in his way when he had to make a move, and in a few seconds the whole stage picture was a little askew, and it looked as if it were his fault; also, in *Scaramouche*, where he played one of the Commedia dell' Arte figures, and wore a long, dragging cloak, one or other of them would contrive to be standing on the end of it when he had a move to make, pinning him to the spot; it was only necessary for them to do this two or three times to put him in terror lest it should happen every time, and he was a man with no ability to defend himself against such harassment.

"They were ugly to Gwenda Lewis, overrunning her very few cues, but Jim Hailey settled that by going to their dressing-room and talking it over with them in language he had learned when he had been in the Navy. Trivial things, but enough to make needless trouble, because a theatrical production is a mechanism of exquisitely calculated details. On tour it was useless to threaten them with dismissal, because they could not be replaced, and although there was a tariff of company fines for unprofessional conduct it was hard for Macgregor to catch them red-handed.

"Their great triumph had nothing to do with performance, but with the private life of the company. I fear this will embarrass you, Roly, but I think it has to be told. The great passion the Cantab felt for Audrey Sevenhowes was everybody's business; love and a cough cannot be hid, as the proverb says. I don't think Audrey was really an ill-disposed girl, but her temperament was that of a flirt of a special order; such girls used to be called cock-teasers; she liked to have somebody mad about her, without being obliged to do anything about it. She saw herself, I suppose, as lovely Audrey, who could not be blamed for the consequences of her fatal attraction. I am pretty sure she did not know what was going on, but Charlton and Woulds began a campaign to bring that affair to the boil; they filled the Cantab full of the notion that he must enjoy the favours of Miss Sevenhowes to the fullest—in the expression they used, he must 'tear off a branch' with Audrey—or lose all claim to manhood. This put the Cantab into a sad state of self-doubt, because he had never torn off a branch with anybody, and they assured him that he mustn't try to begin with the Sevenhowes, as he might expose himself as a novice, and become an object of ridicule. Might make a Horlicks of it, in fact. They bustled the poor boob into thinking that he must have a crash course in the arts of love, as a preparation for his great conquest; they would help him in this educational venture.

"It would have been nothing more than rather nasty joking and manipulation of a simpleton if they had kept their mouths shut, but of course that was not their way. I disliked them greatly at that time, but since then I have met many people of their kind, and I know them to be much more conceited and stupid than really cruel. They both fancied themselves as lady-killers, and such people are rarely worse than fools.

"They babbled all they were up to around the company; they chattered to Eric Foss, who was about their own age, but a different sort of chap; they let Eugene Fitzwarren in on their plan, because he looked wordly and villainous, and they were too stupid to know that he was a past president of the Anglican Stage Guild and a great worker on behalf of the Actors' Orphanage, and altogether a highly moral character. So very soon everybody in the company knew about it, and thought it a shame, but didn't know precisely what to do to stop the nonsense.

"It was agreed that there was no use talking to the Cantab, who wasn't inclined to take advice from anybody who could have given him advice worth having. It was also pretty widely felt that interfering with a young man's sexual initiation was rather an Old Aunty sort of thing to do, and that they had better let nature take its course. The Cantab must tear off a branch some time; even C. Pengelly Spickernell agreed to that; and if he was fool enough to be manipulated by a couple of cads, whose job was it to protect him?

"It became clear in the end that Mungo Fetch was elected to protect him, though only in a limited sense.—No, Roly, you can't possibly want to go to the loo again. You'd better sit down and hear this out.—The great worriers about the Cantab were Holroyd and Macgregor, and they were worrying on behalf of Sir John and Milady. Not that the Tresizes knew about the great plot to deprive the Cantab of his virginity; Sir John would have dealt with the matter summarily, but he was in hospital in Vancouver, and Milady was much bereft by his absence and telephoned to the hospital wherever we were. But Macgregor and Holroyd felt that this tasteless practical joke somehow reflected on those two, whom they admired wholeheartedly, and whose devotion to each other established a standard of sexual behaviour for the company that must be respected, if not fully maintained.

"Holroyd kept pointing out to Macgregor that the Cantab was in a special way a charge delivered over to Sir John by his Mum, and that it was therefore incumbent on the company as a whole—or the sane part of it, he said—to watch over the Cantab while Sir John and Milady were unable to do so. Macgregor agreed, and added Calvinist embroideries to the theme; he was no great friend to sex, and I think he held it against the Creator that the race could not be continued without some recourse to it; but he felt that such recourse should be infrequent, hallowed by church and law, and divorced as far as possible from pleasure. It seems odd, looking back, that nobody felt any concern about Audrey Sevenhowes; some people assumed that she was in on the joke, and the others were confident she could take care of herself.

"Charlton and Woulds laid their plan with gloating attention to detail. Charlton explained to the Cantab, and to any man who happened to be near, that women are particularly open to seduction in the week just preceding the onset of their menstrual period; during this time, he said, they simply ravened for intercourse. Furthermore, they had to be approached in the right way; nothing coarsely direct, no grabbing at the bosom or anything of that sort, but a psychologically determined application of a particular caress; this was a firm, but not rough, placing of the hand on the waist, on the right side, just below the ribs; the hand should be as warm as possible, and this could easily be achieved by keeping it in the trousers pocket for a few moments before the approach. This was supposed to impart special, irresistible warmth to the female liver; Liesl tells me it is a very old belief."

"I think Galen mentions it," said Liesl, "and like so much of Galen, it is just silly."

"Charlton considered himself an expert at detecting the menstrual state of women, and he had had his eye on Miss Sevenhowes; she would be ripe and ready to fall when we were in Moose Jaw, and therefore the last place in which the Cantab could achieve full manhood would be Medicine Hat. He approached Morton W. Penfold for information about the altars to Aphrodite in Medicine Hat, and was informed that, so far as the advance agent knew, they were few and of a Spartan simplicity. Penfold advised against the whole plan; if that was the kind of thing they wanted, they had better put it on ice till they got to Toronto. Anyhow he wanted no part of it. But Charlton and Woulds had no inclination to let their great plan rest until after Sir John had rejoined the company, for though they mocked him, they feared him.

"They played on the only discernible weakness in the strong character of Morton W. Penfold. His whole reputation, Charlton pointed out, rested on his known ability to supply anything, arrange anything, and do anything that a visiting theatrical company might want in Canada; here they were, asking simply for an address, and he couldn't supply it. They weren't asking him to take the Cantab to a bawdy-house, wait, and escort him home again; they just wanted to know where a bawdy-house might be found. Penfold was touched in his vanity. He made some inquiries among the locomotive crew, and returned with the address of a Mrs Quiller in Medicine Hat, who was known to have obliging nieces.

"We were playing a split week, of which Thursday, Friday, and Saturday were spent in Medicine Hat. On Thursday, with Charlton and Woulds at his elbow, the Cantab telephoned Mrs Quiller. She had no idea what he was talking about, and anyways she never did business over the phone. Might he drop in on Friday night? It all depended; was he one of them actors? Yes, he was. Well, if he come on Friday night she supposed she'd be t'home but she made no promises. Was he comin' alone? Yes, he would be alone.

"All day Friday the Cantab looked rather green, and Charlton and Woulds stuck to him like a couple of bridesmaids, giving any advice that happened to come into their heads. At half past five Holroyd sent for me in the theatre, and I found him in the tiny stage-manager's office, with Macgregor and Morton W. Penfold. 'I suppose you know what's on tonight?' said he. '*Scaramouche*, surely?' I said. 'Don't be funny with me, boy,' said Holroyd; 'you know what I mean.' 'Yes, I think I do,' said I. 'Then I want you to watch young Ingestree after the play, and follow him, and stay as close to him as you can without being seen, and don't leave him till he's back in his hotel.' 'I don't know how I'm going to do that—' I began, but Holroyd wasn't having it. 'Yes, you do,' he said; 'there's nothing green about you, and I want you to do this for the company; nothing is to happen to that boy, do you understand?' 'But he's going with the full intention of having something happen to him,' I said; 'you don't expect me to hold off the girls with a gun, do you?' 'I just want you to see that he doesn't get robbed, or beaten up, or anything worse than what he's going for,' said Holroyd. 'Oh, Nature, Nature, what an auld bitch ye are!' said Macgregor, who was taking all this very heavily.

"I thought I had better get out before I laughed in their faces; Holroyd and Macgregor were like a couple of old maids. But Morton W. Penfold knew what was what. 'Here's ten dollars,' he said; 'I hear it's the only visiting card Old Ma Quiller understands; tell her you're there to keep an eye on young Ingestree, but you mustn't be seen; in her business I suppose she gets used to queer requests and odd provisos.' I took it, and left them, and went off for a good laugh by myself. This was my first assignment as guardian angel.

"All things considered, everything went smoothly. After the play I left Macgregor to do some of my tidy-up work himself, and followed the Cantab after he had been given a back-slapping send-off by Charlton and Woulds. He didn't walk very fast, though it was a cold January night, and Medicine Hat is a cold town. After a while he turned in to an unremarkable-looking house, and after some inquiries at the door he vanished inside. I chatted for a few minutes with an old fellow in a tuque and mackinaw who was shovelling away an evening snowfall, then I knocked at the door myself.

"Mrs Quiller answered in person, and though she was not the first madam I had seen—now and then one of the sisterhood would appear in search of Charlie, who had a bad habit of forgetting to settle his bills—she was certainly the least remarkable. I am always amused when madams in plays and films appear as wonderful, salty characters, full of hard-won wisdom and overflowing, compassionate understanding. Damned old twisters, any I've ever seen. Mrs Quiller might have been any suburban housewife, with a dyed perm and bifocal specs. I asked if I could speak to her privately, and waggled the ten-spot, and followed her into her living-room. I explained what I had come for, and the necessity that I was not to be seen; I was just someone who had been sent by friends of Mr Ingestree to see that he got home safely. 'I getcha,' said Mrs Quiller; 'the way that guy carries on, I think he needs a guardeen.'

"I settled down in the kitchen with Mrs Quiller, and accepted a cup of tea and some soda crackers—her nightly snack, she explained—and we talked very comfortably about the theatre. After a while we were joined by the old snow-shoveller, who said nothing, and devoted himself to a stinking cigar. She was not a theatre-goer herself, Mrs Quiller said—too busy at night for that; but she liked a good fillum. The last one she seen was *Laugh, Clown, Laugh* with Lon Chaney in it, and this girl Loretta Young. Now there was a sweet fillum, but it give you a terrible idea of the troubles of people in show business, and did I think it was true to life? I said I thought it was as true as anything dared to be, but the trials of people in the theatre were so many and harrowing that the public would never believe them if they were shown as they really were. That touched the spot with Mrs Quiller, and we had a fine discussion about the surprises and vicissitudes life brought to just about everybody, which lasted some time.

"Then Mrs Quiller grew restless. 'I wonder what's happened to that friend of yours,' she said; 'he's takin' an awful long time.' I wondered, too, but I thought it better not to make any guesses. It was not long till another woman came into the kitchen; I would have judged her to be in her early hard-living thirties, and she had never been a beauty; she had an unbecoming Japanese kimono clutched around her, and her feet were in slippers to which remnants of Caribou still clung. She looked at me with suspicion. 'It's okay,' said Mrs Quiller, 'this fella's the guardeen. Anything wrong, Lil?' 'Jeez, I never seen such a guy,' said Lil; 'nothin' doing *yet*. He just lays there with the droops, laughin', and talkin'. I never heard such a guy. He keeps sayin' it's all so ridiculous, and would I believe he'd once been a member of some Marlowe Society or something. What are they, anyway? A bunch o' queers? But anyways I'm sick of it. He's ruining my self-confidence. Is Pauline in yet? Maybe she could do something with him.'

"Mrs Quiller obviously had great qualities of generalship. She turned to me. 'Unless you got any suggestions, I'm goin' to give him the bum's rush,' she said. 'When he come in I thought, his heart's not in it. What do you say?' I said I thought she had summed up the situation perfectly. 'Then you go back up there, Lil, and tell him to come back when he feels better,' said Mrs Quiller. 'Don't shame him none, but get rid of him. And no refund, you understand.'

"So that was how it was. Shortly afterward I crept from Mrs Quiller's back door, and followed the desponding Cantab back to his hotel. I don't know what he told Charlton and Woulds, but they hadn't much to say to him from then on. The odd thing was that Audrey Sevenhowes was quite nice to him for the rest of the tour. Not in a teasing way—or with as little tease as she could manage—but just friendly. A curious story, but not uncommon, would you say, gentlemen?"

"I say it's time we all had a drink, and dinner," said Liesl. She took the arm of the silent Ingestree and sat him at the table beside herself, and we were all especially pleasant to him, except Magnus who, having trampled his old enemy into the dirt, seemed a happier man and, in some strange way, cleansed. It was as if he were a scorpion, which had discharged its venom, and was frisky and playful in consequence. I taxed him with it as we left the dinner table.

"How could you," I said. "Ingestree is a harmless creature, surely? He has done some good work. Many people would call him a distinguished man, and a very nice fellow."

Magnus patted my arm and laughed. It was a low laugh, and a queer one. Merlin's laugh, if ever I heard it.

(7)

Eisengrim was altogether in high spirits, and showed no fatigue from his afternoon's talking. He pretended to be solicitous about the rest of us, however, and particularly about Lind and Kinghovn. Did they really wish to continue with his narrative? Did they truly think what he had to say offered any helpful subtext to the film about Robert-Houdin? Indeed, as the film was now complete, of what possible use could a subtext be?

"Of the utmost possible use when next I make a film," said Jurgen Lind. "These divergences between the acceptable romance of life and the clumsily fashioned, disproportioned reality are part of my stock-in-trade. Here you have it, in your tale of Sir John's tour of Canada; he took highly burnished romance to a people whose life was lived on a different plateau, and the discomforts of his own life and the lives of his troupe were on other levels. How reconcile the three?"

"Light," said Kinghovn. "You do it with light. The romance of the plays is theatre-light; the different romance of the company is the queer train-light Magnus has described; think what could be done, with that flashing strobe-light effect you get when a train passes another and everything seems to flicker and lose substance. And the light of the Canadians would be that hard, bright light you find in northern lands. Leave it to me to handle all three lights in such a way that they are a variation on the theme of light, instead of just three kinds of light, and I'll do the trick for you, Jurgen."

"I doubt if you can do it simply in terms of appearances," said Lind.

"I didn't say you could. But you certainly can't do it without a careful attention to appearances, or you'll have no romance of any kind. Remember what Magnus says: without attention to detail you will have no illusion, and illusion's what you're aiming at, isn't it?"

"I had rather thought I was aiming at truth, or some tiny corner of it," said Lind.

"Truth!" said Kinghovn. "What kind of talk is that for a sane man? What truth have we been getting all afternoon? I don't suppose Magnus thinks he's been telling us the truth. He's giving us a mass of detail, and I don't doubt that every word he says is true in itself, but to call that truth is ridiculous even for a philosopher of film like you, Jurgen. What's he been doing to poor old Roly? He's cast him as the clown of the show—mother's boy, pompous

Varsity ass, snob, and sexual non-starter—and I'm sure it's all true, but what has it to do with our Roly? The man you and I work with and lean on? The thoroughly capable administrator, literary man, and smoother-of-the-way? Eh?"

"Thank you for these few kind words, Harry," said Ingestree. "You save me the embarrassment of saying them myself. Don't suppose I bear any malice. Indeed, if I may make a claim for my admittedly imperfect character, it is that I have never been a malicious man. I accept what Magnus says. He has described me as I no doubt appeared to him. And I haven't scrupled to let you know that so far as I was concerned he was an obnoxious little squirt and climber. That's how I would describe him if I were writing my autobiography, which I may do, one of these days. But what's an autobiography? Surely it's a romance of which one is oneself the hero. Otherwise why write the thing? Perhaps you give yourself a rather shopworn character, like Rousseau, or H.G. Wells, and it's just another way of making yourself interesting. But Mungo Fetch and the Cantab belong to the drama of the past; it's forty years since they trod the boards. We're two different people now. Magnus is a great illusionist and, as I have said time after time, a great actor: I'm what you so generously described, Harry. So let's not fuss about it."

Magnus was not satisfied. "You don't believe, then," said he, "that a man is the sum and total of all his actions, from birth to death? That's what Dunny believes, and he's our Sorgenfrei expert on metaphysics. I think that's what I believe, too. Squirt and climber; not a bad summing-up of whatever you were able to understand of me when first we met, Roly. I'm prepared to stand by it, and when your autobiography comes out I shall look for myself in the Index under S and C: 'Squirts I have known, Mungo Fetch', and 'Climbers I have encountered, Fetch, M.' We must all play as cast, as my contract with Sir John put it. As for truth, I suppose we have to be content with the constant revisions of history. Though there is the odd inescapable fact, and I still have one or two of those to impart, if you want me to go on."

They wanted him to go on. The after-dinner cognac was on the table and I made it my job to see that everyone had enough. After all,

I was paying my share of the costs, and I might as well cast myself as host, so far as lay in my power. God knows, that piece of casting would be undisputed when the bill was presented.

"As we made the return journey across Canada, a change took place in the spirit of the company," said Magnus; "going West it was all adventure and new experiences, and the country embraced us; as soon as we turned round at Vancouver it was going home, and much that was Canadian was unfavourably compared with the nests in the suburbs of London toward which many of the company were yearning. The Haileys talked even more about their son, and their grave worry that if they didn't get him into a better school he would grow up handicapped by an undesirable accent. Charlton and Woulds were hankering for restaurants better than the places, most of them run by Chinese, we found in the West. Grover Paskin and Frank Moore talked learnedly of great pubs they knew, and of the foreign fizziness of Canadian beer. Audrey Sevenhowes, having squeezed the Cantab, threw him away and devoted herself seriously to subduing Eric Foss. During our journey West we had seen the dramatic shortening of the days which has such ominous beauty in northern countries, and which I loved; now we saw the daylight lengthen, and it seemed to be part of our homeward journey; we had gone into the darkness and now we were heading back toward the light, and every night, as we went into those queer little stage doors, the naked bulb that shone above them seemed less needful.

"The foreignness of Canada seemed to abate a little at every sunset, but it was not wholly gone. When we played Regina for a week there was one memorable night when five Blackfoot Indian chiefs, asserting their right as tribal brothers of Sir John, sat as his guests in the left-hand stage box: it was rum, I can tell you, playing *Scaramouche* with those motionless figures, all of them in blankets, watching everything with unwinking, jetty black eyes. What did they make of it? God knows. Or perhaps Sir John had some inkling, because Morton W. Penfold arranged that he should meet them in an interval, when there was an exchange of gifts, and pictures were taken. But I doubt if the French Revolution figured largely in their scheme of things. Milady said they loved oratory, and perhaps they were proud of Soksi-Poyina as he harangued the aristocrats so eloquently.

"Sir John had rejoined us by that time, and it was a shock when he appeared in our midst, for his hair had turned almost entirely grey during his time in the hospital. Perhaps he had touched it up before then, and the dye had run its course; he never attempted to return it to its original dark brown, and although the grey became him, he looked much older, and in private life he was slower and wearier. Not so on the stage. There he was as graceful and light-footed as ever, but there was something macabre about his youthfulness, in my eyes, at least. With his return the feeling of the company changed; we had supported Gordon Barnard with all our hearts, but now we felt that the ruler had returned to his kingdom; the lamp of romance burned with a different flame—a return, perhaps, to gaslight, after some effective but comparatively charmless electricity.

"I had a feeling, too, that the critics changed their attitude toward us on the homeward journey, and it was particularly evident in Toronto. The important four were in their seats, as usual: the man who looked like Edward VII from *Saturday Night;* the stout little man, rumoured to be a Theosophist, from the *Globe;* the smiling little fellow in pince-nez from the *Telegram;* and the ravaged Norseman who wrote incomprehensible rhapsodies for the *Star.* They were friendly (except Edward VII, who was jocose about Milady), but they would persist in remembering Irving (whether they had ever actually seen him, or not), and that bothered the younger actors. Bothered Morton W. Penfold, too, who mumbled to Holroyd that perhaps the old man would be wise to think about retirement.

"The audiences came in sufficient numbers, and were warm in their applause, particularly when we played *The Lyons Mail.* It was another of the dual roles in which Sir John delighted, and so did I, because it gave me a new chance to double. If Roly had been looking for it, he would have found the seed of his Jekyll and Hyde play here, for it was a play in which, as the good Leserques, Sir John was all nobility and candour, and then, seconds later, lurched on the stage as the drunken murderer Dubosc, chewing a straw and playing with a knobbed cudgel. There was one moment in that play that never failed to chill me: it was when Dubosc had killed the driver of the mail coach, and leaned over the body, rifling the pockets; as he did it, Sir John whistled the 'Marseillaise' through his teeth, not loudly, but with such terrible high spirits that it summoned up, in a few seconds, a world of heartless, demonic criminality. But even I, enchanted as I was, could understand that this sort of thing, in this form, could not last long on the stage that Noel Coward had made his own. It was acting of a high order, but it was out of time. It still had magic here in Canada, not because the people were unsophisticated (on the whole they were as acute as English audiences in the provinces) but because, in a way I cannot explain, it was speaking to a core of loneliness and deprivation in these Canadians of which they were only faintly aware. I think it was loneliness, not just for England, because so many of these people on the prairies were not of English origin, but for some faraway and long-lost Europe. The Canadians knew themselves to be strangers in their own land, without being at home anywhere else.

"So, night by night, Canada relinquished its hold on us, and day by day we became weary, not perhaps of one another, but of our colleagues' unvarying heavy overcoats and too familiar pieces of luggage; what had been the romance of long hops going West—striking the set, seeing the trucks loaded at the theatre and unloaded onto the train, climbing aboard dead tired at three o'clock in the morning, and finding berths in the dimmed, heavily curtained sleeping-car— grew to be tedious. Another kind of excitement, the excitement of going home, possessed us, and although we were much too professional a company to get out of hand, we played with a special gloss during our final two weeks in Montreal. Then aboard ship, a farewell telegram to Sir John and Milady from Mr Mackenzie King (who seemed to be a great friend of the theatre, though outwardly a most untheatrical man), and off to England by the first sailing after the ice was out of the harbour.

"I had changed substantially during the tour. I was learning to dress like Sir John, which was eccentric enough in a young man, but at least not vulgar in style. I was beginning to speak like him, and as is common with beginners, I was overdoing it. I was losing, ever so little, my strong sense that every man's hand was against me, and my hand against every man. I had encountered my native land again, and was reconciled to all of it except Deptford. We passed through Deptford during the latter part of our tour, on a hop between Windsor and London: I found out from the conductor of the train that we would stop to take on water for the engine there, and that the pause would be short, but sufficient for my purpose; as we chugged past the gravel pit beside the railway line I was poised on the steps at the back of the train, and as we pulled in to the station, so small and so familiar, I swung down onto the platform and surveyed all that was to be seen of the village.

"I could look down most of the length of our main street. I recognized a few buildings and saw the spires of the five churches— Baptist, Methodist, Presbyterian, Anglican, and Catholic—among the leafless trees. Solemnly, I spat. Then I went behind the train to the siding where, so many years ago, Willard had imprisoned me in Abdullah, and there I spat again. Spitting is not a ceremonious action, but I crowded it with loathing, and when I climbed back on the train I felt immeasurably better. I had not settled any scores, or altered my feelings, but I had done something of importance. Nobody knew it, but Paul Dempster had visited his childhood home. I have never returned.

"Back to England, and another long period of hand-to-mouth life for me. Sir John wanted a rest, and Milady had the long trial of waiting for her eyes to be ready for an operation—they called it 'ripening' in cases of cataracts then—and the operation itself, which was successful in that it made it possible for her to see with thick, disfiguring lenses that were a humiliation for a woman who still thought of herself as a leading actress. Macgregor decided to retire, which was reasonable but made a gap in the organization on which Sir John depended. Holroyd was a thoroughgoing pro, and could get a good job anywhere, and I think he saw farther than either Sir John or Milady, because he went to Stratford-on-Avon and stayed at the Memorial Theatre until he too retired. Nothing came of the Jekyll and Hyde play, though I know the Tresizes tinkered with the scenario for years, as an amusement. But they were comfortably off for money—rich, by some standards—and they could settle down happily in their suburban home, which had a big garden, and amuse themselves with the antiques that gave them so much delight. I visited them there often, because they kept a kind interest in me, and helped me as much as they were able. But their influence in the theatre was not great; indeed, a recommendation from them took on a queer look in the hands of a young man, because to so many of the important employers of actors in the London theatre in the mid-thirties they belonged to a remote past.

"Indeed, they never appeared at the head of a company again. Sir John had one splendid appearance in a play by a writer who had been a great figure in the theatre before and just after the First World War, but his time, too, had passed; his play suffered greatly from his own illness and some justifiable but prolonged caprice on the part of the star players. Sir John was very special in that play, and he was given fine notices by the press, but nothing could conceal the fact that he was not the undoubted star, but 'distinguished support in a role which could not have been realized with the same certainty of touch and golden splendour of personality by any other actor of our time'—so James Agate said, and everybody agreed.

"There was one very bad day toward the end of his life which, I know, opened the way for his death. In the autumn of 1937, when people were thinking of more immediately pressing things, some theatre people were thinking that the centenary of the birth of Henry Irving should not pass unnoticed. They arranged an all-star matinee, in which tribute to the great actor should be paid, and as many as possible of the great theatre folk of the day should appear in scenes selected from the famous plays of his repertoire. It should be given at his old theatre, the Lyceum, as near as possible to his birthday, which was February 6 in the following year.

"Have you ever had anything to do with such an affair? The idea is so splendid, the sentiment so admirable, that it is disillusioning to discover what a weight of tedious and seemingly unnecessary diplomacy must go into its arrangement. Getting the stars to say with certainty that they will appear is only the beginning of it; marshalling the necessary stage-settings, arranging rehearsals, and publicizing the performance, without ruinously disproportionate expense, is the bulk of the work, and I understand that an excellent committee did it with exemplary patience. But inevitably there were muddles, and in the first enthusiasm many more people were asked to appear than could possibly have been crowded on any stage, even if the matinee had been allowed to go on for six or seven hours.

"Quite reasonably, one of the first people to be asked for his services was Sir John, because he was the last actor of first-rate importance still living who had been trained under Irving. He agreed that he would be present, but then, prompted by God knows what evil spirit of vanity, he began to make conditions: he would appear, and he would speak a tribute to Irving if the Poet Laureate would write one. The committee demurred, and the Poet Laureate was not approached. So Sir John, with the bit between his teeth, approached the Poet Laureate himself, and the Poet Laureate said he would have to think about it. He thought for six weeks, and then, in response to another letter from Sir John, said he didn't see his way clear to doing it.

"Sir John communicated this news to the committee, who had meanwhile gone on with other plans, and they did not reply because, I suppose, they were up to their eyes in complicated arrangements which they had to carry through in the spare time of their busy lives. Sir John, meanwhile, urged an ancient poet of his acquaintance, who had been a very minor figure in the literary world before the First World War, to write the poetic tribute. The ancient poet, whose name was Urban Frawley, thought a villanelle would do nicely. Sir John thought something more stately was called for; his passion for playing the literary Meddlesome Mattie was aroused, and he and the ancient poet had many a happy hour, wrangling about the form the tribute should take. There was also the great question about what Sir John should wear, when delivering it. He finally decided on some robes he had worn not less than twenty-five years earlier, in a play by Maeterlinck; like everything else in his wardrobe it had been carefully stored, and when Holroyd had been summoned from Stratford to find it, it was in good condition, and needed only pressing and some loving care to make it very handsome. This valet work became my job, and in all I made three journeys to Richmond, where the Tresizes lived, to attend to it. Everything seemed to be going splendidly, and only I worried about the fact that nothing had been heard from the committee for a long time.

"There was less than a week to go before the matinee when at last I persuaded Sir John that something must be done to make sure that he had been included in the programme. This was tactless, and he gave me a polite dressing-down for supposing that when Irving was being honoured, his colleagues would be so remiss as to forget Irving's unquestioned successor. I was not so confident, because since the tour I had mingled a little with theatre people, and had learned that there were other pretenders to Irving's crown, and that Sir Johnston Forbes-Robertson and Sir Frank Benson had been spoken of in this regard, and Benson was still living. I took my scolding meekly, and went right on urging him not to leave things to chance. So, rather in the spirit of the Master of Ballantrae giving orders to the pirates, he telephoned the secretary of the committee, and talked, not to him, but to his anonymous assistant.

"Sir John told him he was calling simply to say that he would be on hand for the matinee, as he had been invited to do some months before; that he would declaim the tribute to Irving which had been specially written by that favoured child of the Muses, Urban Frawley; that he would not arrive at the theatre until half past four, and he would arrive in costume, as he knew the backstage resources of the theatre would be crowded, and nothing was further from his mind than to create any difficulty by requiring the star dressing-room. All of this was delivered in the jocular but imperative mode that was his rehearsal speciality, with much 'eh' and 'quonk' to make it sound friendly. The secretary's secretary apparently gave satisfactory replies, because when Sir John had finished his call he looked at me slyly, as if I were a silly lad who didn't understand how such things were done.

"It was agreed that I should drive him to the theatre, because he might want assistance in arranging his robes, and although he had an old and trusted chauffeur, the man had no skill as a dresser. So, with lots of time to spare, I helped him into the back seat in his heavy outfit of velvet and fur, climbed into the driver's place, and off we went. It was one of those extremely class-conscious old limousines; Sir John, in the back, sat on fine whipcord, and I, in front, sat on leather that was as cold as death; we were separated by a heavy glass partition, but from time to time he spoke to me through the speaking tube, and his mood was triumphal.

"Dear old man! He was going to pay tribute to Irving, and there was nobody else in the world who could do it with a better right, or more reverent affection. It was a glory-day for him, and I was anxious that nothing should go wrong.

"As it did, of course. We pulled up at the stage door of the Lyceum, and I went in and told the attendant that Sir John had arrived. He wasn't one of your proper old stage doormen, but a young fellow who took himself very seriously, and had a sheaf of papers naming the people he was authorized to admit. No Sir John Tresize was on the list. He showed it to me, in support of his downright refusal. I protested. He stuck his head out of the door and looked at our limousine, and made off through the passage that led to the stage, and I stuck close to him. He approached an elegant figure whom I knew to be one of the most eminent of the younger actor-knights and hissed 'There's an old geezer outside dressed as Nero who says he's to appear; will you speak to him, sir?' I intervened; 'It's Sir John Tresize,' I said, 'and it was arranged that he was to speak an Epilogue—a tribute to Irving.' The eminent actor-knight went rather pale under his make-up (he was rigged out as Hamlet) and asked for details, which I supplied. The eminent actor-knight cursed with brilliant invention for a few seconds, and beckoned me to the corridor. I went, but not before I was able to identify the sounds that were coming from the stage as a passage from *The Lyons Mail;* the rhythm, the tune of what I heard was all wrong, too colloquial, too matter-of-fact.

"We made our way back to the stage door, and the eminent actor-knight darted across the pavement, leapt into the limousine beside Sir John, and began to talk to him urgently. I would have given a great deal to hear what was said, but I could only catch scraps of it from where I sat in the driver's seat. 'Dreadful state of confusion … can't imagine what the organization of such an affair entails … would not for the world have slighted so great a man of the theatre and the most eminent successor of Irving ... but when the proposal to the Poet Laureate fell through all communication had seemed to stop ... nothing further had been heard ... no, there had been no message during the past week or something would certainly have been done to alter the program ... but as things stand ... greatest reluctance ... beg indulgence ... express deepest personal regret but as you know I do not stand alone and cannot act on personal authority so late in the afternoon....'

"A great deal of this; the eminent actor-knight was sweating and I could see in the rear-vision mirror that his distress was real, and his determination to stick to his guns was equally real. They were a notable study. You could do wonders with them, Harry: the young actor so vivid, the old one so silvery in the splendour of his distinction; both giving the quality of art to a common human blunder. Sir John's face was grave, but at last he reached out and patted the knee in the Hamlet tights and said, 'I won't say I understand, because I don't; still, nothing to be done now, eh? Damned embarrassing for us both, quonk? But I think I may say a little more than just embarrassing for me.' Then Hamlet, delighted to have been let off the hook, smiled the smile of spiritual radiance for which he was famous, and did an inspired thing: he took the hand Sir John extended to him and raised it to his lips. It seemed under the circumstances precisely the right thing to do.

"Then I drove Sir John back to Richmond, and it was a slow journey, I can tell you. I hardly dared to look in the mirror, but I did twice, and both times tears were running down the old man's face. When we arrived I helped him inside and he leaned very heavily on my arm. I couldn't bear to hang around and hear what he said to Milady. Nor would they have wanted me.

"So that was how you knifed him, Roly. Don't protest. When the stage doorman showed me that list of people who were included in the performance, it was signed by you, on behalf of the eminent actor-knight. You simply didn't let that telephone message go any farther. It's a pity you couldn't have been on hand to see the scene in the limousine."

Magnus said no more, and nobody else seemed anxious to break the silence. Ingestree appeared to be thinking, and at last it was he who spoke.

"I don't see any reason now for denying what you've said. I think you have coloured it absurdly, but your facts are right. It's true I devilled for the committee about that Irving matinee; I was just getting myself established in the theatre in a serious way and it was a great opportunity for me. All the stars who formed the committee heaped work on me, and that was as it should be. I don't complain. But if you think Sir John Tresize was the only swollen ego I had to deal with, you'd better think again; I had months of tiresome negotiating to do, and because no money was changing hands I had to treat over a hundred people as if they were all stars.

"Yes, I got the call from Tresize, and it came just at the time when I was hardest pressed. Yes, I did drop it, because by that time I had been given a programme for that awful afternoon that we had to stick to or else disturb I can't think how many careful arrangements. You saw one man disappointed; I saw at least twenty. All my life I've had to arrange things, because I'm that uncommon creature, an artist with a good head for administration. One of the lessons I've learned is to give no ground to compassion, because the minute you do that a dozen people descend upon you who treat compassion as weakness, and drive you off your course without the slightest regard for what happens to you. You've told us that you apprenticed yourself to an egoism, Magnus, and so you did, and you've learned the egoism-game splendidly; but in my life I've had to learn how to deal with people like you without becoming your slave, and that's what I've done. I'm sorry if old Tresize felt badly, but on the basis of what you've told us I think everybody else here will admit that it was nobody's fault but his own."

"I don't think I'm ready to admit that," said Lind. "There is a hole in your excellent story: you didn't tell your superior about the telephone call. Surely he was the man to make final decisions?"

"There were innumerable decisions to be made. If you've ever had any experience of an all-star matinee you can guess how many. During the last week everybody was happy if a decision could be made that would stick. I don't remember the details very clearly. I acted for what seemed the best."

"Without any recollection of being told how to carry a chair, or that unfortunate reference to your father's shop, or the disappointment about Jekyll-and-Hyde in masks and meem?" said Magnus.

"What do you suppose I am? You can't really imagine I would take revenge for petty things of that sort."

"Oh yes; I can imagine it without the least difficulty."

"You're ungenerous."

"Life has made me aware of how far mean minds rely on generosity in others."

"You've always disliked me."

"You didn't like the old man."

"No. I didn't."

"Well, in my judgement at least, you killed him."

"Did I? Something had to kill him, I suppose. Something kills everybody. And when you say something you often mean somebody. Eventually something or somebody will kill us all. You're not going to back me into a corner that way."

"No, I don't think you can quite attribute Sir John's death to Roly," said Lind. "But a not very widely understood or recognized element in life—I mean the jealousy youth feels for age—played a part in it. Have you been harbouring ill-will toward Roly all these years because of this incident? Because I really think that what Sir John was played a large part in the way he died, as is usually the case."

"Very well," said Magnus; "I'll reconsider the matter. After all, it doesn't really signify whether I think Roly killed him, or not. But Sir John and Milady were the first two people in my life I really loved, and the list isn't a long one. After the matinee Sir John wasn't himself; in a few weeks he had flu, which turned to pneumonia, and he didn't last long. I went to Richmond every day, and there was one dreadful afternoon toward the end when I went into the room where Milady was sitting; when she heard my footstep she said, 'Is that you, Jack?' and I knew she wasn't going to live long, either.

"She was wandering, of course, and as I have told you I had learned so much from Sir John that I even walked like him; it was eerie and desolating to be mistaken for him by the person who knew him best. Roly says I ate him. Rubbish! But I had done something that I don't pretend to explain, and when Milady thought he was well again, and walking as he had not walked for a year, I couldn't speak to her, or say who I was, so I crept away and came back later, making it very clear that it was Mungo Fetch who had come, and would come as long as he was wanted.

"He died, and at that time everybody was deeply concerned about the war that was so near at hand, and there were very few people at the funeral. Not Milady; she wasn't well enough to go. But Agate was there, the only time I ever saw him. And a handful of relatives were there, and I noticed them looking at me with unfriendly, sidelong glances. Then it broke on me that they thought I must be some sort of ghost from the past, and very probably an illegitimate son. I didn't approach them, because I was sure that nothing would ever make it clear to them that I was indeed a ghost, and an illegitimate son, but in a sense they would never understand.

"Milady died a few weeks later, and there were even fewer at her funeral; Macgregor and Holroyd were there, and as I stood with them nobody bothered to look twice at me. Odd: it was not until they died that I learned they were both much older than I had supposed.

"The day after we buried Milady I left England; I had wanted to do so for some time, but I didn't want to go so long as there was a chance that I could do anything for her. There was a war coming, and I had no stomach for war; the circumstances of my life had not inclined me toward patriotism. There was nothing for me to do in England. I had never gained a foothold on the stage because my abilities as an actor were not of the fashionable kind, and I had not been able to do any better with magic. I kept bread in my mouth by taking odd jobs as a magician; at Christmas I gave shows for children in the toy department of one of the big shops, but the work was hateful to me. Children are a miserable audience for magic; everybody thinks they are fond of marvels, but they are generally literal-minded little toughs who want to know how everything is done; they have not yet attained to the sophistication that takes pleasure in being deceived. The very small ones aren't so bad, but they are in a state of life where a rabbit might just as well appear out of a hat as from anywhere else; what really interests them is the rabbit. For a man of my capacities, working for children was degrading; you might just as well confront them with Menuhin playing 'Pop Goes the Weasel'. But I drew streams of half-crowns from tiny noses, and wrapped up turtles that changed into boxes of sweets in order to collect my weekly wage. Now and then I took a private engagement, but the people who employed me weren't serious about magic. It sounds odd, but I can't put it any other way; I was wasted on them and my new egoism was galled by the humiliation of the work.

"I had to live, and I understood clocks. Here again I was at a disadvantage because I had no certificate of qualification, and anyhow ordinary cleaning and regulating of wrist-watches and mediocre mantel clocks bored me. But I hung around the clock exhibition in the Victoria and Albert Museum, and worked my way into the private room of the curator of that gallery in order to ask questions, and it was not long before I had a rather irregular job there. It is never easy to find people who can be trusted with fine old pieces, because it calls for a kind of sympathy that isn't directly hitched to mechanical knowledge.

"With those old clocks you need to know not only how they work, but why they are built as they are. Every piece is individual, and something of the temperament of the maker is built into them, so the real task is to discern whatever you can of the maker's temperament and work within it, if you hope to humour his clock and persuade it to come to life again.

"In the States and Canada they talk about 'fixing' clocks; it's a bad word, because you can't just fix a clock if you hope to bring it to life. I was a reanimator of clocks, and I was particularly good at the *sonnerie*—you know, the bells and striking apparatus—which is especially hard to humour into renewed life. You've all heard old clocks that strike as if they were being managed by very old, arthritic gnomes; the notes tumble along irregularly, without any of the certainty and dignity you want from a true chime. It's a tricky thing to restore dignity to a clock that has been neglected or misused or that simply has grown old. I could do that, because I understood time.

"I mean my own time, as well as the clock's. So many workmen think in terms of their own time, on which they put a value. They will tell you it's no good monkeying with an old timepiece because the cost of the labour would run too close to the value of the clock, even when it was restored. I never cared how long a job took, and I didn't charge for my work by the hour; not because I put no value on my time but because I found that such an attitude led to hurried work, which is fatal to humouring clocks. I don't suppose I was paid as much as I could have demanded if I had charged by the hour, but I made myself invaluable, and in the end that has its price. I had a knack for the work, part of which was the understanding I acquired of old metal (which mustn't be treated as if it were modern metal), and part of which was the boundless patience and the contempt for time I had gained sitting inside Abdullah, when time had no significance.

"I suppose the greatest advantage I have had over other people who have wanted to do what I can do is that I really had no education at all, and am free of the illusions and commonplace values that education brings. I don't speak against education; for most people it is a necessity; but if you're going to be a genius you should try either to avoid education entirely, or else work hard to get rid of any you've been given. Education is for commonplace people and it fortifies their commonplaceness. Makes them useful, of course, in an ordinary sort of way.

"So I became an expert on old clocks, and I know a great many of the finest chamber clocks, and lantern clocks, and astronomical and equation clocks in the finest collections in the world, because I have rebuilt them, and tinkered them, and put infinitesimal new pieces into them (but always fashioned in old metal, or it would be cheating), and brought their chimes back to their original pride, and while I was doing that work I was as anonymous as I had been when I was inside Abdullah. I was a back-room expert who worked on clocks which the Museum undertook, as a special favour, to examine and put in order if it could be done. And when I had become invaluable I had no trouble in getting a very good letter of recommendation, to anybody whom it might concern, from the curator, who was a well-known man in his field.

"With that I set off for Switzerland, because I knew that there ought to be a job for a good clock-man there, and I was certain that when the war came Switzerland would be neutral, though probably not comfortable. I was right; there were shortages, endless problems about spies who wouldn't play their game according to the rules, bombings that were explained as accidental and perhaps were, and the uneasiness rising toward hysteria of being in the middle of a continent at war when other nations use your neutrality on the one hand, and hate you for it on the other. We were lucky to have Henri Guisan to keep us in order.

"I say 'we', though I did not become a Swiss and have never done so; theirs is not an easy club to join. I was Jules LeGrand, and a Canadian, and although that was sometimes complicated I managed to make it work.

"I presented my letter at the biggest watch and clock factories, and although I was pleasantly received I could not get a job, because I was not a Swiss, and at that time there were many foreigners who wanted jobs in important industries, and it was probable that some of them were spies. If I were going to place a spy, I would get a man who could pass for a native, and equip him with unexceptionable papers to show that he was a native; but when people are afraid of spies they do not think rationally. Still, after some patient application I wrangled an interview at the Musée d'Art et d'Histoire in Geneva, and after waiting a while Jules LeGrand found himself once more in the back room of a museum. It was there that one of the great strokes of luck in my life occurred, and most uncharacteristically it came through an act of kindness I had undertaken. There must be a soft side to my nature, and perhaps I should have trusted it more than I have done.

"I was living in a pension, the proprietor of which had a small daughter. The daughter had got herself into deep trouble because she had broken her father's walking stick, and as the stick had been a possession of her grandfather it had something of the character of an heirloom. It was no ordinary walking-stick, but one of those joke sticks that fashionable young men used to carry—a fine Malacca cane, but with a knob on the top that did a trick. The knob of this particular specimen was of ivory, carved prettily like the head of a monkey; but when you pressed a button in its neck the monkey opened its mouth, stuck out a red tongue, and rolled its blue eyes up to heaven. The child had been warned not to play with grandfather's stick, and had predictably done so, and jammed it so that the monkey was frozen in an expression of idiocy, its tongue half out and its eyes half raised.

"The family made a great to-do, and little Rosalie was lectured and hectored and deprived of her allowance for an indefinite period, and the tragedy of the stick was brought up at every meal; everybody at the pension had ideas either about child-rearing or the mending of the stick and I became thoroughly sick of hearing about it, though not as sick as poor Rosalie, who was a nice kid, and felt like a criminal. So I offered to take it to my workroom at the Musée and do what I could. Mending old toys could not be very different from mending old clocks, and Rosalie was growing pale, so clearly something must be done. The family had tried a few watch-repair people, but none of them wanted to be bothered with what looked like a troublesome job; it is astonishing that in a place like Geneva, which numbers watch mechanics in the thousands, there should be so few who are prepared to tackle anything old. Something new delights them, but what is old seems to clog their works. I suppose it is a matter of sympathetic approach, which was my chief stock-in-trade as a reanimator of old timepieces.

"The monkey was not really difficult, but he took time. Releasing the silver collar that kept the head in position without destroying it; removing the ivory knob without damage; penetrating the innards of the knob in such a way as to discover its secrets without wrecking them: these were troublesome tasks, but what someone has made, someone else can dismantle and make again. It proved to be a matter of an escapement device that needed replacing, and that meant making a tiny part on one of my tiny lathes from metal that would work well, but not too aggressively, with the old metal in the monkey's works. Simple, when you know how and are prepared to take several hours to do it; not simple if you are in a hurry to finish. So I did it, and restored the stick to its owner with a flowery speech in which I begged forgiveness for Rosalie, and Rosalie thought I was a marvellous man (in which she was quite correct) and a very nice man (in which I fear she was mistaken).

"The significant detail is that one evening after the museum's working day was done I was busy with the walking-stick when the curator of my department walked through the passage outside the small workshop, saw my light, and came in, like a good Swiss, to turn it off. He asked what I was doing, and when I explained he showed some interest. It was a year later that he sent for me and asked if I knew much about mechanical toys; I said I didn't, but that it would be odd if a toy were more complex than a clock. Then he said, 'Have you ever heard of Jeremias Naegeli?' and I hadn't. 'Well,' said he, 'Jeremias Naegeli is very old, very rich, and very much accustomed to having his own way. He has retired, except for retaining the chairmanship of the board of So-and-So'—and he mentioned the name of one of the biggest clock, watch, and optical equipment manufacturers in Switzerland—'and he has collected a great number of mechanical toys, all of them old and some of them unique. He wants a man to put them in order. Would you be interested in a job like that?'

"I said, 'If Jeremias Naegeli commands several thousand expert technicians, why would he want me?' 'Because his people are expected to keep on the job during wartime,' said my boss; 'it would not look well if he took a first-rate man for what might appear to be a frivolous job. He is old and he doesn't want to wait until the war is over. But if he borrows you from the museum, and you are a foreigner not engaged in war production, it's a different thing, do you understand?' I understood, and in a couple of weeks I was on my way to St Gallen to be looked over by the imperious Jeremias Naegeli.

"It proved that he lived at some distance from St Gallen on his estate in the mountains, and a driver was sent to take me there. That was my first sight of Sorgenfrei. As you gentlemen know, it is an impressive sight, but try to imagine how impressive it was to me, who had never been in a rich house before, to say nothing of such a gingerbread castle as that. I was frightened out of my wits. As soon as I arrived I was taken by a secretary to the great man's private room, which was called his study, but was really a huge library, dark, hot, stuffy, and smelling of leather furniture, expensive cigars, and rich man's farts. It was this expensive stench that destroyed the last of my confidence, because it was as if I had entered the den of some fearsome old animal, which was precisely what Jeremias Naegeli was. It had been many years—in Willard's time—since I had been afraid of anyone, but I was afraid of him.

"He played the role of great industrialist, contemptuous of ceremony and without an instant to spare on inferior people. 'Have you brought your tools?' was the first thing he said to me; although it was a silly question—why wouldn't I have brought my tools?—he made it sound as if I were just the sort of fellow who would have travelled across the whole of Switzerland without them. He questioned me carefully about clockwork, and that was easy because I knew more about that subject than he did; he understood principles but I don't suppose he could have made a safety-pin. Then he heaved himself out of his chair and gestured to me with his cigar to follow; he was old and very fat, and progress was slow, but we crawled back into the entrance hall, where he showed me the big clock there, which you have all seen; it has dials for everything you can think of—time at Sorgenfrei and at Greenwich, seconds, the day of the week, the date of the month, the seasons, and the signs of the zodiac, the phases of the moon, and a complex *sonnerie*. 'What's that?' he said. So I told him what it was, and how it was integrated and what metals were probably used to balance one another off with enough compensation to keep the thing from needing continual readjustment. He didn't say anything, but I knew he was pleased. 'That clock was made for my grandfather, who designed it,' he said. 'He must have been a very great technician,' I said, and that pleased him as well, as I meant it to do. Most men are much more partial to their grandfathers than to their fathers, just as they admire their grandsons but rarely their sons. Then he beckoned me to follow again, and this time we went on quite a long journey, down a flight of steps, through a long corridor, and up steps again into what I judged was another building; we had been through a tunnel.

"In a tall, sunny room in this building there was the most extraordinary collection of mechanical toys that anyone has ever seen; there can be no doubt about that, because it is now in one of the museums in Zürich, and its reputation is precisely what I have said—the most extensive and extraordinary in the world. But when I first saw it, the room looked as if all the little princes and princesses and serene highnesses in the world had been having a thoroughly destructive afternoon. Legs and arms lay about the floor, springs burst from little animals like metal guts, paint had been gashed with sharp points. It was a breathtaking scene of destruction, and as I wandered here and there looking at the little marvels and the terrible damage, I was filled with awe, because some of those things were of indisputable beauty and they had been despoiled in a fit of crazy fury.

"It was here that the old man showed the first touch of humanity I had seen in him. There were tears in his eyes. 'Can you mend this?' he asked, waving his heavy stick to encompass the room. It was not a time for hesitation. 'I don't know that I can mend it all,' I said, 'but if anybody can do it, I can. But I mustn't be pressed for time.' That fetched him. He positively smiled, and it wasn't a bad smile either. 'Then you must begin at once,' he said, 'and nobody shall ever ask you how you are getting on. But you will tell me sometimes, won't you?' And he smiled the charming smile again.

"That was how I began life at Sorgenfrei. It was odd, and I never became fully accustomed to the routine of the house. There were a good many servants, most of whom were well up in years, as otherwise they would have been called away for war work. There were also two secretaries, both invalidish young men, and the old Direktor— which was what everybody called him—kept them busy, because he either had, or invented, a lot of business to attend to. There was another curious functionary, also unfit for military service, whose job it was to play the organ at breakfast, and play the piano at night if the old man wanted music after dinner. He was a fine musician, but he can't have been driven by ambition, or perhaps he was too ill to care. Every morning of his life, while the Direktor consumed a large breakfast, this fellow sat in the organ loft and worked his way methodically through Bach's chorales. The old man called them his prayers and he heard three a day; he consumed spiced ham and cheese and extraordinary quantities of rolls and hot breads while he was listening to Bach, and when he had finished he hauled himself up and lumbered off to his study. From that time until evening the musician sat in the secretaries' room and read, or looked out of the window and coughed softly, until it was time for him to put on his dress clothes and eat dinner with the Direktor, who would then decide if he wanted any Chopin that evening.

"We all dined with the Direktor, and with a severe lady who was the manager of his household, but we took our midday meal in another room. It was the housekeeper who told me that I must get a dinner suit, and sent me to St Gallen to buy one. There were shortages in Switzerland, and they were reflected in the Direktor's meals, but we ate extraordinarily well, all the same.

"The Direktor was as good as his word; he never harried me about time. We had occasional conferences about things I needed, because I required seasoned metal—not new stuff—that his influence could command from the large factories in the complex of which he was the nominal ruler and undoubted financial head; I also had to have some rather odd materials to repair finishes, and as I wanted to use egg tempera I needed a certain number of eggs, which were not the easiest things to get in wartime, even in Switzerland.

"I had never dealt with an industrialist before, and I was bothered by his demand for accurate figures; when he asked me how much spring-metal of a certain width and weight I wanted I was apt to say, 'Oh, a fair-sized coil,' which tried his temper dreadfully. But after he had seen me working with it, and understood that I really knew what I was doing, he regained his calm, and may even have recognized that in the sort of job he had given me accuracy of estimate was not to be achieved in the terms he understood.

"The job was literally a mess. I set to work methodically on the first day to canvass the room, picking up everything and putting the component parts of every toy in a separate box, so far as I could identify them. It took ten days, and when I had done I estimated that of the hundred and fifty toys that had originally been on the shelves, all but twenty-one could be identified and put into some sort of renewed life. What remained looked like what is found after an aircraft disaster; legs, heads, arms, bits of mechanism and unidentifiable rubbish lay there in a jumble that made no sense, sort it how I would.

"It was a queer way to spend the worst years of the war. So far as work and the nurture of my imagination went, I was in the nineteenth century. None of the toys was earlier than 1790, and most of them belonged to the 1830s and '40s, and reflected the outlook on life of that time, and its quality of imagination—the outlook and imagination, that's to say, of the kind of people—French, Russian, Polish, German—who liked mechanical toys and could afford to buy them for themselves or their children. Essentially it was a stuffy, limited imagination.

"If I have been successful in penetrating the character of Robert-Houdin and the sort of performance he gave, it is because my work with those toys gave me the clue to it and his audience. They were people who liked imagination to be circumscribed: you were a wealthy bourgeois papa, and you wanted to give your little Clothilde a surprise on her birthday, so you went to the very best toymaker and spent a lot of money on an effigy of a little bootblack who whistled as he shined the boot he held in his hands. See Clothilde, see! How he nods his head and taps with his foot as he brushes away! How merrily he whistles 'Ach, du lieber Augustin'! Open the back of his case—carefully, my darling, better let papa do it for you—and there is the spring, which pumps the little bellows and works the little barrel-and-pin device that releases the air into the pipes that make the whistle. And these little rods and eccentric wheels make the boy polish the boot and wag his head and tap his toe. Are you not grateful to papa for this lovely surprise? Of course you are, my darling. And now we shall put the little boy on a high shelf, and perhaps on Saturday evenings papa will make it work for you. Because we mustn't risk breaking it, must we? Not after papa spent so much money to buy it. No, we must preserve it with care, so that a century from now Herr Direktor Jeremias Naegeli will include it in his collection.

"But somebody had gone through Herr Direktor Naegeli's collection and smashed it to hell. Who could it be?

"Who could be so disrespectful of all the careful preservation, painstaking assembly, and huge amounts of money the collection represented? Who can have lost patience with the bourgeois charm of all these little people—the ballerinas who danced so delightfully to the music of the music-boxes, the little bands of Orientals who banged their cymbals and beat their drums and jingled their little hoops of bells, the little trumpeters (ten of them) who could play three different trumpet tunes, the canary that sang so prettily in its decorative cage, the mermaid who swam in what looked like real water, but was really revolving spindles of twisted glass, the little tightrope walkers, and the big cockatoo that could ruffle its feathers and give a lifelike squawk—who can have missed their charm and seen instead their awful rigidity and slavery to mechanical pattern?

"I found out who this monster was quite early in my long task. After I had sorted the debris of the collection, and set to work, I spent from six to eight hours a day sitting in that large room, with a jeweller's glass stuck in my eye, reassembling mechanisms, humouring them till they worked as they ought, and then touching up the paintwork and bits of velvet, silk, spangles, and feathers that had been damaged on the birds, the fishes, monkeys, and tiny people who gave charm to the ingenious clockwork which was the important part of them.

"I am a concentrated worker, and not easily interrupted, but I began to have a feeling that I was not alone, and that I was being watched by no friendly eye. I could not see anything in the room that would conceal a snooper, but one day I felt a watcher so close to me that I turned suddenly and saw that I was being watched through one of the big windows, and that the watcher was a very odd creature indeed—a sort of monkey, I thought, so I waved to it and grinned, as one does at monkeys. In reply the monkey jabbed a fist through the window and cursed fiercely at me in some Swiss patois that was beyond my understanding. Then it unfastened the window by reaching through the hole it had made in the glass, threw up the sash, and leapt inside.

"Its attitude was threatening, and although I saw that it was human, I continued to behave as if it were a monkey. I had known Rango pretty well in my carnival days, and I knew that with monkeys the first rule is never to show surprise or alarm; but neither can you win monkeys by kindness. The only thing to do is to keep still and quiet and be ready for anything. I spoke to it in conventional German—"

"You spoke in a vulgar Austrian lingo," said Liesl. "And you took the patronizing tone of an animal-trainer. Have you any idea what it is like to be spoken to in the way people speak to animals? A fascinating experience. Gives you quite a new feeling about animals. They don't know words, but they understand tones. The tone people usually use to animals is affectionate, but it has an undertone of 'What a fool you are!' I suppose an animal has to make up its mind whether it will put up with that nonsense for the food and shelter that goes with it, or show the speaker who's boss. That's what I did. Really Magnus, if you could have seen yourself at that moment! A pretty, self-assured little manikin, watching to see which way I'd jump. And I did jump. Right on top of you, and rolled you on the floor. I didn't mean to do you any harm, but I couldn't resist rumpling you up a bit."

"You bit me," said Magnus.

"A nip."

"How was I to know it was only meant to be a nip?"

"You weren't. But did you have to hit me on the head with the handle of a screwdriver?"

"Yes, I did. Not that it had much effect."

"You couldn't know that the most ineffective thing you could do to me was to hit me on the head."

"Liesl, you would have frightened St George *and* his dragon. If you wanted gallantry you shouldn't have hit me and squeezed me and banged my head on the floor as you did. So far as I knew I was fighting for my life. And don't pretend now that you meant it just as a romp. You were out to kill. I could smell it on your breath."

"I could certainly have killed you. Who knew or cared that you were at Sorgenfrei, mending those ridiculous toys? In wartime who would have troubled to trace one insignificant little mechanic, travelling on a crooked passport, who happened to vanish? My grandfather would have been angry, but he would have had to hush the thing up somehow. He couldn't hand his granddaughter over to the police. The old man loved me, you know. If he hadn't, he would probably have killed me or banished me after I smashed up his collection of toys."

"And why did you smash them?" said Lind.

"Pure bloody-mindedness. For which I had good cause. You have heard what Magnus says: 'I looked like an ape. I still look like an ape, but I have made my apishness serve me and now it doesn't really matter. But it mattered then, more than anything else in the world, to me. It mattered more than the European War, more than anybody's happiness. I was so full of spleen I could have killed Magnus, and enjoyed it, and then told my grandfather to cope with the situation, and enjoyed that. And he would have done it.

"You'd better let me tell you about it, before Magnus rushes on and puts the whole thing in his own particular light. My life was pretty much that of any lucky rich child until I was fourteen. The only thing that was in the least unusual was that my parents—my father was Jeremias Naegeli's only son—were killed in a motor accident when I was eleven. My grandfather took me on, and was as kind to me as he knew how to be. He was like the bourgeois papa that Magnus described giving the mechanical toy to little Clothilde; my grandfather belonged to an era when the attitude toward children was that they were all right as long as they were loved and happy, and their happiness was obviously the same as that of their guardians. It works pretty well when nothing disturbs the pattern, but when I was fourteen something very disturbing happened in my pattern.

"It was the beginning of puberty, and I knew all about that because my grandfather was enlightened and I was given good, if rather Calvinist, instruction by a woman doctor. So when I began to grow rather fast I didn't pay much attention until it seemed that the growth was too much for me and I began to have fainting fits. The woman doctor appeared again and was alarmed. Then began a wretched period of hospitals and tests and consultations and head-shakings and discussions in which I was not included, and after all that a horrible time when I was taken to Zürich three times a week for treatment with a large ray-machine. The treatments were nauseating and depressing, and I was wretched because I supposed I had cancer, and asked the woman doctor about it. No, not cancer. What, then? Some difficulty with the growing process, which the ray treatment was designed to arrest.

"I won't bore you with it all. The disease was a rare one, but not so rare they didn't have some ideas about it, and Grandfather made sure that everything was done that anyone could do. The doctors were delighted. They did indeed control my growth, which made them as happy as could be, because it proved something. They explained to me, as if it were the most wonderful Christmas gift any girl ever had, that if they had not been able to do wonders with their rays and drugs I would have been a giant. Think of it, they said; you might have been eight feet tall, but we have been able to halt you at five foot eleven inches, which is not impossibly tall for a woman. You are a very lucky young lady. Unless, of course, there is a recurrence of the trouble, for which we shall keep the most vigilant watch. You may regard yourself as cured.

"There were, of course, a few side effects. One cannot hope to escape such an experience wholly unscathed. The side effects were that I had huge feet and hands, a disfiguring thickening of the skull and jaw, and surely one of the ugliest faces anyone has ever seen. But wasn't I lucky not to be a giant, as well?

"I was so perverse as not to be grateful for my luck. Not to be a giant, at the cost of looking like an ape, didn't seem to me to be the greatest good luck. Surely Fortune had something in her basket a little better than that? I raved and I raged, and I made everybody as miserable as I could. My grandfather didn't know what to do. Zürich was full of psychiatrists but my grandfather belonged to a pre-psychiatric age. He sent for a bishop, a good Lutheran bishop, who was a very nice man but I demolished him quickly; all his talk about resignation, recognition of the worse fate of scores of poor creatures in the Zürich hospitals, the necessity to humble oneself before the inscrutable mystery of God's will, sounded to me like mockery. There sat the bishop, with his snowy hair smelling of expensive cologne and his lovely white hands moulding invisible loaves of bread in the air before him, and there sat I, hideous and destroyed in mind, listening to him prate about resignation. He suggested that we pray, and knelt with his face in the seat of his chair. I gave him such a kick in the arse that he limped for a week, and rushed off to my own quarters.

"There was worse to come. With the thickening of the bones of my head there had been trouble with my organs of speech, and there seemed to be nothing that could be done about that. My voice became hoarse, and as my tongue thickened I found speech more and more difficult, until I could only utter in a gruff tone that sounded to me like the bark of a dog. That was the worst. To be hideous was humiliating and ruinous to my spirit, but to sound as I did threatened my reason. What was I to do? I was young and very strong, and I could rage and destroy. So that is what I did.

"It had all taken a long time, and when Magnus first saw me at the window of his workroom I was seventeen. I had gone on the rampage one day, and wrecked Grandfather's collection of toys. It was usually kept locked up but I knew how to get to it. Why did I do it? To hurt the old man. Why did I want to hurt the old man? Because he was at hand, and the pity I saw in his eyes when he came to see me—I kept away from the life in the house—made me hate him. Who was he, so old, so near death, so capable of living the life he liked, to pity me? If Fate had a blow, why didn't Fate strike him? He would not have had to endure it long. But I might easily live to be as old as he, trapped in my ugliness for sixty years. So I smashed his toys. Do you know, he never said a word of reproach? In the kind of world the bishop inhabited his forbearance would have melted my heart and brought me to a better frame of mind. But misfortune had scorched all the easy Christianity out of me, and I despised him all the more for his compassion, and wondered where I could attack him next.

"I knew Grandfather had brought someone to Sorgenfrei to mend the toys, and I wanted to see who it was. There was not much fun to be got out of the secretaries, and I had exhausted the possibilities of tormenting Hofstätter, the musician; he was poor game, and wept easily, the feeble schlemiel. I had spied on Magnus for quite a time before he discovered me; looking in the windows of his workroom meant climbing along a narrow ledge some distance above ground and as I looked like an ape I thought I might as well behave like one. So I used to creep along the ledge, and watch the terribly neat, debonair little fellow bent over his workbench, tinkering endlessly with bits of spring and tiny wires, and filing patiently at the cogs of little wheels. He always had his jeweller's glass stuck in one eye, and a beautifully fresh long white coat, and he never sat down without tugging his trousers gently upward to preserve their crease. He was handsome, too, in a romantic, nineteenth-century way that went beautifully with the little automata he was repairing.

"Before my trouble I had loved to go to the opera, and *Contes d'Hoffmann* was one of my favourites; the scene in Magnus's workroom always reminded me of the mechanical doll, Olympia, in *Hoffmann*, though he was not a bit like the grotesque old men who quarrelled over Olympia. So there it was, Hoffmann inside the window and outside, what? The only person in opera I resembled at all was Kundry the monstrous woman in *Parsifal*, and Kundry always seemed to be striving to do good and be redeemed. I didn't want to do good and had no interest in being redeemed.

"I read a good deal and my favourite book at that time was Spengler's *Der Untergang des Abendlandes*—I was not a stupid girl, you understand—and from it I had drawn a mishmash of notions which tended to support whatever I felt like doing, especially when I wanted to be destructive. Most adolescents are destructive, I suppose, but the worst are certainly those who justify what they do with a half-baked understanding of somebody's philosophy. It was under the banner of Spengler, then, that I decided to surprise Magnus and rough him up a bit. He looked easy. A man who worried so much in private about the crease of his trousers was sure to be a poor fighter.

"The surprise was mine. I was bigger and stronger but I hadn't had his experience in carnival fights and flophouses. He soon found out that hitting me on the head was no good, and hit me a most terrible blow in the diaphragm that knocked out all my breath. Then he bent one of my legs backward and sat on me. That was when we had our first conversation.

"It was long, and I soon discovered that he spoke my language. I don't mean German; I had to teach him proper German later. I mean that he asked intelligent questions and expected sensible answers. He was also extremely rude. I told you I had a hoarse, thick voice, and he had trouble understanding me in French and English. 'Can't you speak better than that?' he demanded, and when I said I couldn't he simply said, 'You're not trying; you're making the worst of it in order to seem horrible. You're not horrible, you're just stupid. So cut it out.'

"Nobody had ever talked to me like that. I was the Naegeli heiress, and I was extremely unfortunate; I was used to deference, and people putting up with whatever I chose to give them. Here was little Herr Trousers-Crease, who spoke elegant English and nice clean French and barnyard German, cheeking me about the way I spoke. And laying down the law and making conditions! 'If you want to come here and watch me work you must behave yourself. You should be ashamed, smashing up all these pretty things! Have you no respect for the past? Look at this: a monkey orchestra of twenty pieces and a conductor, and you've reduced it to a boxful of scraps. I've got to mend it, and it won't take less than four to six months of patient, extremely skilled work before the monkeys can play their six little tunes again. And all because of you! Your grandfather ought to tie you to the weathervane and leave you on the roof to die!'

"Well, it was a change from the bishop and my grandfather's tears. Of course I knew it was bluff. He may have hoped to shame me, but I think he was cleverer than that. All he was doing was serving notice on me that he would not put up with any nonsense; he knew I was beyond shame. But it was a change. And I began, just a little, to like him. Little Herr Trousers-Crease had quality, and an egoism that was a match for my own.

"Now—am I to go on? If there is to be any more of this I think I should be the one to speak. But is this confessional evening to know no bounds?"

"I think you'd better go ahead, Liesl," said I. "You've always been a great one to urge other people to tell their most intimate secrets. It's hardly fair if you refuse to do so."

"Ah, yes, but dear Ramsay, what follows isn't a tale of scandal, and it isn't really a love-story. Will it be of any interest? We must not forget that this is supposed to provide a subtext for Magnus's film about Robert-Houdin. What is the real story of the making of a great conjuror as opposed to Robert-Houdin's memoirs, which we are pretty much agreed are a bourgeois fake? I don't in the least mind telling my side of the story, if it's of any interest to the film-makers. What's the decision?"

"The decision is that you go on," said Kinghovn. "You have paused simply to make yourself interesting, as women do. No—that's unjust. Eisengrim has been doing the same thing all day. But go on."

"Very well, Harry, I shall go on. But there won't be much for you in what I have to tell, because this part of the story could not be realized in visual terms, even by you. What happened was that I came more and more to the workroom where little Herr Trousers-Crease was mending Grandfather's automata, and I fell under the enchantment of what he was able to do. He has told you that he humoured those little creatures back into life, but you would have to see him at work to get any kind of understanding of what it meant, because only part of it was mechanical. I suppose one of Grandfather's master technicians—one of the men who make those marvellous chronometers that are given to millionaires by their wives, and which never vary from strict time by more than a second every year—could have mended all those little figures so that they worked, but only Magnus could have read, in a cardboard box full of parts, the secret of the tiny performance that the completed figure was meant to give. When he had finished one of his repair jobs, the little bootblack did not simply brisk away at his little boot with his miniature brush, and whistle and tap his foot: he seemed to live, to have a true quality of being as though when you had turned your back he would leap up from his box and dance a jig, or run off for a pot of beer. You know what those automata are like: there is something distasteful about their rattling merriment; but Magnus made them *act*—they gave a little performance. I had seen them before I broke them, and I swear that when Magnus had remade them they were better than they had ever been.

"Was little Herr Trousers-Crease a very great watchmaker's mechanic, then? No, something far beyond that. There must have been in him some special quality that made it worth his while to invest these creatures of metal with so much vitality and charm of action. Roly has talked about his wolfishness; that was part of it, because with that wolfishness went an intensity of imagination and vision. The wolfishness meant only that he never questioned the overmastering importance of what he—whoever and whatever he was—might be doing. But the artistry was of a rare kind, and little by little I began to understand what it was. I found it in Spengler.

"You have read Spengler? No: it is not so fashionable as it once was. But Spengler talks a great deal about what he calls the Magian World View, which he says we have lost, but which was part of the *Weltanschauung*—you know, the world outlook—of the Middle Ages. It was a sense of the unfathomable wonder of the invisible world that existed side by side with a hard recognition of the roughness and cruelty and day-to-day demands of the tangible world. It was a readiness to see demons where nowadays we see neuroses, and to see the hand of a guardian angel in what we are apt to shrug off ungratefully as a stroke of luck. It was religion, but a religion with a thousand gods, none of them all-powerful and most of them ambiguous in their attitude toward man. It was poetry and wonder which might reveal themselves in the dunghill, and it was an understanding of the dunghill that lurks in poetry and wonder. It was a sense of living in what Spengler called a quivering cavern-light which is always in danger of being swallowed up in the surrounding, impenetrable darkness.

"This was what Herr Trousers-Crease seemed to have, and what made him ready to spend his time on work that would have maddened a man of modern education and modern sensibility. We have paid a terrible price for our education, such as it is. The Magian World View, in so far as it exists, has taken flight into science, and only the great scientists have it or understand where it leads; the lesser ones are merely clockmakers of a larger growth, just as so many of our humanist scholars are just cud-chewers or system-grinders. We have educated ourselves into a world from which wonder, and the fear and dread and splendour and freedom of wonder have been banished. Of course wonder is costly. You couldn't incorporate it into a modern state, because it is the antithesis of the anxiously worshipped security which is what a modern state is asked to give. Wonder is marvellous but it is also cruel, cruel, cruel. It is undemocratic, discriminatory, and pitiless.

"Yet here it was, in this most unexpected place, and when I had found it I apprenticed myself to it. Literally, for I begged Herr

Trousers-Crease to teach me what he knew, and even with my huge hands I gained skill, because I had a great master. And that means very often an exacting, hot-tempered, and impatient master, because whatever my great countrymen Pestalozzi and Froebel may have said about the education of commonplace people, great things are not taught by blancmange methods. What great thing was I learning? The management of clockwork? No; any great craft tends at last toward the condition of a philosophy, and I was moving through clockwork to the Magian World View.

"Of course it took time. My grandfather was delighted, for what he saw was that his intractable, hideous granddaughter was quietly engaged in helping to repair what she had destroyed. He also saw that I improved physically, because my agony over my sickness had been terribly destructive; physically I had become slouching and simian, and as Magnus saw at once, I made my speech trouble far worse than it was, to spite myself and the world. Magnus helped me with that. Re-taught me, indeed, because he would not tolerate my uncouth mutterings, and gave me some sharp and demanding instruction in the manner of speech he had learned from Lady Tresize. And I learned. It was a case of learn to speak properly or get out of the workroom, and I wanted to stay.

"We were an odd pair, certainly. I knew about the Magian World View, and recognized it in my teacher. He knew nothing of it, because he knew nothing else: it was so much in the grain of the life he had lived, so much a part of him, that he didn't understand that everybody else didn't think—no, not think, feel—as he did. I would not for the world have attempted to explain it to him, because that would have endangered it. His kind was not the kind of mind that is happy with explanations and theories. In the common sense of the expression, he had no brains at all, and hasn't to this day. What does it matter? I have brains for him.

"As his pupil, is it strange that I should fall in love with him? I was young and healthy, and hideous though I was, I had my yearnings— perhaps exaggerated by the unlikelihood that they could find satisfaction. How was I to make him love me? Well, I began, as all the beginners in love do, with the crazy notion that if I loved him enough he must necessarily respond. How could he ignore the devotion I offered? Pooh! He didn't notice at all. I worked like a slave, but that was no more than he expected. I made little gestures, gave him little gifts, tried to make myself fascinating—and that was uphill work, let me assure you. Not that he showed distaste for me. After all, he was a carnival man, and had grown used to grotesques. He simply didn't think of me as a woman.

"At least, that is how I explained it to myself, and I made myself thoroughly miserable about it. At last, one day, when he spoke to me impatiently and harshly, I wept. I suppose I looked dreadful, and he became even more rough. So I seized him, and demanded that he treat me as a human creature and not simply as a handy assistant, and blubbered out that I loved him. I did all the youthful things: I told him that I knew it was impossible that he should love me, because I was so ugly, but that I wanted some sort of human feeling from him.

"To my delight he took me quite seriously. We sat down at the workbench, and settled to a tedious task that needed some attention, but not too much, and he told me about Willard, and his childhood, and said that he did not think that love in the usual sense was for him, because he had experienced it as a form of suffering and humiliation—a parody of sex—and he could not persuade himself to do to anyone else what had been done to him in a perverse and terrifying mode.

"This was going too fast for me. Of course I wanted sexual experience, but first of all I wanted tenderness. Under my terrible appearance—I read a lot of old legends and I thought of myself as the Loathly Maiden in the Arthurian stories—I was still an upper-class Swiss girl of gentle breeding, and I thought of sexual intercourse as a splendid goal to be achieved, after a lot of pleasant things along the way. And being a sensible girl, under all the outward trouble and psychological muddle, I said so. That led to an even greater surprise.

"He told me that he had once been in love with a woman, who had died, and that he could not feel for anyone else as he had felt for her. Romance! I rose to it like a trout to a fly. But I wanted to know more, and the more I heard the better it was. Titled lady of extraordinary charm, understanding, and gentleness. All this was to the good. But then the story began to slide sidewise into farce, as it seemed to me. The lady was not young; indeed, as I probed, it came out that she had been over sixty when he first met her. There had been no tender passages between them, because he respected her too much, but he had been privileged to read the Bible to her. It was at this point I laughed.

"Magnus was furious. The more he stormed the more I laughed, and I am sorry to say that the more I laughed the more I jeered at him. I was young, and the young can be horribly coarse about love that is not of their kind. From buggery to selfless, knightly adoration at one splendid leap! I made a lot of it, and hooted with mirth.

"I deserved to be slapped, and I was slapped. I hit back, and we fought, and rolled on the floor and slugged each other. But of course everyone knows that you should never fight with women if you want to punish them; the physical contact leads to other matters, and it did. I was not ready for sexual intercourse so soon, and Magnus did not want it, but it happened all the same. It was the first time for both of us, and it is a wonder we managed at all. It is like painting in water-colours, you know; it looks easy but it isn't. Real command only comes with experience. We were both astonished and cross. I thought I had been raped; Magnus thought he had been unfaithful to his real love. It looked like a deadlock.

"It wasn't, however. We did it lots of times after that—I mean, in the weeks that followed—and the habit is addictive, as you all know, and very agreeable, if not really the be-all and end-all and cure-all that stupid people pretend. It was good for me. I became quite smart, in so far as my appearance allowed, and paid attention to my hair, which as you see is very good. My grandfather was transported, because I began to eat at the family table again, and when he had guests I could be so charming that they almost forgot how I looked. The Herr Direktor's granddaughter Fräulein Orang-Outang, so charming and witty, though it is doubtful if even the old man's money will find her a husband.

"I am sure Grandfather knew I was sleeping with Magnus, and it must have given him severe Calvinist twinges, but he did not become a great industrialist by being a fool; he weighed the circumstances and was pleased by the obvious balance on the credit side. I think he would have consented to marriage if Magnus had mentioned it. But of course he didn't.

"Nor would I have urged it. The more intimate we became, the more I knew that we were destined to be very great friends, and probably frequent bed-mates, but certainly not a happy bourgeois married couple. For a time I called Magnus Tiresias, because like that wonderful old creature he had been for seven years a woman, and had gained strange wisdom and insight thereby. I thought of him sometimes as Galahad, because of his knightly obsession with the woman we now know as Milady, but I never called him that to his face, because I had done with mocking at his chivalry. I have never understood chivalry, but I have learned to keep my mouth shut about it."

"It's a man's thing," said I; "and I think we have seen the last of it for a while on this earth. It can't live in a world of liberated women, and perhaps the liberation of women is worth the price it is certain to cost. But chivalry won't die easily or unnoticed; banish chivalry from the world and you snap the mainspring of many lives."

"Good, grey old Ramsay," said Liesl, reaching over to pat my hand; "always gravely regretting, always looking wistfully backward."

"You're both wrong," said Magnus. "I don't think chivalry belongs to the past; it's part of that World View Liesl talks so much about, and that she thinks I possess but don't understand. What captured my faith and loyalty about Milady had just as much to do with Sir John. He was that rare creature, the Man of One Woman. He loved Milady young and he loved her old and much of her greatness was the creation of his love. To hear people talk and to look at the stuff they read and see in the theatre and the films, you'd think the true man was the man of many women, and the more women, the more masculine the man. Don Juan is the ideal. An unattainable ideal for most men, because of the leisure and money it takes to devote yourself to a life of womanizing—not to speak of the relentless energy, the unappeasable lust, and the sheer woodpecker-like vitality of the sexual organ that such a life demands. Unattainable, yes, but thousands of men have a dab at it, and in their old age they count their handful of successes like rosary beads. But the Man of One Woman is very rare. He needs resources of spirit and psychological virtuosity beyond the common, and he needs luck, too, because the Man of One Woman must find a woman of extraordinary quality. The Man of One Woman was the character Sir John played on the stage, and it was the character he played in life, too.

"I envied him, and I cherished the splendour those two had created. If, by any inconceivable chance, Milady had shown any sexual affection for me, I should have been shocked, and I would have rebuked her. But she didn't, of course, and I simply warmed myself at their fire, and by God I needed warmth. I once had a hope that I might have found something of the sort for myself, with you, Liesl, but my luck was not to run in that direction. I would have been very happy to be a Man of One Woman, but that wasn't your way, nor was it mine. I couldn't forget Milady."

"No, no; we went our ways," said Liesl. "And you know you were never much of a lover, Magnus. What does that matter? You were a great magician, and has any great magician ever been a great lover? Look at Merlin: his only false step was when he fell in love and ended up imprisoned in a tree for his pains. Look at poor old Klingsor: he could create gardens full of desirable women, but he had been castrated with a magic spear. You've been happy with your magic. And when I gained enough confidence to go out into the world again, I was happy in a casual, physical way with quite a few people, and some of the best of them were of my own sex."

"Yes, indeed," said Magnus. "Who snatched the Beautiful Faustina from under my very nose?"

"Oh, Faustina, Faustina, you always bring her up when you feel a grievance. You must understand, gentlemen, that when my grandfather died, and I was heir to a large fortune, Magnus and I realized a great ambition we had in common; we set up a magic show, which developed and gained sophistication and gloss until it became the famous *Soirée of Illusions*. It takes money to get one of those things on its feet, as you well know, but when it is established it can be very profitable.

"You can't have a magic show without a few beautiful girls to be sawn in two, or beheaded, or whisked about in space. Sex has its place in magic, even if it is not the foremost place. As ours was the best show in existence, or sought to become the best, we had to have some girls better than the pretty numskulls who are content to take simple jobs in which they are no more than living stage properties.

"I found one in Peru, a great beauty indeed but not far evolved in the European sense; a lovely animal. I bought her, to be frank. You can still buy people, you know, if you understand how to go about it. You don't go to a peasant father and say, 'Sell me your daughter'; you say, 'I can open up a splendid future for your daughter, that will make her a rich lady with many pairs of shoes, and as I realize you need her to work at home, I hope you won't be offended if I offer you five hundred American dollars to recompense you for your loss.' He isn't offended; not in the least. And you make sure he puts his mark on an official-looking piece of paper that apprentices the girl to you, to learn a trade—in this case the trade of sempstress, because actress has a bad sound if there is any trouble. And there you are. You wash the girl, teach her to stand still on stage and do what she is told, and you clout her over the ear if she is troublesome. Quite soon she thinks she is a great deal more important than she really is, but that can be endured.

"Faustina was a thrill on the stage, because she really was stunningly beautiful, and for a while it seemed to be good business to let curious people think she was Magnus's mistress; only a few rather perceptive people know that great magicians, as opposed to ham conjurors, don't have mistresses. In reality, Faustina was my mistress, but we kept that quiet, in case some clamorous moralist should make a fuss about it. In Latin America, in particular, the clergy are pernickety about such things. You remember Faustina, Ramsay? I recall you had a wintry yearning toward her yourself."

"Don't be disagreeable, Liesl," I said. "You know who destroyed that."

"Destroyed it, certainly, and greatly enriched you in the process," said Liesl, and touched me gently with one of her enormous hands.

"So there you have it, gentlemen," she continued. "Now you know everything, it seems to me."

"Not everything," said Ingestree. "The name, Magnus Eisengrim—whose inspiration was that?"

"Mine," said Liesl. "Did I tell you I took my degree at the University of Zürich? Yes, in the faculty of philosophy where I leaned toward what used to be called philology—quite a Teutonic specialty. So of course I was acquainted with the great beast-legends of Europe, and in Reynard the Fox, you know, there is the great wolf Eisengrim, whom everyone fears, but who is not such a bad fellow, really. Just the name for a magician, don't you think?"

"And your name," said Lind. "Liselotte Vitzlipützli? You were always named on the programmes as Theatre Autocrat—Liselotte Vitzlipützli."

"Ah, yes. Somebody has to be an autocrat in an affair of that kind, and it sounds better and is more frank than simply Manager. Anyhow, I wasn't quite a manager: I was the boss. It was my money, you see. But I knew my place. Manager I might be, but without Magnus Eisengrim I was nothing. Consequently—Vitzlipützli. You understand?"

"No, gnädiges Fraulein, I do not understand," said Lind, "and you know I do not understand. What I am beginning to understand is that you are capable of giving your colleagues Eisengrim and Ramsay a thoroughly difficult time when it is your whim. So again—Vitzlipützli?"

"Dear, dear, how ignorant people are in this supposedly brilliant modern world," said Liesl. "You surely know *Faust*? Not Goethe's *Faust*, of course; every Teuton has that by heart—both parts of it— but the old German play on which he based his poem. Look among the characters there, and you will find that the least of the demons attending on the great magician is Vitzlipützli. So that was the name I chose. A delicate compliment to Magnus. It takes a little of the sting out of the word Autocrat.

"But an autocrat is what I must be now. Gentlemen, we have talked for a long time, and I hope we have given you your subtext. You have seen what a gulf lies between the reality of a magician with the Magian World View and such a pack of lies as Robert-Houdin's bland, bourgeois memoirs. You have seen, too, what a distance there is between the pack of lies Ramsay wrote so artfully as a commercial life of our dear Eisengrim, and the sad little boy from Deptford. And now, we must travel tomorrow, and I must pack my two old gentlemen off to their beds, or they will not be happy for the plane. So it is time to say good night."

Profuse thanks for hospitality, for the conversation, for the pleasure of working together on the film *Un Hommage à Robert-Houdin,* from Lind. A rather curious exchange of friendly words and handshakes between Eisengrim and Roland Ingestree. The business of waking Kinghovn from a drunken stupor, of getting him to understand that he must not have another brandy before going home. And then, at last, we three were by ourselves.

"Strange to spend so many hours answering questions," said Liesl.

"Strange, and disagreeable," said Eisengrim.

"Strange what questions went unasked and unanswered," said I.

"Such as——?" said Liesl.

"Such as 'Who killed Boy Staunton?'" said I.

3

Le Lit de Justice

(1)

"You know the police in Toronto are still not satisfied that you told them all you know about Staunton's death?"

"I told them all I thought proper."

"Which wasn't everything?"

"Certainly not. The police must work with facts, not fancies and suppositions. The facts were simple. I met him, for the first time in my life, when I visited you at your school in Toronto on the night of November 3, 1968; we went to your room and had a talk that lasted less than an hour. I accepted his offer to drive me back to my hotel. We chatted for a time, because we were both Deptford boys. I last saw him as he drove away from the hotel door."

"Yes. And he was found less than three hours later in the harbour, into which he appeared to have driven in his powerful car, and when the police recovered the body they found a stone in his mouth."

"So I understand."

"If that had been all there was to it, would the police still be wondering about you?"

"No indeed."

"It was my fault," said Liesl. "If I had been more discreet, the police would have been satisfied with what Magnus told them. But one has one's pride as an artist, you know, and when I was asked a question I thought I could answer effectively I did so, and then the fat was in the fire."

Would anyone who saw us at this moment have thought we were talking about murder? I was convinced that Magnus had murdered Staunton, and with reason. Was not Staunton the initiator of most of what we had heard in the subtext of the life of Magnus Eisengrim? If, when both he and I were ten years old, Percy Boyd Staunton had not thrown a snowball at me, which had instead hit Mrs Amasa Dempster, bringing about the premature birth of her son Paul and robbing her of her wits, would I at this moment be in bed with Magnus Eisengrim and Liselotte Vitzlipützli in the Savoy Hotel, discussing Staunton's death?

We had come to this because we were inclined to share a bed when we had anything important to talk about. People who think of beds only in terms of sexual exercise or sleep simply do not understand that a bed is the best of all places for a philosophical discussion, an argument, and if necessary a showdown. It was not by chance that so many kings of old administered justice from their beds, and even today there is something splendidly parliamentary about an assembly of concerned persons in a bed.

Of course it must be a big bed. The Savoy had outfitted Magnus's room with two splendid beds, each of which was easily capable of accommodating three adults without undue snuggling. (The Savoy is above the meanness of "single" beds.) So there we were, at the end of our long day of confession and revelation, lying back against the ample pillows, Liesl in the middle, Magnus on her left, and I on her right. He wore a handsome dressing-gown and a scarf he twisted around his head when he slept, because he had a European fear of draughts. I am a simple man; a man of blue pyjamas. Liesl liked filmy night-robes, and she was a delightful person to be in bed with because she was so warm. As I grow older I fuss about the cold, and for some reason I feel the cold for an hour or so after I have removed my artificial leg, as of course I had done before climbing in with them. My chilly stump was next to Liesl.

There we lay, nicely tucked up. I had my usual glass of hot milk and rum, Liesl had a balloon glass of cognac, and Magnus, always eccentric, had the glass of warm water and lemon juice without which he thought he could not sleep. I am sure we looked charmingly domestic, but my frame of mind was that of the historian on a strong scent and eager for the kill. If ever I was to get the confession that would complete my document—the document which would in future enable researchers to write "Ramsay says ..." with authority— it would be before we slept. If Magnus would not tell me what I wanted to know, surely I might get it from Liesl?

"Consider the circumstances," she said. "It was the final Saturday night of our two weeks' engagement at the Royal Alexandra Theatre in Toronto; we had never taken the *Soirée of Illusions* there before and we were a huge success. By far our most effective illusion was *The Brazen Head of Friar Bacon,* second to last on the programme.

"Consider how it worked, Ramsay: the big pretend-brass Head hung in the middle of the stage, and after it had identified a number of objects of which nobody but the owners could have had knowledge, it gave three pieces of advice. That was always the thing that took most planning; the Head would say, 'I am speaking to Mademoiselle Such-A-One, who is sitting in Row F, number 32.' (We always called members of the audience Madame and Monsieur and so forth because it gave a tiny bit of elegance to the occasion in an English-speaking place.) Then I would give Mademoiselle Such-A-One a few words that would make everybody prick up their ears, and might even make Mademoiselle squeal with surprise. Of course we picked up the gossip around town, through an advance agent, or the company manager might get a hint of it in the foyer, or even by doing a little snooping in handbags and pocket-books—he was a very clever old dip we valued for this talent. I was the Voice of the Head, because I have a talent for making a small piece of information go a long way.

"We had, in the beginning, decided never to ask for questions from the audience. Too dangerous. Too hard to answer effectively. But on that Saturday night somebody shouted from the gallery—we know who it was, it was Staunton's son David, who was drunk as a fiddler's bitch and almost out of his mind about his father's death— 'Who killed Boy Staunton?'

"Ramsay, what would you have done? What would you expect me to do? You know me; am I one to shy away from a challenge? And there it was: a very great challenge. In an instant I had what seemed to me an inspiration—just right in terms of the Brazen Head, that's to say; just right in terms of the best magic show in the world. Magnus had been talking to me about the Staunton thing all week; he had told me everything Staunton had said to him. Was I to pass up that chance? Ramsay, use your imagination!

"I signalled to the electrician to bring up the warm lights on the Head, to make it glow, and I spoke into the microphone, giving it everything I could of mystery and oracle, and I said—you remember what I said—*He was killed by the usual cabal: by himself, first of all; by the woman he knew; by the woman he did not know; by the man who granted his inmost wish; and by the inevitable fifth, who was keeper of his conscience and keeper of the stone.* You remember how well it went."

"Went well! Liesl, is that what you call going well?"

"Of course; the audience went wild. There was greater excitement in that theatre than the *Soirée* had ever known. It took a long time to calm them down and finish the evening with *The Vision of Dr Faustus*. Magnus wanted to bring the curtain down then and there. He had cold feet—"

"And with reason," said Magnus; "I thought the cops would be down on us at once. I was never so relieved in my life as when we got on the plane to Copenhagen the following morning."

"You call yourself a showman; It was a triumph!"

"A triumph for you, perhaps. Do you remember what happened to me?"

"Poor Ramsay, you had your heart attack, there in the theatre. Right-hand upper stage box, where you had been lurking. I saw you fall forward through the curtains and sent someone to take care of you at once. But would you grudge that in the light of the triumph for the *Soirée*? It wasn't much of a heart attack, now, was it? Just a wee warning that you should be careful about excitement. And were you the only one? Staunton's son took it very badly. And Staunton's wife! As soon as she heard about it—which she did within an hour—she forgot her role as grieving widow and was after us with all the police support she could muster, which luckily wasn't enthusiastic. After all, what could they charge us with? Not even fortune-telling, which is always the thing one has to keep clear of. But any triumph is bound to bring about a few casualties. Don't be small, Ramsay."

I took a pull at my rum and milk, and reflected on the consuming vanity of performers: Magnus, a monster of vanity, which he said he had learned from Sir John Tresize; and Liesl, not one whit less vain, to whom a possible murder, a near-riot in a theatre, an outraged family, and my heart attack—*mine*—were mere sparks from the anvil on which she had hammered out her great triumph. How does one cope with such people?

One doesn't; one thanks God they exist. Liesl was right; I mustn't be small. But if I was allowed my own egoism, I must have the answers I wanted. This was by no means the first time the matter of the death of Boy Staunton had come up among the three of us. On earlier occasions Magnus had put me aside with jokes and evasions, and when Liesl was present she stood by him in doing so; they both knew that I was deeply convinced that somehow Magnus had sent Staunton to his death, and they loved to keep me in doubt. Liesl said it was good for me not to have an answer to every question I asked, and my burning historian's desire to gather and record facts she pretended to regard as mere nosiness.

It was now or never. Magnus had opened up to the film-makers as he had never done to anyone—Liesl knew a little, I presume, but certainly her knowledge of his past was far from complete—and I wanted my answers while the confessional mood was still strong in him. Press on, Ramsay: even if they hate you for it now, they'll get cool in the same skins they got hot in.

One way of getting right answers is to venture a few wrong answers yourself. "Let me have a try at identifying the group you called 'the usual cabal,'" I said. "He was killed by himself, because it was he who drove his car off the dock; the woman he did not know, I should say, was his first wife, whom I think I knew quite well, and certainly he did not know her nearly so well; the woman he did know was certainly his second wife; he came to know her uncomfortably well, and if ever a man stuck his foot in a bear-trap when he thought he was putting it into a flower-bed, it was Boy Staunton when he married Denyse Hornick; the man who granted his inmost wish I suppose must have been you, Magnus, and I am sure you know what is in my mind—you hypnotized poor Boy, stuck that stone in his mouth, and headed him for death. How's that?"

"I'm surprised by the crudeness of your suspicions, Dunny. 'I am become as a bottle in the smoke: yet do I fear thy statutes.' One of those statutes forbids murder. Why would I kill Staunton?"

"Vengeance, Magnus, vengeance!"

"Vengeance for what?"

"For what? Can you ask that after what you have told us about your life? Vengeance for your premature birth and your mother's madness. For your servitude to Willard and Abdullah and all those wretched years with the World of Wonders. Vengeance for the deprivation that made you the shadow of Sir John Tresize. Vengeance for a wrench of fate that cut you off from ordinary love, and made you an oddity. A notable oddity, I admit, but certainly an oddity."

"Oh, Dunny, what a coarsely melodramatic mind you have! Vengeance! If I had been as big an oddity as you are I would have embraced Boy Staunton and thanked him for what he had done for me. The means may have been a little rough, but the result is entirely to my taste. If he hadn't hit my mother on the head with that snowball—having hidden a rock in it, which was dirty play— I might now be what my father was: a Baptist parson in a small town. I have had my ups and downs, and the downs were very far down indeed, but I am now a celebrity in a limited way, and I am a master of a craft, which is a better thing by far. I am a more complete human being than you are, you old fool. I may not have had a very happy sex-life, but I certainly have love and friendship, and much of the best of that is in bed with me at this moment. I have admiration, which everybody wants and very few people achieve. I get my living by doing what I most enjoy, and that is rare indeed. Who gave me my start? Boy Staunton! Would I murder such a man? It is to his early intervention in my life I owe what Liesl calls the Magian World View.

"Vengeance, you cry. If anybody wanted vengeance, it was you, Dunny. You lived near Staunton all your life, watched him, brooded over him, saw him destroy that silly girl you wanted—or thought you wanted—and ill-wished him a thousand times. You're the man of vengeance. I never wanted vengeance in my life for anything."

"Magnus! Remember how you withheld death from Willard when he begged for it! What did you do today to poor Roly Ingestree? Don't you call that vengeance?"

"I admit I toyed with Roly. He hurt people I loved. But if he hadn't come back into my life by chance I should never have bothered about him. I didn't harbour evidence of his guilt for sixty years, as you harboured that stone Staunton put in the snowball."

"Don't twist, Magnus! When you and Staunton left my room at the College to go back to your hotel you took that stone, and when next it was seen the police had to pry it out of poor Staunton's jaws, where it was clenched so tight they had to break his teeth to get at it!"

"I didn't take the stone, Dunny; Staunton took it himself."

"Did he?"

"Yes. I saw him. You were putting your box back in the book-shelves. The box that contained my mother's ashes. Dunny, what on earth made you keep those ashes? It was ghoulish."

"I couldn't bear to part with them. Your mother was a very special figure in my life. To me she was a saint. Not just a good woman, but a saint, and the influence she had in my life was miraculous."

"So you've often told me, but I knew her only as a mad-woman. I had stood at the window of our miserable house trying not to cry while Boy Staunton and his gang shouted 'Hoor!' as they passed on their way to school."

"Yes, and you let the police think you had never met him until the night he died."

"Perfectly true. I knew who he was, when he was fifteen and I was five. He was the Rich Young Ruler in our village, as you well know. But we had never been formally introduced until you brought us together, and I presumed that was what the police were talking about."

"A quibble."

"An evasion, possibly. But I was answering questions, not instructing my questioners. I was working on advice given me long ago by Mrs Constantinescu: don't blat everything you know, especially to cops."

"You didn't tell them you knew that Boy had been appointed Lieutenant-Governor of the province when nobody else knew it."

"Everybody knew it was in the air. I knew it the second night he came to the theatre, because he had the letter of appointment in the inner pocket of his handsome dinner jacket. Liesl has told you we had a member of our troupe—our company manager—who welcomed important patrons in the foyer. I suppose our man found out that the rumour had become a fact by means which I always thought it better not to investigate too closely. So I knew. And the Brazen Head could have spilled the beans that evening, from the stage, but Liesl and I thought it might be just a teeny bit indiscreet."

"That was another thing you didn't tell the police. Boy Staunton came twice to the *Soirée of Illusions*."

"Lots of people used to come twice. And three and four times. It's a very good show. But you're right; Staunton came to see me. He was interested in me in the way people used to be interested in Sir John. I suppose there was something about my personality, as there was about Sir John's, that had a special attraction for some people. My personality is a valuable part of our bag of tricks, as you very well know."

Indeed I did. And how it had come pressing off the screen in *Un Hommage à Robert-Houdin*! I had always thought personal attributes lost something in the cinema; it seemed reasonable that a photograph of a man should be less striking than the man himself. But not when the art of Lind and that rumpot of genius Kinghovn lay behind the photograph. I had sat in the little viewing-room at the B.B.C. entranced by what I saw of a Magnus more vivid than ever I had seen him on the stage. True, his performance was a tiny bit stagy, considered as cinematic acting, but it was a staginess of such grace, such distinction and accomplishment, that nobody could have wished it otherwise. As I watched I remembered what used to be said of stage favourites when I was a boy: they were *polished*. They had enviable repose. They did nothing quite the way anyone else did it, and they had an attitude toward their audiences which was, quite apart from the role they were playing, splendidly courteous, as if a great man were taking friendly notice of us. I had thought of this when Magnus told us how Sir John accepted applause when he made his first entrance in *Scaramouche,* and later gave those curtain-speeches all across Canada, which seemed to embrace audiences of people who yearned mutely for such attention. Magnus had this polish in the highest and most subtle degree, and I could understand how Boy Staunton, who was a lifelong hero-worshipper and had not got it out of his system even at the age of seventy would have responded to it.

Polish! How Boy had honed and yearned after polish! What idols he had worshipped! And as a Lieutenant-Governor elect I could imagine how he coveted what Magnus displayed on the stage. A Lieutenant-Governor with that sort of distinction—that would astonish the Rubes!

We were silent for a while. But I was full of questions, mad for certainties even though I understood there were no certainties. I broke the silence.

"If you weren't the man who granted his inmost wish, who was it? I have swallowed the pill that I was 'the inevitable fifth, who was keeper of his conscience and keeper of the stone'—though I accept that only as Liesl's oracular phraseology. But who granted his wish? And what was the wish?"

This time it was Liesl who spoke. "It could very well have been his son, Ramsay. Don't forget David Staunton, who represented continuance to his father. Have you no understanding of how some men crave for continuance? They see it as their immortality. Boy Staunton who had built up the great fortune, from a few fields of sugar-beets to a complex of business that was known all over the world. You must pardon my nationalist bias, but it is significant that when Staunton died—or killed himself, as it was supposed—his death was reported at some length in our *Neue Zürcher Zeitung.* That paper, like the *London Times,* recognizes only the most distinguished achievements of the Angel of Death. Their obituary columns are almost the Court Circular of the Kingdom of God. Well, who inherits an important man's earthly glory? People like Staunton hope it will be a son.

"A son Staunton had, we know. But what a son! Not a disgrace. One might find the spaciousness of tragedy in a disgrace. David Staunton was a success; a notable criminal lawyer, but also a sharp critic of his father's life. A man whose cold eye watched the glorious Boy growing older, and richer, and more powerful, and was not impressed. A man who did not admire or seek to emulate his father's great success with women. A man who understood, by tie of blood and by a child's intuition, the terrible, unappeasable hunger that lies at the bottom of ambition like Boy Staunton's. I don't know whether David ever understood that consciously; but he thwarted his father's terrible craving to be everything, command everything, and possess everything, and he did it in the way that hurt most: he refused to produce a successor to himself. He refused to continue the Staunton line and the Staunton name and the glory that was Staunton. That was pressing the knife into the vital spot. But don't jump to conclusions: the man who granted his inmost wish wasn't David Staunton."

"Aren't you doing a lot of fancy guessing?"

"No. Staunton told Magnus and Magnus told me."

"It was one of those situations Liesl is always talking about," said Eisengrim. "You know: a man reaches the confessional time in his life. Sometimes he writes an autobiography; sometimes he tells his story to a group of listeners, as I have been doing. Sometimes there is only one listener, and that was how it was with Staunton.

"Surely you remember what it was like in your room that night of November 3? Staunton and I had clicked, in the way people sometimes do. He wanted to know me: I was more than commonly interested in him because he was from my past, and not at all what one would have predicted for the fattish, purse-proud kid who had shouted 'Hoor' at my mother. You understood that we'd clicked, and you didn't like it at all. That was when you decided to spill the beans, and told Staunton who I was, how he had literally brought about my birth, how you knew about the rock in the snowball and had kept it all those years. You even had my mother's ashes in a casket. And through it all Staunton was cool as a cucumber. Denied everything that he had not—quite honestly, I believe—forgotten. Chose to regard the whole affair as something only very remotely connected with himself. Considering the way you went at him, I thought he showed enviable self-possession. But he said some sharp things about you.

"When we were in his car, driving down the long avenue from the school, he expanded on what he'd said. He cursed you very thoroughly, Dunny. Told me that for boyhood friendship he had kept an eye on your money all through the years, and made you secure and even well-off. Befriended you and brought you to the notice of really important people—people in a very big way of business—as a guest in his house. Confided in you when his first marriage was going on the rocks, and was patient when you sided with his wife. Put up with your ironic attitude toward his success, because he knew it had its root in jealousy.

"He was offended that you never mentioned Mary Dempster—he never spoke of her as my mother—and her long years in asylums; he would have been glad to help a Deptford woman who had come to grief. And he was angry and hurt that you kept that damned stone on your desk to remind you of a grudge you had against him. A stone in a snowball! The kind of thing any boy might do, just for devilment. He would never have thought the dark, judgmatical Ramsay blood in you was so bitter with hate—you, who had made money out of saints!

"It was then I began to know him. Oh yes, I came to know him quite well during the next hour. We'd clicked, as I said, but I've always distrusted that kind of thing since I first clicked with Willard. It's unchancy. There was sympathy of character, I suppose. There was a wolfishness in Boy Staunton that he kept very well under, and probably never recognized in himself. But I know that wolfishness. Liesl has told you I have a good measure of it in myself, and that was why she suggested I take the professional name of Eisengrim, the name of the wolf in the old fables; but the name really means the sinister hardness, the cruelty of iron itself. I took the name, and recognized the fact, and thereby got it up out of my depths so that at least I could be aware of it and take a look at it, now and then. I won't say I domesticated the wolf, but I knew where his lair was, and what he might do. Not Boy Staunton. He had lived facing the sun, and he had no real comprehension of the shadow-wolf that loped after him.

"We wolves like to possess things, and especially people. We are unappeasably hungry. There is no reason or meaning in the hunger. It just exists, and possesses you. I saw it once, in myself, and though I didn't know what it was at the time, I knew that it was something that was at the very heart of my being. When we played *Scaramouche* through Canada, I had a little meeting with Sir John, every night, just before Two, two; we had to stand in front of a mirror, to make sure every detail of costume and make-up was identical, so that when I appeared as his double the illusion would be as perfect as possible. I always enjoyed that moment, because I am wolfish about perfection.

"There we stood, the night I speak of; it was in Ottawa, in his dressing-room at the old Russell, and we had a good mirror, a full-length one. He looked, and I looked. I saw that he was good. An egoist, as only a leading actor can be, but in his face, which was old under the make-up, there was gentleness and compassion toward me, because I was young, and had so much to learn, and was so likely to make a fool of myself through my driving greed. Compassion for me, and a silvery relish for himself, too, because he knew he was old, and had the mastery of age. But in my face, which was so like his that my doubling gave the play a special excitement, there was a watchful admiration beneath which my wolfishness could be seen—my hunger not just to be like him but to *be* him, whatever that might cost him. I loved him and served him faithfully right up to the end, but in my inmost self I wanted to eat him, to possess him, to make him mine.

"He saw it, too, and he gave me a little flick with his hand as though to say, 'You might let me live out my life, m'boy. I've earned it, eh? But you look as if you'd devour my very soul. Not really necessary, quonk?' Not a word was spoken, but I blushed under my make-up. And whatever I did for him afterward, I couldn't keep the wolf quiet. If I was a little sharp with Roly, it was because I was angry that he had seen what I truly thought I had kept hidden.

"That was how it was with Boy Staunton. Oh, not on the surface. He had a lovely glaze. But he was a devourer.

"He set to work to devour me. He went at it with the ease of long custom, and I don't suppose he had an instant's real awareness of what he was doing. He laid himself out to be charming, and to get me on his side. When he had finished damning you, Dunny, he began to excuse you, in a way that was supposed to be complimentary to me: you had lived a narrow, schoolmaster's life, and had won a certain scholarly reputation, but he and I were the glittering successes and breathed a finer air than yours.

"He was extremely good at what he was doing. It is not easy to assume an air of youth successfully, but when it is well done it has extraordinary charm, because it seems to rock Age, and probably Death, back on their heels. He had kept his voice youthful, and his vocabulary was neither stupidly up-to-the-minute nor flawed with betraying fossil slang. I had to keep reminding myself that this man must be seventy. I have to present a professional picture of physical well-being, if not actually of youth, and I know how it is done because I learned it from Sir John. But Boy Staunton—an amateur, really—could teach me things about seeming youthful without resorting to absurdities. I knew he was eager to make me his own, to enchant me, to eat me up and take me into himself. He had just discovered a defeat; he thought he had eaten you, Ramsay, but you were like those fairy-tale figures who cut their way out of the giant's belly.

"So, not at all unlike a man who loses one girl and bounces to another, he tried to eat me.

"We really must talk, he said. We were driving down from your school to my hotel, and as we were rounding Queen's Park Circle he pulled off the road into what I suppose was a private entry beside the Legislature; there was a porte-cochère and a long flight of steps. It won't be long before this is my personal entrance to this building, he said.

"I knew what he was talking about; the appointment that would be announced next morning; he was full of it."

"I'll bet he was," I said; "it was just his thing—top dog in a large area—women curtsying to him—all that. And certainly his wife wanted it, and engineered it."

"Yes, but wait: having got it, he wasn't so sure. If you are one of the wolfish brotherhood you sometimes find that you have no sooner achieved what you wanted than you begin to despise it. Boy's excitement was like that of a man who thinks he has walked into a trap."

"Well, the job isn't all fun. What ceremonial appointment is? You drive to the Legislature in a carriage, with soldiers riding before and behind, and there is a lot of bowing, because you represent the Crown, and then you find you are reading a speech written by somebody else, announcing policies you may not like. If he didn't want to be a State figurehead, he should have choked off Denyse when she set to work to get him the job."

"Reason, reason, reason! Dunny, you surely know how limited a part reason plays in some of our most important decisions. He coveted the state landau and the soldiers, and he had somehow managed to preserve the silly notion that as Lieutenant-Governor he would really do some governing. But already he knew he was mistaken. He had looked over the schedule of duties for his first month in office, and been dismayed by the places he would have to go, and the things he would have to do. Presenting flags to Boy Scouts; opening a home for old people; eating a hundredweight of ceremonial dinners to raise money to fight diseases he'd rather not hear about. And he couldn't get out of it; his secretary made it clear that there was no choice in the matter; the office demanded these things and he was expected to deliver the goods. But that wasn't what truly got under his skin.

"Such appointments aren't done in a few days, and he had known it was coming for several weeks. During that time he had some business in London and while he was there he had thought it a good idea to take care of the matter of his ceremonial uniform. That was how he put it, but as a fellow-wolf I knew how eager he must have been to explore the possibilities of state finery. So—off to Ede and Ravenscroft to have the job done in the best possible way and no expense spared. They happened to have a uniform of the right sort which he tried on, just to get the general effect. Even though it was obvious that the uniform was for a smaller man, the effect was catastrophic. 'Suddenly I didn't look like myself at all,' he said; 'I looked old. Not shaky old, or fat old, or grim old, but certainly old.'

"He expected me to sympathize, but wolf should never turn to wolf for sympathy. 'You are old,' I said to him. 'Very handsome and well preserved, but nobody would take you for a young man.' 'Yes,' he said, 'but not old as that uniform suggested; not a figurehead. I tried putting the hat a little on one side, to see if that helped, but the man with the measuring-tape around his neck who was with me said, *Oh no, sir; never like that,* and put it straight again. And I understood that forever after there would always be somebody putting my hat straight, and that I would be no more than the animation of that uniform, or some version of it.'

"As one who had spent seven years as the cunning bowels of Abdullah I didn't see that fate quite as he did. Of course, Abdullah wasn't on the level. He was out to trounce the Rubes. A Lieutenant-Governor can't have any fun of that kind. He is the embodiment of everything that is correct, and on the level, and unsurprising. The Rubes have got him and he must do their will.

"'I have lost my freedom of choice,' he said, and he seemed to expect me to respond with horror. But I didn't. I was enjoying myself. Boy Staunton was an old story to you, Dunny, but he was new to me, and I was playing the wolf game, too, in my way. I had not forgotten Mrs Constantinescu, and I knew that he was ready to talk, and I was ready to hear. So I remembered old Zingara's advice. Lull 'em. So I lulled him.

"'I can see that you're in a situation you never would have chosen with your eyes open. But there's usually some way out. Is there no way out for you?'

"'Even if I found a way, what would happen if I suddenly bowed out?' he said.

"'I suppose you'd go on living much as you do now,' I told him. 'There would be criticism of you because you refused an office you had accepted, under the Crown. But I dare say that's been done before.'

"I swear I had nothing in particular in mind when I made that comment. But it galvanized him. He looked at me as if I had said something of extraordinary value. Then he said: 'Of course it was different for him; he was younger.'

"'What do you mean?' I said.

"He looked at me very queerly. 'The Prince of Wales,' he said; 'he was my friend, you know. Or rather, you don't know. But many years ago, when he toured this country, I was his aide, and he had a profound effect on me. I learned a great deal from him. He was special, you know; he was truly a remarkable man. He showed it at the time of the Abdication. That took guts.'

"'Called for guts from several of his relatives, too,' I said. 'Do you think he lived happily ever after?'

"'I hope so,' said he. 'But he was younger.'

"'I've said you were old,' said I, 'but I didn't mean life had nothing for you. You are in superb condition. You can expect another fifteen years, at least, and think of all the things you can do.'

"'And think of all the things I can't do,' he said, and in a tone that told me what I had suspected, because with all the fine surface, and bonhomie, and his careful wooing of me I had sensed something like despair in him.

"'I suppose you mean sex,' I said.

"'Yes,' he said. 'Not that I'm through, you know; by no means. But it isn't the same. Now it's more reassurance than pleasure. And young women—they have to be younger and younger—they're flattered because of what I am and who I am, but there's always a look you surprise when they don't think you're watching: He's-amazing-for-his-age-I-wonder-what-I'd-do-if-he-had-a-heart-attack-would-I-have-to-drag-him-out-into-the-hall-and-leave-him-by-the-elevator-and-how-would-I-get-his-clothes-on? However well I perform—and I'm still good, you know—there's an element of humiliation about it.'

"Humiliation was much on his mind. The humiliation of age, which you and I mustn't underestimate, Dunny, just because we've grown old and made our age serve us; it's a different matter if you've devoted your best efforts to setting up an image of a wondrous Boy; there comes a time when the pretty girls think of you not as a Boy but as an Old Boy. The humiliation of discovering you've been a mug, and that the gorgeous office you've been given under the Crown is in fact a tyranny of duty, like the Crown itself. And the humiliation of discovering that a man you've thought of as a friend—rather a humble, eccentric friend from your point of view, but nevertheless a friend—has been harbouring evidence of a mean action you did when you were ten, and still sees you, at least in part, as a mean kid.

"That last was a really tough one—disproportionately so—but Boy was the kind of man who truly believes you can wipe out the past simply by forgetting it yourself. I'm sure he'd met humiliations in his life. Who hasn't? But he'd been able to rise above them. These were humiliations nothing could lift from his heart.

"'What are you going to do with the stone?' I asked him.

"'You saw me take it?' he said. 'I'll get rid of it. Throw it away.'

"'I wouldn't throw it a second time,' I said.

"'What else?' said he.

"'If it really bothers you, you must come to terms with it,' I said. 'In your place I'd do something symbolic: hold it in your hand, re-live the moment when you threw it at Ramsay and hit my mother, and this time *don't* throw it. Give yourself a good sharp knock on the head with it.'

"'That's a damned silly game to play,' he said. And would you believe it, he was pouting—the glorious Boy was pouting.

"'Not at all. Consider it as a ritual. An admission of wrongdoing and penitence.'

"'Oh, balls to that,' he said.

"I had become uncomfortable company: I wouldn't be eaten, and I made peculiar and humiliating suggestions. Also, I could tell that something was on his mind, and he wanted to be alone with it. He started the car and very shortly we were at my hotel—the Royal York, you know, which is quite near the docks. He shook hands with the warmth that I suppose had marked him all his life. 'Glad to have met you: thanks for the advice,' said he.

"'It's only what I would do myself, in the circumstances,' I said. 'I'd do my best to swallow that stone.' Now I swear to you that I only meant what I said symbolically—meaning to come to terms with what the stone signified. And he seemed not to notice.

"'I meant your advice about the Abdication,' he said. 'It was stupid of me not to have thought of that myself.'

"I suddenly realized what he meant. He was going to abdicate, like his hero before him. But unlike his Prince of Wales he didn't mean to live to face the world afterward. There it is, Dunny: Liesl and I are convinced that the man who truly granted his inmost wish, though only by example, was the man who decided not to live as Edward VIII.

"What should I have done? Insisted that he come to my room, and plied him with hot coffee and sweet reasonableness? Not quite my line, eh? Hardly what one expects of a brother wolf, quonk?"

"You let him leave you in that frame of mind?"

"Liesl likes to talk about what she calls my Magian World View. She makes it sound splendid and like the Arabian Nights and dolls it up with fine phrases from Spengler—"

"Phantasmagoria and dream-grotto," said Liesl, taking a swig of her cognac; "only that's not Spengler—that's Carlyle."

"Phantasmagoria and dream-grotto if you like," said Magnus, "but—and it is a vital *but*—combined with a clear-eyed, undeluded observation of what lies right under your nose. Therefore—no self-deceiving folly and no meddlesome compassion, but a humble awareness of the Great Justice and the Great Mercy whenever they choose to make themselves known. I don't talk about a Magian World View; I've no touch with that sort of thing. In so far as it concerns me, I live it. It's just the way things strike me, after the life I've lived, which looks pretty much like a World of Wonders when I spread it out before me, as I've been doing. Everything has its astonishing, wondrous aspect, if you bring a mind to it that's really your own—a mind that hasn't been smeared and blurred with half-understood muck from schools, or the daily papers, or any other ragbag of reach-me-down notions. I try not to judge people, though when I meet an enemy and he's within arm's length, I'm not above giving him a smart clout, just to larn him. As I did with Roly. But I don't monkey with what I think of as the Great Justice—"

"Poetic justice," said Liesl.

"What you please. Though it doesn't look poetic in action; it's rough and tough and deeply satisfying. And I don't administer it. Something else—something I don't understand, but feel and serve and fear—does that. It's sometimes horrible to watch, as it was when my poor, dear old master, Sir John, was brought down by his own vanity, and Milady went with him, though I think she knew what the truth was. But part of the glory and terror of our life is that somehow, at some time, we get all that's coming to us. Everybody gets their lumps and their bouquets and it goes on for quite a while after death.

"So—here was a situation when it was clear to me that the Great Justice had called the name of Boy Staunton. Was it for me to hold him back?

"And to be frank why would I? You remember what was said in your room that night, Dunny. You're the historian: surely you remember everything important? What did I say to Boy when he offered me a lift in his car?"

I couldn't remember. That night I had been too overwrought myself by the memories of Mary Dempster to take note of social conversation.

"You don't remember? I do: I said—'What Ramsay tells me puts you in my debt for eighty days in Paradise, if for nothing in this life. We shall call it quits if you will drive me to my hotel.'"

"Eighty days in Paradise?"

"I was born eighty days before my time. Poor little Paul. Popular opinion is very rough on foetuses these days. Horrid little nuisances. Rip 'em out and throw them in the trash pail. But who knows what they feel about it? The depth psychologists Liesl is so fond of think they have a very jolly time in the womb. Warm, protected, bouncing gently in their beautiful grotto light. Perhaps it is the best existence we ever know, unless there is something equally splendid for us after death—and why not? That earliest life is what every humanitarian movement and Welfare State seeks to restore, without a hope of success. And Boy Staunton, by a single mean-spirited action, robbed me of eighty days of that princely splendour. Was I the man to fret about the end of his life when he had been so cavalier about the beginning of mine?"

"Oh, Magnus, that's terribly unjust."

"As this world's justice goes, perhaps. But what about the Greater Justice?"

"I see. Yes, I really do see. So you let him dree his weird?"

"You're getting really old, Dunny. You're beginning to dredge up expressions from your Scotch childhood. But it says it all. Yes, I let him dree his weird."

"I can very well understand," I said, "that you wouldn't have got far explaining that to the police."

Liesl laughed, and threw her empty brandy balloon against the farthest wall. It made a fine costly crash.

(2)

"Ramsay."

"Liesl! How kind of you to come to see me."

"Magnus has been asleep for hours. But I have been worrying about you. I hope you didn't take it too badly—his suggestion that you played rather a crucial part in Staunton's death."

"No, no; I faced that, and swallowed it even before I joined you in Switzerland. While I was recovering from my heart attack, indeed. In an old Calvinist like me the voice of conscience has always spoken long before any mortal accuser."

"I'm glad. Glad that you're not grieving and worrying, that's to say."

"Boy died as he lived: self-determined and daring, but not really imaginative. Always with a well-disguised streak of petulance that sometimes looked like malice. The stone in the snowball: the stone in the corpse's mouth—always a nasty surprise for somebody."

"You think he gobbled the stone to spite you?"

"Unquestionably. Magnus thinks I kept the stone for spite, and I suppose there was something of that in it. But I also kept it to be a continual reminder of the consequences that can follow a single action. It might have come out that it was my paperweight, but even if it didn't, he knew I would know what it was, and Boy reckoned on having the last word in our lifelong argument that way."

"What a detestable man!"

"Not really. But it's always a good idea to keep your eye on the genial, smiling ones, and especially on those who seem to be eternally young."

"Jealousy, Ramsay, you battered antique."

"A little jealousy, perhaps. But the principle holds."

"Is that what you are making notes about, on all that excellent Savoy notepaper?"

"Notes for a work I have in mind. But it's about Magnus; he told me, you know, that the Devil once intervened decisively in his life."

"He likes to talk that way, and I am sure it is true. But life is a succession of decisive interventions. Magnus himself intervened in my life, and illuminated it, at a time when I needed an understanding friend even more than I needed a lover. It wasn't the Devil that sent him."

"Why should it be? God wants to intervene in the world, and how is he to do it except through man? I think the Devil is in the same predicament. It would be queer, wouldn't it, if the Devil had only made use of Magnus that one time? And God, too: yes, certainly God as well. It's the moment of decision—of will—when those Two nab us, and as they both speak so compellingly it's tricky work to know who's talking. Where there's a will, there are always two ways."

"That's what you're making notes about? And you hope to untangle it? What vanity!"

"I'm not expecting to untangle anything. But I'm making a record—a document. I've often talked to you about it. When we're all gone—you dear Liesl, though you're much the youngest, and Magnus—there may be a few who will still prove a point with 'Ramsay says …'"

"Egoist!"